A PLACE OF BIRDS

Nineteen-year-old Susanna Elliot rebels against her strict Quaker background, which alienates her from her family and community. She is rejected by the doctor she admires and is refused permission to take her dead brother's place in the family business. She flees to join her two cousins on their mission to China and all three leave Falmouth for Shanghai aboard a schooner owned by Lowell Hawke. Hawke's daring exploits have made him a legend along the Chinese coast and Susanna finds herself involved in danger—and love ...

A PLACE OF BIRDS

A PLACE OF BIRDS

by

Jane Jackson

Magna Large Print Books
Long Preston, North Yorkshire,
England.

British Library Cataloguing in Publication Data.

Jackson, Jane
A place of birds.

A catalogue record for this book is
available from the British Library

ISBN 0-7505-1289-X

First published in Great Britain by Robert Hale Ltd., 1997

Published in Large Print 1998 by arrangement with Robert Hale Ltd.

Magna Large Print is an imprint of
Library Magna Books Ltd.
Printed and bound in Great Britain by
T.J. International Ltd., Cornwall, PL28 8RW.

With love and gratitude to Mike,
for all the laughter.
And to Dot, who had faith.

Chapter One

'No!' Samuel Elliot quivered with agitation. 'What you ask is impossible.'

'But, Father, I'm perfectly capable—'

'Did you not hear me?' He shook his head despairingly. 'You would try the patience of a saint.' Susanna watched him reclaim control over both his expression and emotions. 'I don't doubt your ability,' he said, with the careful fairness she admired and hated in equal measure, 'but I cannot permit admiration for your achievements to influence my decision.'

'Why not? How can you praise my intelligence and abilities yet refuse to let me use them?'

'Susanna, my position as an Elder demands *every* member of my family observe the same high standards of correct behaviour I set myself. Your reluctance to conform causes me great pain.'

She felt her face flame. 'I'm sorry.' Guilt battled with resentment. 'But please, may I not—?'

'No. Assisting at a time of crisis is one thing; what you are asking is quite another. And out of the question.' His stern features softened. 'I am sure with thought and prayer you will find a more appropriate use for your talents among the many charities we support. Women have no place in business or politics. Both are worlds for

9

which they are completely unsuited.' He picked up his newspaper, signalling the matter closed.

Her eyes brimming with tears of disappointment and frustration she fled to the sanctuary of her room.

'Captain Willis must have gone mad, that's all I can say,' the seaman in the corner bed shouted at his hard-of-hearing neighbour. 'No good will come of it, you wait and see.'

Startled out of her introspection Susanna thrust aside the memories and glanced quickly over her shoulder.

'Don't take no notice, miss,' gasped the sailor at whose bedside she sat. The congestion in his lungs made each breath a struggle but his exhausted face was creased in a grin. 'He believes giving a ship the wrong name will bring her bad luck.'

A stray curl fell across her forehead. She tucked it back out of sight beneath her close-fitting white bonnet and indicated the almost-full page resting on her writing-case.

'Shall I give them your love?'

He nodded, wheezing. Susanna finished writing and turned the page towards him so he could sign it. But when he made no move to take the pen she understood at once. 'If you're not feeling up to it ... .'

The sailor nodded quickly. 'You sign it and put my name underneath.'

Her twice-weekly visits to the Seamen's Home and Infirmary had started back in the spring after her parents had insisted she accompany them to a Friends' Charity Committee meeting.

One of the speakers had been Doctor Edward Arundell. Supposedly in his early thirties his springy thatch of rust-coloured hair and spattering of freckles made him look much younger. But his eyes swiftly shattered the illusion of boyishness.

His remarks about seamen with families suffering keenly from lack of contact with them had persuaded her to make the infirmary the focus of her charity work.

Hunger for knowledge and a series of excellent tutors meant she was, at nineteen, far better educated than most girls of her age and background. Her language skills enabled many of the foreign sailors to send word to their families and enjoy some conversation in their own tongue.

The seamen treated her with touching respect. But despite confiding intimate details about their lives and families, most hated admitting they could not write even their name. Her innate sensitivity enabled them to save face.

'I just want you to know, miss,' the sailor wheezed shyly, 'seeing you do make my day. There isn't many would bother with the likes of us. Especially not girls as pretty as you.'

Astonished, Susanna looked up. *Pretty? Her?* At every family gathering she attracted disapproval. *No one else in the family has green eyes. Something should be done about that hair, it's far too thick and curly. A mouth like that denotes a sensual temperament, she'll need a firm hand.*

She hadn't chosen her looks. She didn't want

11

to be different. So she tried hard to be as meek and decorous as her plain brown dress which had neither crinoline nor bustle to give it style and not a single ribbon or piece of lace as trimming.

'Thank you, Mr Roberts. I'm glad my visits help.'

'Oh they do, miss.' He stifled another cough.

Printing the sailor's name beneath her own signature Susanna opened her writing-case and took out an envelope, angling herself to make the most of the wintery light.

There were two windows in this, the infirmary's main ward, but no curtains to gather dust. A gas pipe circled the room just below the high ceiling with five thin feeder pipes running down the white-painted walls to glass-bowled lamps, one above each of the four beds and one just inside the door. A coal fire glowed in the black iron grate, brightening the gloomy November afternoon.

A sudden shout came from outside the ward, a man's voice harsh with pain and fear.

'Poor bastard,' Roberts shook his head. ''Scuse me, miss. Brung in last night he was, raving with fever.'

Another cry echoed through the ward, falling away to a desperate babble.

'Off again, is he?' the seaman in the corner bed called out. 'I looked in this morning when I went for a p— when I had a wash. He hasn't got long.'

'He's Portuguese,' Susanna murmured.

Mr Roberts's shaggy eyebrows shot up. 'How

do you know that, then?'

'My father is a cargo broker. He's also principal shareholder in a number of schooners and steamships which make regular trips to Portugal. I recognize the language; I can speak it a little.'

Roberts's astonishment became a frown of warning. 'Best keep your distance. You being a lady and all.'

'He's right,' the other seaman added. 'A lot of these foreigners—' He shook his head. 'Come from the gutter they do. The only women they know is whores, begging your pardon, miss. Better leave him to the doctor.'

'Whassamatter?' his deaf neighbour peered at each of them. 'What's going on? Tea coming, is it?'

'Not yet,' the seaman yelled. 'Have a nap. I'll wake you when it's time.'

The Portuguese shouted again. The desperation in his voice worried Susanna. Surely something could be done to help him?

'Think you'll catch the post, miss?' Mr Roberts clamped his lips tightly as his chest heaved.

Realizing he needed to clear his lungs and was trying to spare her the unpleasantness Susanna stood up and replaced the hard wooden chair against the wall.

'I'll do my best. I hope you feel better tomorrow.' Nodding to the other men she picked up her writing-case and the letter and left the ward. Behind her Mr Roberts released a choking bubbling cough. As she opened the dispensary door to fetch her cloak another

13

heart-rending cry came from the small side-room.

She hesitated. Albert, the infirmary's odd-job man, was busy outside. Lewis, who helped in the dispensary and acted as Edward's assistant during operations, had already gone.

Where was Edward? It was totally unlike him to ignore a patient's suffering. Among seamen Doctor Edward Arundell was spoken of with something approaching reverence for his insight, patience and kindness. Which made it all the more strange that with her he could be so blindly insensitive. She must be far better at hiding her feelings than she'd thought.

Her conscience pricked. She hadn't known Edward's wife but, like everyone else, she had been shocked by the tragedy. Katharine's death had been so sudden, so unexpected. She had borne her other two children without any problem.

Edward's response to the loss of his wife and baby had been to bury himself in his work. And the sailors' gratitude for his care and attention ensured his name was known far beyond the port of Falmouth. She knew he valued her visits to the infirmary.

'The men regard you as a treasure,' he had told her, smiling.

What about you? she had longed to ask. *What am I to you?* Surely one day soon he would see beyond her Quaker drab to the woman beneath?

She looked up and down the passage in an agony of indecision. The sailors had warned her to stay clear. But she couldn't simply ignore the man's anguished cries. She would reassure him that he hadn't been forgotten then go and find Edward. As she opened the side-ward door a fetid stench made her recoil.

The man in the bed moved restlessly. His face was gaunt and swarthy with several days' beard. His hair had come out in patches leaving uneven clumps and thin dark strands. Bloodshot eyes, sunk deep in their sockets, had a febrile glitter and his prominent cheekbones were flushed with hectic colour. A yellow gummy substance had gathered at the corners of his cracked lips. He moaned, his face contorting, still unaware of her presence.

Breathing as lightly as she could she crossed to the bed. He looked on the brink of death. Christian charity demanded that any man, no matter what his background, was entitled to a few words of comfort.

'Teresa?' he rasped with glimmering hope.

'No.' She spoke haltingly in his own language. 'Please try to rest. I'll find the doctor.'

'Teresa.' He grimaced. His skin was mottled with reddish-brown spots. One hand shot out and fastened around her wrist. He started to babble, pulling her closer. The gust of putrid breath made her gag.

She tried to wrench her arm loose but his grip was maniacally strong. Her writing-case fell to the floor and fright arrowed through her. 'Please, let go. I can't understand you. You are talking too fast.'

Her words were drowned by his frenzied

pleas. Struggling in earnest now she tore at his fingers. 'Stop it. Let *go!*'

The Portuguese twisted her wrist over and pressed into her hand a small disc about two inches across. Its carved surface was so dirty the colour was impossible to determine. Heaving himself up off the pillow he tried to drag her towards him. She jerked frantically backwards.

'*Eu amo-te,* Teresa. I love you.' He closed his hand over hers pressing the edges of the disc against her fingers. 'This cost me everything—*aaaagh.*' His lips drew back in a snarl of pain and his eyelids flickered closed.

Tearing herself free she snatched up the letter and her writing-case from the floor and ran out. In the dispensary she leaned against the bench gulping for air. Suddenly she began to shiver. Her breath caught in a sob and hot tears slid down her cheeks. She raised her hand to wipe her eyes. But where he had held her she could smell the sickly, rotting odour.

A bitter taste rose in her throat and she lurched across to the stone sink beneath the window. Reaching out to turn on the single tap she realized she was still clutching the disc. Dropping it in the sink she seized the soap and scrubbed her hands, working up a thick creamy lather. The men in the ward had warned her; she had no one to blame but herself. But that *smell* ...

Blinking away tears she rinsed off the suds then bent forward and cupped the icy water over her burning face. It took her breath away but she felt better. As she dried herself her gaze fell on

16

the disc. She turned on the tap once more and, using plenty of soap, gave it a thorough wash. Her hands ached from the cold water but she had stopped trembling.

The medallion was pink jade carved with a Chinese motif. Her Uncle George had been in China during the first Opium War. He had described steep mountains and flat plains, wide rivers and terraced fields, pirate-infested waters and typhoons. A land where people wore red to celebrate birth and marriage, and white to mourn their dead; where black was the only acceptable colour for hair and eyes. 'They'd call you a devil,' he'd said, laughing. Then he had told her about the Honourable East India Company. 'A British trading venture begun in 1600, which acquired a prestige unequalled since the days of the Phoenicians.' He told her how it had spread its operations from India to China. And how, after the company lost its monopoly in 1833, free-traders scrambled to set up new trading houses. 'Jardine Matheson, Dent, Beale, Hawke: adventurers who cared nothing for regulations or the legality of what they were trading. They bribed the mandarins. Any custom-house officials foolish enough to interfere were simply brushed aside.'

Susanna had listened, wide-eyed, to his tales. But when she asked him about the war, and about the opium that caused it, his face had darkened. 'I'll not speak of that,' he'd said. 'What's past is done and best forgotten. You let it be, understand?'

After he died she had continued to scour

17

the newspapers, eager to learn more about this strange land. But her parents disapproved of her interest in a country still ignorant of Christianity. So she had tried to concentrate on things they *did* approve of. But their world was so narrow, so limited, she felt as if she were suffocating.

Susanna hung the towel on its hook. The dispensary had its own peculiar smell—a mixture of herbs, camphor, gas and carbolic—familiar, comforting, and safe. Suddenly all the bottles rattled as the outside door crashed open. With a violent start she thrust the Chinese medallion into the pocket of her dress and ran out.

Two men wearing the thick trousers, boots and stained canvas smocks of fishermen staggered up the passage carrying a makeshift stretcher on which a white-faced boy lay keening in agony. Behind them, his tall, slightly stooping figure instantly recognizable, came Edward. Her heart gave a sharp kick.

The gold pin in his maroon silk cravat and the fine cloth and immaculate cut of his frock coat proclaimed him a man of wealth. But slimy mud smeared his trousers and caked shoes normally polished to a mirror shine. As the men drew level, their weather-beaten faces strained with effort and anxiety, the one at the back shot her an anguished glance.

''Tis my boy, Colin. The shoring collapsed and 'is leg was trapped under the boat.'

'Oh, Mr Treneer, I'm so sorry.' As they trudged past she caught a poignant glimpse of a dirty bare foot no bigger than her own.

The lower part of one trouser leg was ripped and through the muddy blood-soaked cloth she caught the gleam of jagged white bone. This new horror was too much. Her head swam and she pressed her fingers to her mouth.

'First door on the right,' Edward called. 'Just put the stretcher on the table. Don't try to move him.' He paused beside Susanna. 'Is Lewis still here?'

Swallowing hard she shook her head. 'He left while I was on the ward.'

'What about Albert?'

'He's still outside unblocking that drain.'

'Then it'll have to be you. Come on.' He started down the passage to where the men were carefully manoeuvring the stretcher in through the doorway.

'M-me?' she gasped, gripping the door jamb. He *couldn't* expect her to—

Edward turned back. 'Yes, you. I need an assistant.'

She gaped at him. 'But I'm not—I can't—'

'*I* can't do this alone. And if I don't act soon the boy will die.' His blunt summary of the situation made her cringe. 'Surely you don't want that on your conscience?'

'Of course not,' she retorted appalled. 'But—'

'No buts,' he interrupted. 'Please. We haven't time. When you first started your visits you told me it was because you wanted to do something really useful. Well, this is your chance. I don't know if I can save the boy's leg. I'll do my damnedest. But I need your help. Do you understand?'

19

Moistening parched lips and deliberately shutting out the clamour of parental warnings she nodded.

Flashing her one of his rare smiles he strode down the corridor. She followed, her thoughts flying in all directions like sparks from a firework.

'We had the boat up on the foreshore,' George Treneer was saying. 'It was only minor repairs, see?' Susanna tried desperately to blank out the boy's screams as he was transferred from the makeshift stretcher to the operating-table. The room smelled of blood, fish, and sewage-tainted mud.

'I asked 'un if he'd checked the wedges.' George's normally cheerful face was haggard and grey. 'Always in a rush he is. "Boats don't earn no money on the beach, father", he'd say to me.'

'Susanna, will you fetch two buckets of water, one boiling and one cold.' As Edward glanced across at her, George's words echoed in her head. *The shoring collapsed and his leg was trapped under the boat.* She tried desperately to push the all-too-vivid image from her mind. 'Then go to the dispensary.'

Returning to the operating-room, her arms full, she saw Edward bent over the boy while the two fishermen hovered uncertainly near the door.

'Get them out of here,' he muttered.

Setting bowls, bandages and bottles down on a metal trolley, she ushered the men into the passage. 'Doctor Arundell thinks it would be

20

better if you went home now, Mr Treneer.'

The fisherman's craggy face was ashen and there was agony in his eyes. 'I can't jest leave 'un.'

'Your son is in good hands,' Susanna tried to reassure him. 'The doctor will do all he can.'

'I knew that. That's why I sent Jacko to fetch 'un. The other doctors've got no time fer the likes of we.' George Treneer craned his neck to see past Susanna. 'Can't I do nothing to help?'

'Honestly, Mr Treneer, it's best if you go home. You know how news travels in this town.' Susanna laid a hand on his arm. 'Think how your wife will feel if she hears it from someone who wasn't even there. You should be the one to tell her. She'll need your comfort. And reassurance that Colin is receiving the very best care.'

Reluctantly he nodded. 'Ais, I s'pose you're right.' He glanced at her hand on his arm then raised moist eyes to hers. 'Yer father should be proud of 'e.'

She gave him a brief smile and said nothing. According to her family her fondness for physical contact was yet another of her failings. Yet instinct told her that a simple touch often provided greater comfort, conveyed more sympathy, and showed deeper concern than a hundred earnest words.

Clearing his throat awkwardly the other man spoke for the first time. 'Lose 'is leg, will 'e?'

She understood what lay behind the question and why George Treneer had been unable to

21

ask it. Shooting nets in rough seas and gutting fish on a heaving slippery deck required two strong legs.

'Doctor Arundell will do everything in his power to avoid that,' she replied firmly.

'When can I come and see 'un?'

She spread her hands. 'I don't—'

'Susanna!' Edward's summons was urgent.

'Perhaps tomorrow evening, just for a moment, if he's strong enough. Please excuse me, I have to go.' Heart pounding she gritted her teeth and returned to the operating-room.

Chapter Two

Edward had taken off his frock coat and rolled up his shirt sleeves, exposing pale sinewy forearms dusted with freckles. A clean white apron covered him from chest to knee.

'There's one for you by the sink,' he said. 'Hurry up and wash your hands.'

Susanna had never seen any of the doctors who visited her family wear aprons or wash their hands, but Edward would not be giving her these strange instructions without a very good reason.

Moments later she approached the table. Edward was bent over the shaking boy, his voice low and reassuring.

'This will put you to sleep for a while and the pain will stop. Just breathe naturally. That's

22

it.' Drop by careful drop he was pouring liquid through a metal spout attached to a large brown bottle on to a gauze-lined mask made of thin perforated metal which he held over the boy's nose and mouth.

'Here, you take over. Two or three more drops should be enough.'

'What is it?' Her voice sounded thin.

'Ether. I must get the dirt out of that wound otherwise there'll be precious little chance of saving his life, never mind his leg.'

Susanna wanted to run, to get out before she saw things she would never be able to forget.

The boy's eyelids were half-closed. Tremors racked him. Despite the coolness of the room his ashen face was sheened with perspiration.

If she ran how would she live with herself? Edward needed her. *There was no one else.* Rigid with tension she took his place.

'That's fine,' he reassured, moving away to complete his preparations.

Her hands were shaking so badly it took every ounce of her concentration to hold the metal spout steady over the mask. The sweet pungent scent of the anaesthetic enveloped her in waves. She went hot then cold and her long-sleeved, high-necked dress of brown serge clung heavily to her clammy body.

'Don't get too close.'

As Edward's warning penetrated the fog in her head Susanna realized she had been breathing in the fumes, and turned her face aside.

The boy had stopped groaning and lay utterly still, eyes closed, his face as white as the sheet beneath him. Lifting the boy's arm Edward allowed it to fall back on the table. 'He's well away. You can put those down,' he indicated the bottle and mask. 'There, on the trolley. Susanna?' She glanced up nervously. 'You're doing fine.' He placed an empty bucket on a stool alongside the table. Picking up another bottle he poured some colourless liquid into an enamel bowl full of water. The strong acrid smell of carbolic caught in Susanna's throat. 'Now come round here.' Gently he lifted the boy's leg so it extended beyond the edge of the table and over the bucket. Then to her horror he parted the torn flesh with his thumbs to expose the glistening jagged edge of the broken bone.

'Use that small bowl as a dipper and pour the antiseptic over the wound. But not too fast.'

Nausea tightened her throat and prickled her skin with sweat. Blackness crowded the edge of her vision and she felt herself sway.

'Susanna,' he said sharply. 'Come along, pull yourself together.'

Her green eyes, huge and shocked, flew to his face. 'D-don't sh-shout at me,' she stammered. 'You're used to all this, I'm not.'

'I'm not shouting,' he said carefully, 'and I'm not angry.' The skin around his nostrils was pinched and white. 'But this is no time to have an attack of the vapours. Stop worrying about how *you* feel. Think about the boy. And if you can't face that, don't think at all. Just do exactly as I tell you. All right?'

'I'm sorry.' The words emerged jerkily as her breath caught and with a shaking hand she

24

carefully irrigated the wound with antiseptic solution.

Several tense and silent minutes later he told her to stop. The sound of the broken bones being restored to their proper position made her flinch.

Heart thumping, eyes steadfastly lowered so as not to betray the chaos inside her, Susanna allowed him to place her hands on the boy's leg.

'Make sure you hold it perfectly still.'

She nodded, not trusting herself to speak as he spread a fawn-coloured, dough-like material with a pungent, biting smell on to the wound and over a wide area around it.

'The putty will stop the carbolic acid being washed out of the dressing by normal wound discharge.'

After a moment it dawned on her that in explaining what he was doing he was treating her as an equal. She darted a look at him, but he had turned away to reach for a towel.

After wiping his hands Edward picked up a square of thin tin sheet from the trolley and moulded it over the putty. 'This was originally used to line the chests that carry tea from China. And if it keeps moisture *out,* it should also hold it *in.* It's important that the carbolic doesn't simply evaporate.'

He splinted and bandaged the leg. 'That's it.' He straightened up. 'Now all we can do is wait.'

The crisis was over. But its aftermath of exhaustion and elation left Susanna dizzy and light-headed. She clung to the trolley, her legs tingling and rubbery.

'Are you all right?'

Edward's voice seemed to come from far away. With a tremendous effort she fought off the blackness that threatened to engulf her and sucking in a deep breath raised her head and gave him a glassy smile. 'I'm fine.'

He nodded, then gave a rueful shrug. 'I—er—I shouldn't have shouted at you. You did remarkably well. In fact I have to say you're a constant surprise.'

'Why? I'm not stupid. Or is it because I'm young? Time will soon remedy that.' Her frustration tumbled out, unstoppable. 'I *want* so much to learn but you would not believe the difficulties I face.'

'I have never,' he said gravely, 'met a young woman like you.'

Normally she was able to keep her feelings well hidden. Emotion was considered untidy. Control was all. But she had been waiting and hoping for so *long*. Hot-cheeked and flustered she began to gather up the debris.

Bending over the still unconscious boy Edward gently lifted one closed eyelid then checked his pulse. 'Hold the door for me will you?' He moved to the head of the table. 'I'll wheel our young patient along to the ward.'

'How long will Colin be staying?'

'It will be four days before I know whether or not the wound is infected,' he answered obliquely.

'Is there anything more I can do?'

'No, thank you. You've done quite enough.'

She lifted one shoulder, a small uncertain movement. 'I'm sorry. Only it was such a shock—'

'For heaven's sake, Susanna, don't apologize.' He made a wry face, the corners of his mouth turning down. 'You'll make me feel even worse. You were quite remarkable. Very few young women could have done what you did. In fact, I can't think of one.'

Eyes lowered she held the door open, pierced by guilt for her sinful pride.

He manoeuvred the wheeled table out into the passage then paused. 'Actually, there is something you could do. Will you take a message to Mrs Bennett? Tell her I won't be back for dinner.'

Ever since meeting Edward she had wondered what his home was like. To see for herself his treasured possessions was something she had dreamed about.

'One more thing; there are several medical journals on the desk in my study. Could you bring them back for me?'

Crossing the infirmary yard she drew in a deep breath to clear the ether fumes and those other dreadful odours from her lungs. The sky was pearl-coloured and fast-moving ragged-edged clouds threatened rain before nightfall.

Grove Place was a terrace of tall, dignified town houses set in small front gardens with paved paths leading to wide stone steps and pillared porches. Susanna lifted the polished brass knocker set high on the white-painted front

27

door and let it fall twice. Across the busy road, crowded with horse buses and private carriages taking shoppers home from town, waves slapped against the sea wall.

The gusting wind, redolent of seaweed, tar and horse droppings, whined in the rigging of two huge, five-masted barques anchored in the inner harbour. She knew from her brother William that they had recently arrived from South America, one carrying nitrates and guano, the other a mixed cargo of wool, cotton, and hides. They dwarfed a trio of brigs moored nearby.

Quay punts bustled to and fro on the grey choppy water, ferrying men and supplies from jetties to ships. Boats of every size and rig were built and repaired in the yards that stretched along the bar as far as the docks. To her left the town of Falmouth ran along the water's edge past the gasworks, Market Strand and Pye's Cellars as far as the Greenbank Hotel where the inner harbour narrowed to merge with Penryn River.

Since childhood, the ever-changing scene on the water had fascinated her. She had once confided to her mother that she wished she had been born a boy so she could see the places Uncle George and her father talked about. Even their names had an exotic, mysterious sound: Foochow, Samarang, Madras, Singapore.

Her mother had told her not to be so silly. Men might travel and explore, it was in their nature; but a woman's place was at home taking care of the family. Instead of indulging

28

in fanciful notions she should put more effort into thinking of others. The Friends ran many charities and an extra pair of hands was always welcome.

Accepting that such desires indicated a serious weakness in her character Susanna tried hard to banish them. But occasionally she was overwhelmed by a longing for escape so intense that she ached.

Behind her the door opened. 'Can I help you?'

The maid wore a small lace-edged apron over her black afternoon dress and a frilly cap sat on top of her fair frizzy curls.

'I'd like to see Mrs Bennett, please. I have a message from Doctor Arundell.'

The red floor tiles gleamed with polish. A faint scent of beeswax and lemons hung on the air. At the far end of the hall a thickly carpeted staircase with cream-painted balusters curved past a large window and out of sight.

Shown into the drawing-room Susanna was left alone as the maid bustled out. She had never seen so much colour. The richness of it all took her breath away. Beneath heavy drapes of crimson brocade looped back by ties of braided silk, lace curtains with scalloped edges shrouded the large windows, assuring privacy.

The paintwork and ceiling were palest cream, the walls dark green. A gilt chandelier with five branches, each topped by a frosted glass bowl, was suspended from the carved ceiling rose. A mahogany bookcase covered one wall. The others were hung with pictures; delicate watercolours in pastel shades, and oil paintings with pigment so lavishly applied the artist might have been sculpting his vision on to canvas. Plants cascaded glossy green leaves over the lace mats or polished surfaces on which they stood.

She moved silently across the Indian carpet and, unable to resist the urge to touch, drew her fingertips across the back of a red velvet armchair piled with squashy cushions and through the silky fringes of a Paisley square thrown over the back of the matching sofa.

A massive fern-like plant in a shiny brass pot filled the empty fireplace. Candlesticks, tiny ornaments, and miniatures encased in silver lined the mantelpiece. But her attention was caught by a large and ornate gilded frame hanging above it.

Her parents were strict in their observance of the rules governing Quaker life. There were no pictures in their home, no ornaments, *and no mirrors*. These were condemned as an invention of the Devil, encouraging the sins of vanity and pride.

Guilt wrestled with curiosity: and lost. She saw high cheekbones, a small straight nose, wide, full-lipped mouth and narrow chin. She studied dark brows arched like the wings of a bird, and thick lashes that fringed almond-shaped eyes the colour of new grass.

Lifting her hand she watched the image touch the hollow of one flushed cheek and felt the smooth elasticity of skin warm beneath her fingertips. *Who are you?*

The door opened and she swung round guiltily.

'Good afternoon. I'm Constance Bennett. I'm told you have a message for me?' The voice was cool, matching the expression. Artfully applied cosmetics made it impossible to guess her age. Honey-coloured hair was elegantly styled, her figure voluptuous.

Susanna tried to ignore the unease and envy that pricked like thorns as she looked at the dress of violet and lavender silk trimmed with ribbons and lace and gathered into a fashionable bustle. Constance Bennett was no ordinary housekeeper.

'Doctor Arundell asked me to tell you that there has been an emergency at the infirmary and he will not be back for dinner tonight.'

Constance inclined her head graciously. 'Thank you. Ellen will show you out.'

'He also asked me to collect some medical journals. They are on the desk in his study.'

'Dear Edward.' She gave a tinkling laugh but her eyes were cold. 'So forgetful. You mustn't let him take advantage, Miss Elliot.'

Not sure how to respond Susanna simply smiled politely as Constance glided out, returning a few moments later with the journals.

Hurrying back to the infirmary Susanna wondered at the housekeeper's antagonism. Recalling the sitting-room with its lush furnishings and vibrant colour she pictured herself taking tea there with Edward. The image entranced her.

Edward was in the dispensary, pounding a

reddish resin into powder with a brass mortar and pestle. Placing the journals on the bench she edged closer, intrigued.

'What are you making?'

'A powder of kino and calomel for our patient with congestion of the lungs.'

Our patient. Susanna thought she might burst with happiness. She screwed up her courage. 'Could I learn how to make medicines?'

Edward smiled. 'I think you could learn anything you put your mind to.'

Glowing, Susanna gazed up at him. 'I meant will you teach me? Please?' She indicated the mortar and pestle in his hands. 'If I did some of the basic preparation you would have more time for important things.'

Edward eyed her thoughtfully. 'This is not a job normally done by a woman.'

'According to my family, there is much about me that is not *normal.*' She shrugged, pretending it didn't hurt. 'But you said yourself you could not have operated on Colin Treneer without my help.'

'An extra pair of hands would certainly be useful,' he admitted. 'But what about your other commitments? Your parents might—'

'Nothing,' she broke in quickly, 'is more important than what I'm doing here.'

'All right. Now you really should go home. It will be getting dark soon. Good night, Susanna. And thank you.'

Brimming with happiness she flashed him a brilliant smile as she opened the door. 'Goodnight, Edward.' This was the most important day of her life.

At the bottom of the lane she stopped on the pavement and looked back over her shoulder at the Seamen's Home. Inside the three-storeyed, red-brick building furnishings were spartan, but she had seen tough men hardened by months at sea in atrocious conditions reduced to tears of gratitude for the luxury of a hot meal, a clean bed and medical aid. Many were decent God-fearing men who returned to their families as often as they could. But others eyed her in a way she found disconcerting.

She had seen some a few days after their release from the infirmary staggering through the streets, drunk and cursing. If they could not get a berth on a ship they often ended up among the ruffians and thieves who skulked in the narrow alleys and passageways of the waterfront at night, scavenging like rats. Yet each of them was somebody's son.

She was finding it ever more difficult to reconcile a loving merciful God with the squalor and suffering she saw every day.

Fishermen wearing thick jerseys trudged up from the town quay, their oilskins folded into the large square basket each carried over his arm, their pasty dinners eaten many hours ago.

Pulling her cloak more closely around her Susanna walked on. Though her teeth chattered and her gloveless hands were frozen she was glowing inside. At last Edward had begun to see her in a new light. If, as her parents claimed, marriage was the only permissible ambition for a woman then Edward was the only man she could even consider marrying. For if he were to accept her—not just into his life but into his work as well—then maybe she would find the fulfilment she craved.

But Edward was a Catholic. And for her to marry a non-Quaker meant she would be disowned by the Society of Friends. Her father was an Elder, a position of respect and seniority within the Church. Her mother sat on numerous committees and was actively involved in every charity supported by Friends.

Her disownment would affect their standing among their peers. And though she found the constraints of their lifestyle suffocating she loved them dearly. Having been taught to obey them in all things the enormity of what she was considering filled her with agonizing guilt.

Chapter Three

Her hands composed on her lap, Susanna kept her face carefully impassive. Like her mother Maria and older sister Frances sitting either side of her she wore a simple white bonnet and beneath her drab cloak a plain grey dress.

How she envied them their tranquillity and patience. As the silence dragged Susanna took a folded handkerchief from her pocket. Hands hidden by her cloak she uncovered the pink jade medallion and ran her fingertips over its carved surface.

She ought to have given it to Edward to return to the Portuguese. After all, it had not been given to *her*, but to the person his fever-racked mind believed she was. But it was unusual and beautiful and she had never owned any jewellery or pretty trinkets. Perhaps she could look after it for a few days. Then she would give it back.

Edward lived in a home bursting with colour yet what he did for his fellow human beings required more courage, dedication, and sheer hard work than any activity undertaken by Friends. He was unlike any other man of her acquaintance. And from what he had said yesterday, he thought the same of her.

She imagined Edward cupping her face in those wonderful healing hands. Then his arms enfolding her, drawing her close against his body as he lowered his head and his lips—Frances's elbow in her ribs made her gasp. She bent her head hoping her bonnet would hide the betraying flush.

The cold bare room had remained hushed for almost half an hour. Yet in a manner which seemed totally spontaneous awareness that the period of silent worship had ended spread through the assembly in the space of a breath. Susanna was sure the Elders had some prearranged signal.

Maria turned to her daughters, her round face calm and serene. 'Come, girls.'

As they started towards the door Susanna saw John Tregelles place a restraining hand on her father's sleeve and murmur in his ear. Her father's reproachful gaze left her in no doubt

35

that she was the subject of the whispered remarks. Who had she offended now?

'Richard will be joining us for dinner,' Frances said importantly, falling into step beside her.

Susanna glanced quickly round. 'I didn't see him.'

'He didn't come. His mother is poorly.'

'Again? I'm sorry to hear that. She seems to be suffering rather a lot of ill-health.'

'She worries about being a burden to Richard. But who else can she turn to?'

'Her husband?' Susanna suggested mildly.

'Mr Webber's *weakness* makes him unreliable.'

Privately Susanna thought that living with Mrs Webber's endless demands and complaints would drive the strongest man to drink.

'You will try to be pleasant, won't you?'

'He doesn't make it easy.'

'What do you mean?' Though short and rounded like their mother Frances had sharp elbows and a sharp tongue. Even her features were pointed.

'He's always so critical. Haven't you noticed?'

'No.' Frances's eyes widened in genuine surprise. 'I've never found him so.'

Susanna smiled wryly. 'Well, you wouldn't. How could he find fault with someone who exemplifies all the best qualities of Quaker womanhood?'

Uncertainty drew Frances's heavy brows together. 'Are you teasing me?'

'No, of course not. Fran, why do you find it so difficult to accept a compliment?'

Wriggling uncomfortably beneath her dreary

36

grey-brown cloak Frances sniffed. 'Compliments encourage vanity.'

Susanna felt a surge of pity for her serious dutiful sister. 'No they don't. Being good at something doesn't mean you're vain. It just proves you are using the talents God gave you. I think that's far more useful than sitting in silence for hours.'

'Susanna!' Frances looked round quickly to make sure no one else had overheard. 'No wonder Richard thinks you dangerous.'

Dangerous? She opened her mouth to make a crushing retort but thought better of it. Frances was not responsible for Richard. 'I would enjoy Richard's company more if he did not concern himself quite so much with *my* affairs.'

'Your behaviour is his concern, or will be very soon.' They followed Hester Trethown and her mother out on to the cobbled street.

The wind funnelling up Quay Hill from the harbour swirled around their ankles and lifted the hem of Hester's dress. Quickly she grasped a handful of the billowing skirt. A swift shake and it was once again in place, decorously brushing the tops of her shoes.

'Did you see that?' Frances was scandalized.

'Yes,' Susanna smiled, 'I saw. Fran, what did you mean about Richard? Why should what I do—'

'Red stockings! Hester was wearing *red stockings!*'

'Shh. There's no need to tell everyone.' Susanna watched Hester with new respect and

37

a pang of envy. 'It's no one else's business anyway.'

'She'll go to Hell,' Frances announced with utter conviction.

Susanna looked at her in bewilderment. At twenty three Frances had the outlook and attitudes of her mother's generation. Yet was that so surprising? When Susanna recalled her childhood it was Frances she remembered bathing her knees when she fell down, Frances who told her bedtime stories and taught her prayers.

William's birth had been difficult and during Maria's long recuperation both parents relied heavily on their eldest daughter. As soon as her strength returned Maria took over once more. But by then duty and responsibility had become Frances's security and her prison.

'Hester go to Hell?' Susanna mocked gently. 'For wanting a little colour in her life?'

'Don't you care about your immortal soul?'

'Of course I do. I just happen to believe God has more important things to worry about than the colour of Hester Trethown's stockings.'

'Oh!' Frances squeaked. 'I believe you say these things quite deliberately to shock me.'

Seeing her sister's eyes full of tears Susanna swallowed her exasperation. 'Fran, what you said about Richard. What did you mean?'

Two splotches of pink appeared high on Frances's cheeks. With sudden childlike excitement, the more endearing for being so rare, she confided, 'We are to be married before Christmas after all.'

'*Before* Christmas?'

Frances stiffened. 'What's wrong with that?'

'Nothing. I didn't mean—'

'I don't think you care about my happiness.'

'Of course I do.' Susanna clasped her sister's cold hand. 'Fran, I wish you all the joy in the world. It's just—' She stopped herself. What possible objection could she make? It would not be fair to allow her dislike of him to spoil her sister's happiness.

'It's just what?' Frances asked suspiciously.

'Nothing. Nothing at all. For your sake I will try to think of Richard as part of our family.'

'Thank you. You see as your brother-in-law and ... my husband!'—Frances's colour deepened—'Richard is bound to take an interest in your welfare. I know he is concerned about the amount of time you spend at the Seamen's Hospital.'

A lightning flash of anger lanced through Susanna. But the arrival of her brother stopped her making the comment she would have instantly regretted.

'Fran, Mother wants you. Something to do with the infants school.' He caught Susanna's hand. 'Come on, I'll race you home. You might even win. My feet are so cold I can hardly feel them.'

'I'm not running. Your legs are twice as long as mine.' She tucked her arm through his and they set off along the narrow pavement past closed shops with thick wooden shutters over their windows to prevent them being smashed by the drunken seamen for which this end of the town was notorious.

Though two years younger, William had always been her closest friend and ally. In his eyes she could do no wrong. As the rest of the family frequently took the opposite view his unquestioning loyalty and approval had always been an enormous comfort.

'Did you know that the wedding had been brought forward?' she enquired as they turned into Swanpool Street.

'Whose wedding?' He shortened his loping stride as the hill grew steeper. In the last two years he had shot up and still seemed not quite used to his new height. The bitter wind tousled his fair hair and whipped colour into his cheeks.

'Frances and Richard's of course.'

'Oh yes. There's no reason to wait now.'

'What do you mean?'

'You know they were looking for a house to rent—'

'Have they found somewhere then?'

William pulled a face. 'In a manner of speaking. Richard and his mother have decided that it would be foolish for him to go to such expense when the Webber house is quite big enough for them all. Poor Fran.'

'It might not be charitable to say so but I think it's a very bad idea. If she isn't careful she'll find herself looking after the whole family.'

'I hadn't thought of that.'

Susanna looked quickly at her brother. 'What did you mean then, *poor Fran?*'

40

'Marrying *Richard*. He's such a stuffed shirt. Still,' he shrugged, 'Fran's the same. In fact when you think about it they're a perfect match. If Fran can cope with Richard's mother they'll probably be very happy together. And Fran will have a whole regiment of baby stuffed shirts.'

Susanna thumped his arm. 'Will, that's awful.'

'No, it's not, it's true. But I'm glad for them, really. After all neither of them has been besieged by suitors. Richard might be Fran's only chance.'

'For goodness' sake, she's not that old.'

'Yes she is. I'm not talking in years. Some people are born old. Fran's like that. She never climbed trees with me like you did, or fished for tadpoles. And she hates horses.'

'You have to understand about Fran,' Susanna began.

'I do,' William said. 'She's a good person. She works terrifically hard and never looks for praise like so many of the women. In fact, it seems to make her uncomfortable. Fran's trouble is she doesn't know how to have fun.' He shrugged. 'I think that's sad.'

William had voiced her own thoughts.

He nudged her. 'Want to go for a ride later?'

'On a Sunday?' Susanna dragged air into her heaving lungs. 'We'd never get away with it.'

Crossing Woodlane they arrived at Wodehouse Place. The elegantly proportioned house was set

41

at an angle to the road. Tall trees and shrubs enclosed the front garden and gave privacy from neighbouring properties.

Susanna glanced at the few remaining flowers and the cloud of plume-like seeds on the white clematis as she followed William up the steps to the porch. Soon even those would be gone.

Samuel Elliot stood at the head of the table carving a large joint of beef. Susanna and William sat on his right, Richard and Frances on his left. Maria was at the far end opposite her husband.

Richard tucked the starched napkin into the top of his waistcoat. 'Teaching children to read and write is not enough. Bible study is vital. Only through religion will they be led away from crime and dependence upon the charity of others.' His mouse-brown hair was receding at the temples and so thin on top his pink scalp showed through.

'Well said,' Samuel nodded, as he transferred slices of beef, crisp and brown on the outside and succulent pink in the middle, on to plain white plates.

Susanna's gaze flickered from Richard's fleshy features to Frances. Though her eyes were fixed on her fiancé her expression gave nothing away.

What did she *feel?* Susanna wondered. Was there a kinder, more gentle side to Richard that only Frances knew? She hoped so. Frances often spoke of beliefs she shared with Richard, but she had never mentioned love.

'Children must be taught what joy is to be found in hard work and thriftiness,' Richard declared. 'It is our responsibility to set a proper example to the lower classes.'

'Indeed,' Samuel murmured.

Susanna caught William's eye. He gave his head an almost imperceptible shake. She read the warning but wisdom was drowned by anger.

'Richard, do you know Gutheridge's Yard, Sedgmond's Court and Rose Cottages?'

His lips pursed. 'Pretty names, but not, I'm afraid, familiar.'

Irony twisted Susanna's mouth. 'I did not really expect them to be. They are slums on the north side of Well Lane. They are filthy, dark and overcrowded. Disease is rife because there is no proper water supply or sewage disposal. But the children who live there know all about hard work and thriftiness. If they live to reach the age of six they are sent out to earn a few coppers by sweeping chimneys or packing fish. They dodge horses' hooves and the wheels of heavy carts to run errands. And if, as so often happens, they are injured and cannot work they look after their smaller brothers and sisters. How much joy do you suppose they know?'

'Susanna!' Frances gasped.

Drawing himself up Richard gazed down his pudgy nose. 'It is not for us to question God's purpose.'

Flinching as William kicked her ankle, Susanna bit her tongue hard, remaining silent

43

as her mother smoothly turned the conversation to Richard's prospects for advancement.

The uniformed maid bustled to and fro from the trolley with dishes of roast potatoes, braised leeks, mashed parsnip and swede, placing them in a row down the centre of the plain white cloth.

After setting a pot of horseradish sauce and two jugs of rich steaming gravy on the table she pushed the trolley back against the wall and returned to the kitchen.

Though he was one of the town's most successful ship-owners and cargo brokers, Samuel's Quaker conscience required that everything in his house should be plain and functional. His only means of proclaiming his status, while not offending his conscience or his peers, was to ensure that his furniture, while devoid of decoration or ornament, was of the very best quality.

The dining-table, matching chairs and long sideboard were solid oak. The cutlery was silver and the napkins finest Irish linen. But the cream-painted walls were bare. There were no rich carpets on the polished wood floors and the windows were curtained with plain beige linen rep.

Susanna felt no spiritual uplift in this monochrome austerity and with each passing day her sense of separateness and emotional starvation grew harder to bear.

When plates had been passed down the table and everyone was served, Samuel said grace and the meal began.

Chapter Four

'Susanna?'

She looked up with a start. Everyone was staring at her. Normally she was able to follow her own train of thought while still keeping one ear tuned to the general conversation. Today she had lost track. Someone had spoken to her. But who? A sideways flicker of William's eyes was all she needed to warn her. She might have guessed.

'Would you mind repeating that, Richard?' She flashed him her sweetest smile and was delighted to see him momentarily disconcerted.

Dabbing his mouth with his napkin he stretched his chin forward and cleared his throat. 'Susanna, I wish you to understand that my only reason for speaking out is because of the esteem in which I hold your family. A family which, on marriage to my dear Frances, I will embrace as my own.'

'Indeed, Richard, I understand your motives perfectly.'

He blinked then continued, 'Then you will know I have only your welfare at heart when I tell you that the amount of time you are spending with Doctor Arundell at the Seamen's Home and Infirmary is causing much comment.'

Skilfully disguised as concern his words were as deliberate and lethal as a dagger-thrust.

Susanna flushed as shock and anger tingled through her. But she forced herself to remain calm. 'I would be surprised if Doctor Arundell's work was not arousing interest. His experiments with antisepsis are saving lives which would otherwise almost certainly have been lost.'

'I think you are deliberately misunderstanding me.' His small eyes glittered with malevolence. 'I have no interest in Doctor Arundell, though I would have expected a professional man to conduct himself with far more prudence and circumspection. As for his *experiments*, I know Doctor Tuffery considers them a complete waste of time. My concern is for the reputation of this family. When a man who should know better permits a young unmarried woman to—'

'The patients care nothing for my age or marital status, Richard.' Susanna broke in as fury at his impertinence overrode good manners. 'They are too occupied with trying not to die.'

'Susanna!' A frown marred Maria's normally serene countenance. But Susanna knew her mother's censure was directed less at her blunt words than at her second lapse of etiquette in arguing with a guest at the dinner-table.

'I apologize, Mama.' Susanna set her knife and fork neatly on her plate. Placing her crumpled napkin beside her water glass she started to rise.

'May I be excused?'

'No.' Samuel intervened and gestured for her to resume her seat.

She had known that sooner or later this would happen. It had been brewing for weeks. Richard

46

was nothing more than a catalyst.

As she sat down again his expression of regret was contradicted by the spite in his eyes. *Why?* she wondered. *What have I ever done to him?* Then she remembered the first time he had come to the house.

Her father and William were at the office, her mother out visiting relations, and Frances at a meeting. She had been in the drawing-room sorting and listing linen given by other Friends for the poor mothers' lying-in-home.

'If you please, miss.' Agnes had poked her head round the door. 'There's a gentleman to see Miss Frances.'

'Has he brought the slates and chalk for the day school?'

The maid shook her head. 'I didn't see none, miss. He's holding a bunch of flowers.'

Susanna's brows climbed. The only gentlemen to call on Frances were those connected with her charitable work.

'I expect she'll be back any minute, miss.'

Detecting a note of anxiety Susanna interpreted it as concern that once frightened off this rare bird might not return.

'Then you had better show him in, Agnes.'

The maid disappeared returning a few moments later. 'Mr Richard Webber, miss.'

'Good afternoon, Mr Webber.' Susanna closed the ledger in which she had been listing the linen and walked towards him offering her hand. His fingers were damp and soft. She fought the urge to wipe her hand down her skirt. 'Isn't it lovely to see some sun at last?'

He jutted his fleshy chin forward as if his collar was tight. 'Good afternoon, Miss Elliot.' He seemed unable or unwilling to meet her eyes.

Because of his father's fondness for alcohol and his mother's ill-health he often cut a rather lonely figure among the other Quaker families. 'What beautiful flowers,' she smiled, indicating the sheaf of daffodils and jonquils he carried. Had they been simply a random choice? Or was he aware that they signified the desire for returned affection? 'Their fragrance is truly the breath of spring.'

'Indeed,' Richard agreed, with ill-concealed impatience. 'Has your sister been informed that I am here?'

Drawing on the good manners that had been drummed into her since early childhood Susanna swallowed her instinctive antipathy towards this pompous little man only a few years older than herself. 'I'm afraid Frances is not back yet.'

His frown was accusing as though this were somehow her fault. 'Not back? Where is she then?'

His supercilious manner rasped across her nerve ends like a grater. But he was the first man ever to bring flowers for Frances. If she had to bite her tongue to keep him here until her sister returned then that was what she would do. But her cheeks were beginning to ache with the effort of maintaining her smile.

'Frances had a committee meeting this afternoon. You know how they can overrun.

48

I'm sure she will be here shortly.' Ignoring Richard's sniff of irritation she indicated the sofa. 'Do come and sit down.'

His expression grew even more disapproving. 'I think not, Miss Elliot. In fact I think it would be best if I leave and return at a more convenient time.'

'Please, that really isn't necessary.' Frances would be devastated if she came back only to find she had missed him. She would assume Susanna had not made enough effort to make him feel welcome. 'Don't go,' she entreated. 'You are not keeping me from anything urgent.'

He tilted his head back, his porcine gaze oddly bright as his mouth pursed in righteous indignation. 'So you would amuse yourself by trying to entice your sister's suitor? Shame on you, Miss Elliot.'

Shock drove all the breath from her body. 'I? Entice *you?*' She burst out laughing. 'How could you possibly think—? The idea is utterly ridiculous.'

His mouth sagged open. He seemed stunned by her reaction.

Her laughter had been involuntary. Her remarks intended simply to put his mind at rest, to assure him she had no designs upon his person. But his crimson flush of humiliation indicated severely wounded pride. Scorn at his conceit in imagining she found him the least bit attractive battled with rising anger that he dared assume she would do something so hurtful. But for Frances's sake she had to ignore her own feelings and try to make amends.

Footsteps on the path outside made her look quickly towards the window. As the front door slammed she turned to him.

'Mr Webber, I love my sister and would never do anything to hurt her. I trust you feel the same?'

The door opened and Frances whirled in, an unaccustomed blush softening her pointed face. Susanna had never seen her look so pretty.

'Do forgive me, Richard.' She sounded breathless, yet Frances *never* ran. She took great pride in her ability to plan her days so that without a minute being wasted her progress from one task to another was smooth and unhurried.

'I was at a committee meeting concerning the infant school.' As the tension registered her gaze flickered uncertainly to Susanna and her smile faded.

In that instant Susanna saw through the public image of her conscientious and hard-working older sister to the vulnerability beneath. A wave of protectiveness washed over her.

'My dear, you are an example to us all.' Richard's patronizing smirk made Susanna's hand itch with thoroughly unchristian desire to slap his fat red face.

Turning her back on him she smiled reassuringly at Frances and picked up the ledger.

'Mr Webber arrived only moments ago. I am surprised you did not meet on the doorstep. Look at the flowers he's brought you, aren't they beautiful?'

Frances's bewilderment revealed her low self-esteem as she gazed first at the flowers then at the man who carried them. *No man had ever brought her flowers before.* Her surprise was edged aside by a dawning smile of wholly feminine delight and pride. But with a visible effort she straightened her face.

Susanna wanted to cry out to her not to feel guilt for her moment's pleasure. The flowers were beautiful. And whatever her own opinion of the man carrying them if seeing him made Frances happy who was she to interfere? Gathering up the linen and her ledger she went to the door.

'Please excuse me, I really must finish this today. I'll ask Agnes to bring some tea, shall I?'

'Yes, thank you,' Frances said over her shoulder before turning back to her visitor. 'Oh Richard, how kind of you. Of all spring flowers I like these the best.'

Susanna closed the door, not wanting to hear his reply.

Richard continued to visit. Once Frances had jolted her by asking why she didn't like him.

'What are you talking about?' Susanna had feigned surprise. 'Whatever makes you think that?'

'Well, whenever Richard calls you always seem to be rushing off somewhere.'

'Am I? I hadn't noticed.' It couldn't be sinful to lie when the motive was to avoid hurting someone you loved. 'Anyway,' she smiled, 'Richard comes to see *you,* not me. You must have lots to talk about. If I stayed I'd only be in the way.'

'So you have nothing against him then?' Frances persisted, clearly wanting confirmation.

Apart from the fact that he's a petty, pompous, self-righteous prig with an unpleasant tendency to hector and a hugely inflated opinion of himself? 'I don't think he's good enough for you.'

Frances's expression mirrored her astonishment. But within moments she was her normal matter-of-fact self. 'Don't be silly,' she said briskly. 'Richard has a secure position with excellent prospects. It is my good fortune to be marrying such a man.' Her small tight smile brought a lump to Susanna's throat.

'Oh Fran,' she whispered.

Their eyes met. For one brief instant Frances's gaze was naked and self-knowing. 'I do not wish to be an object of pity all my life.'

Susanna grasped her sister's hand tightly. 'Does he make you happy?' If he did she could forgive him much. But if he ever hurt this awkward brave sister of hers ...

Frances lowered her head blushing as she nodded. 'I never imagined any man—' Whatever she had been about to confide remained unsaid, held back by her innate reticence. Instead she looked up. 'Father admires his ambition. Did you know Richard has been invited to sit on the infant school committee? He's very well thought of among the Friends.'

Susanna had made the appropriate responses, gritting her teeth as her sister continued to list Richard Webber's virtues.

52

'Susanna,' her father's voice broke into her thoughts. 'You must not blame Richard. The matter had already been brought to my attention. I was simply waiting for an appropriate moment to discuss it with you.'

Glancing at her sister's fiancé Susanna saw his malicious pleasure at her discomfort replaced by the sudden fear that he might have gone too far.

'I am not angry, Father,' she lied. 'Just disappointed and a little surprised. Didn't our Lord use the parable of the Good Samaritan to tell us that we should tend the sick and wounded?'

Her father sighed. 'Why can you not be more like your brother and sister? Frances is an exemplary daughter. She has never given us a moment's worry. And though William is only seventeen he is proving a great asset to the business. His willingness and sunny disposition are more than adequate compensation for his lack of scholarship.'

As William's brows climbed, Susanna's urge to laugh was almost irresistible. She bit the inside of her lip so hard she tasted blood.

'But you—' her father shook his head. 'You are blessed—or perhaps cursed—with an intelligence too great for your own good. It causes restlessness of spirit and a lack of foresight regarding the results of your impetuous behaviour. I welcome and applaud your desire to be of service. However, it is simply not acceptable that a girl of your age should be making regular and unchaperoned visits to the Seamen's Mission and Hospital. I am surprised Doctor Arundell has not mentioned this to you.'

'Doctor Arundell has far more important matters on his mind.'

To her surprise her father nodded. 'I will accept that bereavement may temporarily have clouded his judgement.'

Susanna swallowed. 'I meant he was more concerned for his patients. Father, Doctor Arundell not only welcomes my help he depends upon it. He has told me so.' She longed for a drink but didn't dare pick up her water glass. Keeping her trembling hands under the table out of sight she twined them tightly together. 'Were it not for Doctor Arundell the sick and injured sailors—not to mention the poor in the town—'

'He is, I am sure, most dedicated. But Falmouth has other doctors who are equally caring for the plight of the poor—'

'Forgive me, Father, but that is not so. Certainly the town has other doctors. And they may well shake their heads and tut when they speak of the poor, but most of them prefer to devote their attention to wealthy patients. They have no time left for those suffering the ills which accompany extreme poverty.'

Samuel opened his mouth to speak but Susanna raced on. 'Father, you are always telling us that philanthropy is a saving grace and how important it is that we show kindness and charity to those less fortunate than ourselves.

Isn't that what I am doing? I know many girls *enjoy* running the Bible classes and Sunday schools or helping in the soup kitchen, but I know very few who would be willing, even if they were able, to do what I do.'

'Such vanity, Susanna,' Samuel reproved as she stopped for breath. 'I am prepared to concede that your actions, while misguided, spring from a genuine desire to help.' Relief left Susanna weak. 'However, this family enjoys a certain standing both in the business community and among the Friends. I will not have our good name jeopardized.'

'But—'

'What your father is trying to say,' Maria interjected, 'is that Quaker women of our class must exercise care in our choice of charitable work. What we do reflects on our menfolk.'

'But the Friends in Falmouth contribute regularly to the Seamen's Home and Infirmary.'

'Susanna, neither your father nor I doubt the value of the infirmary or Dr Arundell's work, but he is not a Friend.'

'He cannot be thought less of for that,' Susanna responded at once.

Her parents exchanged a fleeting glance. 'Of course not,' Maria said, 'but if he were a Friend he would have greater understanding for *your* position.'

'He does unders—' she began.

'You see, Susanna,' Samuel continued inexorably, 'in committing yourself exclusively to one charity you are neglecting others equally worthy. While Dr Arundell's care for his patients

55

is beyond question, he has taken advantage of your compassion.'

'He hasn't.' Susanna shook her head vigorously. 'It is you who don't understand.'

'Susanna,' Maria tapped the table, 'please be silent. It is time you listened. You have a kind heart. But while your desire to help the suffering is commendable your conceit is not. Generations of Quaker women have spent long arduous hours doing the traditional charity work of which you are so dismissive.'

'What else is there for them to do, Mama?' The words erupted out of her in a torrent of frustration. 'They have servants to look after their homes; nurses and tutors for their children. Painting and music which women of our class outside the Society enjoy are forbidden to us. *Of course* Quaker women devote themselves to charitable work. They would go mad with boredom if they did not.'

'That will do!' Samuel thundered. 'Your wilfulness is unbecoming to a young woman. A period of work in the soup kitchen might teach you greater humility.'

Throwing herself back in her chair Susanna bent her head seething with anger and resentment. Not at her father, for he was an honourable man who expected even more of himself than he did of his family. Her rage centred on Richard who had deliberately provoked the scene.

'And now let us spare our guest further embarrassment and talk of other things.' Samuel turned to his elder daughter. 'Frances, have you told Richard about the success of your sewing class?'

The tension was broken and conversation resumed as plates were gathered up and dessert served.

Susanna was mortified and furious to feel a tear spill over and slide down her cheek leaving a cool trail on her hot skin.

Her father leaned towards her. 'You may leave the table if you wish.'

Excusing herself Susanna walked from the room without a backward glance. But all the way to the door she was aware of Richard's malicious gaze like a dagger-blade between her shoulders.

Chapter Five

Pausing only to put on outdoor shoes and her thick cloak Susanna let herself out of the house and ran swiftly down the road to Grove House Farm where the family's horses were stabled.

What was she to do? To openly defy her father by refusing to help in the soup kitchen was out of the question. But nor could she give up her visits to the infirmary. Especially now Edward had promised to teach her about medicines. She tensed as a shadow fell across the doorway.

'It's only me,' William said. The mare whickered gently and nudged him with her satiny nose. Opening his hand he fed her the expected sugar lumps.

'What have you done to Richard to make him dislike you so?'

'It was months ago, a silly misunderstanding. He thought I was laughing at him. I wasn't. But ...' She shrugged helplessly. 'Richard might wear plain clothes and a righteous expression but he's a boring, spiteful, hypocritical snob.'

William grinned. 'And those are his good points.'

Susanna threw her arms around her brother. 'Oh, Will, what would I do without you?'

He hugged her with clumsy affection. 'Miss me, I hope. But you'll never have to do without me. I shall look after you when you become a cantankerous old lady terrifying the Elders with your strange ideas.'

'They're not strange. I'm doing something good and worthwhile. And I'm not going to give it up. But if Father asks you about me what will you say?'

'Me? I'm in an office all day struggling with manifests and bills of lading. How would I know where you are or who you're with?'

Susanna planted a kiss on the downy cheek he hadn't yet begun to shave. 'You're my best friend, Will.'

'So can I beg a favour? It's the company ledgers. Father's clerks have explained but I just can't seem to—' He lifted one hand in a gesture of helplessness. 'Look, you've spent time down there. You're much better at that sort of thing than I am.' He gave a wry grin. 'You're better than me at most things.'

58

'Will, that's rubbish.'

'Oh, I don't mind,' he said cheerfully. 'I like you this way. You're never boring, not like most of the girls we know.'

Susanna squeezed his arm. 'Of course I'll help you. We can spend an hour on it tonight if you like.'

'Really?' He beamed with relief. 'What about that ride?'

'Mother asked me to visit the Braithwaites. They weren't at Meeting this morning. Since Uncle George died Mother feels she ought to keep an eye on them.'

William's eyebrows disappeared in the hair that flopped over his forehead. 'They're grown women. I mean, they're almost middle-aged.'

'You know what Mother's like with *family*. She's concerned that Meredith's cold might have gone to her chest.'

'There's certainly enough of it.'

'Will, that's not polite.'

'Do you know what cousin Meredith reminds me of? A bolster full of blancmange.'

'*Will!*' Susanna spluttered with laughter.

'I don't mind calling on them. But if we went for a trot round the castle first we would arrive back at Lansdowne Road in time for afternoon tea.'

'Honestly, William, you organize your entire life around food.'

'I'm still growing,' he defended himself. 'I need constant nourishment. There's a lot of me to fill. And Lucy makes wonderful fruit cake.'

Horses saddled, they mounted up and rode

down Swanpool Street. Glancing through tall wrought-iron gates marking the back entrance to Arwenack Estate Susanna glimpsed the long, covered rope walk and caught the faint odours of dry jute and tar. In the morning dozens of men would be at work twisting together fibres of manila to make ropes as thick as a man's arm.

At the bottom of the street the stench of rotting fish, stale beer, wet sawdust, and other less pleasant smells wafted up from the narrow hill leading down to the north arm of the quay. Men's voices raised in song issued from the open doorway of one of the hotels. Halfway down the steep slope surrounded by a knot of shouting onlookers two men were brawling, a sight so common at this end of town neither remarked on it.

As they passed the Seamen's Home and approached the terrace of grand houses on Grove Place, Susanna offered a silent prayer for Colin Treneer's recovery knowing she wished it for Edward's sake as much as the boy's.

'Hey,' William moved up alongside her. 'Isn't that—?'

'Doctor Arundell, yes.' Susanna felt warmth flood her body at the sight of the tall, red-haired figure.

'This wind certainly is sharp, you've gone all pink. What did I say?' he demanded as she flashed him an anguished glare.

Standing on the pavement alongside a small landau Constance Bennett looked elegant in a close-fitting emerald coat with black velvet

60

frogging, her upswept hair crowned by a tiny hat of emerald silk and black ostrich feathers. Shepherding Edward's children into the waiting carriage Constance climbed in after them. 'We should be back by five.'

'Give them my regards.' As the landau pulled away he walked quickly back up the steps and into the house.

'I wonder if she hopes to marry him?' William mused.

Susanna's astonishment was drowned by dismay. 'She can't.'

'Why not?'

'Well.' Susanna scrabbled for a legitimate-sounding reason. 'For a start, he's still officially in mourning.'

'I didn't mean right now,' William said patiently. 'Though it must be nearly a year since his wife died. But it would make sense, wouldn't it? They're about the same age and she's been a widow for ages. And as they are distantly related the children would be getting a stepmother they've known all their lives. So all things considered—'

'Don't, Will!' Though it had never occurred to her before the idea seemed all too appallingly possible.

William frowned in surprise. 'What's the matter?'

'Have you heard something?' It took all her courage to ask. Through his work in the office and visits to other places of business William met far more people than she did.

'About Mrs Bennett and Doctor Arundell?

No. And Elliot's office knows what's going on almost before it happens.' His broad grin faded. 'Su, what *is* the matter? You look awful.'

'Just because people expect something to happen doesn't mean that it will,' she said desperately.

'True. But why should you care? As long as you are able to continue your work—' Comprehension spread slowly across his face. 'Oh.'

She attempted a self-mocking smile. But her mouth trembled and she turned her head away.

'Does he know how you feel?'

'I don't know. I don't think so.'

'You haven't told him?'

'Of course I haven't!' She was shocked.

William's bafflement returned. 'Why not?'

'Will, how could I? You know perfectly well that convention requires the *man* to make the first move.'

'You care little for convention in other matters,' he pointed out reasonably.

'I know. But this is different. I *can't* speak before he does. It would compromise us both. And I would hate him to think me fast.' Though Richard's accusation had been totally unfounded it still rankled.

'You?' William started to laugh. 'How could he possibly think that? You're either at home, at the infirmary, or out on visits to the old and sick. What time do you have to be a social butterfly? You haven't had a caller who wasn't related to the family in some way.'

'Edward doesn't know that. Anyway, it's not a subject easily raised when we are discussing a patient's illness or treatment.'

'True.' After a few moments William said dubiously, 'He is quite old.'

'He's nothing of the sort,' Susanna retorted. 'I doubt he's much more than thirty ... or thereabouts,' she amended. 'In any case it is quite usual for men to be several years older than their wives. Father is ten years older than mother. A man needs to have established himself before he can support a family.'

'I expect you're right,' William agreed mildly.

The tension drained out of her. That was one of the things she loved best about Will. He might question, or offer an opinion. But he refused to argue.

Their horses' hooves echoed hollowly as they trotted under the railway arch and up the steep curving hill on to Castle Drive with its spectacular view of the docks and the crowded anchorage of the Fal Estuary.

Susanna gazed down over thickly wooded slopes stripped bare by the autumn gales. Birds had picked the tangled brambles clean of berries, and the bracken was brown and flattened by recent heavy rain. White-capped waves of inky blue crashed against jagged grey rocks flinging spray that glittered like splintered glass high into the crisp air and filling clefts in the dark rock with creamy foam.

Screaming gulls hung on the wind and puffball clouds raced across the sapphire sky playing hide and seek with the sun.

'Do you know what I think?' William said. 'I think he must like you a lot.'

Susanna searched his face longing for him to be right. But Will was two years younger than she. What could he know? *He was a man wasn't he?* And men had far more freedom. They lived much wider lives.

'What makes you think so?'

'Come on, Su,' he grinned. 'Didn't you tell me you assisted at an operation yesterday? You said he's going to *teach* you. You must be very special for him to do that.'

Lifting her face to the bright sunshine she breathed in deeply. The air was invigorating. Will's words even more so. 'You could be right.'

'I *am* right,' he insisted. 'Look, if you are having a difficult time because of gossip and disapproval what must it be like for him? I expect his colleagues are giving him a real roasting.'

Susanna stared at him. She had been so immersed in her own problems it had never occurred to her that Edward might be facing similar attack. 'If that is so, Will, then I have no choice.'

'You're not going to give it up?' His expression hovered between surprise and disappointment.

Susanna shook her head, fired with new determination. 'No. I'm not.'

William grinned. 'I didn't think you would. Good for you. But you'll have to be more discreet. Father is in a difficult position, being an Elder.'

'Do you think I don't know that?' Susanna cried. 'Some of the Overseers—and John Tregelles is one of them—seem bent on making trouble. I think they are really enjoying Father's embarrassment.'

William nodded. 'But think a minute. How does John Tregelles, or any of the Overseers, know what Doctor Arundell has been teaching you?'

Susanna stared at him, frowning. 'They don't.'

'Exactly. Don't you see? They *can't* know anything about your work at the infirmary. Not unless you or the doctor have told them, which you haven't. They just want to cause trouble for Father because of his stand against change within the Society. Your activities are simply a convenient stick to beat him with.'

'Will, that's monstrous. Are you sure?'

He nodded. 'I hear things. At Meetings, and in the office. Because I'm quiet, people forget I'm there. It's sad really. They are all honest decent God-fearing men, yet they squabble like children. They can't condemn you for visiting the sick. The only moral delinquency they can charge you—or Father—with, is failing to ensure you are properly chaperoned. So is there anyone you could ask to accompany you when you go to the hospital?'

Susanna started to shake her head then her mouth widened in a smile of delight. 'Molly Treneer. Colin's mother. I expect she'll visit him as often as she can. If I arrive and depart with her—'

'It will be seen that you are dutifully observing all the necessary proprieties. Your critics, and Father's, will have the wind taken right out of their sails.' William radiated contentment. 'Once you're inside who is to know what you do?'

'You're wicked.'

'I know. I've got this terrible sister who leads me astray.'

Susanna's shift of balance as she gathered up the reins was all the mare needed. 'In that case let's canter.' Ears pricked, the mare danced sideways.

'It's Sunday,' William reminded. 'You'll get into trouble.'

'Who's to know?' Susanna demanded recklessly.

'You're on!' William dug his heels into his horse's sides.

Reaching the fork that led up to the castle Susanna reluctantly reined the mare in. Arriving on her cousins' doorstep scarlet-cheeked and out of breath would raise even more questions about her behaviour.

Oak Villa stood plain square and solid in a small front garden separated from the pavement by black-painted iron railings and a berberis hedge. Narrow glass panels surrounded the top half of the white front door protected by a stone porch on either side of which was a large bay window.

'You go on in,' William directed. 'I'll see to the horses.'

Handing him the mare's reins Susanna tucked her escaping curls back under her bonnet and after brushing the dust from her grey dress, pulled her cloak straight and started up the path while William led the horses away to the stable where hay nets and water buckets were always kept full.

'Susanna!' Lucy beamed with pleasure. Wiry and straightbacked she had skin like fine tissue paper and eyes as bright and sharp as a bird's. Her hair was the same colour as her plain fawn dress. She wore it drawn into a simple knot high on the back of her head. 'How lovely to see you. Have you come alone?'

'No, William is with me.' Susanna pulled off her thin riding gloves and unfastened her cloak, handing both with a smile to the maid who had opened the door. 'He'll join us as soon as he's seen to the horses.'

'Come on in by the fire. Mary,' she addressed the maid, 'we'll have tea now. Bring plenty.' She turned to Susanna with a knowing smile. 'William's appetite will not have lessened since his last visit.'

Bobbing respectfully the girl left, and Susanna followed her cousin across the room. The mahogany bureau, tall bookcases, and the library chair with its buttoned leather seat and padded arms brought back vivid memories of her Uncle George. Two wooden rocking chairs stood either side of the hearth, each with a flattened cushion covered in dark green wool.

In the grate orange flames consumed a tumble of logs. They shifted and a shower of sparks flew up the chimney. The room was warm and smelled of apples.

As Susanna sat in one chair Lucy took the other and began to rock gently. 'Are your parents both well?'

'Yes thank you. They were worried when you did not come to Meeting this morning. Is Meredith's cold worse?'

'No, it's actually quite a bit better.' Lucy's gentle mouth lifted at the corners. 'But you know Meredith.'

Susanna nodded. 'Pneumonia?'

'At the very least.'

'What does Doctor Vigurs say?'

'That there is nothing more he can do.' Lucy sighed. 'He's a kind man and remarkably patient. But that was not the wisest choice of words.'

Shaking with barely controlled laughter, Susanna covered her mouth. 'Did he prescribe anything?'

'He couldn't. We already have everything. There isn't an inch of space on Meredith's bedside table.' She rocked quietly for a few moments. 'I expect you've heard. We've been turned down.'

'Oh *no*.' Sympathy and dismay wiped the smile from Susanna's face. 'Lucy, I'm so sorry. Is that why Meredith took to her bed?'

'She's terribly disappointed. She was so sure, you see. We had sounded out opinion before making our formal application and we'd been led to believe we'd get a favourable response.'

'So what happened?'

'Meredith presented our petition, that we be allowed to travel to China and set up a Quaker

68

Mission there. I must admit I was worried. You know how the senior Friends distrust religious enthusiasm, and this concern is so dear to Meredith's heart.'

Susanna nodded quickly, all too familiar with her older cousin's volatile nature.

'But she was inspired.' Lucy gazed into the flames. 'She spoke with humility and restraint, yet no one could have doubted the strength of her vocation. We were told the deliberations would take a little while. Naturally we assumed that to mean a few days, perhaps even a week or two.'

'But that was back in May.'

'Indeed it was. And despite our requests to the monthly and quarterly select meetings no one could tell us if a decision had been reached. Then last week we received a letter. It was ...' she paused, 'very much to the point. It advised us to stay at home and mind our business.'

The bluntness of the refusal stunned Susanna. 'I don't know what to say.'

Lucy met her shock with a gentle smile of resignation. 'There is nothing to be said, my dear. It is most unlikely anything will persuade them to change their minds. Fortunately we are quite comfortably off. As you know Father left us a financial interest in the shipyard. But we have nothing to do with the day-to-day running of the business. Uncle Joshua and your cousin Charles handle that side of things. Regardless of the committee's advice, I don't think they would welcome interference from two maiden ladies, do you?'

'How can you take it so calmly?'

Lucy shrugged her thin shoulders. 'What choice do I have? Meredith was devastated. She is going to need a lot of support.' She glanced round at the sound of voices in the hall.

Chapter Six

The door opened and Meredith swept in, majestic and determined. From a severe centre parting her brown hair coiled in a small tight bun just above the white collar of her grey bombazine dress. Though the cold which had confined her to bed for several days had miraculously vanished Susanna noticed new lines around her eyes and mouth.

'Susanna! What a lovely surprise. It seems such a long time since we saw you or your parents. I expect they're busy. I've never known anyone work as hard for as many good causes as your dear mother. I really don't know how she does it. And looking after a family as well. Though you are all growing away now. My, just look at you.'

Susanna stood up to greet her cousin. It was the only way to avoid the sensation of being swamped by the gush of words. Meredith didn't set out to overwhelm people, but her physical size, forceful personality and effusive speech combined to leave recipients of her attention feeling slightly battered. She smiled

70

back. 'Mother was worried when you didn't come to Meeting. She asked me to call and make sure all was well. Lucy was just telling me you've been poorly.'

Meredith threw up her hands. 'Lucy does fuss. A slight indisposition, nothing serious. But it left me a little languid. Of course, having a delicate chest—' she placed one hand on the bosom that curved like a garden roller from just below her chin—'I am forced to take care. I find a day or two in bed with a light nourishing diet and plenty of rest is usually quite sufficient to restore me.' She peered closely at Susanna. 'You look a little flushed. I hope you are not sickening for something. I really cannot afford to—'

'I'm fine,' Susanna reassured quickly. 'William and I came around the Castle Drive.'

'William is with you?' Meredith's face lit up.

Susanna nodded. Her brother's natural charm made him the most popular member of the entire Elliot/Braithwaite family. 'Yes, he's—'

'Right here.' William poked his tousled head around the door.

'Meredith hasn't been well,' Susanna signalled a warning. William understood immediately.

'I'm so sorry to hear that. How rotten for you.'

'It was nothing.' Meredith sighed valiantly. 'I may be a martyr to my chest but I'm not going to let it get the better of me. Anyway, I'm so glad you've both come. You'll be able to give the wonderful news to your parents.'

'I'm sure they'll be as delighted as we are to hear you are recovered,' William said gravely.

Susanna looked away, not daring to catch his eye.

'No doubt they will. But that wasn't the wonderful news,' Meredith corrected, as she lowered herself into the rocker Susanna had vacated. The door opened to admit the maid pushing a trolley. The top tier held fine bone china, linen napkins and a silver tea service. On the bottom were two plates of sandwiches, one of freshly baked scones, dishes of raspberry jam and thick clotted cream, and a fruit cake.

'Gosh.' A wide grin split William's face as he gazed at the spread.

'Just a morsel to stave off starvation until you get home,' Lucy said drily.

'This *is* nice,' Meredith beamed. 'We don't often have company for afternoon tea. Not that we indulge ourselves like this every day. It wouldn't be right.'

'Oh I don't know,' William patted his flat stomach. 'I think I could get used to it.'

'Just look at him,' Meredith sighed. 'Like a string bean.'

'I'm still growing,' he protested. 'Lucy, you spoil me.'

'It's not *all* for you, young man.'

Meredith sighed again. 'I wish I had a better appetite.' Ignoring the sandwiches she leaned forward to spoon jam thickly on to a scone before piling it high with cream.

'Any news from the select committee yet?' William reached for another sandwich.

'Yes. We've been turned down,' Lucy replied.

'Oh I say. What bad luck.' He grimaced

sympathetically. 'I suppose that's it then.'

Lucy opened her mouth but Meredith forestalled her. 'No. That most certainly is not *it.*' She dabbed the corners of her mouth firmly with her napkin. 'The select committee have rejected our services. That is their privilege.' Her poker-straight spine signalled affront and indignation. 'But they cannot stop us.' She paused then announced dramatically, 'We will go to China independently.'

William stopped in mid-chew. It was obvious to Susanna that Meredith's announcement had come as a complete surprise to Lucy.

'There are other missions,' Meredith continued. 'Lowell mentioned one when he wrote last Christmas.'

'The London Missionary Society?' Lucy shook her head. 'But they only use—'

'No,' Meredith broke in impatiently, 'not them. That other one.'

Lucy's frown cleared. 'Oh, yes. Mr Hudson Taylor's organization: the China Inland Mission.'

'But if each mission is run by a particular church—' Susanna began.

'Not this one,' Meredith broke in.

'It's non-sectarian,' Lucy explained. 'And like the Society of Friends it favours the evangelical approach.'

'I am quite sure they will appreciate our offer.' Meredith beamed and picked up another scone. 'But if for some reason they are not able to accept our services then we will set up our own mission. We have a vocation, don't we,

Lucy?' Meredith's face was transformed. 'And with faith, we shall move mountains.'

'I wish I had your religious conviction,' Susanna blurted. 'It must be wonderful to be so *sure.*' Her own life seemed so full of obstacles and uncertainty.

'Er, Meredith,' William said, 'perhaps you haven't seen the reports in the newspapers—'

'We read *Lake's Falmouth Packet* and *Cornwall Advertiser* every week,' she answered. 'For news of Lowell's exploits.'

'Excuse me,' Susanna said, 'but who is Lowell?'

Meredith's eyes widened in astonishment. 'Lowell Hawke. You must have heard of him. He's one of the finest clipper-ship captains in the China Seas.'

'I have,' William said quickly. 'He's broken all kinds of records and pioneered new routes through some of the most dangerous waterways around the China coast.'

'Two of the seamen in the infirmary were talking about a Captain Hawke several weeks ago,' Susanna said. 'One of them called him the Devil incarnate.'

Meredith snorted. 'No doubt the sailor was a lazy no-good who had been dismissed for dereliction of duty.' She beamed with pride. 'Lowell is our cousin.'

'A very distant cousin,' Lucy amended gently. 'His grandmother was our grandfather's sister.'

'Then I'm surprised he hasn't warned you,' William said. 'During the past few months we've had a number of senior officers from ships trading with the treaty ports in the office and they've all said the same thing.'

Meredith rolled her eyes. 'What *are* you talking about?' She took a large mouthful of cream-laden scone.

He hunched his shoulders. 'I feel awful. I'd hate to be the one to spoil your plans.'

Meredith laughed. 'Don't be silly. How could you possibly spoil anything? It's all decided. All that remains is for us to finalize arrangements.'

'What exactly are you trying to say, William?' Lucy prompted quietly.

'That foreigners are not welcome in China. Without official backing you might find things much more difficult than you imagine.'

Meredith opened her mouth but before she could speak Lucy leaned forward and touched her sister's knee. 'Why don't we give William a chance to explain more fully? I know we read the newspapers but their view of the social and political situation might be less accurate than that of men who have actually been there and seen for themselves. Isn't that so, William?'

'Did you know,' Meredith turned to Susanna, 'next year when more submarine cables have been laid, messages sent from the Far East by electric telegraph will take only a few hours?'

'Quite so,' Lucy agreed, before Susanna could comment. 'But in the meantime the more we can learn about the situation in China the better we will be prepared for whatever lies ahead.'

With a sniff Meredith settled back in her chair, rocking vigorously.

'According to Captain Hutchinson,' William

said, 'missionaries who venture outside the foreign settlements are constantly being harassed and forced to move on. As they can't stay in one place more than a few days it's impossible for them to make any converts, or even to teach.'

'But why are the Chinese so set against missionaries?' Susanna asked.

It was Lucy who answered. 'Because they hold them responsible for the greatest uprising in Chinese history, the Taiping Rebellion. They hate all foreigners. But especially the English.'

'Why?' Susanna was acutely aware of the jade medallion nestling against her skin inside the bodice of her dress. Wary of leaving it at home in case it was discovered, and afraid it might be lost if it fell from her sleeve or a pocket, she had hung it around her neck on a loop of strong thread.

'Back in 1618,' Lucy explained, 'the Emperor of China was warned in a mysterious letter that his country would be subdued by a grey-eyed people. When English ships reached the Canton River some years later the Chinese saw that the crews had blue eyes. Terrified the prophecy was going to come true the Emperor tried to ban all Christians from his country.'

'But surely that doesn't apply now?' Susanna set her cup and saucer on the small table. 'The English have been trading with the Chinese for ages.'

'Where would we be without tea?' Meredith picked up her cup, holding it out for Susanna to refill.

'But not through choice,' William said. 'Father

told me it was the English who first introduced opium to China. Even though it's widely used by the court, as well as by ordinary people who want to sell things to us so they can buy more of it, the Chinese have tried twice to stop it being imported. But each time the ban led to a war which they lost. And under the terms of surrender they were forced to make more concessions and give us greater trading rights. Not just us, but Americans, French, and Parsees from India as well.'

'It's not really surprising that they don't like foreigners very much,' Susanna murmured.

'The Chinese authorities hate missionaries even more than they hate opium,' Lucy added. 'Because it was a Chinese schoolteacher convert to Christianity who started the Taiping movement.'

'Do you know what Taiping means?' Meredith sniffed in derision. 'It means *Great Peace*. But what began as a religious crusade was taken over by ruffians and criminals who wanted to bring down the ruling dynasty. Half the country was ravaged in an orgy of wanton destruction. Villages were burned, crops destroyed. Hundreds of thousands died.'

'Many more were left homeless and starving.' Lucy's quiet voice held more sadness than anger.

'The point is,' Meredith declared briskly, 'since the rebellion collapsed nearly six years ago China has been awash with lost souls who desperately need guidance to bring them God's grace and help them find salvation.'

77

William looked worried. 'I think it sounds rather dangerous.'

Meredith's smile was one of total certainty. 'We will be doing the Lord's work and He will protect us. It will not be an easy task. But what a glorious challenge!' She turned to her sister. 'I think I shall write to Mr Thomas Hanbury in Shanghai and tell him of our plans.'

'Is he a missionary?' Susanna enquired.

Meredith shook her head. 'No. He's a merchant. But he's one of us, a Friend, and is very highly thought of by both the English and the wealthy Chinese. Lowell said that when there was some trouble in the settlement over high taxes and oppressive magistrates the Chinese merchants were so impressed by Mr Hanbury's reputation for honesty they gave him all their money for safe-keeping until the problems were sorted out.' The twin grooves between her brows deepened. 'Susanna, you've hardly eaten a thing. What's the matter with you?'

'Nothing, truly. I was just so interested in all your plans.' She transferred a small slice of fruit cake to her plate.

'Well, that's our news,' Meredith announced. She studied the cake then helped herself to a large wedge. 'What about you two? What have you been doing? Do you still help those poor unfortunate seamen write letters to their loved ones, Susanna? And as for you, young man,' she continued before Susanna could reply, 'your father must be so proud. It's a man's dream to have his son follow him into the family business. Has Uncle Samuel found his profits are falling?'

William's eyes widened and he looked helplessly at Susanna who gulped, coughing as a cake crumb went down the wrong way.

'Meredith!' Lucy chided as Susanna mopped her streaming eyes with her napkin.

'What?' Meredith gazed at them in bewilderment. 'It's not an unreasonable question. I know Uncle Joseph is finding a difference at the shipyard. And by *difference* I mean the dividends are down. Apparently these dreadful smelly steamers don't need repairing as often as brigs and schooners. I suppose that's because they don't carry all those masts and spars and aren't thrown about so much in storms.'

Lucy, William and Susanna exchanged glances of dawning realization.

'Do you mean have Father's profits fallen because merchants are asking for their goods be transported by steam rather than sail?' William enquired carefully.

Meredith raised her eyes to the ceiling. 'Isn't it perfectly obvious that's what I was asking?'

'Actually, no,' William said with a grin. 'But thanks to Father's foresight Elliot's is actually doing better than ever.'

'But Uncle Samuel owns and manages schooners not steamers.'

William nodded. 'They work the routes that the steamers don't want or can't manage, and routes on which there is more cargo than steamships available to carry it. But where speed of delivery influences the price a cargo will fetch, Father is using steamers. In fact he's bought one and is talking about buying shares in a new steamship line.'

'He's always been a shrewd businessman,' Meredith said admiringly. 'I know our father thought very highly of him. I think it's such a shame though.'

'What is?' Susanna set her empty plate on the table and wiped her mouth. Meredith was well informed and had a lively mind but following her train of thought was impossible.

'The way he *suffers* so much. I mean I could understand it if he was a failure. It's not so long ago that bankruptcy meant having to leave the Society. But to agonize over being successful and earning lots of money, well, I find that most peculiar.'

Susanna and William exchanged a glance. They agreed but loyalty forbade them saying so.

'Would anyone like another cup of tea?' Lucy enquired. 'Susanna, how about you? William, I'm sure you could manage another scone.'

Susanna smiled gratefully. Lucy spent a large part of her life rescuing people from Meredith's tactlessness with such quiet charm the incident was immediately forgotten. There wasn't a mean bone in Meredith's substantial body. But she said what she thought without stopping to consider what effect it might have.

'Honestly, Lucy, I'm full. It was a lovely tea.'

'I wish I had room for more,' William mourned. 'But I can't manage another mouthful.' He stood up. 'It's been lovely seeing you both.'

80

'Are you going?' Meredith's face fell.

'I wish we didn't have to.' William leaned down and kissed her cheek. 'But we'll be expected to go to Meeting again this evening.' He tugged on the bell-pull beside the fireplace. 'And Susanna has promised to help me with some accounts procedures I'm having difficulty with.' He grinned. 'It's really useful having a brainy sister.'

'I wish Father agreed with you,' Susanna murmured.

'Uncle Samuel is a very devout man,' Lucy spoke so that only Susanna could hear. 'But he perceives change in any form as a threat.' Lucy laid a hand lightly on her arm. 'He does love you, Susanna. Try to remember that.'

'I know,' Susanna whispered, her eyes pricking. 'But Lucy, I can't be what he wants. And he won't let me do what *I* want.'

'Are you sure you know what that is?' Lucy asked gently. 'You might *think* you do. But you are still very young.'

Mary arrived with Susanna's cloak and William's coat.

'I'll go and get the horses,' William said. 'Thanks again, Lucy.' He kissed her. 'Bye, Meredith. Good luck with your arrangements.' He loped out.

'Don't leave it so long before your next visit,' Meredith called.

Susanna waited until the maid was out of earshot then confided as she fastened her cloak around her shoulders, 'I assisted Doctor Arundell with an operation yesterday.'

81

Lucy stiffened and with a swift glance across at her sister whispered, 'You did *what?*'

'Edward—Doctor Arundell needed help and there wasn't anyone else. The boy might have died. He would certainly have lost his leg. I wanted so much to tell Mother and Father about it, to make them see that though I'm not naturally good like Fran and I can never mean as much to them as William, they can still be proud of me.'

'And did you tell them?'

Shaking her head Susanna saw Lucy let out the breath she'd been holding. 'I'm already in disgrace for visiting the infirmary without a chaperone. For that sin I have to work in the soup kitchen.' She smiled, torn between laughter and tears. 'What punishment would I have received for being unchaperoned while helping to save a boy's life?'

'Oh my dear,' Lucy whispered, her face full of compassion.

'What's going on?' Meredith demanded. 'What are you two muttering about?'

Lucy turned. 'Susanna was just telling me that she'll be helping in the soup kitchen for a few weeks.'

'Really? I used to take a turn down there myself. Of course, that was quite a while ago. I have so many other demands on my time now. And I'm going to be even more busy with all the preparations to make for our mission to China. I can't leave it all to Lucy can I, dear? You know how you fuss.'

Lucy's fingers tightened on Susanna's arm,

82

cutting off the spirited defence before a word could be uttered. 'It's all right,' she whispered. 'She doesn't mean it the way it sounds. She worries you see, and this is her way of hiding it.'

Susanna gave her cousin a quick fierce hug. 'You're a wonderful person, Lucy.'

'Come and see us again soon.'

'I will,' Susanna promised. She leaned forward to kiss the papery cheek.

'I shall look forward to hearing about your patient's progress,' Lucy whispered.

With a grateful smile Susanna hurried out to join her brother for the ride home.

Chapter Seven

Setting his knife and fork together on the plate Lowell Hawke picked up his wine glass and looked past the other seven still bent over their food. He ate too quickly. It was a habit he'd acquired during his first weeks at sea. Below deck his midshipman's rank had counted for little. With the other lads he had learned to grab what he could and cram it down fast.

At sea, food was reduced from a pleasure to be lingered over to mere fuel for survival. Tonight, despite the perfection of the meal and the elegant surroundings, the old habit had prevailed. Adjustment required energy and he was too damn tired.

The oak chair was solid and comfortable, the tablecloths and napkins crisply starched and dazzling white. Shielded by frosted glass bowls, gas mantles on the crimson-papered walls suffused the large room with soft light. The muted murmur of conversation mingled with the soft scrape of cutlery on fine china and the clink of wine bottle against crystal glass. So soothing was the sound that Lowell had to fight the desire to let his eyes close. They felt gritty and were still sore from the chill wind and salt spray.

Waiters dipped and whirled like swallows between the tables as they removed the debris of one course and presented another. At another table a woman laughed. It was a long time since he'd heard that sound. She laughed again, her head tilted back. In the candlelight her pale throat had the lustre of polished marble. A poor comparison he decided, taking a mouthful of wine. Marble was cold whereas a woman's skin—He stared into his glass.

'Do you find England much changed since your last visit, Captain?'

Rousing himself, Lowell looked across the bowl of hot-house flowers which added their delicate fragrance to air rich with the savoury aromas of braised onions and roast meat. He saw corn-coloured hair slicked down with pomade and a very new formal black jacket a shade too large for the bony young frame. There was less than a decade between them yet Lowell felt as old as time. Exhaustion made him terse.

'As I arrived only thirty-six hours ago and

did not leave the docks until this afternoon I have seen too little of England to form an opinion.'

For weeks his world had been the deck of his ship and the confines of his day cabin. For much of the voyage he had slept fewer than five hours a night.

Leaving too late to take part in the race to England with the new season's tea he had still driven his crew to make the fastest passage possible.

'We need those guns,' Ellis had thundered. 'We're virtually under siege. The imperial troops should be protecting us from thieves and looters not bloody well assisting them! Protesting to the mandarins is a waste of time. All they do is shrug and pretend the soldiers are beyond their control. Too many of our people are dying, Hawke. I know the governor has sent gun-boats, but with six hundred miles of the Yangtze river to patrol, what chance is there of one of them being here at Kewkiang when it's needed? In any case the pirate junks and lorchas outnumber them by fifty to one.'

Ellis had been trembling with anger and frustration. 'We must have protection. Those yellow bastards have no intention of honouring the treaty. It's time they were taught a lesson.' He had thrust a soft leather bag heavy with gold coins into Lowell's hand. 'Get us what we need. I don't care how. But do it fast and do it soon.'

'Your pardon, Captain.' The brusque response had caused the most junior member of the

London branch of Hawke and Son to blush scarlet.

Lowell shook his head. 'No, it is I who should apologize. I appear to have left my manners aboard my ship.'

'That's all right.' The young man smiled shyly, wriggling like a puppy.

'How many days did your passage actually take, Captain?' Henry Bowles's plummy voice held a note of challenge.

Lowell switched his gaze to the tall company secretary. In the three years since they'd last met, Henry had changed little. The silver-grey hair which he wore longer than was strictly fashionable in Victorian society gave him a poetic appearance totally at odds with his true personality. If the milk of human kindness had ever flowed through Henry's veins it had long since curdled. But when the occasion demanded he could display exceptional charm—the cold calculating mind hidden from all but those astute enough to recognize the mask for what it was.

'One hundred and eight days.'

Henry's patrician brows rose. 'Captain Keys only took ninety-nine.'

'Captain Keys loaded in Foochow.' Lowell responded more sharply than he intended. He should have slept this afternoon but there had been too much to do. 'The tea is ready for shipping from Foochow in June, *before* the southwest monsoon reaches its full strength.'

'Is it indeed? Then why weren't you among those taking advantage of this?'

'Because in June I was ...' *negotiating a pact with a warlord* 'elsewhere,' Lowell replied easily. 'In coastal trading you go where the cargoes take you. I loaded at Shanghai. The tea isn't ready there until July or August. I'd say we made pretty fair time considering we hit a typhoon off Swatow and more storms at the Cape.'

'I still think—'

Lowell leaned forward. Resting one elbow on the gleaming damask cloth, he toyed with the stem of his glass. 'Henry, the speed and accuracy with which you can calculate the profit per cubic foot of storage space for a dozen different cargoes whose prices might have changed between collection and delivery is quite awe-inspiring. But—' suddenly his quiet voice had the edge of an unsheathed blade—'you have never set foot on my ship, nor, I suspect, on any other. A man who passes judgement on matters about which he knows nothing risks making a fool of himself.'

Though Henry's aquiline nostrils whitened his control was superb. With a languid movement which conveyed boredom with the conversation he beckoned the waiter.

His point made, Lowell sat back smiling pleasantly.

'Is it true what we read in the papers, Captain?' Terence Barker, the chief clerk, peered over his pince-nez. 'Are the China Seas really infested with pirates?' He seemed both intrigued and appalled by the possibility.

'It is,' Lowell replied evenly.

The young clerk's eyes rounded with awe.

'Have you ever been attacked by pirates, Captain?'

Swallowing a yawn Lowell nodded. 'It's an occupational hazard in that part of the world.'

'Please, Captain,' the young clerk begged, 'do tell us. What happened?'

Lowell glanced round the table. Two of the ladies were gazing at him with wide-eyed admiration. Used to this reaction he took little notice of it. Some people were easily impressed. The expression of the third woman was more speculative.

'I was young midshipman on the *Guinivere*. We were on our way through the Gaspar Straits into the Java Sea. But the wind had come round and was against us.'

As he spoke memories sucked him back through time. He was once more on the clipper's deck. On either side of the ship, islands, steep and thickly wooded, rose out of the water their summits shrouded in mist. Above the crack of canvas, creaking ropes, and the hiss of the water along the hull he could hear monkeys chattering and shrieking in the trees. Birds he couldn't see screamed eerily.

The sun was already low on the horizon and Lowell felt a twist in his gut as he realized they would have to anchor where they were for the night. Darkness made it impossible for the lookouts to take soundings or spot the tell-tale shadows of reefs and shoals lurking just beneath the surface. Powerful currents surged around the submerged rocks. Once in their grip *Guinivere* would be dragged on to the jagged black teeth which would bite through her sturdy hull as easily as a soaked biscuit.

As the anchor was dropped, Lowell scrambled aloft with the other boys to reef in all the upper sails. They worked feverishly in silence, the tropical night enfolding them like thick black velvet. Sweat trickled down his back. The air was stifling, heavy with the fetid stench of decaying vegetation.

In the silence the coughing roar sounded very close. Lowell started. The boy balanced next to him gasped, his foot slipping through the rope on which he was standing. He began to arch backwards, arms flailing wildly. Hooking one arm around the spar to which they had been tying the sail Lowell grabbed the boy's shirt and slammed him forward against the topmast. A flailing fist caught him a glancing blow high on his right cheek making his eyes water and his head ring. Wrapping his arms around the mast the boy gulped. 'Th-Thanks.' He swallowed again. 'What was that?'

Lowell blinked hard. He could barely see and his cheek stung painfully. 'A tiger, I think.'

'Oi, you lads!' The first mate's voice floated up to them. 'Stop fooling about, and get that gear stowed.'

'Aye-aye, *sir*,' Lowell shouted down. He turned to the boy whose face was just a pale blur in the darkness. 'Are you all right?'

''Course I am.' The boy's robust claim ended with another gulp. 'You can let go now.'

Lowell was surprised how difficult it was to unclench his fingers and release the bunched

89

material in order to finish tying up the sail.

Back on deck they exchanged wary glances as seamen rushed to and fro carrying grape and canister shot to load the sixpounders. In the galley the poker was heating in the fire ready to light the fuses. Two men carrying rifles ran to the fo'c'sle head and the poop. Lowell's heart was thumping and his muscles tightened in mingled excitement and fear.

The captain shouted for attention and in the sudden silence Lowell heard a soft splash. Whirling round he glimpsed a ripple of phosphorescence as something disturbed the dark water. He knew an instant's agonizing uncertainty. *What if he shouted and it was only a fish?* He stared into the blackness, straining his eyes, not daring to breathe in case he missed anything. Then he saw it again, closer this time.

He opened his mouth to scream a warning. At the same instant the lookout on the poop fired his rifle bellowing, 'Proas on the port quarter!' The next few minutes were a mind-numbing hell. The cannons roared and men shouted, labouring furiously to reload and fire again. Lowell crouched on the deck, digging the metal canisters loaded with shot from their boxes and passing them to the men manning the guns, his head spinning with the noise. Steel clashed on steel, spears entered living flesh with a wet thud, the wounded screamed. His stomach heaved at the acrid pungency of explosive, the hot sweet smell of blood and the sour sweat of fear.

It ended as suddenly as it had started.

Crawling to the side he peered over and caught a quick glimpse of a wounded man being dragged from the water on to the single outrigger. Then the proas vanished, swallowed up in the darkness. He had slumped to the deck, his head bent over his hunched knees, shaking uncontrollably.

'I can only imagine it is a most unpleasant experience,' the chief clerk's pursed lips indicated severe disapproval.

'Mmm,' Lowell agreed expressionlessly. 'Especially when one is only twelve.' He watched the two women exchange a horrified glance. He knew what they were thinking. *What had he been doing there? How could his parents have allowed it? etc. etc.* Attempting to explain would only add to their confusion. Far better that everyone continued to believe the family stood united.

'Pirates are only one of the dangers we face in those waters. There are also an unpleasantly large number of uncharted reefs and banks. Believe me, given the circumstances I made remarkably good time.' Raising the glass to Henry in mock salute, Lowell took a large gulp. How soon could he get away? If he didn't get some sleep ...

'Do you realize—' Gilbert Kirby looked round the table—'Captain Hawke brought his ship into the docks only yesterday morning? Yet by last evening most of the tea had been landed, weighed, and the duty paid.' His jubilant manner lightened the atmosphere at once. Nearing sixty, Gilbert had run the London branch of Hawke and Son for almost a quarter of a century.

'Before nightfall upwards of eighty chests of that same tea was already on its way to the far corners of the British Isles.' Gilbert paused, smiling around the table. 'And, as some of it was bought by retailers right here in London, I venture to say that by last evening—less than twenty-four hours after Captain Hawke sailed into the Thames mind you—his cargo was being served at the tea tables of our capital city. Supplying the demand, ladies and gentlemen. That is the bedrock of Hawke and Son's success. And I for one am proud to be a part of it.' He raised his glass, beaming around the table.

Raising the goblet to his lips Lowell surveyed those who had been invited in his honour to the fashionable and expensive restaurant on this cold wet November night. Did they see it as the prodigal's return? Four men, faces flushed with food, wine and self-congratulation above their starched white collars, and between them—birds of paradise amid magpies—three wives.

Gowned in rainbow-hued taffeta and lace, their elaborate hairstyles crowned with egret feathers and glittering ornaments, they displayed varying amounts of lavishly jewelled cleavage. Two picked daintily at the food on their plates, too tightly laced to swallow more than a few mouthfuls, the other ...

As she lifted her glass he noticed her fingers were short and strong-looking. Quite different from Marjorie's. Marjorie had long slender fingers and skin so translucent the veins showed in a delicate blue tracery. Marjorie's hands fluttered like caged birds, and clung. *He was trapped. The strands that bound him gossamer-fine and quite unbreakable.*

He clenched his teeth feeling a muscle jump in his jaw as he thrust thoughts of his wife to the back of his mind behind the barrier. He took another gulp of the bright ruby wine seeking escape from the pain.

The woman caught his eye. Holding his gaze she slowly passed the glass back and forth across her lower lip. Then with a barely perceptible smile she tipped it and swallowed. In spite of his resolve Lowell's body stirred. Beneath heavy lids her eyes gleamed. Then she looked serenely away: a warm attractive woman confident of her allure. Both knew that before the evening was over a time and place would be agreed.

Filling his mouth with Château-Latour Lowell tried to wash away the taste of his treachery.

'And your brother, Captain?' Gilbert Kirby enquired. 'Is he well?'

Exhaustion and the distracting sexual signals of Henry's wife had caused Lowell's concentration to lapse. But Kirby's query, on the surface a routine politeness, brought him to instant alertness.

'He's fine,' Lowell lied smoothly, his mind filling with images of his elder brother as he used to be. Tall and fair-haired, John resembled their father in appearance. He in contrast, was shorter, more thickset, and had inherited their mother's dark colouring. John had violet eyes which attracted adoring women in droves. His own were light grey—*like ice on the sea* was how his youngest sister had once described them—and

93

their effect was very different. Younger women seemed wary of him. Those with more experience apparently considered him a challenge.

The last time he had seen his brother, the golden boy, repository of all their father's hopes, John had been drunk and despairing, his physical and mental disintegration all too visible in the distortion of his once-handsome features.

'We were hoping he might accompany you,' Gilbert continued. Beneath the disappointment, well hidden as good manners demanded, Lowell detected curiosity. 'Your father did mention the possibility of Mr John coming over the year before last. But I believe business in Hong Kong prevented him making the voyage. Naturally we are all keen to meet the heir to Hawke and Son, the future hand on the helm so to speak. In the interests of continuity you understand.'

'Naturally.' Lowell allowed archness to edge his smile. 'However, as my father is in excellent health, don't you think it's perhaps a little premature to be discussing his successor?'

Gilbert Kirby's smile stiffened then faded as his features rapidly rearranged themselves to reflect his shocked denial. 'I did not mean—' He cleared his throat. 'Captain, it is my dearest wish that Joseph Hawke continues, for as long as it pleases God to spare him, to lead this company to even greater success.'

'A noble sentiment, Mr Kirby.' Lowell raised his glass. 'Let us all drink to that.' But as the wine slid down his throat it left behind a bitter taste.

He had been fighting all his life: fighting his father; fighting to free himself from his brother's shadow; fighting for the right to follow his own star.

He had wanted to go to sea since he was old enough to frame the words. But Joseph Hawke had been determined that both his sons should follow him into the trading company he had inherited from his father-in-law and built up into one of the major merchant houses on the China coast.

John accepted the future mapped out for him; Lowell did not. His mother was reduced to tears and his father to near-apoplexy by his stubborn refusal. No one seemed to care what he wanted.

Eventually, convinced it was just a whim, his father apprenticed him to one of the hardest clipper-captains on the China Seas.

'You say this is what you want, boy, let's see how you deal with it.'

'Joseph, you can't. He's only a child,' his mother pleaded.

'If he's old enough to defy me and spurn a future that would have most lads his age grovelling with gratitude, he's old enough to find out what shipboard life is really like. I wager he'll be scuttling back home in a month. A typhoon or two and the whole ridiculous notion will be out of his system once and for all, you wait and see.'

But contrary to his father's expectations and, Lowell suspected, those of Captain McKenzie, commander of the *Guinivere*, he thrived. Life was hard, the work strenuous and demanding. Not only was it a severe test of physical fitness, but the young midshipmen also had to study geography, physics and nautical astronomy, plus at least one of the Chinese dialects. They were expected never to lose their temper, to demonstrate at all times steadiness and courage, and to remain cool under provocation.

Lowell found it ironic that his father's fierce opposition to his chosen profession should have bred in him precisely those qualities which helped him succeed.

Guinivere was a tea-clipper, one of an elite band whose exploits were legendary. But Lowell soon learned there was another far more lucrative commodity being traded along the China coast.

Chapter Eight

'Come, William.' Samuel rose from the breakfast-table. 'Today you'll be working with Norman. He will show you how to calculate the profits each boat has made on her year's trading and how they are to be divided.'

William dropped his napkin beside his plate and pushed back his chair. 'As each boat has sixty-four shares it's just a matter of checking the names of the shareholders against the name of the boat. Am I right, Father?'

Samuel's habitual dourness was replaced by

a smile of pleasure. 'Indeed you are, William. I was beginning to wonder if the financial side of the business was beyond your grasp.'

'I feel much more confident now.' As he followed his father out William shot Susanna a grin of gratitude.

'I must go too,' Frances said. 'Richard thinks his mother might benefit from some of my blackcurrant cordial. I shall take some over before I go to the infant school.'

Susanna rose too but was stopped by her mother.

'Would you go down into town for me? I have a great deal to do this morning.'

Realizing reluctance would provoke questions, she forced herself to smile and look willing. 'Of course.'

'I need more writing paper and envelopes. Mr Nance knows our preference. Also a reel of cotton thread, a packet of fine needles, and two skeins of ivory silk. And call into the chemist's and ask Mr Hosking for a packet of dried dill and a small bottle of peppermint oil.'

'Is father suffering with his stomach again?' At her mother's nod Susanna's shoulders drooped. 'It's me, isn't it?'

'Not entirely.' Maria took several silver coins from a soft kid drawstring purse in the bureau and gave them to Susanna. 'Your father has a thriving business which demands a great deal from him. He also takes very seriously the responsibility of being an Elder. More seriously perhaps than some others do.'

Susanna gripped the handle of her basket with

both hands. 'I really don't mean to cause him shame.'

'We both know that, Susanna. But continually apologizing does not make a virtue out of a vice. If you were to think more carefully before you speak or act you would spare yourself, and us, a lot of pain.'

But you don't approve of the things I want. So what am I to do? I cannot simply forget about them. As Susanna was about to seize this rare opportunity for a heart-to-heart talk Maria turned away.

'I trust you will not be going to the Seamen's Home this morning,' she called over her shoulder, as she walked briskly out into the hall.

'No, Mother,' Susanna answered truthfully. She had an important errand of her own.

Closing the front door behind her she glanced up at the sky. Unable to sleep she had listened to a gusty wind hurl rain against the window like handfuls of gravel. But now the heavy cloud was breaking up to reveal patches of blue. As she gazed down at the panorama of coastline and water a ray of bright sunshine illuminated the gorse-covered hillside across the inner harbour.

It was an omen Susanna decided, her spirits lifting. Starting down the path, the air fresh on her face, she could smell damp earth, frying bacon, and the yeasty fragrance of newly baked bread.

Built along the side of several hills, Falmouth's streets ran in tiers parallel to the water. Crossing the terraces and descending narrow slopes and flights of stone steps Susanna emerged at Church Corner between the cab rank and the King's Head Hotel. The horses stood placidly, coats brushed, tack clean and polished, while the drivers sucked on their pipes and blew plumes of fragrant smoke through pursed lips as they chatted.

Though it was not much after nine, the town's main thoroughfare was busy. Women with red, chapped hands carrying baskets of fish or laundry, screeched at children with runny noses and ragged oversized clothes to mind the carts thundering by on heavy iron wheels.

Shopkeepers in dark suits or crisp white aprons smiled and wished her good morning as they stood in their doorways discussing trade while their apprentices washed down steps, windows and tiled entrances.

The sickly-sour reek of spilled beer and stale tobacco smoke billowed from one open door where the ale-house keeper was sweeping the previous night's wet sawdust out on to the street. Within moments the golden drift had been ground into the dirt by passing wheels and tramping boots.

On the opposite side of the road the gas works added its own pungency to the odours of new leather and wet paint, the sharp tang of ripe cheese and the rich aroma of roasting coffee.

On the sea-side of the street, a group of men were busy with picks and shovels. As Susanna drew level with the recently started hole a passer-by alongside her bawled at one of them, 'Dear life, Perce, what are 'e doing now? Tidn' a week since you was all in a trench down Market Strand.'

The workman squinted up. Leaning on his shovel he pushed back his flat cap and scratched his scalp before settling the cap in place once more. 'Got another bleddy leak, 'aven't us,' he snorted. 'I tell 'e, I spend so much time under this bleddy street I feel like a bleddy mole.'

Suppressing a grin Susanna moved on. Beyond the bend in the road where Church Street became Market Street scorched rubble was all that remained of several shops and houses. The fire, rumoured to have started in a store behind the shops, had completely destroyed the buildings on the seaward side of the street creating a hole like a gaping mouth in which the blackened and broken masonry resembled stumps of rotten teeth.

She paused alongside the imposing Doric columns and iron railings fronting the Falmouth Subscription rooms. Her father often met his ships' captains here in the evening, preferring to keep business quite separate from domestic life, Though at this moment he was sure to be in his office several hundred yards away in Arwenack Street, she could not prevent herself darting a wary guilt-filled glance at the windows. Then, taking a deep breath, she crossed the road and entered the dark narrow passage that led up to Snow's Court.

The granite-lined gutter running down the steep cobbled court still bore traces of soap suds and other less savoury waste. Lines of washing stretched from one side to the other attached to pulleys hammered into the walls of the cramped houses. Some of the small-paned, upstairs windows stood open and bedding hung over the sill to air.

The front door of the house nearest her opened and a scrawny woman with a pale, careworn face emerged, wearing an apron made of coarse sacking over her grubby brown calico skirt. The sleeves of her blouse were rolled up and she leaned sideways against the weight of the bucket she was carrying.

'Good morning,' Susanna smiled. The woman looked at her briefly with no change of expression then tipped the contents of the bucket into the gutter. Susanna's nostrils flared at the sour stench and she looked quickly away from the yellow stream. The woman turned to go in. 'Excuse me,' Susanna raised her voice. 'Could you tell me where Mrs Treneer lives?'

The woman gestured with her thumb to the next house and still without speaking went back inside.

'Thank you so much,' Susanna muttered and walked up the slippery cobbles to the stone step and knocked on the rough door.

From inside a voice shouted, 'Timmy, if you're playing your silly games again, I'll—' The door was snatched open by a short, sturdy woman with a rosy complexion and thick, wheat-coloured hair pulled back into an untidy knot. 'Oh,' she blinked. 'Sorry, dear, I thought you was—' Then recognition spread across her face. 'Why, Miss Elliot, what you doing here?' Fear eclipsed her smile and one red, work-roughened hand flew to her mouth. 'Is it Colin? Something gone wrong, has it?'

Susanna shook her head quickly. 'Not as far as I know. Actually I've come to ask if you are going in to see him today.'

Molly Treneer's eyes closed in relief. Beneath her white apron her sprigged blouse and navy skirt were faded but both looked clean and fresh and had been carefully mended.

'Yes, I'm going in this afternoon. 'Ere, George told me what you done and how you was helping the doctor. Never seen nothing like it he said. And the doctor told 'un when he went in yesterday, if it 'adn't been fer you ...'

Edward had praised her to George? Susanna hid her pleasure lest it should seem like vain pride but there was a warm glow in the pit of her stomach.

Molly's eyes brimmed suddenly. 'It don't bear thinking about.' Snatching up the hem of her apron she wiped away her tears. 'Look at me. Some daft I am.' She tried to smile but her lips trembled. 'Tidn' like 'e died. The doctor says 'e got a good chance. It's just—'

'It must have been a dreadful shock for you.'

Susanna glanced up and down the cobbled court and saw that several women had come out of their houses. One was sweeping her front doorstep while two others checked to see if their washing was dry. While appearing to ignore her their curiosity and suspicion were obvious. 'Do you think I might come in for a moment?'

Molly stepped back at once pulling the door wider. 'Where's me manners? Tidn' what you're used to, mind.'

Sympathizing with a defensive pride she understood only too well, Susanna simply ignored it. 'I won't keep you a moment. I expect you're busy. But it is important.'

'You'd best sit down.' Molly gestured to the high-backed wooden settle standing at right-angles to the deep hearth where a large blackened pot hung from an iron hook over a crackling fire. Though gloomy the small room was warm and clean. 'I 'aven't long been back meself.'

'Have you been shopping?'

Molly's laugh was harsh. 'No, my 'andsome. I do my shopping at the end of the day when things is cheapest. I been out cleaning since five.' She pulled a wooden chair from beneath the scrubbed table and sagged wearily on to it. 'The fishing haven't been good lately. We was all right when I had my job at Geach's. But the fire put paid to that.' She tucked stray wisps of hair up into the knot at the back of her head.

'What happens to your other children while you're out?'

'If George is fishing I drop them down Mother's. They aren't left to fend for theirselves,' she added quickly. 'I don't hold with that. Since Mary had the measles she can't hear proper. And Jennet is a real 'andful. Father is good as gold with them. If the tide's out he takes them down where the coasters unload to pick up coal from the beach. Mr Johns pretends not to notice.

103

Partial to sea bass he is'—Molly tapped the side of her nose—'so George see him right. But now we won't have Colin's money coming in ...' Her face creased with worry.

'That's partly why I'm here,' Susanna said.

Molly's back straightened. 'We don't want no charity. Don't take me wrong, but George don't hold with that.'

'No, that wasn't—The truth is I've come to ask for your help.'

'*Me?* Help you?'

Susanna nodded and explained her need for a chaperone on her visits to the infirmary. Excitement stirred as another idea began taking shape at the back of her mind, but she wouldn't mention it yet. One step at a time. 'So could we meet at Church Corner? Say two o'clock?'

As Molly ducked her head in agreement Susanna added, 'I'd like to bring something. I thought perhaps some fruit, a dozen eggs and maybe a cake? It's not charity,' she insisted hastily. 'After all, it is you who are helping me. It's simply a token of appreciation. Please?' She stood up and on impulse held out her hand.

After a moment's hesitation Molly gave a decisive nod. 'All right then.' Wiping her palm quickly on her apron she gripped Susanna's.

As the family ate their midday meal, Susanna waited for an opportune moment to make her announcement. Swallowing the last mouthful of his apple pie and custard, her father wiped his mouth with his napkin then turned to her.

'And what will you be doing this afternoon?'

Susanna had thought long and hard about the

best way to phrase it. She didn't feel comfortable with an outright lie. But nor could she risk her father doubting that her actions were driven by a genuine desire to be of help to others. If one of those she helped was Edward, and if in helping him she found pleasure, was that so wrong? 'I am accompanying Mrs Treneer to visit her son. She is naturally most anxious about his condition.'

Samuel frowned. 'How did this arrangement come about?'

'I saw her when I was in town this morning doing some shopping for Mother.' Susanna saw her mother nod in reply to her father's questioning glance. 'Apparently Mr Treneer told his wife of my help when Colin arrived at the infirmary. As he is out fishing he cannot accompany her and she is worried about going to the infirmary by herself She knows I have been a regular visitor.'

'I see. Presumably Mrs Treneer will wish to visit her son as often as she can?'

Susanna's mouth felt dry. 'I imagine so. They seem to be a very close family.'

'Do they have other children?' Frances asked.

'Two little girls of ten and six. The elder one is deaf.'

Samuel pushed back his chair and stood up. 'I have no objection to you accompanying Mrs Treneer. I'm sure that when it is time for her to leave she will be comforted by your presence.' He glanced across at his wife. 'I know myself how hard it is to leave the bedside of a loved one who is suffering.'

This rarely revealed side to her father startled and intrigued Susanna, hinting at an aspect of her parents' relationship only they knew.

'Thank you, Father.' She lowered her eyes demurely to hide her relief. But he had made himself abundantly clear. Her visits to the infirmary could continue *on one condition:* she was to arrive and leave with Molly Treneer.

Forty minutes later, Susanna escorted her chaperone through the infirmary door and along the passage. Though Molly's head was high she was visibly nervous.

As they passed the side ward Susanna saw Albert was pushing a mop over the bleached floorboards. He glanced up, clicking his tongue.

'I think the doctor believe I got four pairs of 'ands. Tis too much fer one person. I can't be everywhere at once.'

Initially Susanna had worried about Albert who gave the impression of being seriously overworked. Her tentative questions had elicited a knowing smile from Edward. 'Albert loves his job. Complaining is his way of making sure we understand how necessary he is. You watch him. When all the beds are full or we have an emergency operation which means extra cleaning up on top of his usual work he manages his duties with surprising speed. Equally, when the ward is quiet he has perfected the knack of expanding each task to take much longer so he still appears very busy.'

Susanna had been amazed to observe that Edward was right. Now when Albert grumbled, she either smiled and ignored his moans knowing he didn't really mean them, or commiserated and told him how much he was appreciated.

'It's marvellous how you cope, Albert.'

'Good job someone think so,' he grunted.

'Is Doctor Arundell in his office?'

Albert leaned on his mop. 'He've gone 'ome fer a bath and change of clothes. Here all night he was. Wanted to keep an eye on the youngster. Then this one went.' He jerked his thumb over his shoulder and Susanna saw the bed which had been occupied by the Portuguese was stripped to the bare frame. 'Good thing too,' Albert was matter-of-fact. 'He was in some bad way. Any'ow what with one thing and another the doctor wadn' off his feet fer nigh on twenty-four hours. He'll be back again directly.' His gaze switched to Molly. 'How 'e doing, then?'

'With my boy in 'ere? How do 'e think?'

Like Molly's husband, Albert came from a fishing family but intractable seasickness had prevented him joining his brothers. Learning of this Susanna had immediately understood his need to feel that the infirmary could not run without him.

'Always something, innit?' Albert sighed sympathetically. 'Still, 'e idn' doing too bad. Least 'e's still 'ere.' With these words of intended comfort he went back to his mopping.

Taking Molly's arm Susanna piloted her into the main ward. The Portuguese's death had shaken her. She wasn't sure why, everyone had expected it. And during the few minutes she had spent with him his suffering had been dreadful to watch.

'What's the matter? Something wrong is it?'
Molly's voice was thin and nervous.

'No, not at all. Here we are.' As they
entered the ward two of the patients glanced
in their direction. Another was huddled under
the covers snoring. 'Good afternoon,' Susanna
smiled, receiving mumbled greetings in return.

Colin's bed was nearest the door, the
bedclothes humped over a frame which kept
all weight off his legs. He was propped up on
pillows, his face chalk white but for dark circles
like sooty thumbprints beneath his closed eyes.

'Dear life, my poor little man. What do 'e
look like?'

Susanna pulled the wooden chair round so
Molly could face her son. 'Sit down, you'll
be much more comfortable. I expect Doctor
Arundell has given him something for the
pain. But if you talk he'll be able to hear
you.'

'Honest?' Molly whispered, visibly uneasy as
she glanced over her shoulder at the other
occupants of the ward who, with touching
courtesy, looked quickly away.

Susanna smiled. 'Yes, really.'

'What shall I talk about?' Molly hissed,
twisting the basket handle so it creaked beneath
her gleaming knuckles.

Pressing her down gently Susanna put the
basket by her feet. 'Just tell him what the
family's been doing: the kind of things you
would tell him if he'd been away for a while.
It's the sound of your voice that's important.'

Molly swivelled round admiring and curious.

'How d'you know all this stuff?'

Susanna lifted her shoulders. 'I've watched. And I've talked to the men after the doctor has given them medicines to ease their pain. They looked just like Colin does now. But they told me later that it gave them great comfort to hear my voice. I expect you'd like some privacy, so—'

Molly tensed. 'Where are you going?'

'Just across the passage to fetch pen and paper in case any of the sailors want letters written. I'll only be a moment.'

Albert had finished his mopping. The window in the small room stood half-open and cool air blowing over the wet boards carried the acrid smell of chloride of lime to Susanna's nostrils.

'You've certainly done a very thorough job.'

'Doctor's orders. Before I come in 'ere I 'ad to burn the mattress and put all the bedding in to soak in that there carbolic stuff.'

Unease stirred in Susanna. 'Whatever for? Usually sulphur candles are enough to—'

'I 'abn' got time to stand 'ere yapping. I need four pairs of 'ands fer all I got to do.' Snatching up the mop and bucket he shut the door and hurried away down the passage.

Susanna stared after him in astonishment. She had never seen him move so fast. As she started across the passage towards the dispensary the outside door opened and Edward entered. His posture betrayed a weariness that wrenched her heart. Then he looked up.

109

Chapter Nine

'Good afternoon, Susanna.'

After the quick warmth in his eyes this polite formality was a crushing disappointment. With a calm that had all the strength and resilience of an eggshell she folded her hands.

'Good afternoon, Edward. What marvellous news.'

'What?'

'I was just talking to Albert. He says Colin is stable. Well, *he's still here* was how he put it. I gather you worked all night.'

'I must speak to Albert about his gossiping.'

'It wasn't gossip. Truly. He was simply saying how busy you had been. Your dedication to your patients should be a source of pride. It is certainly not a weakness to be hidden.' She broke off, her cheeks burning. She hadn't meant to say so much. But she desperately wanted him to understand she was not an outsider to be kept at a distance.

The corners of his mouth flickered. 'I stand rebuked. But is pride not a sin? Forgive me, I should not tease. At least there has been no deterioration. That alone is cause for hope.'

'I'm so glad for you.' She made no attempt to hide her admiration.

As their eyes locked, the crease between his brows deepened. 'Susanna—'

110

'Mrs Treneer came in with me,' she said quickly. It was enough that she had penetrated his armour of professional reserve. Her happiness was so intense she imagined it radiating from her like sunlight. 'I took her through to the ward so she could sit with her son. I hope that was all right?'

Edward nodded. Detecting a trace of relief, Susanna guessed he was glad she had recognized the need while in the infirmary to keep their relationship strictly professional. It wasn't easy, for when else did she see him?

'Her presence will comfort him. Other than relieve his pain there is little I can do until it is time to change the dressings. Will she be able to visit regularly?'

'I hope so,' Susanna said fervently. 'For if she can't then I won't be able to come either.'

He looked startled. 'Why not? I thought—not two days ago you were asking to work in the dispensary. Was it the operation? I realize that—'

'It has nothing to do with the operation. Nor is it my choice to stay away. Do you really think me so weak and fickle?' She did not give him the chance to respond. 'It seems I have embarrassed my father by visiting the infirmary without a chaperone.'

His blank expression reminded her of Richard's condemnation of Edward's indifference to any concerns but his own. She pushed the memory away. Edward spent every day dealing with situations of life and death. It was perfectly understandable if details of etiquette slipped his mind. Especially as they did not directly affect him.

'My visits may continue provided I arrive and leave with Colin's mother.' Bitterness overwhelmed her. 'Thus people who have no interest in the work I do may be reassured that at least I am observing all the proprieties.'

'That's all right then.'

For now perhaps. But what would she do when Colin left the infirmary?

As they entered the ward, Molly was holding her son's limp hand and talking softly to him. Seeing Edward she started to get up.

'Please don't move, Mrs Treneer.'

'I don't want to be no trouble, Doctor.'

'Come as often as you wish. Colin is very weak at the moment but your presence will be a great comfort to him.'

'That's what Miss Elliot said.'

Darting Susanna a glance that made her squirm, Edward nodded. 'I'll be back again later, Mrs Treneer. If you have any questions I'd be happy to answer them. Will you come with me, Miss Elliot?' He led the way across to the dispensary and opened the door. 'I understand your desire to offer reassurance but in future I would prefer that you did not discuss a patient's condition—'

'I didn't,' Susanna cried. 'You told me when I first started here that anything I learned about the patients was not to be spoken of to anyone. I have never broken that confidence. I simply told her the medicine might make Colin sleepy but if she sat and talked to him he would know she was there.'

'What makes you so sure?' Edward's tone was more curious than condemning.

'When I was twelve I had scarlet fever and was delirious for twenty-four hours. But I remember my mother sitting beside my bed telling me that my brother William had fallen out of a tree while trying to retrieve his kite. And the seamen have sometimes mentioned things I've said when they appeared to be quite unconscious.'

'I see.' Edward was non-committal. 'Perhaps now would be a good time to begin your instruction.'

Susanna was ecstatic. 'What would you like me to do? Shall I wash my hands?' As he moved about the dispensary collecting bottles and jars off the shelves and items from the banks of wooden drawers she went to the sink. But as the cold water ran over her wrists she shuddered, remembering the last time she had stood there.

'Oh Susanna.' She glanced round quickly. It was the first time she'd ever heard Edward laugh. 'Your enthusiasm is a tonic by itself. If I could bottle it how much easier my job would be.'

Filled with a happiness she had never imagined, she crossed to stand beside him.

'Because most of our patients spend the greater part of their lives cold, wet, exhausted and hungry, their general health is often poor. Mr Roberts for example. As well as inflammation of the lungs he has an ulcer on his left shin which refuses to heal. He has had it nearly a year.'

'Poor man. Will you be able to cure it?'

'I hope so. I shall treat it with the powder you are about to make.' Taking a small lump of camphor from a jar he placed it in a marble mortar which he handed to Susanna. 'You cannot grind this all at once. It must first be broken into smaller pieces. Strike it gently with direct blows.' Holding the mortar against her midriff she did as he directed. The camphor cracked and separated. 'Now, one piece at a time, first bruise it then rub the pestle round until it is ground to powder.' Taking a bottle from the middle shelf of the glass-fronted cupboard he measured three drops into the mortar. 'Spirits of wine helps camphor powder more easily.'

Opening a wooden box he removed a pair of brass scales and set them on the bench.

'Developments in anaesthetics and antiseptic procedures have greatly reduced the number of post-operative deaths.' He placed a tiny flat square weight on to one of the concave brass circles suspended from the overhead arm by three fine chains. Susanna's gaze darted from mortar to scales. She didn't want to miss a thing. 'Unfortunately, there are too many cases where we simply do not know enough or the patients reach us too late.' He spooned white powder from a brown glass jar with a wide top into the other dish.

'Like the Portuguese?'

The jar slipped from Edward's hand making her jump as it clattered against the scales before landing with a thud on the bench. 'What do you know of him? I left strict instructions that no one was to enter that room. Didn't Albert tell you?'

'When I arrived Albert wasn't in the infirmary.' Susanna defended herself. 'Nor were you. I heard this terrible moaning and shouting. I recognized the language. That's how I knew he was Portuguese. The poor man was in great distress.'

'But you didn't go in?' At her hesitation his expression darkened. She wanted to explain but he didn't give her the chance. 'Did you touch him? Or anything belonging to him?'

She could understand him being cross. She had disobeyed an order, albeit unwittingly. But he had never used that tone with her before, a sharp anxiety that made her nervous. Placing the mortar and pestle carefully on the wooden bench she wiped her palms down her skirt, recalling the dreadful appearance and nauseating smell of the raving man.

'I only wanted to reassure him he hadn't been forgotten. His cries were truly piteous.'

'Susanna, your motives are not in question. But I *wish*—No matter, it is too late now.'

'What do you mean, too late? What was wrong with him?' She recognized Edward's expression as the one he adopted on the ward when patients asked questions he did not wish to answer.

'Did you touch him?' he repeated.

'He seized my arm and would not let go. I—the smell—' Her stomach contracted.

115

Edward's mutter sounded suspiciously like a curse. Crossing to the sink he rinsed his hands. 'I want you to tell me exactly what happened from the moment you entered the side ward.'

Twining her fingers together she recounted all that had happened.

'And then you came straight in here?'

She nodded. 'I was—distressed. I didn't want anyone to see me.'

'What did you do then?'

'I washed my hands and rinsed my face.'

The slight shift in his expression sent a dart of fear through her. 'Susanna, this is important. Think carefully. Did you touch your face or wipe your eyes before you washed your hands?'

She went over the sequence again in her mind. 'No,' she said slowly. 'I came in, shut the door and leaned against it for a moment. I raised my hands but the smell—' She shuddered violently. 'I went straight to the sink and turned on the tap. I washed my hands then rinsed my face.'

'And the jade disc?'

'I washed that too.' Her hand strayed to her throat where it lay hidden next to her skin. As Edward's gaze followed the movement she realized too late what she had done. Reluctantly she felt for the loop of thread. 'You'd better have this.'

The delicate pink medallion lay on his flattened palm. 'You don't want to part with it, do you?'

She shook her head.

'Why? After such an unpleasant experience ...?'

Susanna bit her lip then the words burst out. 'My family are *plain* Quakers.' She grasped the drab material of her dress. 'All my clothes are like this. I have never owned any jewellery, nothing pretty or colourful. That medallion ...' She gazed at it with longing. 'It's just so beautiful. I think it's Chinese.'

He handed it back to her. 'Why don't you ask John Burton at the Old Curiosity Shop? He has a shopful of rare objects from all over the world.'

'I can keep it?' Susanna was startled. 'But what about his next of kin? Or Teresa?'

'Susanna, the man was not lucid enough to give even his own name. So there is no way of tracing his family, or the girl. If you would like it then have it. Tell me, in the past two days have you noticed any feeling of feverishness? Any chills? Anything at all out of the ordinary?'

Squirrelling the jade quickly away inside her dress she shook her head. 'No. Nothing at all.'

'Even so,' he said quietly, 'I think I should examine your eyes and the glands in your neck. Would you like Mrs Treneer to be present?'

'Why?' Susanna was apprehensive.

'She is your chaperone, is she not?'

'No, I meant why is an examination necessary?'

'A precaution, that's all. While you are in the infirmary I am responsible for your safety.'

Already riven with guilt over her disobedience

117

she was anxious not to cause further trouble. 'There seems little point in disturbing Mrs Treneer for something which will take only a few moments.' The nervousness that thinned her voice sprang from more than one source. 'Please do whatever you feel is necessary.'

Edward beckoned her forward. 'Come and stand in front of the window.' His fingers felt cool against her fiery cheeks as he turned her face. Aware of her deepening blush she sought escape behind her lowered lashes. 'No, look up,' he directed, apparently oblivious to the effect his nearness and touch were having on her. He gently thumbed her eyelids down one after the other. 'Now look to the right ... and the left.' Their faces were only inches apart. He slid his hands to her neck and with sensitive fingertips palpated the glands beneath her jaw and at the back of her skull. Her shiver had nothing to do with fear.

'Please, Edward, I have a right to know. What was wrong with him?'

He stared into space with frowning concentration, relying on his sense of touch to identify what he could not see. His voice was carefully emotionless. 'He had the pox.'

'But I've seen smallpox. His spots were nothing like that. And that smell—I've never known—'

'Susanna.' His hands were gentle on her shoulders. 'It wasn't smallpox. The Portuguese died of syphilis.'

As the implications registered, her eyes widened in horror.

As her father's office was surrounded by inns and ale-houses she was used to seeing seamen accosted by the gaudily dressed women with painted faces and glassy hopeless eyes who loitered beneath the hissing gas lamps. Her mother referred to them as 'Poor unfortunates for whom we must pray' but would not explain why. And while helping distribute gifts of food and clothing to the destitute families of dead sailors, she had overheard snatches of low-voiced conversation concerning 'man's base nature' and 'the wages of sin', and deduced that sometimes sailors died because of what they did with those women.

Since coming to the infirmary she had occasionally walked in on banter between the patients in which the pox had been referred to in tones that ranged from anxious to bawdy. But because they instantly changed the subject she had not realized the same word referred to two very different diseases. The shock was like a sudden drenching with icy water.

'Listen to me. Are you listening?' She nodded, her head wobbling like a flower too heavy for its stem. 'It's possible for syphilis to be passed on by simple hand-to-hand contact with a sufferer who has open sores. The infection is transferred to the moist tissues of the eyes and mouth then enters the bloodstream.'

She stared at him, her horror deepening as fear for herself was joined by another appalling thought. 'Oh no! Colin—the operation— I touched—held—'

'Exactly.' His face was grim. 'Now do you

understand why I issued those instructions? And why I took the precaution of examining you? But you are not infected, Susanna.'

'H-how c-can you b-be s-so s-sure?' There was a faint roaring in her ears and the walls rippled as if she were seeing them through a heat-haze.

'Because the infection shows itself within a matter of hours in the form of a fever and swollen glands.'

The roaring grew louder and the room darkened, closing in on her. 'I feel ... strange.'

She was vaguely aware of Edward's arm around her and a scraping noise. Then she was eased down on to the tall stool normally kept beneath the bench. The relief was incredible. From somewhere in the distance she heard Edward telling her to bend forward. Giving in to the gentle pressure on her back she obeyed. Suddenly his supporting arm had gone. Engulfed by a sense of loss she was too weak and shaky to move. Then she felt cold water on the nape of her neck. The acrid sting of ammonia under her nose caught in her throat and made her eyes water. But it cleared her head and she felt better almost at once. She straightened carefully.

'You really are perfectly all right,' Edward repeated. 'Washing your hands immediately should have removed any risk of infection. But I'm sure you understand I wanted to be absolutely sure.'

'I've never fainted before.' Her surprise made him smile.

'It's perfectly understandable. You did have rather a shock.'

She screwed up her courage. 'Edward, you—you'll still teach me how to prepare medicines?' As he regarded her in silence, his brows lifting, she added quickly, 'I promise faithfully to follow your instructions. Please, Edward. Coming here ...' *seeing you* ... it trembled on the tip of her tongue but some sixth sense stopped her, 'means everything to me.'

'I should say no.' He seemed to be talking as much to himself as to her. 'But your visits give great comfort to the patients. Having an attractive, intelligent young woman interested in their welfare not only exerts a definite civilizing influence, it seems to speed recovery.'

She was amazed and delighted. 'Really?'

He nodded. 'Melancholy and boredom depress the spirit. This is especially true of men with little or no education who are conditioned to hard physical work and who take pride in their skills. For them illness is a sign of weakness, a cause for shame. My own days are too full for me to spend time talking with them. I desperately need more staff. In fact, I am preparing a report for the committee. The trouble is I haven't had time to finish it.'

This was just the opening she needed. 'I started to tell you earlier that in future my visits would depend on Mrs Treneer's availability. But though she wants to see Colin at least every other afternoon it just won't be possible.'

'Why not?'

'Because the Treneers have two more children

and very little money. Fishing has been poor lately. And with Colin unable to work for several weeks money will be even more scarce. Molly has two cleaning jobs: one in the morning at an ale-house, another in the afternoons at the fish market.' Susanna grimaced at the thought of what both jobs involved. 'There are simply not enough hours in the day for her to fulfil all her obligations and still find time to visit Colin regularly. Yet if she does not ...' She shrugged helplessly.

'I see.' Edward regarded her with a thoughtful frown. 'You appear to know the family. How would you describe Mrs Treneer?'

'She's a woman of strong moral character. She lives in poor surroundings but her children are clean and so is her home.'

'Do you consider she has a level head and a strong constitution?'

Susanna smiled. 'Running a home, caring for a husband and three children—one of whom is disabled—and earning extra money from two cleaning jobs? She would put many men to shame.'

'I think that answers my question. It seems to me that several problems could be solved if Mrs Treneer were to come and work at the infirmary. Would you not agree?'

'It's a wonderful idea! Oh Edward, I couldn't bear not to come. You cannot imagine—the chance to learn, to assist you—it's everything—' She looked away, blushing furiously.

He was brisk. 'Perhaps you will come with me while I speak to Mrs Treneer? I've been considering employing a nurse for some time but I didn't know of anyone suitable.' He paused. 'I would miss your help, Susanna. We all appreciate what you do here.'

'Thank you.' His words said so much and yet so little.

Chapter Ten

Lowell gazed down with almost clinical detachment at the sweat-glazed woman beneath him. He could feel her urgency, her need. Her heat and musky scent of arousal enveloped him. Yet despite the intense intimacy of the moment, skin hot on slippery skin, it was as if he stood outside himself observing, heartsick at what he was doing and at the need for it.

The house had the cold staleness of a place unlived in.

'It belongs to friends of mine,' she had said as he followed her through the echoing hall where white-shrouded furniture stood ghostly and unfamiliar in the half-light. 'They're abroad for the winter. So much more discreet than an hotel don't you think?'

He hadn't argued. He had spoken very little. Life at sea provided few opportunities to practise small talk. Besides what was there to say? Both knew why they were there. She seemed quite unperturbed by the lack of conversation. That alone would have reassured him she was no novice in these matters, her possession of a key to her friends' house simply confirmed it. She had even brought candles.

'I can do without a fire,' she had smiled, her dark eyes bold and hungry. 'But I must have light. Making love in the dark is like eating meat without salt. There's no piquancy, no savour.'

A fusty odour of disuse had wafted from the sheets. Now damp and creased they smelled of her perfume. He did not care for it.

The candles flickered. The house was large and elegantly proportioned, but a raw wind blew outside and with no fires to warm the high-ceilinged rooms, draughts feathered like chilly breath across his sweating back.

Yet she seemed oblivious to the cold. Her eyes were closed, the fine folds of her lids shiny. At forehead and temples her hair, wet with perspiration, was a darker shade of gold and clung to her skin in snail-like curls. The tip of her tongue slid over her parted lips to moisten them.

His body quickened and as the tremor rippled through him she clutched his shoulders and arched her back, her hips thrusting upwards.

'Don't stop.' Her voice was both plea and husky command, her features tight with frowning concentration.

As he looked down, for an instant Lowell saw not Henry's wife but his own. *Dear God, if only—*

'I do love you, Lowell. You must believe that.' How many times had he heard those words, heard the desperation in Marjorie's voice as tears spilled over her thick lashes? How many times had he seen her pale, drawn face contort with anguish at her failure? 'I want to be a dutiful wife to you.'

Dutiful? Was that what it meant to her? 'I know'. How many times had he said it? Trying to hide his despair. Trying to reassure her. He did believe she loved him. But what kind of love was it? How could she love him yet recoil when he reached for her? How could she love him yet tremble when he kissed her—not from desire or even shyness, but from fear and loathing? And how could he prove to her she had nothing to fear when the lightest brush of his fingers or lips made her flinch?

She had tried. He gave her credit for that. 'Go on,' she had whispered the last night of their disastrous honeymoon, forcing the words between bloodless lips as she lay, rigid as a corpse, against him. She had closed her eyes in an effort to hide her terror and disgust but they had screamed silently at him from her shrinking flesh. 'I want to please you, Lowell,' she had murmured, her voice catching on a sob quickly—valiantly—suppressed. 'Do whatever you wish. I am your wife now.' Tears had slid from the corners of her eyes and soaked the hair at her temples.

For a moment he had considered taking her at her word so great was his disappointment and frustration. It was no crime to rape your own wife. Instead, clamping his jaws tight not trusting himself to speak, he had flung on his clothes and slammed out into the night. With a seaman's instinct he had found a crowded noisy tavern and drunk himself steadily into a stupor.

One compensation for the demands of life aboard a tea-clipper had been the esteem and approval lavished by women from all levels of society on the crews braving wind and storm as they raced home across the world's oceans with their precious cargo. Like the other junior officers he had taken full advantage of this admiration. In contrast to some of his shipmates who simply used women he discovered that he *liked* them, which meant his experiences had neither jaded nor coarsened him. Instead he had learned. He had begun to understand what women enjoyed and wanted. And their pleasure increased his own.

He had been attracted to Marjorie from the first moment he met her. Beneath her natural shyness lurked a sense of playfulness and fun. She was intelligent yet possessed the same soft womanly qualities he remembered in his mother.

His father had tried to dissuade him. 'Not that one, boy. Something wrong there.' But he was so used to his father arguing against or disapproving of everything he did he dismissed the warning as just more of the same. Marjorie was always so warm and affectionate towards him that he did not question the physical limits she imposed on their courtship, convincing himself that her refusal to allow him more than a chaste kiss or two was a sensible refusal to play with fire, a reluctance to defy

126

the convention that a bride should go to her marriage bed a virgin. She told him as much, promising that once they were married things would be different, her anxiety arousing his protective instincts.

Self-control had not been easy but the depth of her gratitude for his restraint had surprised and touched him. When frustration grew unbearable he quietly sought release elsewhere, ashamed of his weakness but reassuring himself that once he and Marjorie were married he would never again cross the threshold of such places.

It never occurred to him that Marjorie's behaviour was governed by anything other than social convention. Why should it? She told him often how much she loved him and looked forward to being his wife. His own father might not have welcomed the match but Marjorie's parents were clearly delighted.

'Of course they are,' Joseph had exploded. 'Marjorie is twenty-three, the same age as you. She's not a bad-looker and she's never been short of suitors. So why have none of them married her? Eh? Tell me that.'

Lowell had hung on to his temper. 'I have no idea. Perhaps they proposed and she turned them down. In any case that is no one else's business but hers. Stay out of it, Father. Don't meddle in things that don't concern you.'

'Don't concern me? Despite all the grief you've caused you're still my son: *that's* what makes it my business. I'll tell you why she's still single and you'd do well to listen. It's because there's something not right about that girl.

127

You'd see it for yourself if you were thinking with your brain instead of your balls.'

Fighting the urge to hit his father Lowell strode towards the door. Joseph's voice followed him.

'It's in the family; look at her mother. I'm all for a wife respecting her husband, that's as it should be, but the way that woman behaves isn't natural.'

Lowell had noticed how Helen Hill always deferred to her husband, her eyes nervously seeking him out before she responded to even the most innocuous of remarks. Her mother was shy, Marjorie explained.

'I'm telling you, Lowell,' Joseph warned. 'Something's wrong. Wed that girl and you'll regret it.'

Lowell had refused to listen. He needed a wife and Marjorie loved him.

So they were married, Marjorie ethereal in her white gown, her cheeks pale as she pledged herself body and soul to him. *One flesh.*

That had been five and a half years ago. Two thousand nights. And Marjorie was still a virgin.

Silent laughter, mocking, agonized, ate like acid into his soul. He wanted to hurt her, to make her suffer as he had. His mother and sisters had died because of him. He was married but had no wife.

He tightened his arm around the figure beneath him. He would take pleasure where and when he felt the need. And he would give it. Fair exchange was no robbery. But no involvement. No emotion. That was for fools. He began to move again, slowly.

She writhed against him. 'Yes,' she whispered. 'Oh yes.'

At first restrained, carefully controlled, his movements gradually became faster and more forceful. Lust, loneliness, rage and lacerating hurt spiralled into a vortex that drew him to its core. *Damn you, bitch. Damn you to hell.* Henry's wife, or his own? At that moment he could not have said. Nor did he care.

As he thrust deeper he felt his control begin to slip. He closed his eyes and his head arched back. *Oh God it felt good, so good. No more anger. No more pain, just hunger and excitement.* His heartbeat thundered in his ears and his breathing was ragged and shallow. Conscious thought began to fade. He was vaguely aware of her head thrashing on the pillow as her nails dug into his shoulders. Then she gave a strangled cry and her body convulsed, shuddering in wild spasms.

Panting, he drove deeply into her again and again, seeking, reaching ... With an explosive groan he dissolved, melting into the sweet oblivion of total physical release.

As soon as the pulsing faded he rolled away, collapsing on his back one arm across his eyes, his chest heaving.

Beside him Henry's wife lay spent and languorous, her legs tangled in the rumpled sheets.

There was a smile in her husky voice as she sighed with contentment. 'That was ...' she paused, concluding thoughtfully, 'a revelation. Tell me, Captain, how long do you expect to remain in London? Perhaps we might—'

'I think not.' Sitting up he swung his legs over the edge of the bed and with his back to her pushed both hands through his tousled hair.

'Why not?' Though her tone was level he detected surprise and pique.

He glanced over his shoulder. 'My dear, think of the risk to your reputation.' He had long-since ceased to be astonished at the number of women whose husbands knew little and cared even less about affording their wives pleasure in the marital bed. Having for the first time enjoyed what they ordinarily endured a few were loath to let him go. Usually this tactful reminder was sufficient to prompt a sigh and a reluctant nod of agreement. She, however, was of a different calibre. She simply gazed at him, her tangled hair spread over the pillow, her eyes heavy-lidded.

'That is my concern, Captain,' she reproved lightly, 'not yours. A gentleman would surely humour me?' She raised her brows, smiling.

Lowell smiled back. She had spirit and intelligence and he admired both. But she was Henry's wife. 'No doubt. But as a mere seafarer I cannot claim such distinction.'

She sat up tossing back her hair and linking her hands loosely about her raised knees. 'A seaman you may be, Captain, but describing yourself as a mere anything is humbug, as you very well know. Do me the courtesy of being honest. You owe me that.'

Lowell inclined his head briefly. 'Of course. Forgive me. This ...' Looking at the rumpled bedclothes he toyed with the idea of using seaman's language to describe the afternoon's activity. From her abandoned hungry response to him he knew the words would not shock her. But he knew too her desire for honesty was not that strong. 'This was truly a delightful interlude and I will treasure the memory. But one cannot repeat something unique.'

She met his gaze, her face hardening imperceptibly. 'You express yourself with great precision, Captain. Do I take it you are declining my invitation? An invitation, may I say, frequently sought but rarely extended.'

'I appreciate the honour you do me. And were circumstances different ...'

'Spare me your excuses, Captain,' she snapped. 'I see I was mistaken. Indeed you are no gentleman. I suggest you leave.' Her tone was icy. 'At once.'

'As you wish.' With a lithe movement Lowell scooped up his scattered garments from the floor and padded naked across the room. He saw her lips part in astonishment as he bowed gravely. 'Your servant, ma'am.' Closing the door behind him he allowed himself a weary smile. She had thought to avenge his slight by watching him struggle, awkward and embarrassed, into his clothes. Only once had he done that. There wouldn't be a second time.

Ignoring the muffled thud of a pillow hurled against the door he dressed quickly in the dark and within minutes was letting himself out of the

131

house into the dusk of early evening. Turning up the collar of his greatcoat he looked up and down the road. Gas lamps shed pools of yellow light on to the pavement. In the distance he heard the brisk clop of horses' hooves as a cab crossed the junction. He turned towards it.

A bath would wash off the sweat and smell of illicit love and a stiff drink would take away the bitter taste. But what would wipe out the shame and self-disgust? Anger burned in him. But it was shot through with a terrible pity for his damaged wife. He lifted his face to the cold sky, wanting to howl like a dog.

Reaching the junction and the busy, well-lit main road he hailed a cab. Using a technique perfected over five long, wretched years he shut his blighted marriage out of his mind and focused his thoughts on Sir Andrew Cathcart's invitation to dine with him at the Traveller's Club.

He had met the baronet briefly on his last trip to England three years ago. It had been at a party marking the retirement of the captain with whom he had served his apprenticeship. James Mackenzie had introduced them with the cryptic remark that Lowell's career might bear watching.

Cathcart had smiled politely but made no comment and, after a few moments' bland conversation, moved on. Lowell had shrugged inwardly and forgotten the incident. Until this morning when the hotel manager had handed him the note. What could Cathcart want?

Chapter Eleven

Sitting at her father's massive oak desk Susanna finished translating the letters he had drafted. The final one of the four was addressed to a Spanish wine shipper worried about collection and delivery of his cargo should the squabble over who should succeed Queen Isabella—a conflict lurching towards rebellion and civil war—result in a blockade of the northern ports of Gijon, Santander and Bilbao.

Her concentration had shut out the rumble of male voices from the large main office just beyond the half-open door. It was here that the captains, shipowners, shareholders and merchants came, all relying on Samuel Elliot's expertise to find cargoes for their ships and organize the most suitable ship to transport their cargoes.

Slotting the metal-ribbed dipping pen into its holder beside the inkwell Susanna straightened up, flexing shoulders grown stiff from absorption in her task.

She loved coming to the office. It was the hub of a business reaching to the farthest corners of the world: sending mining machinery to South Africa and bringing back fruit and gold; taking salt to Newfoundland then delivering cod to Tuscany; and carrying machinery and steam coal to Brazil, returning with sugar, hides, mahogany and coffee. Occasionally, when the value of the cargo made it worthwhile, her father still sent a ship to China.

She was entranced by the thought of schooners, barques and brigantines whose names she knew—ships she had seen tied up alongside the quays and wharves or anchored in the harbour—crossing the world's oceans to places where exotic peoples in colourful dress observed strange customs.

Making sure each letter was slotted into the flap of its corresponding envelope Susanna sighed. Now she had finished she would have to leave. It was pure good fortune she had been able to come in at all. But with the morning-room taken over by Frances's trousseau, Agnes in the dining-room turning out all the china in preparation for the wedding breakfast, and a meeting of the committee for the rehabilitation of fallen women taking place in the drawing-room, there had been nowhere else for her to work.

Crossing to the open door she held up the letters. 'Father?'

Samuel glanced over the shoulder of his chief clerk—a rotund little man of middle-age whose hunched shoulders, pale complexion, and pince-nez suggested a life spent poring over books with only rare excursions into sunshine. 'Thank you, my dear. I'll be with you directly.'

He turned back to the clerk. 'We can undercut Lashbrook by five per cent and still make a profit. Isn't the *Lady Anne* sailing for Italy tomorrow?'

'Yes, Sir.' The chief clerk consulted the ledger in front of him. 'She's carrying pilchard oil, and will load marble to deliver to Bristol. There would be space in her hold for Mr Ames's cotton goods.'

'If I am still engaged with Captain Stuart when Mr Ames returns, tell him we can offer both a lower price and an earlier delivery date. If he accepts, impress on him the necessity of having the goods on the quay ready for stowing by four this afternoon.'

The clerk nodded. 'What do you wish to do about Captain Styles, sir? He is claiming the conditions under which you purchased the *Sarah* permitted him to remain as master for her next voyage.'

'He is wrong. I made no such concession. Kindly inform him that he is to be off the ship by noon tomorrow. In case he should be tempted to delay his departure, make sure he understands the penalty for trespass. Now, regarding Mr Mabey's cargo of woollens for Spain, I think the extra premium he's prepared to pay makes it worth the risk.' The clerk made a note on his pad. 'Have my share certificates in the Natal Steamship Company arrived yet?'

'Not yet, Sir. But I believe there was a delay on the mail this morning. It is possible they will be delivered this afternoon.'

Half-hidden by the door Susanna listened, awed and amazed at the contrast between her father's ruthlessness and ambition in business and his agonizing over the Quaker principles which governed every aspect of domestic life.

Yet how could she condemn him for hypocrisy when the family's high standard of living and generous donations to the many charities they supported were a direct result of his success?

She should be proud of him. She was. But if he could accept the dichotomy between his puritan conscience and his desire for social prominence and the admiration of his peers in the commercial world, then why could he not accept that she wanted to achieve something? That she had ambitions beyond the normal charity work expected of someone of her class and background?

William pushed the door wide making her jump. 'Father says I am to escort you home.'

'Whatever for? I'm hardly likely to get lost. Anyway, haven't you got work to do?'

William pulled a wry face. 'Father says you need me more than he does.'

Susanna's grin was full of sympathy. 'Oh Will, what have you done?'

'It's what I haven't done.' He heaved a sigh. 'It's those ledgers. I really thought ... I mean you explained it so well ... and I did try ...' He shrugged. Then, like the sun emerging from behind a cloud, his good-natured optimism reasserted itself. 'I'll get the hang of it, I know I will, if I can persuade someone—perhaps a kind *intelligent* sister—to go through it with me again.'

Susanna patted his arm. 'Of course I will. Don't worry. It's not always possible to take everything in first time.'

'Come on, Su, let's not pretend.' He scuffed

the toe of one shoe against a knot in the wood floor. 'This will be the *third* time.'

'So what if it is?' She took her cloak from the hook on the back of the door. 'I don't mind, honestly. I said I'd teach you how to do accounts. And I will.'

'Or perish in the attempt,' he grinned. 'Father says to leave the letters on his desk. He'll sign them later.'

'It really makes me cross,' Susanna said as they emerged on to the busy street. 'If *married* women are allowed the freedom to walk about the town by themselves, why can't I? Oh I know I do, but only on very rare occasions. And usually on an errand for mother. Anyway, how do people know whether or not a woman is married? Wedding rings are not visible beneath a glove. It might be different if they were worn through the nose. It's so stifling.'

'How is Colin coming along?' William enquired, taking her arm as they crossed the road and started up the hill.

Susanna looked at him quickly then let go of her anger. No one understood her better than Will. He was her best friend. 'Progressing well. The dressing was changed for the first time last week. Edward allowed me to watch. He's delighted as the wound shows no sign of putrefaction at all.'

William wrinkled his nose. 'I don't know how you do it. What about Mrs Treneer? Do you think she'll be a good nurse? There have been some dreadful stories in the newspaper about London hospitals where nurses get drunk on duty and are found sleeping off their excesses in the patients' beds.'

Susanna laughed. 'Molly doesn't hold with drink. She's settled in really well. I think the patients were rather shocked to begin with. But when one of them objected to her washing him she soon put him straight. She said he'd do well to remember it was a woman who brought him into the world and saw to all his needs until he could fend for himself, so he could just stop his nonsense. If he preferred Albert to hose him down in the yard she would arrange it, but one way or another he was going to be clean.'

William chuckled in delight. 'How did he take that?'

'In open-mouthed silence. She hasn't had a word of complaint from him since.'

'And Albert? From what you've said in the past I got the impression he doesn't like anyone encroaching on what he considers is his territory.'

'It could have been a problem. But they already knew each other which helped. And their different tasks rarely overlap.'

'What about the children?'

'Fran says Jennet, the younger one, caused a lot of disruption in the class to begin with, but she's much happier now. No one was quite sure what to do about Mary. Being deaf she can't talk properly and other children tend to pick on her. Fran asked Mrs Collins if she would take Mary along to sewing classes at the Meeting House. Mrs Collins says Mary is showing great aptitude with a needle and might eventually make an excellent seamstress.'

'So everything has worked out really well.'
She nodded.

'Then why,' William asked gently, 'aren't you happy?'

'Of course I'm happy. I have a chaperone; Molly has a job that pays well and enables her to see Colin every day; her children are receiving an education that suits their needs and which they would otherwise not have had; the infirmary is running smoothly; everything is fine.' Her wide smile felt horribly false so she hurried on, 'Edward—Doctor Arundell—has been teaching me how to make medicines.'

'I suppose,' he grinned, 'this means you are forced to spend a considerable amount of time with him?'

'Actually, no,' Susanna replied lightly, brushing dust from her skirt to avoid looking at him. 'He's very busy at the moment. Don't forget he has his practice to attend as well as the infirmary. So after he has given me instructions he usually has to rush off somewhere. But he's always back before I leave to check what I've done. He says I learn exceptionally fast.'

Flinging an arm over her shoulder William gave her a quick squeeze. 'I think he's showing enormous faith in you.'

'Oh Will, do you really?'

'Come on, Su. Making medicines is highly skilled work. I mean getting it wrong could kill someone. So for someone as conscientious as Doctor Arundell to leave you to get on with it all by yourself is a terrific compliment.'

The knot of fear began to loosen. What William said made perfect sense. Edward was a very busy man with many demands on his time. His actions were a demonstration of his trust. To interpret them as a means of avoiding her did them both an injustice.

Chapter Twelve

Every surface in the morning-room was covered with tissue paper on which lay camisoles of ivory silk, shifts and pintucked nightgowns of fine cotton lawn, flannel vests and petticoats of cambric and muslin.

A rosewood sofa table was spread with a large white cloth to protect the delicate fabrics heaped upon it. All the lamps were lit and a fire burning brightly in the grate added more light and a welcoming warmth.

As they sewed, Susanna peeped sideways at her sister. The weeks of preparation had wrought a definite change in Frances. She was less prickly. It was as if Richard's proposal had validated her, bestowing a confidence she had previously lacked.

'Fran?' Susanna paused halfway through a stitch. 'When you and Richard are alone does he make love to you?' She found it difficult to imagine Frances and Richard moved by passion.

Frances blushed. 'You know etiquette does not permit us—'

'But he is soon to be your husband. I can't believe he would not have tried to steal a kiss.'

'We have not often been alone. Richard is most considerate of my reputation.'

'But when you were was it nice? Did his lips make you swoon the way the romantic novels say? I know,' she forestalled her sister's scolding, 'we are not supposed to read such books. But it was only one, and I just wanted to see why they are supposed to be so wicked.' She shrugged. 'It certainly wasn't very well written. There was far too much flowery description of appearance and character. But when at last the hero swept the heroine up in his arms ...' She sighed dreamily. 'It was so romantic. Was it like that for you?'

Frances stopped sewing and Susanna saw her fair brows draw together. 'It was ... wet.' Her tone betrayed uncertainty and distaste.

'That's *all?*'

'A lady has a responsibility to restrain excessive ardour in both herself and her lover.'

What *lover?* She tried to contain her exasperation. 'But what harm could a kiss do? You will soon be *married.*'

'Exactly.' Frances was severe. 'Marriage is a serious undertaking. All this talk of kissing is frivolous and out of place.' She resumed her sewing.

About to tease, Susanna noticed her sister's hands were trembling and realized she was far more nervous than she could bring herself to admit. What if she did not enjoy Richard's

141

embraces? Having accepted his proposal presumably she was prepared for the intimacies of marriage. Susanna had not been able to discover exactly what these were, but sleeping in the same bed must surely require husband and wife to enjoy being close to one another? Whenever she thought of Edward in that way she experienced strange sensations deep inside. No doubt that was something else of which she should be ashamed. But it felt so nice.

'Of course it's serious. But can't there be fun as well as responsibilities?'

'You are so ... *superficial*, Susanna. Marriage is the foundation of family life. It should be treated with solemnity and respect.'

'I'm not mocking marriage. I hope I shall soon be making preparations for my own wedding.'

'You?' Frances snorted.

'Why not? And I shall take it every bit as seriously as you do. But I want my marriage to be much more than just an arrangement between families or a partnership for raising children.' She gazed into the blazing fire. 'I want a union of body and soul with the man I love.'

'Susanna! How can you even think such *wicked* thoughts? There must be something wrong with you.'

'Who says they are wicked? Courtship might be strictly controlled by the rules of etiquette, but surely once a couple are wed—'

'You aren't the only one who reads books,' Frances interrupted. 'After my engagement was announced Mother bought me two, specially

142

written for young women preparing for marriage.'

'You never told me.'

'Why should I? You're not the one getting married.'

Not yet, Susanna wanted to respond, but restrained herself. 'So what do they say?'

'That no well-brought-up girl entertains such thoughts. "A wife should be her husband's companion",' Frances quoted. '"And though she must submit to her husband in order to please him, and to fulfil her desire for motherhood, she would otherwise prefer to be relieved from his attentions".'

Behind the triumph on her sister's face Susanna glimpsed relief, but did not immediately register its significance.

'Pray for guidance, Susanna. Until you rid yourself of all these scandalous ideas, how can you even hope to find a serious suitor?'

Susanna lifted her chin. A small voice warned her against rashness. But her sister's disgust coming on top of the day's events goaded her beyond endurance. 'I may already have one.'

As the servant removed their plates, Lowell sat back. 'That was the tastiest steak and kidney I've ever eaten.'

Sir Andrew Cathcart nodded approvingly and dabbed his mouth with his napkin. His silver-grey hair curved back from his temples like two folded wings and his long side-whiskers were neatly trimmed. Because of his girth and the slope of his shoulders—both minimized by the

143

superb cut of his evening clothes—he appeared short. But his face revealed a character much tougher than his physique suggested. He had a deep forehead, a roman nose, and a firm mouth. He was, Lowell guessed, in his mid-fifties.

'Club food is often criticized for being too reminiscent of the nursery or prep school. But personally I prefer it to the mucked-about stuff served in restaurants these days. Can't understand the appeal of such places myself.' He gave a brief shudder. 'A man can't hear himself think with all that female chatter. Give me a club any day. Much more civilized.'

Masking his amusement Lowell glanced around, recalling the previous evening. After a hesitancy over etiquette that felt awkward—like a joint stiffened with age and disuse—he had eased into the appropriate moves and responses. But mentally his adjustment was far from complete.

Yet the double-standards and hypocrisy which characterised English society were as rife in Shanghai as here in London. Perhaps he was simply out of touch. During the past five years he had spent so much time sailing to the wilder shores of China his contact with so-called civilization could be counted in weeks.

Only one other table in the dining-room was occupied, by an elderly man, napkin tucked into his collar, carefully chewing soup.

'It's always quieter in the evenings.' Cathcart smiled. 'Far more suitable.'

The choice of word reminded Lowell of McKenzie's warning. He had gone to see his old

144

captain at Greenwich after receiving Cathcart's invitation, delivered to the ship an hour after it docked.

McKenzie had refused to speculate on what the baronet might want. 'He'll tell ye when he's a mind tae. Just don't be taken in by appearances, lad. A man doesnae reach his position in the Foreign Office just because he inherited a title. Yon baronet has the mind of a serpent and don't you forget it.'

Lowell left, little wiser but greatly intrigued.

'I have never been able to understand the logic'—Cathcart passed the decanter across the table—'in serving a wine of distinction *after* the palate has been dulled by coffee or contaminated by cigar smoke. A vintage port deserves to be treated with more respect.' He passed his glass beneath his nose inhaling appreciatively.

Filling his own glass Lowell lifted it and allowed the tawny wine to slide over his tongue. It was rich, smooth and mellow. He swallowed, belatedly recognizing the compliment implicit in the baronet's choice of wine.

'Excellent,' he agreed. Though the previous night's sleep had blunted his exhaustion, and the interlude with Henry's wife had rid him of a tension that had given him gut-ache and a tendency to snap and snarl, he was still unable to relax.

'The Factory House at Oporto is almost a place of worship for port lovers. Would you care for cheese? How about the Stilton?'

Glancing up impatiently Lowell caught Cathcart's gaze and realised the flow of small talk had been a tactic designed to give his host time to observe and assess. He recalled McKenzie's warning.

Cathcart scooped up the decanter and his glass. 'If you've finished we'll go and make ourselves comfortable.' Across the wide passage a blazing fire welcomed them. Gaslights on the wall either side of the fire hissed softly, adding their gentle illumination to the glow from the flames which cast flickering shadows across the oil paintings hanging on the oak panelling. Button-back armchairs of rich brown leather shiny with use and age were grouped in twos and threes around small tables.

Choosing a corner to one side of the hearth, well out of earshot of two men nursing balloon glasses and puffing on fragrant cigars, Cathcart set the decanter on a slender-legged table at his elbow.

Lowell could wait no longer. 'Why am I here?'

Cathcart pinched the bridge of his nose. The mannerism betrayed weariness.

'Our new Foreign Secretary, Lord Clarendon, does not approve of Prime Minister Disraeli's foreign policy in China. I suspect both of them have only a minimal grasp of the true situation. One of the many problems we have in the Foreign Office is that the intelligence we receive is invariably coloured by the vested interests of the people supplying it.' He looked directly at Lowell. 'You, however, are not a diplomat. Nor, thank God, are you a politician. You were born in China and have lived there

146

all your life. You speak the dialects. And, most important of all, you have access to areas few non-Chinese ever see.'

'Why should you think that?'

Cathcart's smile contained a hint of impatience. 'Come now, Captain Hawke. Your exploits in the Yangtze river are the stuff of legend in waterfront taverns from Macao to Shanghai. Men who have sailed with you are only too delighted to bask in your reflected glory. The legality of your cargoes does not concern me, what I want is information: detailed, accurate information. Supplied directly and exclusively to me on as regular a basis as conditions allow.'

Lowell dark brows climbed. 'A spy?'

'An observer,' Cathcart corrected.

'That's all?'

'For the moment. However, should circumstances—'

'Quite. *Sufficient unto the day* ... ?' Lowell saw Cathcart's features relax into a faint smile. They understood one another.

Pouring himself more wine Cathcart offered the decanter which Lowell declined with a shake of his head. 'Is there some way in which Her Majesty's Government might convey its gratitude for your assistance?'

'I need guns.'

Cathcart's expression did not alter. 'For whom?'

'Among others, British Consular officials at ports up the Yangtze.'

'Why should they need guns?' Cathcart demanded. 'They are there legally under the terms of the peace treaty as representatives of the British Crown.'

'Tell the Chinese that. And tell the two British officials who had their houses set on fire. Under the pretence of helping, local Chinese robbed them of everything they owned. Incidents like these are occurring regularly.' Lowell held his host's gaze. 'If the law cannot or will not protect these people, they must take whatever steps are necessary to protect themselves.'

After a few seconds Cathcart gave an abrupt nod. 'All right. What do you need?'

'A thousand rifles—British Enfield, the .577 calibre that have been converted from muzzle to breech-loading for the new Snider cartridge—plus half a million rounds of ammunition and your guarantee of a continued supply.'

'*What?*'

'Plus Colt .36 single action revolvers, the Navy model, with ammunition.' Lowell's brows formed a single black bar as he thought. 'And seven Gatlings.'

'I beg your pardon?'

'Surely you—'

'I know what a Gatling is,' Cathcart interrupted tartly. 'The deadliest weapon ever invented according to the American whose brainchild it was; ten barrels firing thousands of rounds a minute without risk of jamming or misfire. But it's hardly suitable protection for a consulate.'

Lowell grinned. 'One mounted in the bow of my boat will make damn sure the river pirates don't stop your generous donation to the cause

148

of peace reaching its destination.'

'But *seven?* And why so many rifles and handguns?'

Lowell leaned forward. 'Look, *officially* we may no longer be at war with China, but that hasn't stopped the fighting. To establish and maintain trade in the up-river ports our people have to be protected. There are only two British gunboats to patrol six hundred miles of river, and the imperial war junks steal as much as the *pilongs.*'

'You said *among others.* What others?'

'It seemed expedient to negotiate an alliance.' Lowell shrugged.

Cathcart tossed back a large mouthful of port, heedless of its pedigree. 'With whom?' Strain was audible in his voice.

'Kwang Tsai.'

Cathcart's indrawn breath hissed sharply. 'You're asking Her Majesty's Government to supply arms to a Chinese warlord?'

'No,' Lowell said crisply. 'You *offered.* A token of gratitude in return for my assistance, remember?'

'But giving guns to the Chinese—'

'Kwang Tsai is a realist. He recognizes a fact the dowager empress refuses to accept, that the British are in China to stay. In return for guns with which to defend his territory from rival warlords, he will extend his protection to British traders and missionaries and their families.'

'So the other six Gatlings are for him?'

'Yes.'

'Can we trust him?'

'Can we afford not to?' Lowell replied.

Cathcart tapped his fingertips on the arm of his chair, clearly struggling with the ethics of the situation. After a few moments he gave another brief nod. 'You'd better prepare a full list of the ammunition and spares you'll need.' He rubbed his forehead in a revealing gesture.

'Just one more thing,' Lowell said. 'I want a hideaway gun. Preferably a derringer. The .41 has two barrels but is small enough to be concealed in the hand and can be carried in a waistcoat pocket, up a sleeve, or down a boot.'

'Indeed? How very convenient.' Taking a small white card from an inside pocket Cathcart passed it across. 'Present this, and your list of requirements, at Woolwich Arsenal any time after next weekend.'

A quick glance showed Lowell the card was printed with the simple legend *Smith & Company, Machinery Exports.* 'Thank you.'

Cathcart leaned forward and poured them both more wine. 'Now, what exactly is the situation in China?'

Chapter Thirteen

The Meeting House was full. The window sills had been adorned for the occasion with arrangements of holly and pine cones. Vases of red and white chrysanthemums, signifying love and truth, added welcome colour to the plain room.

Richard had made his declaration, now it was Frances's turn.

'Friends, you are witness this day ...' —she was almost as pale as her bridal gown—'that I take Richard Thomas Webber to be my husband, promising with the Lord's assistance to be a loving and faithful wife until death separate us.'

Her declaration complete, Frances's whole body seemed to unclench. Susanna watched her sister steal a shy glance at the man to whom she had committed the rest of her life. But gazing proudly at the assembled guests he didn't notice as he led her across the room to two chairs placed side by side.

Another minister stood up and, citing the declaration as an allegory of the pledge between man and his Maker, launched into another sermon.

Then it was time for the marriage certificate to be signed. With relatives of both families required to add their names, confirming their approval of the match, the process was slow. Meanwhile Frances and Richard withdrew to the ladies' ante-room to receive good wishes and congratulations from those who had already signed.

'Perhaps you'll be next, Susanna,' Elizabeth Tregelles said just as Mrs Webber shuffled past leaning heavily on a walking stick.

'No man with a care for his good name would have anything to do with her. The

151

girl doesn't know how to behave. She's up at that Seaman's Home all hours,' Mrs Webber confided as though Susanna wasn't there. 'No decent young woman would have anything to do with the place. With the reputation she's getting, her poor parents haven't a hope of marrying her off.'

Marry her off? She was a person, not an inconvenient parcel to be disposed of. 'Will you excuse me?' Without waiting for a reply Susanna walked away.

'There you are, what did I tell you?' Mrs Webber enquired with malicious pleasure, raising her voice to catch the attention of everyone nearby. 'Just look at her. And not a word of apology.'

Susanna's face flamed. What was she supposed to apologize *for*? Her throat thickened and she took a deep breath. As chief bridesmaid she could not leave. She blinked hard and opened her eyes wide to dispel the tears before they could fall. This was Frances's day. Nothing must spoil it. Let them say what they wished. She knew the truth.

With the signing complete the ceremony was over. Watching Richard help his bride into the carriage taking them back to the house Susanna wondered what Frances was feeling. Observing her sister's pallor and fixed smile as she waved through the window Susanna recalled the book on marriage Frances had spoken of and the lines she had quoted.

Religion taught that marriage was supposed to be the closest union on earth. Yet the books implied that marriage changed a man from a courting lover, the soul of delicacy, into a vulgar beast. How? What happened?

Her conscience needled. Such thoughts were sinful. But if marriage was the only acceptable ambition for a woman, how could one not wonder? Besides, since falling in love with Edward—and what other explanation could account for the way being close to him made her heart beat faster and her limbs tremble—her passionate curiosity to experience a man's caresses far outweighed her shame.

Shepherding the other bridesmaids, giggling and chattering excitedly, into one of the fleet of carriages hired to convey guests from the Meeting House back to Wodehouse Place, Susanna imagined her own wedding day. She pictured herself dressed in shimmering white; her hair released from its usual uncomfortable confinement rippling in dark waves down her back and crowned with a simple wreath of orange blossom in the style of a painting by Dante Gabriel Rossetti.

She pictured Edward standing tall and distinguished at her side, her hand drawn through his arm, his fingers resting warm and reassuring on hers as he smiled down at her. But the rest of the image was indistinct, the surroundings blurred. For they could not marry here at the Meeting House and she had never been inside any other place of worship.

Anxiety nibbled at the edges of her happiness and the beautiful image began to fray and dissolve. She clung to her vision. In Edward's love she would find all the strength and support she needed to face the problems a 'mixed' marriage would inevitably raise.

The meal was a triumph: clear soup, dressed crab, cold baked ham with peach chutney and tomato pickle, game pie with bowls of winter salad, roast chicken served with roast potatoes, sprouts, carrots and buttered parsnips, and desserts of fruit jelly with dishes of rich clotted cream, plum tarts, and two huge crystal bowls of trifle.

There were no speeches or toasts but Richard presented each of the bridesmaids with a locket made of his and Frances's hair. Susanna thanked him courteously but couldn't prevent her gaze straying upward to his carefully styled coiffure. Just how much of the hair in the locket was his? He had little to spare. Richard's suddenly heightened colour and the pinching of his mouth showed he knew exactly what she was thinking and hated her for it.

The wedding presents were arrayed on a long table down one side of the drawing-room for everyone to admire. After the meal was over the guests formed knots and groups. Bride and groom circulated separately as custom decreed.

Ignored by some, given distant smiles by others, Susanna stood at one side of the drawing-room looking for William.

'Ah, Susanna.' Richard's voice, soft and gloating, made her spin round. 'With regard to your recent conduct I think I should warn you—'

'Really, Richard, this is hardly the time or the place—'

'On the contrary, these are *exactly* the right circumstances. By marrying your sister I have become the senior male member of this family ... after your father, of course. But he is a very busy man with increasing demands on his time and attention. Therefore I must take the responsibility of improving your standards of behaviour and discipline.' His eyes glittered with malice and anticipation. 'From now on your life will be very different, dear sister-in-law.'

Instinct and a lifetime's training urged Susanna to back down, avoid confrontation. But self-respect and her foolish stubborn pride demanded she remain exactly where she was.

She lifted her chin, one hand rising to seek the jade medallion, invisible beneath her buttoned bodice. She had no idea why but touching the exquisitely carved jade always comforted and reassured her.

'Nothing to say?' he taunted, his gaze dropping to her fingers. Susanna swiftly camouflaged her action by pretending to brush away a crumb.

'Indeed, I have. I find it most peculiar that a man only an hour married should be so concerned with the activities of his wife's sister.' She eyed him with icy contempt. 'I think my father might query your sense of priorities.'

His mouth opened and closed but no sound emerged. Then puce with rage he glanced furtively round to make sure there was no one within earshot. 'You won't get away with this,' he hissed, spittle flying. 'I'll make you give me the respect I deserve.'

'But Richard,' she smiled sweetly, her gaze mirroring disgust, 'I always have.' Turning her back she slipped away through the milling throng.

'I know he's difficult,' William sympathised, 'but just think what life has been like for him. His father drinks and his mother always has something wrong with her.'

Purged of her fury Susanna inhaled deeply. 'I wonder which came first?'

'Who knows?'

'Well, for someone so expert at playing the martyr she certainly has a vicious tongue.'

William nodded. 'Richard can't have had an easy childhood growing up in that atmosphere. He's got no brothers or sisters so there was no one to confide in. I imagine it was pretty lonely for him.'

'That doesn't give him the right to order me about.'

'No, of course it doesn't. But don't you see? Richard has spent his life putting on a brave face, pretending not to be hurt or embarrassed by his parents' behaviour.'

'What has that to do with me?' Susanna demanded.

'Appearances. They mean everything to Richard. It's often that way with people who come from difficult or unhappy backgrounds. And he might feel he's married above his station—'

'He has.'

'Yes, well, he's probably got this mental

picture of how he wants life to be in the future. Everything correct and proper, everyone obeying the rules, doing what is expected of them.'

Susanna stared at her brother. 'And I'm a threat?'

William grinned. 'You certainly are. If we were allowed to gamble, I'd lay money on Richard's bossiness being a cover for anxiety.'

Though she suspected that part of her brother-in-law's antipathy toward her welled from a deeper, darker source, William's theory did make a lot of sense. Linking her arm through his, Susanna gave him a quick hug. 'I wish I had your gift, Will.'

'What gift?'

'You always see the best in people. Even those who don't deserve it. And that includes me.'

'It's tough being a saint,' he grinned. 'Meredith's waving at you. She seems in fine form.'

Susanna followed his gaze and waved back. 'Do you think they'll have heard anything yet?'

'I'd have thought it was a bit too soon.'

'No, we're still waiting,' Meredith replied in answer to Susanna's enquiry. 'In the meantime we are making preliminary preparations. I have been re-reading Mr Hudson Taylor's pamphlets. When I think of the heathen hordes in China my heart bleeds for them. The eleven inland provinces have a total population of nearly two hundred million, yet not a single missionary between them. Is that not a glorious challenge?' Meredith's bolster-like bosom swelled with evangelistic fervour.

'It's certainly an awful lot of people—'

'Lucy has been to see Uncle Joshua,' Meredith steamrollered on. 'He's working with the family solicitor on all the necessary financial arrangements. We want everything sorted out as quickly as possible so that we will be ready to leave the moment the letter arrives.' With a beatific sigh, she folded her hands across her corsetted midriff. 'I leave that side of things to Lucy. She only fusses if she sees me getting tired. She's right of course. I must conserve my energy. There will be so much to do once we get to China. My dear,' she murmured, her gaze sharpening as she looked past Susanna. 'Would you believe that's the *third* slice of cake Mrs Mabey has had? Appreciation is one thing, but *three* slices?' She clicked her tongue. 'I was hoping to take a piece home with me.'

But what if Mr Hudson Taylor turns you down? Susanna could not bring herself to ask.

'We will have to think about booking our passage soon,' Meredith turned back to Susanna. 'Naturally we'll sail from Falmouth. But fewer ships make the voyage now.' Her eyes softened, losing their focus. 'What a different story it was fifteen years ago. Father used to tell us such stories ...' She snapped out of her reverie so sharply that Susanna almost jumped. 'Lucy was wondering whether we should let the house. She says it will only get damp if it's left empty. But I don't know. The thought of strangers sleeping in our beds and eating at our table ... Still.' Her frown cleared and she smiled. 'We'll be strangers in China, won't we? We'll be sleeping in strange beds and eating at strange tables while we go about the Lord's work. Yes,' she nodded firmly, 'we must let the house. Isn't it romantic? Two young people about to set sail on the ocean of matrimony.' Leaving Susanna to follow in her wake she forged her way through the crowd which had gathered at the door to wave Frances and Richard off on their honeymoon.

'What of your young patient?' Lucy enquired softly, as Susanna helped her on with her cloak. 'Is he making good progress?'

'The best,' Susanna whispered. 'His leg has been saved and there has been no putrefaction in the wound at all. Edward was a little concerned when he changed the second dressing as the skin around the wound had been burnt by the carbolic acid. But a new dressing of gauze soaked in a mixture of carbolic and olive oil soothed the raw skin while maintaining the antisepsis.'

'Indeed,' Lucy responded faintly. 'Naturally, I am delighted to hear such good news, but'—she managed a smile—'I have to confess I did not expect to receive quite so much detail.'

'Oh Lucy, how tactless of me. I never thought—'

'I know. Don't look so stricken. I'm quite all right. You just took me by surprise.' Her gaze was both shrewd and troubled. 'You are a remarkable young woman, my dear. I only hope—' Whatever she had been going to say was lost as more guests spilled into the hall, laughing and chatting as they took their leave.

Chapter Fourteen

Turning the glass between his palms Lowell gathered his thoughts. 'In a word, the situation is desperate. According to a mandarin I met in Hangkow, the British are trying to take over China in the same way that we are taking over India. But China is too strong. So, having deliberately tried to impoverish the country by importing opium, we are now sending in missionaries—who are really government agents—to win the hearts and minds of the people by deception and so destabilize the country.'

'I see.'

Lowell continued, 'The treaties have deprived China of sovereignty over her navigable rivers and control of customs revenues. The settlements built by the British, French and Americans in the treaty ports are protected by armed guards, and are beyond the reach of Chinese law. How would you feel if you were an educated Chinese?'

Cathcart's forehead creased in mild perplexity. 'Forgive me for being blunt, but whose side are you on?'

'My own.'

'Very successfully, it would appear.'

Lowell shrugged. 'I was in the right place at the right time.'

'Isn't that carrying modesty a bit far?' Cathcart's smile was shaded with irony. 'Who would have thought smuggling salt could prove so lucrative? And I imagine this will not be the first time you have carried guns. Yet you've never carried opium. Why?'

Lowell felt the familiar tightness in his chest as memories crowded his mind. Of all the rows he'd had with his father, that had been the most bitter.

'I want you to come into the business, as my heir,' his father had announced.

'Oh yes?' Lowell was openly sceptical. They had not seen each other for almost two years. Not since ... he shied away from the recollection. The scene had been painful enough at the time. Later, after the tragedy, the memory of his mother's tears had tortured him for weeks. But how could he have known? And if he had, would he have chosen differently? No, he would not.

He glanced swiftly around. As well as the large mahogany desk and a leather chair the colour of ox-blood, his father's spacious new office contained two superb cut-glass chandeliers fitted with the best spermaceti candles, an elegant French sofa, a low rosewood table and corner cabinets displaying choice items of porcelain and jade figurines. The polished wood floor was partly covered by a Chinese silk carpet. Business was obviously booming.

'Are you listening to me?' Joseph demanded. 'I mean it.'

'What about John?' Now eighteen, Lowell was second mate on the brigantine *Sprite*. No sooner

161

had they tied up alongside the jetty that morning than Lowell had been summoned. Brandishing a letter from Joseph Hawke, Captain Beamish had told Lowell to go ashore at once. He had been oddly brusque but Lowell put that down to annoyance at this interruption to normal procedure.

'What about him?' Joseph snapped.

'He's your heir, remember? Being groomed to take over the company?'

Joseph made an impatient gesture. 'Not any more he isn't. I've washed my hands of him. He's worse than useless. A weakling with no backbone.'

Lowell sprang to his brother's defence. 'He's done his damnedest to live up to your expectations. But nothing is ever good enough for you, is it? He's your son yet you treat him like a coolie.'

Joseph stiffened, his face darkening with anger. 'How dare you speak to me like that!'

'It's time someone did.'

Joseph Hawke suddenly laughed. 'You've got nerve, boy, I'll say that for you.' He leaned forward. 'Just what the company needs. Spirit. Young blood. I thought your brother—' He shook his head. 'I had high hopes for that boy. Didn't I give him the best education money could buy? Didn't I settle his gambling debts? Then there was that other matter. I still shudder when I think of the damage that could have done if it had reached the papers. It cost me a fortune to pay off the girl's family. Silly little bitch. It could have been

162

dealt with discreetly. There are ways; everyone knows that. She didn't have to kill herself.' He snorted indignantly. 'No one could have done more for his son. All wasted. But you've turned out far better than I expected. So I'm giving you a second chance.' Beaming with magnanimity Joseph leaned forward over his massive desk. 'What do you say, boy? Between us we could build this business up to rival Jardine's.'

'No, thank you, Father. I already have a career. At sea.'

'And that's all thanks to me. In case you've forgotten, it was I who apprenticed you to Captain McKenzie.'

'Only because you thought I'd fail,' Lowell shot back. 'You wanted to teach me a lesson and bring me to heel. I survived five years of slave labour in conditions you cannot even begin to imagine.'

'And what have you got to show for it?' Joseph sneered. 'Second mate? What's that compared with what I'm offering?'

'What exactly *are* you offering, Father? A partnership? Shares in the company?'

'Certainly not,' Joseph snapped. Then, as irony twisted Lowell's mouth, he tried to backtrack. 'Not immediately. You have to learn the business first. That's reasonable isn't it?'

'I've already served one apprenticeship. Second Mate might not sound like much to you, but I'm an officer. And I *earned* it. Anyway that's just the start. I intend to be master of my own ship before I'm thirty.'

'Why wait that long?' Joseph came round the

desk and clapped him on the shoulder. 'You've made your point. You don't want to come ashore. But you could still join the company. What if I bought you your own boat? I know of a pretty little schooner that would be just right for you.'

Lowell studied his father. There had to be a catch. 'Why would you do that?'

'I've told you. I want you in the company. You're my son.' Joseph sketched an airy gesture. 'Naturally the schooner would be registered to me until you reach your majority. But what's a couple of years?'

'Three,' Lowell corrected.

'Three then. It's not long. Think of it. Master of your own vessel at twenty-one. How many lads of your age get a chance like that? You'd stay at sea, but you would be working for Hawke & Son. I organize the cargoes, you collect and deliver. A sure market and high profits guaranteed. What more could you ask?'

For an instant Lowell was tempted. Then he recognized the seductive image for what it was, a mirage. It wouldn't be his ship, it would be his father's. And if he joined the company he would be an employee, forfeiting forever his hard-won independence. As for the cargoes, there was only one which guaranteed the return his father quoted.

'No thanks.' Watching his father struggle with shock then bewilderment, Lowell's lips twitched in a bitter smile. *He had been so sure.*

'You owe me, boy,' Joseph hissed.

'For what?'

'Your mother and sisters' lives. They died because of you.'

Lowell flinched. 'No.'

'No? When *Guinivere* was lost your mother nearly went out of her mind. It was weeks before we knew you were safe. When you came home she begged you, *pleaded* with you to leave the sea. But did you listen? Did you care? No, you left her weeping and rushed off to join another ship. You've always been utterly selfish.'

'Of course I cared,' Lowell shouted back. To his horror tears needled his eyelids. 'But I couldn't give up then. Not after all I'd ... I had only just got my promotion. I didn't *know* she was going to die. How could I?' He began to sweat. He had had to bottle up his own grief. His sense of loss had been acute, a physical pain made worse by lacerating guilt. But at sixteen he was a man. A boy might have wept, but for a man to shed tears was shameful. 'Anyway, don't I have the right—?'

'*Right?*' Joseph spat. 'Don't talk to me about rights. What about responsibilities? It was worry about you that caused her ill-health. If it hadn't been for that she and the girls wouldn't have gone to Hong Kong to visit her sister.'

'That's not fair. They didn't go just because of me. The fighting—'

'I don't want to hear your mealy-mouthed excuses,' Joseph roared. 'She'd have come back sooner if she hadn't been so upset over you. She loved John and the girls, but you were always her favourite. Oh, she was careful not to show it, but I knew. She used to accuse me of being

165

too hard on you. Ha!' The sound emerged half sob, half manic laugh. 'Hard? What did I ask? Obedience, that's all. And perhaps a little gratitude. Was that so much? Don't you talk to me about slavery. I may have inherited this company, but it has taken over twenty years of hard work, my work, to build it up to what it is today. When you and John were born I dreamed about you one day following in my footsteps.'

What about our dreams? Lowell wanted to shout, but his father ranted on.

'All that nonsense about you going to sea, I should never have allowed it. A good hiding would have put paid to the whole ridiculous idea. Spare the rod and spoil the child. Well, I did that all right. But for you and your selfishness they would still be alive.'

Lowell stumbled backwards, trying to allow for his father's grief, but injustice stung like salt rubbed into a still-raw wound. 'I miss them too,' he cried. 'It wasn't my fault. It *wasn't*. If you want someone to blame take a long hard look in the mirror.'

Joseph thrust his face forward. 'What the hell do you mean by that?'

'My mother died because of opium,' Lowell shouted. He could feel himself shaking, knew the tremors were visible, inviting mockery. *Get out,* his inner voice urged. But he couldn't, not until he had faced his father with the truth. 'Opium, the cargo that has made you and all the other merchants on the China Coast so wealthy. The Chinese don't want it in their country. But you don't care about that. You

166

don't care about the damage it does or the misery it causes. You're only interested in the huge profits. It was in retaliation against people like *you* that the viceroy sent poisoned flour into Hong Kong's British Compound.'

Joseph rounded furiously on his son. 'You're blaming me? I'm a merchant. To stay in business a merchant trades whatever cargo pays best. The so-called resistance is just political hot air. Even the mandarins who are employed to stop the opium traffic turn a blind eye.'

'Why not?' Lowell yelled. 'You pay them enough.'

'The Chinese buy the stuff, don't they? I simply supply a demand. That's what trade is all about.'

'You're not supplying a demand,' Lowell was scathing. 'You're creating one. You blame me for my mother's death yet you are killing people just as surely as if you had put a gun to their heads and pulled the trigger.'

His father's face contorted in grief and rage. 'What about the viceroy? What he did, putting arsenic in the flour, was murder. Your mother's dead, for Christ's sake. So are Anne and Elizabeth. But I'll have those yellow bastards. One way or another, I'm going to make them pay.'

'Father, don't. Can't you see what's happening? This is destroying you.'

Joseph gave a bark of laughter, his eyes fever-bright. 'Destroying? Don't be ridiculous. I'm one of the most successful men in Shanghai.'

'Your wife is dead, so are your two daughters.

Your eldest son is an alcoholic. How much more *success* do you want? For pity's sake, Father, what does it take to make you realize? Opium brings catastrophe to everyone involved with it.'

'Superstitious nonsense,' Joseph scoffed. 'You'll be talking about curses next.'

Lowell tried once more. 'You don't *need* to deal in the drug. You could still make a good profit trading silk or porcelain, or even jade.'

'You insolent young rip,' Joseph bellowed. 'How dare you tell me how I should run my business. Who do you think you are? Other men have sons who are loyal, sons they can be proud of. What did I spawn? A drunk and a coward.' His mouth curled in disgust.

A *coward?* Clenching his teeth Lowell stared at the floor until his vision cleared and he could trust himself to speak. When he looked up his face was expressionless. 'Then there's nothing more to be said, is there?' He turned to the door.

'I will not tolerate this defiance,' Joseph shrieked. 'I *demand* you obey me. Come back here at once. *Lowell.* If you walk out ... I warn you, you'll be sorry.'

Striding through the outer office where rows of clerks, accountants, and keepers of records sat at high desks, Lowell silently repeated every swearword he could think of. By concentrating on the rage and indignation burning in his gut he was able to bury the hurt and his shattered hopes of reconciliation. He pushed them deep.

Chapter Fifteen

'So everything went off all right?' Molly enquired as they approached the Seamen's Home.

Susanna nodded. 'It was a day we'll all remember.' *Though some of us would prefer not to.*

'All back to normal then.'

'We should be by tomorrow. My parents have gone to Truro today. Father's got a business meeting and mother is visiting Friends who missed the wedding because of illness.'

'So young master William's in the office on 'is own?' Molly grinned. 'That'll please 'un.'

Susanna shook her head. 'He's had to take some urgent papers up to Fowey. Father's got a schooner up there due out on the evening tide.'

'I s'pose he's sailing up? Take 'un ages to go round by the road.'

'He'd much rather have ridden, or taken the coach. He doesn't like the water.'

'Well, at least 'e got a nice calm day.'

Though the dispensary was empty a loosely covered enamel saucepan bubbled on the gas ring. She hoped it would be Edward and not Lewis who returned. Soon, very soon, she was going to have to stand up to her parents for what *she* believed in. This was too important for subterfuge and deceit. She peered at the contents of the various containers, delighted at the speed of her progress.

One of the glass beakers on the bench contained an aromatic resinous-scented liquid she recognized as tincture of myrrh. Inhaling its fragrance she recalled tales of the exotic lands from which it came: India, Arabia, and eastern Africa, and was suddenly overcome with restless yearning.

Unsettled—for wasn't her greatest wish to be with Edward?—she concentrated on recalling the medicinal application of myrrh. Mixed with six ounces of decoction of bark and half a teaspoonful of diluted sulphuric acid it provided great relief for chronic sore throat.

Collecting her writing-case she crossed the passage to the ward where Molly, wearing a starched white apron, was busy changing bed-linen. She greeted Colin with a smile.

'You look better every time I see you.' There were still violet shadows beneath his eyes but his gaze was clear and in his cheeks faint pinkness had replaced the waxy pallor.

He grinned cheekily. 'Well, I would, wouldn' I? Compared with this lot.'

'That's enough from you, my lad,' Molly bundled dirty sheets into a basket. 'Any more lip and you'll feel the back of my hand. You needn't think you're too big neither.'

'Aw, Ma.' Colin rolled his eyes. 'I didn' mean nothin' by it.' He winked at Susanna, reminding her of William at the same age.

Molly spread a fresh sheet on the bed in the far corner while its haggard-faced occupant slumped on a wooden chair, cradling one heavily bandaged arm and fist against the blue and white hospital issue nightshirt. 'Don't you go judging these men by what they look like in 'ere, or by the moanin' they do.' She flipped the blankets neatly into place. 'Tis a known fact men are worse than babies when they're ill. But they've seen more strange places than you've 'ad 'ot dinners, and don't you ferget it.'

'No, Ma,' Colin said meekly.

Susanna was astonished at her chaperone's transformation. On her first visit Molly had been shaking with nerves. Now, less than a month later, she ran the ward with the confidence of someone who'd been doing the job for years.

'Can I get back in now?' the patient whined. 'Tis bleddy cold out 'ere.'

'You jest hold yer noise.' Molly frowned at him. 'You been out to the whatsit this morning?' When he didn't answer she pointed towards the door. 'What are 'ee waiting for? I got better things to do than run back and forth with a po. 'Ere, 'ang on a minute.' With a martyred sigh she pulled one of the thin grey blankets off the newly made bed and wrapped it around his shoulders. 'Go on, my 'andsome. The quicker you're gone the sooner you'll be back.'

Mumbling to himself the seaman shuffled off down the ward as Molly took fresh linen from the metal trolley and patted the huddled mound in the next bed. 'Come on, my bird. Up you get. Doctor'll be along soon.'

Susanna shivered with delightful anticipation.

171

'Good morning, Mr Roberts,' she beamed. 'How are you today?'

'Morning, Miss Elliot. Not too bad at all.' He tapped his chest. 'Tidn' paining me half so much. I dunno what the doctor's giving me, but tis working a treat.'

'Are there any letters you would like me to write?' As he shook his head her relief was tempered with guilt.

'I think I'll wait til I've heard from my Mary. Don't mind, do you, miss? I wouldn't like you to think I'm not grateful.'

'Of course I don't mind.' She was desperate to return to the dispensary. 'I'll see you again soon.'

As she left the ward clutching her writing-case she touched the hidden medallion. An instant's foreboding made her hesitate outside the dispensary. Ignoring it she opened the door. Edward was at the bench and glanced up as she entered.

'Good morning, Susanna. I trust you are well?'

'Good morning, Edward. I'm—' *happy to be sharing this earth, this work, this hour, with you.* 'I'm fine, thank you. I hope I find you the same?'

'A little tired, but—' He shrugged. 'It is rare for a doctor to be anything else.'

She started to close the door.

'I think it might be wiser to leave it ajar.' His head was bent over the powder he was grinding.

'Oh. Of course.' Abashed, it occurred to her

172

that he was concerned she should not be compromised and her heart gave a great leap. 'I was thinking'—she clasped unsteady hands in front of her as she moved toward the bench—'if you delegated certain tasks to an assistant you might not get quite so tired.'

'Possibly.' He poured two teaspoonsful of chloroform on to the powdered camphor. 'But finding someone suitable isn't easy. Now.' He indicated the various beakers, pipkins and mortars. 'Tell me what conditions these preparations might be used for.'

Scanning the array once more Susanna repeated the deductions she had reached earlier. 'And I would guess that this'—she picked up a glass measure and sniffed its contents—'is almond mixture to treat what is left of Mr Roberts's cough.'

'That's quite astonishing, Susanna. You have a remarkably retentive memory.'

'Thank you. But it wasn't all that difficult.' As she recognized the vanity in her remark her colour deepened. 'I mean I find it all so engrossing it's not like work at all.'

'Well, I can only say I am most impressed.'

She turned the measure in her hands. 'I do so want to be of real help to you, Edward.'

'And you are.'

Susanna did not doubt he meant it. But she had hoped for something more. A new warmth in his tone perhaps? A look which acknowledged the special bond between them? Could it be that she had missed it? *Or was he anxious she should not feel compromised?*

The thought cut through the fog of doubt and confusion like a shaft of bright sunshine. That would explain so much. Such as why, since the examination, he had scrupulously avoided even an accidental touch. And why, when their eyes met, he was always first to break the contact by immediately shifting his gaze or turning his head.

Poor Edward. So much effort for her sake. But he couldn't know it was the last thing she wanted—not unless she told him. Not as boldly as that of course. She certainly didn't want him to think her fast. She gathered her courage.

'I imagine the pressures of your work have been much harder to bear since—since your bereavement.' She sensed rather than saw his sidelong glance. 'I'm sorry. I didn't mean to upset you.'

'I'm not upset. The simple fact is that my late wife and I never discussed my work. The subject did not interest her.'

'Oh. So if—when—you contemplate marrying again—'

'I shall not marry again.'

'Not yet, of course. It is still—'

'Not ever.'

The measure slipped from Susanna's nerveless grasp and fell on to its side. For an instant she simply stared at the viscous mixture forming a small pool on the bench. 'You can't mean that,' she whispered.

'You must give me credit for knowing my own mind, Susanna,' he reproved, blending the camphor and chloroform. 'I have been married.

174

I love my two children, but I do not want more. Mrs Bennett runs the domestic side of my life with great efficiency and the children are very fond of her. So though I appreciate your concern I really have no need of it.'

As her precious dreams cracked and crumbled, scattering like dust on the cold wind of reality, she gripped the bench for support. This wasn't the way it was supposed to be. 'Have you no feeling for me at all?'

'You are a young woman of rare qualities whom I hold in great regard. I hope one day you will meet someone worthy of all you have to offer.'

Her hands were ice cold and sweating. She wanted to turn the clock back, make it not have happened. 'Edward—'

'Susanna, I beg you, stop now.' He still didn't look up. 'Words once uttered cannot be recalled. Do not say what you might later regret.'

'Regret?' she repeated incredulously. 'That I love you?'

At last he raised his head, but his eyes were guarded and unreadable. 'I'm sure you sincerely believe that is what you feel. But young women sometimes allow emotion to eclipse common sense. Had you given the matter proper consideration you would have realized that there is no possibility of anything other than friendship between us. All else aside, you are a Quaker, I am a Catholic. I could not, nor would I ever, renounce my religion. Were I to consider remarriage which, as I have said, is not my intention, I would expect my intended bride to belong to the Church of Rome.' She stared at him, agonized. 'Is it not true that if you were to marry outside the Society you would be disowned?'

'Yes.' Her chin quivered. 'But I am already an outsider, both to my family and among the Friends.' This was the first time she had actually put it into words. Doing so clarified everything. Gathering all her courage she raised her eyes to his. 'Edward, with you beside me I could face anything.'

Visibly shaken he turned away. 'I'm sorry. I cannot accept that responsibility.'

The hope that had sustained her through months of family conflict withered and died. She saw with drenching clarity that Edward didn't love her, and considered her love for him an embarrassment. She had made a complete fool of herself.

While she shrivelled inside her face flamed. Perspiration oozed from every pore. She wanted to die.

He cleared his throat. 'I think, under the circumstances, I'll send Albert for a cab to take you home. Don't worry about Mrs Treneer. I'll tell her you developed a headache.' His compassion made it even worse.

'No, no cab,' she said quickly before he could move. Her face felt stiff and her head had begun to pound. 'If you interrupt Albert now it will put him behind with his jobs. Besides I prefer to walk.' To wait while a cab was summoned would only prolong the agony. All she wanted was to get away, to run home to the blessed privacy of her room where no one could see her shame. As she took down her cloak Edward automatically started forward to assist her.

'No,' she said sharply. 'I can manage, thank you.' It took every ounce of strength she possessed to maintain her composure. 'To spare you further embarrassment I will ask William to return the books.'

'Susanna, I want you to understand—'

'I do, Edward, really.' She flashed him a brilliant smile. 'It seems I—I'm sorry—' Her aching throat closed on a wrenching sob. She pulled open the door and ran down the passage. Moments later she was outside in the yard, blinded by scalding tears.

Chapter Sixteen

Curled on her bed, exhausted from weeping, Susanna stared at the high ceiling. Outside the window, dusk had melted swiftly into night. She wished William would come home. He was the only one she could confide in. He might not understand, after all he was only seventeen, but he would listen and sympathize. He wouldn't tell her how stupid she'd been. She could see him now, saying that *Edward* was the fool. That it was *his* loss. Her eyes filled again, the tears sliding down her temples and into her hair. 'Oh Will,' she whispered, 'what am I going to do?'

Downstairs in the hall the grandfather clock

chimed. Swinging her legs over the edge of the bed she sat up, pressing her fingers to her throbbing forehead. Her eyes felt swollen and gritty. Her parents would be back soon. They mustn't see her like this. Crossing to the washstand in the corner she dipped a cloth into the icy water and pressed it to her burning face.

When she could bear the cold no longer she patted herself dry then, freeing her damp untidy hair, she brushed it out, twisted it into a neat coil and replaced her bonnet.

She could never go back to the infirmary. She didn't consider herself a coward but the thought of trying to pretend this morning had never happened—*of glimpsing pity in Edward's eyes.* She shuddered. No doubt her parents would commend her for seeing the error of her ways and suggest alternative charities to which she might devote herself.

Wiping her eyes and blowing her nose she smoothed the counterpane and took a last glance around the room, ensuring all evidence of her wretched stupidity had been neatly tidied away. The doorbell rang, twanging her overstretched nerves.

Who would come calling at this time of day? It was too late for afternoon visiting. Had her parents been home the household would already be at tea. Leaving her room she heard Agnes open the front door, then a low-pitched masculine murmur. *Edward's voice.* She sped down the stairs.

'It's all right, Agnes. I will receive Dr

178

Arundell.' Her heart hammered wildly against her ribs.

'If you please, miss—'

'Later, Agnes,' Susanna hurried forward. 'Oh Edward, I knew you couldn't—'

'Susanna.' He looked shocked and disconcerted.

Glimpsing movement behind him she froze. He was not alone. She made a valiant effort to compose herself. 'Dr Vigurs? What are you doing here?'

'I asked him to accompany me. I thought it best ...'—why wouldn't Edward meet her eyes?—'as he is your family physician.'

'I don't understand.'

The older man came forward on the porch. 'I wonder, my dear, might we come inside?'

Susanna felt her colour rise. 'Yes, yes, of course. Please, do come in.'

Dressed in a cutaway coat and dark trousers, a gold watch-chain looped across his waistcoat, Dr Vigurs drew her hand through the crook of his arm. 'Let's go and sit down.' He led her into the drawing-room where a bright fire burned in the hearth. Glancing over her shoulder Susanna saw Edward murmur a few words to Agnes who bobbed a curtsey and hurried away.

'Forgive me,' Susanna looked from one man to the other, 'but why have you come?'

'You have to be brave, my dear,' Dr Vigurs was sombre. 'I'm afraid there's been an accident.'

She turned cold. 'My parents? What happened? Are they badly hurt? I must—'

'No, no,' Dr Vigurs interrupted. 'Actually we expected to find them here.'

'They have been in Truro all day. They should be back—' she broke off. 'But if—then who—?' Dread curled inside her like poisonous black smoke. She couldn't breathe. She saw Edward turn away, unable to look at her. It wasn't just an accident. It was worse. Far worse. That was why Edward had brought Dr Vigurs. 'No.' She did not recognize the sound of her own voice. She shook her head violently, refusing to acknowledge the unthinkable. 'Not William.'

Dr Vigurs took her hands. His round pink face with its bushy sidewhiskers was sympathetic. 'I'm so sorry, my dear. The boat left Looe just after one o'clock to return to Falmouth. Apparently it ran into a squall off Dodman Point. William was hit by the boom and fell overboard. The crew did all they could but ...' He shook his head sadly.

Susanna closed her eyes. *William.* She imagined him knocked off his feet and scrabbling for purchase on the slippery deck, the sudden stinging shock of the icy water, his terror as it gushed into his nose and mouth, burning and choking him as he gasped for air, fighting desperately as the weight of his sodden clothes dragged him beneath the wind-lashed waves. *William.* Roaring blackness filled her head and she toppled into it.

'How did your father react to your refusal to join the company?' Cathcart enquired.

Lowell's smile was bitter. 'The note that had me excused duties and sent ashore so quickly? It was from my father informing Captain Beamish I would not be returning to the ship.'

'But—'

'Exactly. He had made the decision for me.'

'What did you do?'

'First I tried to convince Captain Beamish that there had been a mistake, that I had no intention of leaving the ship. But he said that as I was still legally under age he could not go against my father's wishes.' Lowell's jaw tightened. The memory of his father's machinations could still provoke an uprush of anger. 'As Hawke & Son was one of the companies for whom the captain carried tea he was not prepared to jeopardize his contract. His advice was to do what my father wanted and be grateful.'

'But you didn't.'

Lowell shook his head. 'I managed to grab my bag before it was handed over to one of Father's servants and went looking for another berth. I knew I had no chance of joining a British ship. My father would have put the word out. And no master with any sense would bite the hand that fed him. So I signed on as second mate aboard an American schooner trading between Shanghai and Nagasaki.'

Cathcart's brows rose. 'That must have been ... *interesting.*'

'It was. Japan had been closed to foreign vessels for two hundred years. We had charts of the coast but they proved notoriously unreliable.

When we finally got ashore we were attacked by *samurai*. Two of the crew were slashed to death. Then there were the traps.'

'Traps?' Cathcart was fascinated. 'What sort of traps?'

'The kind set to catch wild animals. Bamboo-covered pits full of stinking mud. One man drowned before we could get him out.'

'What an appalling place.'

'Oh no. It was absolutely beautiful, completely unspoiled.' Lowell sighed. 'Though once trading started that would change.'

'Were you there long?'

'I made three trips. But on our way down to Hong Kong with a cargo of edible seaweed we were caught in a typhoon and the ship was wrecked!'

'So what did you do then?'

'I went pearl fishing in the outlying islands of the Southern Philippines.' Lowell felt himself smile. That was a time in his life he could look back on with unalloyed pleasure.

'I take it this was not ...' Cathcart gave a small cough—'a totally *legitimate* venture?'

Lowell grinned. 'It wasn't just illegal, it was downright hazardous what with frequent tropical storms and mostly uncharted waters full of submerged reefs.'

'It sounds terrifying.'

'In some ways it was. But watching an oyster shell being opened to reveal a gleaming pearl,' he shrugged. 'For a while you forgot the other dangers.'

'*Other* dangers?'

'It's Spanish territory and the Spanish are very jealous guardians. They fire first, questions come later—*if* there are any survivors.' A shadow crossed Lowell's face. 'Those who are captured invariably wish they had died with their comrades.'

'How did you manage to evade these patrols?'

'We had an advantage. Our skipper was Spanish. I never learned the full story, it's wiser not to pry. But there was bad blood between him and the garrison commander in Jolo. Pearls from the Sulu Archipelago are quite distinctive and highly prized because of their range of colours and fine lustre. By deliberately plundering that area Captain Vicente was not only extracting a very satisfactory revenge, he was also making a fortune for himself and his crew.'

'You included?'

Lowell nodded. 'Pearls paid for my first schooner.'

'You didn't actually dive.'

'No, we used native divers, Malays and Sinhalese.' In his mind's eye he saw Suminten, lithe as a seal, her olive-gold skin silvered by tiny air bubbles as she arrowed down into the limpid depths of the turquoise water holding the stone-weighted line, an open-mesh bag made of woven hemp fibres tied to her slender waist.

He did not speak her language, nor she his. But she entranced him. Her slim body was so fluid and supple that in the water she seemed boneless, as if the azure deeps rather than the forested mountainous island were her natural

183

element. And when her soft dark eyes caught his, her glance swift and shy, his whole body tingled and he felt his face grow red. His shipmates sniggered and made crude remarks, pawing her as she passed and trying to buy her favours.

A fist in the face of the worst offenders had driven them off, earning him a bloody nose and some spectacular bruises. After that Suminten was left alone but Lowell knew his days on the boat were numbered. Memories were long and grudges hoarded. He was careful to watch his back.

Captain Vicente had ten divers working on the boat, a mixed group of young men and girls. Most bore scars from encounters with sharks, swordfish and stingrays. One man had lost his left foot to a salt-water crocodile.

Suminten had a long pale line across one calf and in response to his pointing finger and questioning glance gracefully mimicked the trailing tendrils of a poisonous jellyfish.

He felt sick at the thought of the terrible dangers awaiting her each time she dived. But what could he say? This was her living.

'When diving finished for the day all the crew would gather on deck for the shell opening. The natives were strictly supervised to prevent any of them stealing a pearl.'

He would never know how Suminten had accomplished it. It was their last day. Food was running low. The sky was sullen, the air heavy as another storm approached. The crew were short-tempered, the divers restless and uneasy.

He had been watching her open a pile of gold-lipped oysters, her slim fingers deft and strong. Her batch yielded several large lustrous pearls. Two were creamy white, one had a bronze tint, one was dove-grey, and one gleamed greenish-black. He would have sworn there were no more. He hadn't taken his eyes off her. Yet something must have distracted him just long enough.

When the last of the shells had been opened and the divers began clambering down into their own boat for their final return to the island, Suminten had drawn him into the shadows by the mainmast. Surprise had been followed by delight at the soft pressure of her lips. Then her fingers tightened on his arms in warning and she passed something from her mouth to his. An instant later she disappeared over the side.

He had waited until he was alone before spitting the object into his palm. It was, as he guessed, a pearl. But this one was rose-pink, a colour valued above all others. Her farewell gift to him.

'What made you give up pearling?' Cathcart enquired.

'A number of things. One being that a few minutes after the divers had left we were spotted by a Spanish patrol boat. Captain Vicente decided he had pressed his luck far enough. Believing, rightly, that the storm posed less danger than the Spanish, he set a course for Hong Kong. I got a lift on a coaster to Shanghai and put my pearls in a bank. Then I got a job as mate on a lorcha trading up the Yangtze. I learned the secrets of the river; the tides, currents, and shoals. I learned how and where the sandbars moved from season to season. I learned how to dodge the imperial war junks, and the pirate junks which would slink in from the coast. And I learned to recognize the lorchas sailed by fishermen for whom robbery was a profitable sideline.'

'A remarkable education,' Cathcart commented.

'Oh it was,' Lowell agreed drily. 'Walter Samms was a superb seaman. He was also a drunk. And when he started on the brandy, boat, crew, and cargo became my responsibility.'

'Forgive my asking, but how old were you?'

'Twenty-one.'

'A message, sir.' The servant bowed as he handed Cathcart a folded sheet of paper.

Cathcart scanned the paper then pushed it into his coat pocket. 'My apologies, Captain. I am urgently needed elsewhere.' He turned to the servant. 'George, would you—?'

'Pardon me, sir, I took the liberty of sending for a cab. It is waiting outside.'

'What about you?' Cathcart asked Lowell. 'Shall I have him call a cab for you?'

'Thank you, no.' Lowell set his glass on the table and rose to his feet. 'It's not far to my hotel. I shall enjoy the walk.'

Cathcart extended his hand. 'It has been a most ... instructive evening.'

'Indeed.' Meeting an aristocrat with both a brain and a firm handshake had been a pleasant surprise.

'Perhaps you'd dine with me again before you sail. When are you planning to leave, by the way?'

'The first week in January.'

'Then let's make it the 29th.'

Having received Cathcart's promise of weapons Lowell knew he would be expected to sing for his supper. But the baronet was good company and there were worse ways to spend an evening. 'How kind,' he replied smoothly. 'I shall look forward to it.'

Chapter Seventeen

Rain fell steadily from a sullen sky. A gusting wind, raw-edged and mean, snatched at the cluster of umbrellas. It plastered damp hems to cold ankles, and drove the huddled people deeper into their coats and mantles. It plucked the minister's words from his cold lips and bore away the soft sounds of sorrow.

Susanna lifted her gaze from the oblong hole in the wet earth and the plain oak casket being lowered into it. Her parents stood close together clasping each others' hands, their faces stiff and expressionless. Quakers were not supposed to mourn. Reunion with God was cause for rejoicing not sadness. Grief was selfish—so the theory went.

Susanna felt intense rage stir like a slumbering beast. She looked at Frances clinging to Richard's arm, a handkerchief pressed to her nose, and envied her sister's tears. Next to Frances, Meredith wobbled and jerked with stifled sobs. Lucy appeared calm but her red-rimmed eyes betrayed earlier private weeping. Richard's mother leaned heavily on her stick, her lips pursed, while her husband stared absently into space, swaying slightly.

A polite distance behind the immediate family a large crowd of friends, neighbours, office staff, crew, and shareholders in Samuel's cargo fleet had gathered, together with representatives from many of the town's businesses. They had watched William grow from a baby into a cheerful and popular young man. Many cried unashamedly. 'Such a tragic waste.' Susanna heard the phrase over and over again. 'He was so young, his whole life ahead of him.'

Her eyes burned but she could not weep.

'Much will be required of you during the coming days and weeks,' Dr Vigurs had said as he urged her to drink the tea Agnes had brought. Edward had disappeared. Had she imagined him? 'Your parents will need you to be strong. Having lost their only son their grief will naturally be greater than yours, and their needs must take precedence.'

She had always thought of religious faith as a candle in the soul. In her case a wavering light requiring constant protection against persistent draughts of doubt. As she stared, dry-eyed and ashen-faced at the doctor, the flame flickered and went out, leaving her spirit in impenetrable darkness. A few minutes later her parents had arrived home.

Her mother, usually so strong and capable, collapsed when Dr Vigurs broke the news, her serenity splintering in a piercing scream. Her father turned grey and she watched him visibly shrink inside his skin. She stood by, helpless and ignored, while her parents clung together united and exclusive in their anguish. She fetched and carried for the doctor while he put her mother to bed.

While writing a note to Frances and Richard calling them back from their honeymoon she glimpsed the key to her own survival. Activity. If she kept busy she could hold herself together. Edward's rejection had shattered her dreams. The brutal irony of William's drowning threatened her sanity. But her parents were relying on her and having disappointed them so often in the past she could not let them down now.

Apart from one hour each day at the office, Samuel spent his time with his wife who remained closeted in their bedroom. He emerged only to speak briefly to Elders and ministers about arrangements for the funeral. Susanna took over the running of the household and dealt with the endless deliveries of cards and flowers.

She found the stream of callers exhausting. She was expected to show appreciation for their sympathy and felt herself being sucked dry. She didn't want their commiseration. She wanted William. William had been her dearest friend, her closest ally. How would she manage without him?

189

Doctor Vigurs called several times to see her mother. Always in a hurry he smiled as he passed, told her she was doing a splendid job, and exhorted her to keep it up as everyone was counting on her. No one asked how she felt.

A card arrived from Edward: very formal, addressed to the entire family, and signed 'in sincere sympathy, Edward Arundell'. But he did not come in person. She was both relieved and wretched.

At a rumbling 'Amen' she looked up to see a second minister give the apostolic benediction. Supported by Elders her parents led the way to the carriages. Waiting to follow them, Susanna's gaze strayed past the milling people anxious now to escape the windswept cemetery and chilling rain, to the foam-flecked pewter sea.

Suddenly the clouds parted, darkly purple behind a shaft of pale shimmering light which transformed one small patch of turbulent water into liquid silver. Caught in the radiance was a ship, a stately five-masted barque, outward bound under billowing sails.

She had dreamed wickedly, selfishly, of escape. Now she knew the price. The clouds rolled on, shutting off the light and veiling the ship with a rippling curtain of rain. Turning her back she moved toward the carriage.

It was just over a week since Frances and Richard's wedding. Now all the family were together again. Finding the contrast too gut-wrenchingly poignant Susanna ordered the tables placed in different positions. Her mother fretted at the change but the visible relief of relations

190

entering the dining-room confirmed it had been the right thing to do.

With her mother incapable and Frances fetching and carrying for Mrs Webber the role of hostess fell to Susanna. She helped everyone find seats, offered plates, poured tea, Yet nothing seemed real. Even Mrs Webber's spiteful jibe—that certain people had no right putting on airs and graces and taking so much upon themselves, caused her neither hurt nor anger. It didn't matter. Nothing mattered. *William.*

Feeling her arm gently shaken she looked round to see Lucy close beside her, face puckered in concern.

'Are you all right?'

'Of course.' Susanna's response was automatic.

'You look exhausted.'

'I'm fine.' Most people were genuine in their sympathy but a few were wallowing in the drama. She could see it in their eyes as they gushed platitudes like a fountain spouts water. She wanted to scream at them in fury and disgust. How dare they presume? How could they possibly 'know exactly how you feel, my dear'. It took enormous effort to hide her rage. But she could not, *must not* add to her parents' grief. Yet the constant reminders of William's youth, of his cheerfulness and charm, of the sadness and waste his death represented, and—most bitter of all—how God moved in mysterious ways, were a thousand cuts.

Lucy eyed her shrewdly. 'Have you had any help with all this?'

Susanna shook her head.

'Hasn't Frances—?'

'She's had her own difficulties. Apparently Richard's mother took to her bed the day after the wedding.'

'Oh dear. Considering the awful weather she'd have been wiser to stay at home in the warm.'

'And miss a funeral?' Susanna felt her face contort briefly and fought for control. 'The afternoon they returned they found his mother in bed and his father unconscious on the drawing-room floor. He wasn't ill, just drunk. But Richard said that now Frances was his wife, her first loyalty was to him and *his* family.'

'Surely Frances has visited your parents?'

'Oh yes. But she couldn't stay very long. In any case Mother and Father don't want to talk.'

'It's early days yet.'

Catching a glimpse of her sister, sent by Mrs Webber on yet another errand, Susanna turned back to her cousin. 'Frances has changed.'

Lucy patted her arm. 'Of course she has, my dear. Frances is a married woman now.'

'I think something's wrong.'

'Sharing a house with one's mother-in-law cannot be easy,' Lucy pointed out. 'And Mrs Webber does have a reputation for being perhaps a *little* demanding. Frances will be having to make a great many adjustments.'

'I don't think it's that. Richard's mother can't stand me but she has always spoken well of Frances.'

A faint blush spread across Lucy's papery cheeks. 'It's possible Frances might be finding certain aspects of married life—er—' She cleared her throat. 'I'm told many women find that side of things a little overwhelming at first. She'll be fine once she gets used to it. You'll see.' Lucy patted her arm again, this time with mild desperation.

Susanna was too weary to argue. 'I expect you're right,' she murmured, not believing it for a moment.

Lucy took one of Susanna's hands between her own. 'William was terribly proud of you, you know. He really admired your work at the infirmary. How is that young boy you told me about? The one with the broken leg?'

Susanna swallowed the agonizing stiffness in her throat. 'He's really doing well.'

'When will you be going back? Dr Arundell must be missing your help. It will do you good to get out of the house even if it's only for an hour or two.'

'I won't be going back.' Susanna looked away from her cousin's surprise. The pressure in her chest was crushing, her voice a strangled whisper. 'Lucy, I've been such a fool.'

There was a long pause. 'Oh my dear. I'm so very sorry.'

Susanna closed her eyes tightly then shrugged, hauling her glassy smile back into place. 'My own fault. It doesn't matter. No one else knows. My own silly secret. I must go, Father wants me.'

193

Lucy held her hand a moment longer. 'God—'

'*Don't!*' Susanna whispered fiercely, jerking free. 'Don't preach at me. Not you, Lucy. I couldn't bear it.'

'Hush, you are coping superbly. Don't spoil it now. All I was going to say is that God may give us burdens, but in Him we will find the strength to bear them.'

With a terse shake of her head Susanna started towards her father. He had aged ten years in the past week, tortured by the grief his faith would not permit him to reveal.

Her parents were not religious hypocrites. They had never, like so many, said one thing and done another. Why would a merciful God do this to them? Why take William who had never harmed anyone?

Scalding anger welled up in her again. Live by the rules, you were told, and you would be rewarded. Love God and He would take care of you. She clenched her teeth. There was no God. It was all a lie, a huge confidence trick. She was finished with it.

Dr Vigurs stopped Maria's sedatives but without them she prowled the house at night like a ghost. Already hollow-eyed from anxiety Samuel grew grey with fatigue.

After three nights Susanna asked her father for money and went to the pharmacy. Using what she had learned she made infusions to help her mother sleep, brews to rekindle her appetite, and tisanes to aid her digestion. Her father refused them, declaring he had no need of such things.

As well as overseeing the staff and running the household, coaxing her mother to eat, and writing replies to all the letters of condolence, Susanna took over her mother's visiting of the poor and sick. But there were still too many hours unfilled. She searched desperately for other work to do, anything to keep mind and body occupied.

She knew William was dead, yet when a door slammed she would look up in anticipation, expecting him to walk in. His room was untouched, his books were still in the bookcase. One of his old coats had hung on a nail in the stable until Bryce, the groom, had walked in one day and found her sitting on a hay bale silently rocking to and fro as she hugged it. He had gently taken it from her and escorted her back to the house. She hadn't seen it again.

Maybe if she could have talked about William it would have hurt less. But her father had chosen to deal with the loss of his son by simply refusing to speak of it. She knew this was wrong but when she had dared to question him he had turned on her, his face tormented. 'In God's name, Susanna, respect my wishes in this if nothing else.'

Recognizing his pain as a reflection of her own, she obeyed. But it meant every word that passed between them was rehearsed, edited, bringing new tension to an atmosphere already strained.

The weather turned colder. One morning she opened her bedroom curtains to see frost flowers glistening on the window. A pale sun shone from an oyster sky on to a hazy world bleached of colour.

Her parents had already begun their breakfast. Samuel looked pointedly at the clock then eyed her over his glasses. 'Where are you going today?'

'To the soup kitchen.' She poured milk into her cup then added tea.

'Weren't you there yesterday?'

Susanna nodded. 'Two of Mrs Endean's regular helpers are ill with 'flu.' She looked at the porridge but her stomach heaved in protest, so she took a slice of toast and began to spread it thinly with butter.

He cleared his throat. 'Your new sense of duty has not gone unnoticed. You do not possess your mother's charitable instincts,' he added, ever determined that no child of his should indulge in vanity, 'nonetheless it is pleasing to see that despite the limitations of your youth, inexperience, and wayward character, you are trying to follow her example. Isn't that so, my dear?'

Maria's spoon rested on the congealing remains of her porridge. She looked up slowly, her mind far from her current surroundings.

'My dear, I was just telling Susanna how pleased we are that at last she is placing her duty to others above her own selfish whims.'

Susanna closed her eyes briefly. Even his praise had a cutting edge.

'Yes.' Maria made a visible effort. 'Susanna, next time you see Mrs Endean would you apologize to her for my absence? Tell her I—'

Her forehead creased. She pushed back her chair. 'Would you both excuse me?' Immediately Samuel was at his wife's side his voice gentle as he led her from the room.

Susanna buried her face in her hands. Never in her life had she felt so utterly alone. She straightened, rising as her father returned.

'Your mother isn't well.'

'I'll go and—'

'No, wait.' He rubbed his hands together, uncharacteristically hesitant. 'I—there's—I have a small task for you. It's the dividends.'

The memory of William asking for her help was so clear, the pain so sharp, she almost cried out.

Samuel removed his pince-nez and began to polish them. 'The shareholders have been most patient. But with Christmas almost upon us we cannot keep them waiting any longer. Tomorrow when you have finished your household duties I want you to go down to the office. My chief clerk will explain—'

'It's all right, Father. I know what to do. William—' She stopped as he flinched.

He replaced the glasses. All his movements were made with great care as though he were brittle. Susanna longed to put her arms around him, to give and receive comfort. She desperately wanted to tell him how much she missed her brother, of how she was constantly reminded of things he had done or said.

But she did not.

Chapter Eighteen

'Do you have any idea when he might be back full-time?' The chief clerk wrung his hands. 'You see an hour a day—it's not really ...'

Looking at the open ledgers spread over her father's massive desk Susanna turned the metal-nibbed pen in her fingers. She had sensed tension the moment she entered the office. The truth was she didn't know when her father would return. Anticipating the question she had asked him only to be waved aside.

'Just follow my instructions. Your mother's health is my prime concern at the moment.'

But what was she supposed to tell the chief clerk? Samuel Elliot's success was founded on his judgement and reliability. Any hint that bereavement had affected either would have customers deserting in droves. They sympathized, but European trade was already severely disrupted by the Carlist rebellion in Spain. Germany and France were at war. Paris was under siege. And business was business.

Susanna made a decision. 'Actually, Mr Hosking, I brought a message from my father. But as you were busy when I arrived I thought it best to wait for a more opportune moment.' Through the half-open door she could hear the noise of a busy mid morning in the office. 'My father had expected to return today, but has been unavoidably detained ... on a business matter of some importance.' If she was going to lie she might as well do it properly. 'He—he wants you to write down any queries you may have'—she swallowed—'together with your own suggested course of action. I will take these home with me at the end of the afternoon and relay his instructions to you in the morning.'

'A capital idea.' He washed his hands in a paroxysm of relief at having the responsibility removed from his shoulders. 'A finger on the pulse at all times. Exactly what we have learned to expect from your esteemed father. A remarkable man, Miss Elliot. Not a detail escapes him.'

'So if there is nothing else ...?'

'No, no. Thank you, Miss Elliot.' He indicated the ledgers. 'Are you quite—?' As she nodded, he rubbed his hands again. 'Then I'll leave you to get on.' With a twitch of his hunched shoulders he scurried out.

Sagging back in the big leather chair she gazed down on to the town quay and inner harbour. Frost still lingered in shadowed corners. But the roofs were slowly drying in the slanting sun as meltwater dripped from the eaves. Fishermen, wharfingers, and sailors went about their business on the three arms of the quay, their breath puffing like smoke on the chilly air as they exchanged greetings and bawdy insults.

She pressed the carved jade against her breastbone. She felt so guilty. Not about lying to the chief clerk, that was a necessary evil; her guilt ran far deeper. She had loved

William so much and missed him dreadfully. But if he hadn't died she wouldn't have this opportunity. If she could prove herself able to take his place then at least some good would have come from the catastrophe. It would be her memorial to him.

She was taking a terrible risk but what was the alternative? If her father's continued absence was not already a source of speculation and rumour, it soon would be. How could she stand by and do nothing as the company he had built up over a lifetime disintegrated?

Over the next three days her mother burned with fever and developed a hard dry cough. Dr Vigurs came again and this time diagnosed influenza.

'In my opinion,' he announced, sounding both harassed and impatient as Susanna saw him to the door, 'your mother's emotional state is contributing to her present physical debility.'

'Are you saying it's *her* fault that she's ill? Don't you think she has suffered enough without being blamed for something which is quite clearly outside her control?'

'My dear Miss Elliot!' he spluttered. 'You forget yourself.'

Susanna felt fiery heat flood her cheeks. 'I—I'm sorry. That was unforgivably rude.' Watching the doctor she saw a cockerel shaking out ruffled feathers. *Was she going mad?*

'I am reminding myself,' he said, as he peered at her over his gold-rimmed spectacles, 'that recent events have placed you under a certain strain.' His expression softened. 'Fresh air and exercise, that's what you need. And plenty of good red meat. You're looking pale.' Was he going to pat her on the head? Glancing at his fobwatch he returned it to his waistcoat pocket.

'For your mother's cough I recommend honey and vinegar. She will find it very soothing. A linseed poultice over the lungs might make her more comfortable. She probably won't want to eat but it's important that she drink lots of fluids; water, cordials, and thin beef tea.' He smiled, her lapse forgiven. 'I know I can rely on you.' He strode briskly away to his carriage and his next patient.

By getting up an hour earlier Susanna had time to wash her mother and help her into a clean nightgown while Agnes removed the sweat-drenched sheets and remade the bed with fresh ones. After gently brushing and rebraiding Maria's hair she settled her once more into bed. Next she fetched a fresh glass of honey and vinegar in hot water and coaxed her to drink a few sips. Then she went down to breakfast.

The fourth morning after she had begun work on the dividends she was in the hall putting on her cloak when her father came downstairs. Traces of his former self were re-emerging. He appeared to have folded his grief neatly and stowed it somewhere away from public view.

'Good morning, Father.'

'How are you getting on?' He frowned. 'I hope you are taking care. Accuracy is essential.'

She smoothed her gloves over trembling

fingers. 'I completed the calculations yesterday morning. Mr Hosking is checking them and says I should be able to start delivering the money this afternoon.'

His nod was an acknowledgement not an indication of approval. 'Frances is coming to sit with your mother this afternoon so I shall come down to the office later.'

She forced a smile as her stomach knotted. 'Mr Hosking and the rest of the staff will be delighted to see you.'

He coughed. 'There's to be no fuss. I want everything just as normal.'

Susanna bit the inside of her lip. How could it possibly be *normal* without William?

'Hurry along then.' He was brusque. 'While you're wasting time people are waiting for that money.'

The sun had dipped behind the rooftops as Susanna crossed from Bar Road into Grove Place. The leather pouch, heavy with gold sovereigns when she set out, now contained only the folded paper listing the names of shareholders at this end of town.

She hugged her cloak around her. The air was damp and bitterly cold. On the far side of the river yellow-grey cloud like dirty foam slunk across the sky from the north-west. Shivering she quickened her pace, picturing a warm fire and a mug of hot chocolate. But they were not the only reasons for the new urgency in her stride.

Gazing straight ahead she passed Edward's house. A few moments later she passed the Sailors' Home. As she let out the breath she'd

202

been holding the icy wind funnelling up the slip from the quay hit her with force. She pulled the hood of her cloak over her close-fitting bonnet, holding the thick woollen material over her mouth.

The gas lamps hissed and flickered shedding pale pools of light on to people hurrying along road and pavement, anxious to get home. Jostled by a woman coming the other way Susanna stumbled back against the wall of a shop and glimpsed a familiar figure coming down the street on the opposite side. *Oh no. Not now. That would be too much.* Pulling the hood even further forward she peered through the gloom, suddenly doubtful. She'd *thought* it was ... but with a scarf muffling the lower half of his face and the unfamiliar hat pulled low over his eyes it was difficult to be sure. And why would he wait on the corner of the most notorious street in Falmouth? She must have made a mistake.

The hotel door opened. The man jerked back, not wanting to be seen yet unwilling to move away. Framed in the light a woman with hair hennaed bright orange shivered violently and pulled a thin cloak of tattered red velvet around her. She shouted something over her shoulder which was met with catcalls and coarse male laughter. In the gaslight her face was the colour of stale cod except for the patch of rouge staining each cheek.

Susanna watched the man glance furtively around then murmur something to the woman who looked him up and down. Resting one hand on her hip she asked a question. The man

203

nodded quickly. With a shrug and a sigh the woman jerked her head and turned down into Quay Street. With a last hasty glance behind him the man followed.

Despite the hat, the scarf and the thick dark coat, as soon as he moved Susanna was sure. It *was* him. Then, as the significance of what she had just witnessed dawned on her, shock dried her mouth. She turned up the hill towards home.

Unfastening her cloak with chilled fingers she hung it up, automatically pushing escaped curls into the confining bonnet. As she opened the drawing-room door delicious warmth enfolded her.

Sitting alone by the fire Frances looked up with a start. 'I wanted to visit sooner,' she said quickly. 'But it's difficult—'

'It's all right, Fran,' Susanna broke in, picturing Mrs Webber. 'I understand.' Crouching by the hearth she held her hands out to the dancing flames. 'You look a bit down. Is Mrs Webber being unkind?'

'No, not at all. Well, she has her little ways. But we get along quite pleasantly most of the time.'

'She's extremely lucky to have you for a daughter-in-law.' Susanna sank into the fireside chair opposite her sister's.

'Mother seems much better.' Frances's bright smile looked totally out of place on her pinched face. 'She's just gone to freshen up and have a little rest before tea. I must be on my way too, now you're home. Mrs Webber doesn't like eating alone and Richard won't be back until late. He's at a staff meeting.'

'No—' Susanna stopped herself just in time. Richard's school was at the opposite end of town, almost a half-hour's walk from where she had just seen him in Quay Hill. 'No, stay a while longer,' she amended hastily. 'It seems an age since we've talked.'

'Now I'm married I have so many ...' Suddenly Frances stood up. 'I really ought to—'

'A few more minutes won't hurt. What's wrong? I can see there's something. Can I help?'

A strangled laugh ripped from Frances's throat. 'You? How could you possibly—what would you know about—I can't.'

'Fran, if *I've* noticed, don't you think others will? You know how quickly gossip spreads.'

'Oh no. What have you heard?'

'Nothing.' Susanna reassured her. 'But—'

'I *can't*. It's so ... disloyal.'

Leaning across Susanna touched the white-knuckled hands. 'Nothing you tell me will go beyond these four walls. I give you my solemn promise.'

Sitting on the edge of the cushioned seat Frances raised a face streaked with tears. 'It's Richard.'

Susanna concentrated fiercely on projecting only sympathetic concern. 'What about him?' Did Fran know about his visits to Quay Hill?

'It's so ... shameful,' Frances whispered, huddling forward. 'The first night of our honeymoon ... we had prepared for bed, separately of course, and said our prayers ... and then he told me ...' Her voice faded to a whisper. 'He said he harboured lewd carnal thoughts about me and deserved my utter disdain.'

Susanna stared at her sister. 'But you told me he has always treated you with the utmost respect ...' Frances nodded vigorously. 'Then to say such a thing, especially on your wedding night ... does seem a bit ... *thoughtless.*' Coming from someone so meticulous regarding correct behaviour, and who never lost an opportunity to criticize others, it was not only tactless but brutally insensitive.

'I was startled,' Frances confessed. 'I had not expected such ... bluntness.' Though she was choosing her words with great care her fretting hands and the down-turned corners of her mouth betrayed revulsion. 'But the books said that a wife may not always understand her husband's behaviour. So I told him I was prepared to overlook it. After all, a man's nature is different from a woman's in such matters.'

A shaft of memory pierced Susanna. When Edward had examined her in the dispensary his touch, brief and light, had been confined to her face and neck. Yet every inch of her skin had become instantly and exquisitely sensitive. For weeks just thinking about him had been sufficient to trigger strange palpitations. Not now, of course. She felt nothing now, nothing at all. But she had experienced those feelings.

Was she different from other women? Depraved in some way?

'What did he say?' Susanna swept the memories aside. 'He must have been grateful for your understanding.'

'No.' Frances gave her head a small tight shake. 'He insisted he was unworthy of me. He said he must be punished for his wickedness. Then he took a black riding crop from his suitcase and ...' —nervously she moistened her lips— 'and begged me to beat him.'

Stunned, Susanna stared at her sister's bonneted head. *Beat him?* 'What did you do?'

Frances's head flew up, her face a mask of horror. 'I didn't—'

'No, of course not. I meant what did you say?'

Taking a handkerchief from her sleeve Frances wiped her eyes and nose. 'I told him I forgave him everything. Was he not my husband?' She looked down yet seemed unaware of the hole she was tearing in the fine fabric with her thumbnail. 'He said he did not want forgiveness. He insisted he must be punished.' Her voice caught. 'I know I shouldn't have but I started to cry.' Her face crumpled. 'I was frightened.'

Susanna knelt in front of her sister, covering the tense trembling hands with her own. 'Of course you were.' She struggled to keep her tone gentle as disgust and incredulity fuelled her burning anger. 'Anyone would be.' *Not her. She would probably have laughed and no doubt made matters worse. But she would never have married him in the first place.*

'When he saw I was unable to do what he asked,' Frances hiccupped, 'he put on his dressing-gown and went down the hall to the bathroom. I didn't know what to do. I waited for a while, but I was so tired what with the journey and everything, I got into bed. I must have fallen asleep because I didn't hear him come back.'

'What happened in the morning? Did he apologize? Explain?'

Frances shook her head again. 'When I woke he kissed me on the forehead and got out of bed saying he would dress in the bathroom and take a short walk, then we would breakfast together. He didn't mention ... so naturally I could not. That night he did not ... he made no ... approach. After our meal the following evening he drank brandy.' Despite her misery Frances's voice still held shock at this blatant breaking of the Quaker rules of abstinence. 'When we retired he tried to—' She shuddered. 'Then he began scolding himself for failing me, for not being a proper husband. He pleaded with me to punish him. He said that if I loved him I would help him atone for his sins.' Her tear-wet cheeks reddened. 'The books say a wife should display only shyness and modesty, and indeed that is my natural temperament. But ...' Frances took a deep breath. 'I cast them aside and put my arms around him. I told him that I forgave him with a glad heart, and he had no need of punishment.'

'And?' Susanna prompted, fascinated by this glimpse into the secrets of a marriage.

'He pushed me away.' Frances's chin quivered. 'I don't understand why he was so angry.' She wiped her eyes again. 'Anyway, the next day we received your message calling us home. Since then ... nothing. I don't know what to do.'

'Why don't you go and talk to Dr Vigurs? Perhaps he could explain—'

Frances was aghast. 'I couldn't possibly tell anyone else.'

'Would Richard consider ... ?' As Frances gasped Susanna shook her head. 'No, perhaps not.' If he was too self-centred and inconsiderate to care what effect his peculiar demands might be having on his naive young wife, he would certainly refuse to discuss them with a doctor. 'Well, if the marriage has not been consummated you can get an annulment.'

Frances's eyes grew round with horror. 'I couldn't possibly. There would be a scandal. Think of what that would do to Mother and Father. They've been through so much. And what would Mrs Webber say? She'd blame me. And Richard would be a laughing stock. No.' She sat very straight. 'Anyway, that's not what I want.' Puffy and streaked from weeping her cheeks grew pink. 'I made my vows and I will keep them. Besides, I want—if God wills it, of course—to have children.'

'But surely ... I mean, *how?*'

'It will be all right,' Frances said quickly. 'I'm sure—somehow we'll ...' She jumped up, her face taut with anxiety. 'I should never have ...' As Susanna rose Frances seized her arm. 'You won't say anything, will you? You mustn't.'

'Didn't I promise?' But if *she* had seen Richard in Quay Hill wasn't it possible someone else had? What if *they* talked?

Chapter Nineteen

It was late when Susanna returned to the office the following afternoon.

'... and Charles both have 'flu,' Lucy was saying to a grave-faced Samuel. 'They wanted to know if you could possibly spare one of your staff, just for a few days.'

Samuel shook his head. 'I'm sorry. I had to send my chief clerk home this morning. He was quite clearly unwell and should not have come in at all.'

'Hello, Lucy.'

'Susanna! How nice to see you. What are you doing here?'

'I've just finished delivering dividend payments to the shareholders.' She turned to her father. 'Could I not go? Unless you have something else for me to do here?'

Automatically he started to shake his head. But Lucy clapped her hands together. 'What a wonderful idea! Uncle Joshua does not relish the thought of bringing in an outsider, especially for such a short time. Uncle Samuel, if you could spare Susanna for just a few days I'm sure peace of mind would speed his recovery. No doubt

210

discerning Friends will recognize it as an act of great charity.'

Susanna marvelled. Knowing his objections would centre on what people might think, Lucy had chosen exactly the right words. She forced herself to wait quietly. She desperately wanted the job. It would increase her experience and therefore her usefulness. If she proved equal to it then her father must surely be *bound* to consider her for William's position?

'Well, as these are special circumstances,' her father began, 'and provided Joshua understands that the arrangement is entirely at his own risk—'

Susanna stiffened. Screened from Samuel's view by the wooden counter Lucy's foot slid sideways with gentle pressure. Recognizing the warning Susanna bowed her head. Cyril Hosking had not found a single error when he checked her calculations. What more did she have to do to prove that she was worthy of trust?

'Thank you so much, Uncle Samuel.' Lucy's smile reflected genuine gratitude. How did she do it? How did she keep her patience and her temper and see only the best in people?

'Hmmm.' Samuel eyed his niece with the air of someone who suspects he has been manoeuvred yet cannot perceive how. He turned to Susanna. 'You may as well go along with your cousin.'

'Thank you, Father.'

'Good afternoon, Uncle Samuel. And please give Aunt Maria my fondest regards.'

Dismissing them both with a nod, he turned away.

'Let's go and have a cup of hot chocolate,' Lucy said as they emerged on to the street. 'A warm nourishing drink will soothe your temper and your nerves.'

'Is it that noticeable?'

'Only to me. And only because I understand how frustrated you must feel. Be patient with him, Susanna. He recognizes your intelligence but he's afraid of change. A clever woman learns to bide her time.' Lucy smiled. 'Meredith and I arranged to meet in Mrs Powell's teashop at Church Corner. She'll be delighted to see you.'

'How are all your arrangements progressing?'

'Splendidly. This afternoon I signed the contract for letting the house.'

As Lucy listed all that had been accomplished and the few things remaining to be done, Susanna was startled by a pang of envy.

A bell tinkled above the door as they walked into the teashop. The beamed ceiling was supported by thick baulks of dark and ancient timber. A coal fire burned cheerfully in the blackleaded grate adding an orange-pink glow to the whitewashed walls. The air was fragrant with the scents of spice and saffron, roasting coffee and toasted teacakes. Round tables were spread with pink cloths, and pink glass bowls shaded the gas mantles.

They had just settled themselves at a table by the bow-fronted window when Meredith, laden with bags and packages, whirled in from the gathering dusk like a small hurricane.

212

'Susanna,' she beamed in delight. 'How nice. Lucy, you would not believe what a time I've had. I made a list but do you think I could find it? Fortunately I possess an excellent memory. Hasn't it been cold today? What are we all going to have? I am faint for want of nourishment.'

Concerned, Susanna glanced at Lucy who smiled and gave her head an infinitesimal shake as the tide of words continued to gush from Meredith's mouth.

'That's the problem with a delicate constitution, one can eat so little. Though in this bitter weather I do make a special effort. Who was it said that a hearty meal can protect against the chills and ills of winter? Of course "hearty" is quite beyond me. But I do think I could manage a cup of hot chocolate and a toasted teacake. Susanna, you still look a little peaky. You really must take care of yourself you know. Winter is definitely not my favourite season. I don't like the cold. Mind you, I find too much heat something of a trial. It leaves one so enervated, don't you agree? Now, what are you going to have?'

Awed by Meredith's ability to talk for so long without taking a breath, Susanna was caught unawares. 'Oh, I—er—same, please.'

'And for me,' Lucy smiled at the hovering waitress.

'Isn't this nice?' Meredith twinkled. 'I think we may be permitted one or two little treats before we embark on our great adventure. You cannot imagine how much I am looking forward to it. Naturally, there will be difficulties and privations. But by the grace of Our Lord we will win through.'

Perhaps Meredith was simply accepting that problems were inevitable. After all she was about to venture into a world different from anything she had ever known. No doubt her high colour could be attributed to the biting wind and her rush to get here. But her eyes had a feverish brightness. And a nerve danced in her fleshy cheek.

Glancing at Lucy and seeing no trace of concern Susanna tried to ignore her disquiet. It was perfectly understandable that Meredith's natural ebullience should have risen to an even higher level than usual. 'I do hope you'll find time to write occasionally.'

'Oh I don't think—'

'We will certainly try,' Lucy cut in, gently patting her sister's hand. 'I'm glad to have seen you today, Susanna. I'd be grateful for your advice.'

'*My* advice?'

'Dr Vigurs has prepared a small medical chest for us. However, as we will be in a strange country without easy access to doctors and hospitals I think it might be wiser to keep that for real emergencies. What we need is a selection of remedies for minor discomforts; ailments more inconvenient than dangerous. Would you prepare a list? Or better still, if I give you some money, will you purchase what we need from the apothecary and herbalist?'

Susanna nodded, swallowing the lump in her throat.

'Lucy! What could Susanna possibly know about such things?'

'She did some visiting at the infirmary for a while. Doctor Arundell spoke most highly of her.'

'Really?' Meredith peered at Susanna. 'I'd never have believed—fancy Uncle Samuel—a wonderful man, an example to us all, but such a stickler for *tradition*. And as for permitting—well, it's so *advanced*, isn't it? Not at all what one expects from him. What exactly did you do?'

Knowing better than to speak of her more recent experiences Susanna gave a deprecating shrug. 'I read to the patients and wrote letters for them.'

'I hope they were properly appreciative.'

Recalling Mr Roberts, Susanna smiled. 'I met some very nice people.'

'There you are,' Meredith swivelled to face her sister. 'Didn't I always say Susanna had a good heart? I'm sure it was very interesting.' She began to rummage in a bag, appearing not to have noticed that no one had answered her original question.

As Susanna's fingers traced the outline of the medallion, images flickered through her mind: assisting at Colin's operation, the ravings of the dying Portuguese sailor, grinding camphor in a mortar and pestle in the dispensary, Edward refusing to meet her eyes as he trampled her cherished dreams to dust. 'Indeed, I learned far more than I expected.'

Several days later she opened her bedroom

curtains and looked out onto a white world. Snow clothed roofs and roads. It blanketed the garden and decorated the bare boughs of trees like thick sugar frosting. On the far side of the grey water the white hump of Trefusis headland slumbered beneath a hazy sky the colour of mussel shell and milk.

She started to smile, to turn, to run to the door and shout for William. Then she remembered. Grief stabbed, sharp and deep. Wrapping her arms across her body as if to hold herself together, she closed her eyes and rocked. She wanted to howl, to ease the pain with weeping. But the tears would not come. She wondered sometimes how she could go on. Yet she did. And strangely, part of her life was more satisfying than it had ever been. Her work at Braithwaite's Yard necessitated her dealing directly with the foreman on one hand and ships' masters or owners on the other. Yet she had proved equal to the challenge, winning acceptance and respect—however grudging—from both.

Today was Christmas Eve but there would be no family celebration this year. Frances would be with the Webbers. Her parents would be either at the Meeting House; visiting sick and elderly Friends; or distributing food and blankets to the poor.

She had volunteered to do three full days in the soup kitchen, releasing helpers with young families to spend Christmas with their own children instead of feeding someone else's. Meanwhile she would be spared the ordeal of sitting through endless sermons and listening to prayers to a God she no longer believed in.

Lowell gently swirled the brandy in his balloon glass, sniffing the spirit appreciatively before swallowing. Once again the meal had been simple but well cooked and delicious. After a fortnight spent overseeing repairs to the ship and the stowing of cargo it was pleasant to be once more in the Travellers' Club beside a crackling log fire.

Declining invitations from various members of the London branch of Hawke & Son—none arrived from Henry Bowles—he had spent Christmas Day doing paperwork. It was a job he loathed. But with the sailing date fast approaching he'd had no choice but to shut himself in his cabin and get on with it.

'Could you not have gone tramp-trading up and down the coast?' Cathcart enquired.

'Possibly. But intense competition for cargoes meant there was little profit to be made.' It amused Lowell that the baronet should find details of a seafaring life so absorbing. Whatever his motives there was no doubting his interest. 'Besides, thanks to Walter Samms I know the Yangtze better than most. And I had just bought my first schooner.'

'But why *salt?*'

Lowell shrugged. 'It paid well. The salt market for the whole of the interior of China is based at Eching, a large village on the north bank about eighteen miles above Chinkiang. Salt bought there costs the same as rice, roughly one pound sterling for one hundred and thirty pounds weight. But a few miles further upriver it sells at double the price. I used the profits from the salt to buy silk and cotton. They fetched excellent prices back in Shanghai.'

'How did your father react to your success?'

Lowell felt the cynical smile lift one corner of his mouth. 'He decided the rift between us had lasted long enough.'

'And you accepted this olive branch?'

'On my terms.' He took another mouthful of brandy.

'So all's well that ends well.' Cathcart raised his glass in salute.

'Indeed.' As the spirit burned its way down Lowell recalled his brother's bitterness and jealousy the day he learned of the reconciliation. He had burst into the cabin, slamming the door against the bulkhead.

'Damn you, Lowell. Why the hell did you come back? You must have been making a packet trading on your own, and you didn't have to share the profits.'

Dismissing the mate with a nod Lowell had leaned back against the wooden panelling that formed a wide blunt triangle behind the padded bench seats. 'It isn't a question of money: Father's ill.'

'Ill? He never told me.' Taking a silver hip-flask from his pocket he wrenched off the cap and poured a large measure down his throat. He shuddered and wiped a runner of whisky from his chin with the back of a shaking hand.

'He wouldn't *tell* anyone. You should know that. But you've only got to look at him.'

John made a vague gesture with the hip-flask. 'I haven't been in the office much lately.' He took another swig. Years of dissipation had blurred the once-handsome features. Self-pity had cut creases between his brows and on either side of his mouth. His clothes were spotted and stained and could not disguise the drooping shoulders and beginning of a paunch.

'It's not bloody fair! When you went off to sea, it was *me* who bore the brunt of his anger. *Me* he ranted to about duty and obligations. But nothing I did was ever good enough.' He gave a bitter laugh. 'Not bloody surprising, really. I mean how could I compete with you?'

Lowell stared at him, unexpectedly moved by the despair that underlaid his brother's childish wail. 'What are you talking about? Father disowned me.'

'No, he didn't,' John retorted. 'Not really. Oh, he threatened and made a lot of noise. He was furious with you for disobeying him.' He sucked at the flask again, his face contorting. 'But he admired your spirit and determination. He scoured the papers for news of any ship you were on. What bloody chance did I have? Christ, you've become a legend. That's what you are, *a bloody legend.*' He waved the flask, swaying. 'Acclaimed and notorious. You're the talk of the taverns.'

Leaning his elbows on the chart-strewn table, Lowell held his head in his hands. His glamorous reputation meant nothing to him. He took chances and ran risks, not because he was braver than other men, but because *he didn't care.*

John gave another hard pain-filled laugh. 'Funny, isn't it? I should have been the success. I'm the eldest, and I'm a damn-sight better looking than you. And as father's heir— But people don't realize—' He kicked viciously at the polished deckboards then slumped on to the bench seat opposite, miserable and hopeless. 'So many *demands*, so many *expectations*.' He looked up bleary-eyed. 'I've always been jealous of you.'

Lowell was incredulous. 'What on earth for?'

'You had a burning ambition, a star to follow. You got away.' He lurched to his feet, staggering, his face twisted by anger and jealousy. 'Why did you have to come back? *Damn you.*'

'... future plans for the company?' Cathcart's question broke into Lowell's introspection.

He swiftly gathered his thoughts. 'My father would like to see Hawke & Son on a par with Jardine's or Dent's.'

'Why not? With your father and brother to run things in Shanghai, a successful branch in London, and you pioneering new trade up the Yangtze.' Glancing round, he beckoned the servant. 'Two more brandies, George.'

'Not for me.' Lowell set down his glass. 'Time I got back to my ship.'

'A cab for Captain Hawke, George.' As the servant left, Cathcart said, 'I'll walk you to the door. When do you sail?'

'The day after tomorrow. The lighter arrived from Woolwich Arsenal this morning.'

'Everything satisfactory?'

'Very. Now our people trading up-river in remote villages will be able to insist that the treaties are honoured.'

'I don't really approve of gun-boat diplomacy, but ...'

'Needs must when the Devil drives.' Lowell grinned. They reached the entrance lobby where another servant waited with his greatcoat. Turning to the baronet Lowell held out his hand. 'Thank you. For everything.'

Cathcart shook it firmly. 'God speed, Hawke. I'll be waiting to hear from you.'

Chapter Twenty

Worship over, people moved about the hall greeting one another.

'Susanna, see if you can catch Frances before she takes Mrs Webber home, will you, dear?' Maria turned to join a group of women talking in hushed tones.

Catching the word 'Overseers' Susanna sympathized with the person about to be investigated. Glimpsing her sister she eased through the crowd. Having no desire to speak to Mrs Webber she approached from behind and spoke softly.

'Fran, Mother would like a quick word before you go.' As they moved away Mrs Webber, with astonishing speed and dexterity, reversed her walking stick and hooked the handle around

Susanna's forearm, yanking her to a halt. 'One moment, miss. I want a word with you. Go and see what your mother wants, Frances, but don't be long. Richard has gone to call a cab and will be waiting for us. Go on.' After a brief anxious hesitation Frances hurried away.

'Keep away from my daughter-in-law,' Mrs Webber commanded. 'She's a good biddable girl, and I don't want her head filled with any of your foolish nonsense. You're a bad influence. It's only out of respect for your parents that Visitors haven't been appointed to make a report on your behaviour.'

Susanna stared at the crow-like woman. Dressed in unrelieved black, her plain white bonnet framing features furrowed by years of discontent, Mrs Webber's beady eyes were sharp with spite.

'Tell me, Mrs Webber, what have I done to make you dislike me so?'

After a momentary widening, the eyes narrowed to glittering slits. 'Don't you give me any of your cheek, miss. You're an affront to decent Quaker womanhood. First it was the Seamen's Hospital, then flaunting yourself in your father's office. And now I'm told you're down at Braithwaite's Yard. It's disgusting, that's what it is. *Disgusting!* Stay away from Frances, do you hear? She has a husband to take care of, which is more than you'll ever have.'

Shaking her arm free of the polished wood Susanna walked blindly to the door, and bumped into Lucy.

'Are you all right?'

Taking a deep breath Susanna nodded.

'Mrs Webber?'

'*Why*, Lucy?'

'People fear what they do not understand. Be strong, my dear.'

Susanna made a muffled sound that was half-laugh, half-choking sob. 'I'm tired.'

Meredith bustled up, scarcely able to contain her excitement. 'Has Lucy told you? We've had a letter.' She pressed a hand to her bolster-like bosom, her features suddenly tragic. 'So sad. And the baby too. God does make great demands on his servants.'

Susanna looked helplessly at Lucy who explained.

'Mr Hudson Taylor's wife died in Chinkiang on the 23rd of July. Apparently she'd had consumption of the lungs for some time. Her illness worsened during the summer. Then, just before the birth of her eighth child she suffered an attack of cholera which drained the last of her strength.'

'Poor little mite.' Meredith's eyes filled. 'He lived barely two weeks. Maybe if they'd got him a wet-nurse ...'

'Why didn't they?' Susanna asked.

Lucy's gaze was unflinching. 'They tried. But because of the anger against foreigners, especially the English, no Chinese would offer.'

'But this was a baby,' Susanna cried. 'And the Taylors are missionaries, not opium smugglers or soldiers. What sort of people could stand back and watch an innocent baby die?'

'People who need our help,' Lucy said quietly.

'I'm sure Lucy was afraid that after such news I might have second thoughts,' Meredith confided. 'But regardless of what the letter says I know Mr Taylor will welcome us. It is more important than ever that we are by his side, to assist him in bringing God's message to these wicked heathens.' Excitement lit her face. 'All the legalities are settled and most of the packing done.' The baby's death was forgotten. 'We did have a small setback over our passage. The steamer we hoped to take is already fully booked. But the agents are making enquiries and I'm sure we'll get word very soon. Oh, there's Mrs Lugg. I must catch her before she leaves.'

Watching Meredith cut a path through the chatting groups like a ship in full sail, unease pricked like a thorn.

'Lucy ...'

'Yes?'

She couldn't look so serene and confident if there was anything wrong.

'Nothing.'

The wind was increasing, whipping the sea into heaving grey mounds marbled with white foam. 'All hands to shorten sail!' Lowell shouted. The deck canted beneath his feet as the schooner reared and plunged through the waves. The barometer had been steady and the wind a fresh south-westerly breeze when they sailed out of the Thames.

Sensing a change Lowell had remained on

deck. But wanting to retain the advantage of a good start he had left all sails set. A sudden swing in wind direction and an ominous drop in pressure and it was upon them, a vicious south-easterly gale for which the English Channel was notorious.

Brown-grey cloud hurtled across the sky so low it seemed to brush the mast-heads, releasing torrents of rain which mingled with the spray and cut visibility during the squalls to a few feet.

Waves began to break inboard, the spume-flecked water roaring across the deck and eddying around the hatches. It could not clear the scuppers before the next sea crashed in over the lee gunwale.

He had already ordered the pumps manned. Now his gaze flicked between the figures working aloft and the mountainous waves rushing at them in tumbled confusion from all sides. *Come on, come on.* But his mouth remained shut, his exhortation silent. He knew constant barracking was counter-productive. The crew either ignored it or nursed growing resentment. Both led to trouble.

The jib-boom had gone, broken off like a carrot when the schooner's nose was driven under with the first squall. Responding like a thoroughbred she had shaken herself free of the tons of water as the crew worked like demons.

One by one the sails were being taken in and secured. But as the yard to the gaff topsail was loosed a gust caught the canvas, filling it like a balloon and snatching the rope from the men's desperate grip. Above the howling wind Lowell heard screams as skin was seared from calloused palms. With a deafening crack the sail blew out. A long creaking groan was followed by a rending crash as the topmast snapped, falling in a tangle of ripped canvas and twisted rigging to smash against the foremast.

'Cut her loose!' Lowell ordered the carpenter and two ordinary seamen stationed at the masts with axes. They worked feverishly as the schooner slid into the trough of a huge wave. The mate and wheelman battled to keep her from broaching. If she turned side-on to the wind and waves they were done for.

Not daring to heave-to because of the risk of being pooped by one of the huge waves bearing down on them Lowell ordered two hawsers, one from each quarter, towed behind the vessel to smooth her wake.

Dusk closed in and for the rest of the night they rode the storm. By dawn the gale had blown itself out.

Emerging from the companionway hatch after an hour's sleep Lowell nodded to the wheelman and inhaled deeply, filling his lungs as he looked about him. The sea was still a heaving lumpy mass but the wind had dropped to a gentle breeze and the sky was clear. The sun had not yet risen and a primrose tint on the eastern horizon merged into pale green which became turquoise then aquamarine and finally, high overhead, a freshly washed light blue.

As the first golden rays turned the water to ink and burgundy he made his way forward, checking the damage. They had suffered worse. But this voyage had only just begun. And though time was of the essence with some of the world's most inhospitable oceans still to cross he could not afford to take chances. Repairs must be made. Returning to the stern he gave the wheelman a new course.

Walking through the yard Susanna heard the rhythmic clang of hammer on anvil as she passed the forge. Sawdust formed golden drifts beside sawpits between the timber pool and the dry wood store. She breathed in the smells of oil and hot pitch, the pear-like aroma of varnish, and the coconut scent of manila rope. Strange how quickly she had become accustomed to them.

Workmen nodded, used to her now, and went on talking.

'Well, you know what they say, 'tis an ill wind. I jest 'ope we get a couple in 'ere.'

'Extra work'll mean extra money, and we're always short of both this time of year.'

Before she reached the granite building that housed the sail locker and rope store as well as the yard office she had heard enough to realize that gales in the Channel were bringing an unexpected bonus to the town as ships limped into the harbour for repairs.

At the end of each day she took a cab to Dunstanville Terrace to report the day's happenings to Uncle Joshua. Though out of bed he was still very weak. Sitting in an armchair beside the fire, his knees covered by a rug, he would listen as she related the progress on current jobs, telling him which ships had come in and which had left, giving him invoices to check, letters from suppliers, owners, agents and masters to read, and replies to sign.

At first he had chafed and worried, constantly voicing his doubts about her ability. Biting her tongue she had done exactly as he asked. He had meticulously double-checked her every move until Aunt Eleanor had lost patience.

'For goodness' sake, Joshua! The doctor said it was important you get plenty of rest. The way you're carrying on you might as well be down at the yard yourself. If you didn't think Susanna could do the job, why on earth did you ask her?'

'It was Lucy's idea,' he grumbled, between spasms of coughing. 'She said Susanna's been doing similar work in her father's office.'

'I've always found Lucy a sensible woman.' Eleanor busied herself plumping his pillows and straightening the covers. 'If she believes Susanna can—'

'It isn't Lucy's yard,' he spluttered.

'You won't be around to care,' Eleanor scolded, 'if you don't stop all this fretting.'

While they argued Susanna stood outside in the passage holding the ledgers, silently waiting. She had not received a single word of praise for her efforts. That was understandable. But the constant doubting of her intelligence and undermining of her confidence were harder to endure. *But if enduring them meant she kept the job* ...

So she bit her tongue, was at all times demure and respectful, and continued to carry out her uncle's instructions to the letter. It took a full week for him to accept that the yard was not about to grind to a halt, and was in fact continuing to function efficiently.

After that, though he still wanted a verbal report each evening, he sometimes waved the books aside and skimmed the letters rather than checking every word before adding his signature. There was still no praise, but admonitions were fewer.

Alone in the office, sitting at her cousin Charles's desk, Susanna bent over the ledger trying to shut out the noise of the busy yard as she entered details of invoices and receipts.

Though the work wasn't difficult it required concentration. And because of her daily visits to Uncle Joshua the hours were long. Her father had allowed her to continue only as long as she did not neglect her duties at home, or her charity work, so her evenings too were full.

Laying down her pen she pressed her fingertips to her temples. She was doing everything expected of her. But it was not enough. The emptiness spreading outward like ripples on a pool was eating her away from inside. Soon she would be just a thin shell. She took a deep breath. She was tired that was all. *And she missed Will. She missed him so much.*

At the sound of approaching footsteps she reached for her pen, starting violently as the door opened. She looked up into grey eyes that blinked in surprise beneath frowning black brows.

He glanced swiftly round the office. 'Where's Joshua?' Several days' growth of black stubble covered the lower half of his face.

At this over-familiar reference to her uncle Susanna's fingers tightened on the pen. 'I'm afraid Mr Braithwaite isn't available right now.'

'I see. Would you mind telling me why he isn't available?' Susanna had the unsettling impression that he was amused. Acutely self-conscious she felt hot colour flood her face.

'He's ill with influenza. There's an epidemic.'

'Charles too?'

As she nodded, his gaze flicked lightly over what was visible of her above the desk.

'So, who are you?'

Thick dark hair curled untidily against the collar of his navy jacket, unbuttoned to reveal a grey woollen shirt and a red neckerchief, clothes common along the waterfront. Yet there was something about him she had never encountered among the workmen and crews, or even the owners and masters whose business brought them into the office.

'I'm taking care of things in their absence,' she responded obliquely. 'How may I help you?'

His smile was brief, a flash of white teeth in the dark beard. 'If you have no objection, I'd like to speak to the yard foreman.'

Was he laughing at her? Her cheeks grew hotter. 'Certainly.'

'About storm damage,' he added. His gaze

was disconcertingly direct. It held curiosity, and other things too fleeting for her to recognize.

'I see.'

At the door he bowed politely. 'Good afternoon.'

As it closed quietly behind him she bent once more to the ledger, but the figures were a blur and her pen trembled uncontrollably.

'I shall be returning to the office on Friday,' Joshua Braithwaite announced as Susanna entered the sitting-room. Fully-dressed, he stood with his back to the fire. In an armchair to one side of the hearth, a low table in front of her, Aunt Eleanor was pouring tea. She smiled up at Susanna.

'Isn't it good news? He can't wait to get back.' She gazed fondly up at her husband. 'And I'll be glad to see the back of him. Men are such dreadful patients! Do sit down. Have some tea.'

'I won't, thank you all the same. I didn't expect—I mean, you hadn't said—'

'The doctor came this morning.' Setting the teapot back on the tray she smiled up at her husband. To be honest, I think he's had enough of Joshua's complaining too. I don't suppose you'll be sorry to finish. It can't have been very comfortable for you.'

'I enjoyed the work very much,' Susanna replied at once.

'Did you?' Her aunt's brows arched in surprise. 'Charles is coming by later. Caroline says he's fully recovered apart from a slight

231

cough. Anyway, he's starting back tomorrow morning so you won't need to go in any more.'

Susanna lifted the soft bag containing the ledgers and correspondence folders. 'What about these?' She had known the job was only temporary, but she hadn't expected it to finish so abruptly.

'Oh, just leave them there.' Her uncle indicated a small side table standing between the windows. 'I'll go through them after tea, and Charles can take them with him.' *So that was that.*

'I'm sure your mother will be pleased to have you home,' Aunt Eleanor continued, 'especially now Frances is married and gone.'

With a supreme effort of will Susanna held her smile in place. 'Yes. Well, if you'll excuse me ...'

'You get along,' Aunt Eleanor said comfortably. 'Take care on that path, dear. And give your mother my love.'

'So I was wondering'—hands hidden beneath the table, Susanna nervously twisted her napkin—'if I might go with you in the morning.'

Samuel glanced up from his almost-empty plate. Her own meal was scarcely touched. The few mouthfuls she had forced down lay in a solid lump behind her breastbone.

'What for? The dividends have all been paid.'

'Yes, I know. But I would like'—she swallowed again—'I want to continue training to take William's place.'

Her mother flinched. Her father's head jerked

232

up, his mouth half-open in shock. 'Don't be ridiculous!'

'Father, please. I can do the work. I've proved it.'

Samuel set down his knife and fork. 'Those were purely emergency measures. You cannot possibly take William's place. It's out of the question. I thought I had already made my feelings perfectly clear. Women have absolutely no place in business.'

'But if it weren't for me you wouldn't *have* a business!' She felt as though she were breaking apart inside.

'Stop that at once. Such vanity is—'

'It's *not* vanity. It's the truth. It was me who ran the business while you were here with Mother. *Me!* Cyril Hosking was too frightened to make decisions by himself So when action was needed I got him to make suggestions which he thought you were endorsing. But it was me. I had to take the responsibility—'

'You did *what?*' The blood had drained from her father's cheeks. Now it rushed back, flooding his face and neck a furious crimson. 'I—I'm *appalled.* Such deceit from my own daughter? Susanna, how could you?'

'I had no choice. You—'

'You should have come and told me.'

'I *tried.*' Her voice cracked. 'You wouldn't listen. You were mourning William, and worried about Mother.'

Banging the table with the flat of his hand, making them both jump, Samuel leapt to his feet.

'*Enough,* Susanna! Not another word. Go to your room. *At once.* You will stay there until I decide what's to be done with you.'

She turned in desperation to her mother. But with an infinitesimal shake of her head Maria looked away.

Susanna walked numbly across the hall. She had worked *so hard,* stretching herself to the very limits of her strength. And it had all been for nothing. The void lapped at the edges of her mind. The shell was as thin as a bubble now, and as fragile. If it broke ...

She stopped at the foot of the stairs. After a long moment she turned aside, took her cloak from the peg, and quietly let herself out.

Chapter Twenty-One

Grief twisted its blade in her chest as she ran down the road. All the hopes she had nursed so carefully lay in shreds. What was left?

The mare whinnied softly, velvet-brown eyes reflecting the moonlight as Susanna opened the stable door. Taking a bridle from the hook on the white-washed cob wall she slid it over the mare's head, fastening the buckles with nervous clumsy fingers, then led her out into the yard.

As she released the gate it thudded against the wooden post and a dog started barking furiously inside the farmhouse. Terrified of discovery she threw herself on to the mare's bare back and kicked into a fast canter.

She had questioned and challenged her father on many occasions, but never in her life had she deliberately disobeyed him. Until now. And there was no going back.

At Lansdowne Road she slid shakily to the ground. Leaving the mare contentedly tugging hay from the net she ran up the path and knocked on the front door. A lock of hair had escaped from her bonnet and bounced on her sweating forehead. *They had to be in.* She knocked harder, bruising her knuckles on the solid oak.

A key grated, the knob turned and the door opened, spilling light on to the step and path.

'*Susanna?* What—?'

'I want to go with you, Lucy. You must let me. *Please?*' Susanna's teeth were chattering so violently she could barely form the words. 'I c-can't t-take—' Choking on a sob she shook her head helplessly.

Reaching forward Lucy drew her inside. 'My poor dear girl.' Her voice was full of compassion. 'Whatever's happened?'

'Oh Lucy.' Huge hot tears rolled down Susanna's face. 'I c-can't stay in Falmouth any longer. I don't belong here. I d-don't fit. I can't be what they want. And I'm forbidden to do any of the things I'm good at.' Her thin frame trembled as she clutched her cousin's hands. 'Please let me go with you to China.'

Lucy held her close for a moment then eased her away to study her face. 'Are you absolutely sure that's what you want?'

Susanna nodded fiercely, her whole body wrenched with sobs. 'It's not just Mother and Father: there's Richard, and Mrs Webber, and the Overseers. I can't take any more.' She shuddered, wiping her eyes and nose. 'I'll work hard. I've learned all kinds of things at the infirmary that will be really useful. Please, Lucy, let me go with you.'

'I'd be delighted to have you with us. But the decision isn't mine alone.'

'I don't see why Father should object. I'm just an embarrassment.'

'That's something we'll have to deal with. However, it wasn't what I meant. There's someone else we have to consult first.'

Susanna nodded. 'Meredith. Of course. It's just that—I mean, I thought if *you* agree—'

Taking her arm, Lucy smiled gently. 'Naturally we'll talk to Meredith. But even before that ...' She opened the door into the sitting-room. 'Come along in, my dear.'

Meredith was in her rocking chair beside the roaring fire, her face flushed and shiny. Breaking off her animated conversation she looked up. 'Whatever brings you here? Of course, it's lovely to see you but are you wise to be venturing out—?'

Susanna had stopped listening, her gaze focused on the man whose back was towards her. The navy jacket had been replaced by a frock coat of lustrous broadcloth in charcoal grey. But there was no mistaking the shape of that head. Or the thick dark hair that still curled on his collar. No longer dulled by salt spray it gleamed in the lamplight like polished ebony.

A wave of heat broke over her. *Had he heard?* As he rose to his feet she swivelled towards the door, driven by instinct to flee, and cannoned into Lucy.

'Oh! I'm so sorry.' Sweat stuck her chemise to her back and the medallion to her breast.

Cupping her elbow Lucy led her forward. 'Susanna, this is Captain Hawke. Lowell, may I present my cousin, Susanna Elliot.'

As the grey eyes met hers Susanna recalled vividly William sitting in this very room, repeating the stories he had heard about *Lowell Hawke*. The Devil incarnate. She moistened dry lips.

'Good evening, Captain Hawke.'

'Your servant, Miss Elliot.' Smile and handshake were polite, formal. But curiosity leapt in his gaze. 'We have met before, I believe. At Braithwaite's Yard?'

'Young girls today,' Meredith sighed shaking her head. 'Not a thought in their heads for anyone but themselves.' She beamed at Lowell. 'That is why we think so much of Susanna.'

Susanna's head swam. Black spots danced across her vision. She clenched her toes in an attempt to dispel the strange weakness creeping along her limbs.

'She was at the yard office while Uncle Joshua and Cousin Charles were ill with influenza. But that's not all she's been doing. Not by any means. We lost her dear brother recently. Such a tragedy.' Meredith's chin quivered. 'We all loved

237

William.' Susanna stared at the floor. 'Well, you can imagine how her parents felt—their only son. It was Susanna who took over. And not just the household. Oh no. She saw to it that all the dividends were paid out before Christmas. And she's been a regular visitor at the Seamen's Infirmary, not to mention working right through Christmas in the soup kitchen.'

Her face on fire, Susanna shot a pleading look at Lucy.

'Our cousin is a very special young woman,' Lucy smiled, 'and will be of great help to us in China.'

Lowell's eyes narrowed. 'I was under the impression you required only two berths.'

'Indeed, that was our original plan. But circumstances have changed.'

'I didn't know anything about this,' Meredith said, piqued. 'Why wasn't I told?'

'You've had so much to think about recently,' Lucy soothed, avoiding a direct answer. 'But I'm sure you agree Susanna will be of great help.'

Meredith folded her hands under her vast bosom. 'Fond as I am of her, I can't see—I mean, she's never mentioned—'

'You're right, Meredith,' Susanna broke in quickly. 'I have no calling. But I do have an ear for languages, and I can keep records and accounts. And through my work at the infirmary I've learned a lot about medicine.'

Lowell's expression registered surprise and a quickening interest. 'As I was saying earlier, my ship is not equipped for passengers. I think you would be much more comfortable on a steamer.'

238

'Speed, not comfort, is our priority,' Meredith declared. 'Lowell, dear, we must get to China as quickly as we can. We are urgently needed there.'

He shrugged. 'All the more reason to take a steamer.'

'The problem is,' Lucy explained, 'that all steamer berths are fully booked. There won't be any available for at least a month. But if we came with you, in a month's time we would be one third of the way to China. We are used to simple living and require no special consideration.'

'How can you refuse?' Meredith twinkled up at him. 'Was it not Divine Providence that guided you here? Had it not been for the storm you would not have come into Falmouth. But you did. Family loyalty is so important, don't you think? It is within the family that we learn kindness and generosity.'

He turned his head, a muscle jumping in his jaw. His eye caught hers briefly and once again, as in the yard office, Susanna sensed something shared. Startled she looked away.

'Lowell, I'm sure the repairs to your ship will have been a most unwelcome drain on your resources. It occurs to me,' Lucy said, clearing her throat, 'that our travel expenses might compensate you for a good part of that loss.'

When at last he spoke it took Susanna a second or two to grasp what lay behind his oblique statement.

'The yard foreman tells me repairs will be

239

completed by Wednesday of next week.'

Meredith clapped her hands. 'Wonderful!'

'That will suit us perfectly,' Lucy smiled.

He'd accepted. As his gaze met hers, a dark brow lifting, Susanna touched paper-dry lips with the tip of her tongue. 'I'll be ready.'

'Then if you'll excuse me, ladies, I must take my leave. I shall expect you on the jetty by nine o'clock Thursday morning. I sail on the tide.'

While Lucy saw him out and Meredith launched into the details of her day's activities Susanna reached blindly for a chair. He was so ... polished. Yet that signified nothing. Anyone might acquire the veneer of a gentleman. *William had said some called him a pirate.*

'What if they refuse to let me go?' Susanna whispered as she and Lucy walked up the path.

After sending a message to Samuel and Maria assuring them Susanna was safe and well and would return in the morning, Lucy had put her to bed with a hot water bottle and a cup of hot milk and honey. Meredith had kindly proffered pills and sleeping draughts. But Susanna hadn't needed them, her eyes already closing as she slid down between the sheets.

'The next half-hour will be nothing compared to the difficulties we are likely to face in China,' Lucy chided gently, taking her arm. 'You are sure? It's all right, you know, if you've changed your mind.'

'No,' Susanna shook her head quickly. 'I'm quite sure. I want to go with you, Lucy.'

Her parents received them with cool formality

240

in the drawing-room. Clearly expecting apologies and excuses, Lucy's announcement took them totally by surprise.

'Though she has no calling to preach, Susanna possesses other gifts which—'

As she watched her father shake his head the snakes in Susanna's stomach writhed and coiled.

'The girl has shown herself to be deceitful, wilful, and self-indulgent.'

Hearing his bitter disappointment she was drenched by a sweating wave of shame. But it was followed by a sense of injustice so strong she had to bite her tongue to stop herself crying out.

'Such behaviour requires first punishment, then a period of hard work during which her own desires will be subordinated to the needs of others so she has time to reflect upon her sins.'

'Then you will be comforted to know that working for the China Inland Mission will place Susanna in conditions ideally suited to bring out the best in her character. And that, surely,' Lucy smiled, 'is what we all seek?'

Susanna watched her parents glance uncertainly at one another. Professing belief in forgiveness of sins they could hardly say they *didn't* want redemption for their errant daughter.

'And if Susanna leaves with us next week,' Lucy continued, 'it goes without saying that any allegations concerning her activities or behaviour would have to be dropped.'

'Mmm, well,' her father huffed, 'perhaps, given all the circumstances, it might be for the best.'

What hurt most was their open *relief.* For so long she had been a problem. At last she was about to be solved.

But after that one painful moment there was no time for brooding or introspection. Her recent weeks of hard work paled beside the hectic activity of the next few days.

Her winter gowns were brushed, sponged and pressed; her summer dresses retrieved from storage to be washed and ironed. Hems and buttons were checked. Bonnets were starched, worn items of underwear replaced with new, shoes mended and polished. A sturdy trunk was purchased and packing begun.

Watching her mother arrange tissue-wrapped items with meticulous care, Susanna suddenly understood. Free of restriction now she was leaving she slipped her arms around her mother's waist and held her tightly.

After a moment's utter stillness Maria drew away, brisk and busy. 'Come along now, time's getting on.'

After a visit to the apothecary and herbalist Susanna realized that she dare not rely solely on her memory for the ingredients and dosages of useful remedies. She needed books—specialist books—and knew of only one source.

The morning was crisp. A forget-me-not sky arched above a sparkling sapphire sea, the only colour in a sepia-toned landscape. All trace of snow had gone. But the rutted roads were stiff with frost and ice glazed the puddles, squeaking as it cracked and shattered beneath hooves, wheels and heavy boots.

As she entered his office Edward glanced up, surprise softening to cautious affability.

'Good morning, this is an unexpected pleasure.'

Outside the door her mouth had dried with apprehension at seeing him again. But now to her surprise confidence returned. She was approaching him as an equal. The knowledge was balm to her bruised heart.

'I hope you'll still think so when I tell you why I've come. I'm going away.'

'Anywhere interesting?'

'China, actually.' Scolding herself for unseemly delight at having jolted him, she smiled. 'That's why I'm here. I hope you might be able to help me.'

His brows climbed. 'Me? How?'

'I'm travelling with my two cousins to Shanghai. We are joining the China Inland Mission run by Mr Hudson Taylor.'

'Really?' His expression combined scepticism and surprise.

'I haven't suddenly discovered a religious vocation.' She would not allow him to think her only alternative to him was God. 'The knowledge I gained from assisting you in the dispensary'—she was proud that her voice remained steady despite the sudden rush of painful memories—'will be useful when we reach those parts of the country beyond the range of professional medical aid.'

'I see. And what, exactly, do you want from me?'

'Books, please. I already have one which lists

243

traditional remedies for minor problems, like putting honey on a burn, and oil of cloves for toothache. But—'

'What you need is a Pharmacopaeia. A book that tells you which medicines are suitable for a particular illness, the quantities of each constituent, method of preparation, and appropriate dosages.'

'Yes. I know it's impertinent but'—she pulled a wry face—'who else could I ask?'

Edward's lips twitched. 'Who indeed?' Pushing back his chair he crossed to the bookcases covering almost the whole of one wall. 'While I cannot pretend to understand your reasons for this venture I do not doubt your courage.' He did not look at her, continuing to scan the shelves. 'I have not forgotten your assistance during Colin Treneer's operation.' He opened one of the glass doors. 'So the least I can do is equip you with one or two useful books.' He added drily, 'If only for the sake of your Chinese patients.'

At the door she offered her hand, the respect in his gaze giving her the courage to speak.

'I'm very grateful, Edward. Not just for the books, though they will be invaluable, but for everything I learned here. The important lessons are often the hardest.' The brief pressure of his fingers told her he recognized what she was saying, and what it had cost her.

'I count it a privilege to have known you, Susanna. Goodbye. And good luck.'

The day before they were due to leave, Maria invited Lucy and Meredith, Frances and Richard, and Richard's parents to tea. Anticipating an ordeal, it was even worse than she expected.

'Sorry I'm late.' Flushed and breathless she hung her cloak on the peg and quickly tucked escaping curls under her bonnet. 'The time went so fast.'

'Where *were* you?' Maria lowered her voice, glancing at the drawing-room door.

Smoothing her skirt, Susanna faced her mother. 'Up at Mongleath. I went to say goodbye to Will.'

Maria turned away. 'Wash your hands.'

When Susanna entered a few minutes later the first person she saw was Meredith, purple-faced and animated, hopes and plans pouring in a torrent from saliva-flecked lips. Next to her, malevolent as ever, sat Mrs Webber.

'I cannot understand anyone in their right mind wanting to leave Cornwall. Especially for somewhere *foreign.*' Her sharp features were pinched with contempt and mistrust. 'Heathens, the lot of them. Always have been, always will be. Still, it's an ill wind, as they say.' Looking past her husband who was slumped in a nearby chair, not quite drunk but clearly not sober, she fixed her beady gaze on Susanna. 'At least this family will be spared any more embarrassment.'

Reminding herself that the next day she would start putting several oceans between herself and Mrs Webber, Susanna moved to a chair beside Lucy as Agnes wheeled in the tea trolley.

Meredith immediately craned her neck to see

245

what cakes were being served. Plates and napkins were handed around. Richard was occupying the centre of the sofa. Frances had tucked herself neatly, and distantly, into a corner.

'Susanna, a word?' Inclining his plump body forward Richard beckoned her closer. 'May I ask what contribution you are making to your cousins' brave enterprise?' As she opened her mouth to reply, he smirked. 'Or are you perhaps thinking to find yourself a husband among the colonials? You might have more luck among men far from home.' *Men who are less fussy, more desperate, who will take anything,* his manner implied.

She looked at him calmly. 'You might find this hard to accept, Richard, but I no longer have any desire to marry. From what I have observed, marriage is an arrangement ordered solely for the comfort and convenience of men.'

'And why not? Since it is men who protect and provide for the family?'

And what protection does a wife have from a bullying husband? Catching Frances's stricken expression, Susanna stopped her retort just in time. This was her last evening at home. No matter what the provocation she must not cause her parents upset or embarrassment.

'You're just jealous,' Richard sneered, 'because Frances is married and you're not.'

'Believe me, Richard,' Susanna looked him straight in the eye, 'I wish my sister every possible happiness. But I would not *ever* want to be in her position.'

Uncertainty flickered across his face and, for

an instant, she glimpsed the child he had once been, unattractive, lonely, pathetic. But his self-doubt was swiftly smothered by his conviction of his own superiority.

'You needn't worry about that, miss.' Mrs Webber's tone was as tart as lemons. Invariably deaf to requests for help, her ability to overhear things that were none of her business was quite remarkable. 'No man who cares for his reputation will ever look twice at you. Not until you change your ways and start behaving as a decent Quaker woman should.'

Susanna glanced at Richard's father. His body was present, but where was his mind?

She returned her gaze to his wife. Where had that soul-corroding bitterness sprung from? Disappointment? Her own reaction startled her. She didn't *want* to feel pity for this dried-up shell of a woman who never missed an opportunity to make life difficult for everyone around her.

'You may be certain, Mrs Webber, that your example is one I shall never forget.'

Chapter Twenty-Two

'No, leave that one.'

Ignoring the imperious order, four stone-faced crewmen continued to transfer the trunks and other luggage from the jetty to the boat. Meredith shook her sister's arm. 'Lucy, tell

247

them to put it down. I can't possibly be without my medicines and drops. And I have other important things in that bag. Stop them.'

'Don't worry, We'll sort it all out once we're on board.' Slipping an arm around her, Lucy spoke over her shoulder. 'Will you excuse us, Uncle Samuel? I promise we'll take good care of Susanna.' She turned to her sister. 'Let's go and find our cabin, shall we? Then we can tell the men which bags we want brought down.'

Meredith stopped abruptly, looking askance at the gangplank. 'No, I can't possibly—'

'It's perfectly safe,' Lucy reassured. 'Look, there are even ropes on either side to hold on to.'

'Really, Lucy, sometimes I wonder why I let you talk me into these things. I think perhaps it might be wiser to wait for a steamer.'

'We would still have to use a gangplank to get on board,' Lucy pointed out. 'Besides, we're here now. I'll go first. See? It's easy.'

The sisters tiptoed gingerly across the gangplank leaving Susanna alone with her father.

'I won't come down to the docks,' her mother had announced at breakfast.

The lump in Susanna's throat had made swallowing difficult. But she had forced down a few spoonfuls of porridge and half a cup of tea. She wanted them to remember that, on the day of parting, she had acquitted herself with dignity.

Out in the hall her mother stood by, outwardly composed but white-knuckled, while Susanna fastened her thick cloak with awkward fingers.

248

She felt shivery inside; excited and apprehensive. A new life awaited her. Yet cutting these last ties was more painful than she had expected.

'The cab is loaded.' Samuel came in through the front door. 'Are you ready, Susanna?'

'Goodbye, dear.' Maria's voice was strained. 'May God protect you.'

Embracing her mother Susanna closed her eyes, storing up memories: the scent of her skin, the soft pressure of her bosom, the sudden tightening of her arms before she stepped back. Then Susanna said goodbye to Norah, Agnes and Biddy. Outside, twisting his cap in large raw-boned hands, the groom ducked his head awkwardly as he wished her good luck.

'Thank you, Bryce. And thank you for all you did for William and me.'

Her father cleared his throat, jerking her out of her memories and back to the present. 'Time you were on board. You mustn't keep the captain waiting.'

Realizing any move must come from her she stepped forward bridging the distance between them and gave him a quick fierce hug. 'Goodbye, Father. I'm so sorry I couldn't be—' *all the things you wanted.*

'Yes, well,' he coughed again, jaw rigid, eyes moist. 'You—er—you might write to us now and then. Your mother will want to know how you are.'

She gulped. *She would not cry.* 'Of course I will.'

'That's all right then.' He took out his pocket watch. 'I must go. Early appointment.

249

I—ah—' His composure cracked. 'God bless you, child.' Turning, he walked swiftly down the jetty towards the yard.

'Goodbye, Father.' He wouldn't hear her, but she said it anyway, watching through a haze of tears until the distorted, shimmering figure disappeared.

'When you're *quite* ready, Miss Elliot.'

Lowell Hawke's shout made her jump. She looked up quickly but he was already moving out of sight. The air was sharp, tangy with salt and seaweed. A stiff breeze moulded her skirts to her legs and like a gentle hand on her back pushed her towards the schooner. The ship rode high on the choppy water, tugging against plaited mooring ropes thicker than a man's wrist as if anxious to be free. Two men wearing the rough, stained clothes of dock labourers waited by the huge mooring bollards.

Self-conscious, she stumbled quickly up the gangplank which was immediately pulled in after her. The cluttered deck was a scene of frenzied activity.

'Let go for'ard,' the order was shouted down. Susanna glanced at the four seamen hauling rhythmically on ropes speeding the gaff, from which hung the huge fore-and-aft sail smoothly up the towering foremast. 'Let go aft.' Catching the wind, the schooner surged away from the jetty and out into the wide harbour mouth.

Helped by a boy of about twelve another seaman was stowing loose-meshed sacks of potatoes, swedes, carrots and cabbages in the jolly boat lashed on chocks on top of the hatch above the main hold. Shallow wooden trays containing apples, oranges, half-gallon loaves of bread, large square tins and brown-paper packages, were stacked on the deck.

She looked round uncertain of where to go, bewildered by all the noise: bellowed orders, the creaking windlass, flapping canvas cracking as sails were sheeted in. Feet pounded the deck, men grunted with effort, gulls screamed and underlying it all the hiss and slap of waves against the hull.

'This way, miss.' A stocky man with a dour expression jerked his head towards the stern. The hinged top of the companionway was folded back, the double doors hooked open. Openwork brass stairs spiralled down. Susanna looked up to thank him but he was already hurrying away. Descending carefully she heard Meredith's voice, clearly shocked. 'Oh no. No, there must be some mistake.'

Lowell's reply was edged with impatience. 'I did warn you. Now you must excuse me, I'm needed on deck.'

'But this isn't at all—I mean—how do you expect us—? What are we to do?' Meredith demanded.

As Susanna reached the foot of the stairs, a cramped space containing three doors, the half-open one in front of her was yanked wide. Framed in the opening, Lowell looked back over his shoulder.

'Work it out between yourselves. But decide quickly. I want that luggage off the deck before we clear St Anthony light.' He turned, almost colliding with her as she flattened herself against the bulkhead. With a brief frowning nod he swung himself up the stairs, his solid figure momentarily blocking out the light.

'Well, *I* can't possibly go in there,' Meredith was adamant. 'I'd die of suffocation. And as I shall need you with me, you can't either. Susanna will understand. Ah, there you are,' she beamed. 'We were wondering where you had got to. I'm going to tell one of those men to bring our trunks down. Then we can unpack and get settled. Isn't this an adventure? I have to admit the arrangements are not quite as expected, but we must simply rise above the situation. Come in, come in. Lucy will explain.'

As Meredith clanged up the brass stairs, Susanna looked around. About ten feet deep and at its widest point roughly eight feet across, the cabin narrowed towards the stern so the two padded bench seats formed a shallow V. In the apex at shoulder height a guarded shelf held navigation instruments, tide-tables, papers, books and other sea-junk. Between the seats stood a large triangular-shaped table spread with charts on which lay dividers, a ruler, two pencils and a log book. Above the backs of the padded seats the wood panelling was in two sections, the rearmost slightly recessed. Storage lockers? she hazarded.

Set in the deckhead above the table were a reflecting compass and an open skylight which let in sunshine, fresh air, and the sounds of activity on deck. A brass oil lamp swung on four chains from a hook. And alongside the door through which she had entered, next to a bucket of coal a small black stove radiated welcome warmth. Lucy stood before it, nervously rubbing her palms together with a soft rasping sound. Her expression betrayed rare agitation.

'You'd better tell me.'

'The mate and second mate have generously vacated the two-berth cabin to the left of the stairs which they normally occupy. And the captain has relinquished his own sleeping-quarters here in his day cabin.'

Susanna looked round. 'Where? I can't see ...'

Lucy moved aside a thick dark curtain which had been partly hidden by the chimney pipe. Behind the curtain was a cubbyhole with just enough room for a bunk and a low narrow cupboard on top of which stood an enamel jug and basin. A prism set in the deckhead provided a glimmer of light. Thrusting the curtain into Susanna's stunned grasp Lucy crouched to open the cupboard door. Inside was a bucket with a wooden lid.

'Apparently Lowell had the mate put this in specially. It seems their normal arrangements are somewhat more, ... basic.' As Lucy emerged Susanna dropped the curtain back in place, her heart thudding against her ribs. Her lips were so dry they stuck to her teeth. She had to run her tongue between them before she could speak.

'You mean *I*—?' She gestured at the alcove.

Lucy gave a brief, unhappy nod. 'I'd take it myself, but Meredith—'

253

'Yes, I heard.'

'I'm so sorry, my dear. I never imagined—' She braced her thin shoulders. 'No, this won't do. I have no right to ask it of you.'

'What choice do we have? Apart from leaving the ship. And we can't do that. Not now.' Moistening her lips again Susanna made a valiant stab at nonchalance. 'You warned me conditions in China would be difficult. I shall look on this as practice for what lies ahead. But if I'm in here and you're next door, then where is Captain Hawke to ...?' She glanced round as thumps and footsteps on the companionway stairs heralded the arrival of their trunks and boxes.

'Lucy?' Meredith's call managed to blend demand and helplessness.

'I'm coming.' Lucy hurried out leaving Susanna to stare around the cluttered, functional, intensely masculine cabin. It smelled of sweet resinous wood, of coal and damp wool, and just the faintest whiff of the sulphur candles used for fumigation.

'Captain says you'd best keep this under the bunk.' The stocky seaman backed in with her trunk.

'Thank you. There are some boxes, and a bag.'

'Give us a chance,' he snapped, bent double. 'I only got one pair of 'ands.'

'I'm sorry.' Susanna sprang to hold the curtain back out of his way. 'I didn't mean to—'

Passing her with a surly glance he dragged in

254

the rest of her luggage.

'Thank you, that's most kind.'

He stumped out with an unintelligible grunt. Wondering why he was so cross Susanna pushed the boxes against the bulkhead between the end of the seat and the curtain, and dropped her leather bag on to the bunk. Unpacking was out of the question. There was nowhere to put anything. After a moment's hesitation she left the cabin. The door on the far side of the stairs stood ajar and she could hear Meredith, high-pitched and voluble.

'How are we to find room for everything? I don't want it to go down in the hold. We might never see it again. Look, if you move that one, Lucy—'

Realizing that in the confined space she would be more hindrance than help Susanna went up on deck. The schooner was already clear of the docks and heading out of the Carrick Roads past the castles of Pendennis and St Mawes.

Wrapping her cloak tightly around her she picked her way along the deck until she reached the battened-down hatch of the after hold.

All around her and aloft men were busy, their movements swift and assured as they bent on yet more canvas to supplement the vast sails on the fore, main and mizzen masts. For all the notice they took of her she might have been invisible. But she wasn't offended. After years of having her every move watched and criticized, being ignored was a liberation.

She couldn't see Lowell Hawke. Ashamed of

even looking she gazed out over the starboard quarter. The schooner cut through the deep-blue water leaving a briefly flattened wake of sparkling foam. Moving out into the Atlantic swell the dip and rise became more pronounced, as did the angle of the deck. Yet seated on the hatch-cover, her body already adapting to the rhythm, she hardly noticed.

The town was out of sight, hidden by Pendennis headland. But the cream-painted bulk of the Falmouth Hotel gleaming in the morning sunshine stood out boldly against the surrounding green fields. Just a few short weeks ago Will and she had ridden that way to Lansdowne Road. The view splintered into bright fragments and her breath caught.

'Regrets already, Miss Elliot?'

She spun round. Lowell Hawke's expression gave little away, but his eyes held kindliness as well as curiosity.

'No.' She cleared the thickness from her throat. 'No regrets.'

'Leaving home is a big step for any young woman. To depart for the other side of the world is a bigger step than most.'

Was he simply being tactful? Or did he really understand? Overwhelmed by confusion she quickly bent her head. This was the man who, according to rumour, was guilty of deeds too terrible to recount in front of women. A man welcomed in society's highest circles yet whose name was greeted with awed familiarity in every waterfront bar from Canton to the upper reaches of the Yangtze. *A pirate, a devil.*

Leaping guiltily to her feet she stumbled on the canting deck. He caught her arm.

'You'll soon get your sea legs.'

Horribly embarrassed at having so nearly sprawled at his feet and acutely aware of his hand beneath her elbow she could only stammer her thanks as he guided her aft.

'Susanna?' Emerging from the companionway and clutching one of the folded-back doors, Lucy held up an enamel jug. 'Meredith isn't very well. Could you fetch some hot water?'

'Of course.' She took the jug, gesturing towards the smoking chimney of the caboose. 'There?'

'One moment.' Lowell's tone froze them both. The smiling courteous gentleman had become the ship's master on whose shoulders rested responsibility for everyone on board. Radiating absolute command he was awesome. 'You see the large galvanized iron tank abaft the mainmast? That holds our fresh water. As it has to last the entire voyage every drop is precious. Each morning the day's ration is drawn off into a separate cask. That large one is for the boat's crew, the small one for you ladies.'

Susanna gazed askance at the little barrel. 'B-but what about laundry?' she blurted. 'And bathing?'

'Rain,' he answered succinctly. 'We catch it in tarpaulins and run it off into those butts. The boy, Scally, will bring you each a jugful of

257

hot water with which to wash before breakfast. He'll collect the buckets after. For daytime use a private facility has been rigged up for you in the paint store. That's the door on the starboard side of the wheel shelter. The left-hand side as you look towards the stern,' he explained as she and Lucy exchanged an uncertain glance.

'Thank you, that is most thoughtful,' Lucy murmured, her papery skin faintly pink.

'At sea the main meal is taken in the middle of the day,' he continued. 'You may eat in my day cabin, or in your own.' Picturing the dim curtained cubbyhole Susanna shuddered inwardly. Yet the alternative made her unaccountably nervous. 'If you have any questions feel free to ask Tom Binney. He's the first mate and my deputy.' Lowell indicated a thickset, barrel-chested figure standing, arms akimbo, with two other seamen. In padded smock and thick trousers he looked almost as broad as he was tall. All three had their heads tipped back as they looked up the mainmast.

'Right, if you'll excuse me.' Lowell was already moving away.

'Er—' Tentatively Susanna lifted the jug. 'I know you said—'

'See John-Henry, the cook. Today is an exception,' he warned, 'only because the butts are full.' With a brief nod he strode off along the deck.

'Oh dear,' Lucy murmured

'Yes,' Susanna agreed softly.

258

Chapter Twenty-Three

16 January. We have been at sea two days.

Huddled in a corner between water tank and hatch cover, Susanna inhaled deeply. The air was so cold it stung her nostrils and made her eyes water, but it was clean and fresh. She bent over her journal once more. *I now know where the captain sleeps.*

Lying in her bunk, exhausted but unable to relax, she was acutely aware of him sitting at the table a few feet away on the other side of the curtain. She heard him close the log in which he had been writing up the day's progress, then soft sounds of movement. Carefully moving the thick material she peeped through the crack.

The nearer of the recessed panels above the padded seats stood open. Instead of the storage locker she imagined, the panel hid a sleeping berth. Having removed his boots, but still wearing shirt and trousers, Lowell Hawke was climbing into it.

Shaken, Susanna lay down again, staring into the darkness, her thoughts chaotic. Having pleaded to come she could not now complain particularly as she was enjoying the comfort of the bunk he usually occupied. That realization sent a strange tremor through her. A few moments later she heard another sound. As she identified it her entire body burned with indignation. He was snoring! Hysterical giggles shook her. What would Mrs Webber make of *this?*

Riven with guilt but unable to stop laughing, she nestled down into sheets and blankets brought from home. Inhaling the faint fragrance of dried lavender she quickly smothered the pang of homesickness. She must look forward, not back. Sighing deeply, she tried to relax. If the captain could slumber so easily then the ship must be quite safe. She slid into sleep.

We are in the Bay of Biscay. Poor Meredith is not a good sailor.

'I'm going to die, I know I am.' With another piteous groan Meredith leaned over the bucket once more. Breathing as lightly as possible in the fetid air, Susanna passed the facecloth to Lucy, and carried the basin back to the commode.

'No, you aren't.' Lucy was calm but firm. Meredith fell back on the bunk, eyes closed, her round face greenish-white and glistening. 'God has important work for you.' Lucy gently wiped her sister's sweating forehead with the cool wet cloth. 'Now,' she said as she started to get up, 'you rest while I go and wash the sheets.'

'Don't leave me, Lucy.'

'I won't be long. Susanna will stay.'

With another groan Meredith lurched over the side of the bunk again.

'It's all right, Lucy. I'll do it.' Susanna picked up the stinking bundle.

'No, my dear.' Pale-faced and hollow-eyed, Lucy shook her head. 'I couldn't possibly ask you.'

'You didn't. I'm volunteering. I don't mind, really.' Closing the cabin door she started up the stairs. The prospect of the chore made her own stomach heave. But had it not been for Lucy and Meredith she would still be in Falmouth. This was one small way of showing her gratitude.

'You can't do it in sea-water.' John-Henry looked up from the carrots he was chopping on a board laid across his knees. Squatting on a wooden stool in the snug galley-shack, unshaven, his grey hair straggling from beneath a knitted woollen hat, he looked like a shabby gnome. His rolled-up shirt sleeves revealed arms scarred with old burns.

'No,' she agreed. Nearly all the sailors in the infirmary had had boils and sores caused by the salt in their clothes. 'That's why I came to you. I was wondering ...'

'One bucketful of hot water, that's the best I can do.' He leaned towards the doorway and bellowed, 'Scally!' then looked up at her again. 'And you're only getting that because it rained yesterday.'

'Thank you so much. I'm really grateful.'

John-Henry grunted. 'Go on, then.' He waved her away. 'There's a tin bath round the side there. Mind you bring it back. I got shirts to do for the captain later and I don't want to have to come looking for it.'

Clinging with one hand to the lee rail which tipped all too close to the sea's surface, she trailed sheets, towels, and Meredith's voluminous flannel nightgown alongside the

261

ship to rinse off the worst of the soiling. Then, hands aching from the cold, she soaped off the rest in the tin bath. Aware of being watched by the crew as they went about their business she kept her head bent. Was this the escape she had yearned for?

24 January. We are past the Azores and making good speed in NW winds.

Alone in the day cabin Susanna rubbed the nape of her neck trying to ease the tension that lay across her shoulders like a yoke. As the ship left England further behind, her sense of being in limbo intensified. To escape this, and other feelings she found decidedly unsettling, she sought refuge in her medical books.

She *knew* she could speed Meredith's recovery but her cousin refused to try the tisane of powdered camomile flowers and ginger, or the quassia tonic.

'I'm sure you mean well, dear.' Meredith attempted a wan smile. 'But you save your potions for the Chinese. I've got something from the doctor that suits me very well.'

Checking the bottle of chloral hydrate Susanna saw the level was dropping dangerously fast. 'That's really quite strong. Might it not be wise to try something a little milder?'

'In these terrible conditions? Don't be silly, dear. Anyway, what can you possibly know of such things? Writing letters for sick sailors does not qualify you to offer advice on medical matters. Doctor Vigurs has looked after me since before you were born. He understands my delicate constitution. He said himself he has never known *anyone* suffer with their nerves the way I do.' She plucked at the sheet, her agitation growing. 'I have only to ask and he gives me another bottle. How could you even suggest that he would harm me?'

'No,' Susanna began hastily, 'I wasn't. I didn't mean that.'

'Oh, now I'm all upset.' Meredith's head flopped back against the bunched pillows. 'Lucy.' She beckoned her sister who had just returned from a brief visit topside. 'I don't feel well. Where are my smelling salts? I think I'd better have one of my powders.'

Susanna was aghast. 'I'm so sorry. Lucy, I wasn't criticizing Dr Vigurs, truly. It's just that I'm worried.'

'I know,' Lucy sighed quietly. 'Do you think I'm not?'

As she pushed the Pharmacopoeia away, disquiet nagged at Susanna. In small doses chloral hydrate was an excellent sleeping draught. But Meredith seemed to believe that if one teaspoonful was good two or three would be better. And as she was still taking all her other remedies might not this, rather than seasickness, be the reason for her continuing nausea?

Feeling for the medallion beneath her bodice she unlooped the cord from her neck. As she turned the pink jade in her fingers, awed by its delicate beauty, the pleas of the dying Portuguese sailor echoed in her mind. So much had happened since. She could think of him now without shuddering in horror. Who was Teresa? He had given all he possessed to obtain the pendant for her. Did she wonder where he was, when he would return?

This train of thought led her inevitably to Lowell. When they were both in the cabin she felt jittery and nervous, intensely—almost painfully—aware of him. Terrified he might guess, she often fled to the deck once her chores were done and, weather permitting, found a protected corner out of the crew's way. Yet the moment he came topside, lithe as a cat on the heaving deck, she forgot the view, her journal and her sketch-pad, her gaze drawn helplessly to him.

'Where did you get that?'

She started violently, so deep in her reverie she hadn't heard him come down.

'May I see?' Despite the smile his aura of command was so strong refusal never crossed her mind. He lowered himself on to the bench-seat opposite. 'Do you know what this is?'

'Only that it's Chinese.' Her heart pounded. How *could* a man with a reputation like his make her feel like this? Yet already she had learned there was far more to him than the seamen's tales suggested. Even so ... Though the cabin was not particularly warm, perspiration prickled her back and underarms.

He held it up. 'It's a sacred pi disc. The Chinese believe it embodies the light of the sun and provides a magical link with Heaven.'

His use of the word *magical* didn't come as any great surprise. She knew herself the pendant's mysterious calming effect.

'May I ask how you acquired it?'

264

Her throat was dust-dry. 'It was given to me by a seaman at the infirmary in Falmouth. He—he died.'

'Ah.' He studied her for a moment then handed the medallion back, moving the chart as though looking for something. 'Was he someone special to you?'

'No. Not at all. I didn't even know him. He thought I was someone else.' Realizing she wasn't making sense she tried to explain. 'He was out of his mind with fever. He imagined me to be his ... someone he loved.' She bent her head, cheeks aflame.

'I seem to remember your cousins mentioning your visits to the infirmary.' He paused. 'I'm sure the sailors appreciated being read to.'

Sure she heard amusement, Susanna stiffened. 'They were kind enough to say so. But I did have other tasks as well, some even more rewarding.'

'Such as?'

'Such as helping Edward—Doctor Arundell— with the preparation of medicines.'

His surprise filled Susanna with exultation. Her attraction to him, so strong, and coming so soon after she had believed herself in love with Edward, confused and shamed her, making her spiky. 'I also,' she added defiantly, 'assisted during a surgical operation.'

His brows climbed. 'Oh?'

'Yes.' She dared him to doubt her. 'A young fisherman had his leg crushed when a boat fell on it. Without my help he might well have died. At the very least he would have lost his leg.'

'Really? What exactly did you do?'

She certainly had his full attention now even if scepticism still hovered at the corners of his mouth. But not for long, she'd see to that. *Vanity*, her father's voice thundered in her mind. She shut it out. Her father had never taken her seriously. But Lowell Hawke would. She was weary of hiding her abilities, of pretending to be less than she was so as not to offend other people's ideas of proper behaviour.

'I administered ether to keep him unconscious.' She recalled the ordeal with sickening clarity. 'Then I held the leg while Edward washed out the wound, reset the broken bone, and applied special antiseptic dressings.' She swallowed, the images so vivid and horrific she was amazed at her own achievement.

'*You?*' His open astonishment softened to admiration. 'That must have taken courage.' His expression altered subtly. 'But perhaps your ... esteem ... for the surgeon helped you through the experience?'

Was she so transparent? She clung to the shreds of her dignity. 'Anyone working with Doctor Arundell could not fail to be impressed by his dedication, both to his patients and his family. He is held in great regard by all who know him.' Her conscience pricked as she recalled Edward's bitterness about other Falmouth doctors ridiculing him and refusing even to consider the use of antiseptic techniques.

'I count it an honour to number him among my friends.'

'Of whom you have too few,' he murmured.

266

'*Wh-what?*'

'Come now, Miss Elliot, let us be honest with one another. We are, after all,' his tone held a hint of mischief, 'living in conditions of some intimacy.'

As she stared at him, speechless, he leaned forward resting his arms on the table. His hands were large and strong, the skin golden-brown from years of exposure to wind and sun. 'I'm right though, aren't I?' He sat back, his gaze sliding over her. 'You dress as religious custom dictates, and I imagine you tried very hard to be the daughter your parents wanted. But like a swan among geese you didn't belong.'

Susanna was appalled. 'How—? Has Lucy said—?'

'She's not the type of woman to gossip or betray confidences, you should know that. Besides, she didn't need to. It's perfectly obvious, if one cares to look.' His words hung in the air, resonant with implication.

Quickly gathering up her books she scrambled out from behind the table, awkward in her agitation. 'Please excuse me. You see I promised—'

'Of course.'

Hearing the smile in his voice, she hated him.

After she'd gone Lowell remained where he was, gazing at the chart but not seeing it, uneasy about the direction his thoughts were taking, yet incapable of stopping them.

5 February. We have entered the tropics. I should not complain—Lucy never does and she has more cause than anyone—but the voyage is presenting more difficulties than I ever envisaged.

There was no alternative but to ask John-Henry if he had an old pan or bucket he no longer needed. She quailed at the prospect. But as Lucy had her hands full nursing Meredith who was incapable of anything, she had no choice but to take responsibility for doing what was necessary for all three of them.

She remembered how frightened she had been that first time, her terror deepened by guilt that somehow she must have done something to cause it. Her mother, with averted eyes and a pinker than usual complexion, had said only that the event marked a girl's transition to womanhood and would occur regularly. While leaving her still confused, the explanation at least reassured her she was not dying.

She was instructed that each month she should place the cloths in a covered bowl by her wash-stand. The bowl was collected when Agnes made the bed, and the cloths—clean and ready to be used again—replaced in the drawer the following day. It never occurred to her to wonder who washed them and how that person might feel about the task. She knew now.

'What d'you want it for?' John-Henry demanded, frowning.

It had been too much to hope that he wouldn't ask. 'S-some-er-small items of washing.'

Crimson with embarrassment she tucked an escaped curl behind her ear, startled for a moment not to feel the crisp confining cotton. Waking with a headache as well as stomach cramps, she had glared at the hated bonnet then, crumpling it into a ball, stuffed it down the side of her trunk.

Entering her cousins' cabin bareheaded she had felt acutely self-conscious. But Lucy had simply smiled as she handed over the washing. Meredith hadn't even noticed.

'Ahhh,' John-Henry said suddenly, nodding. 'The flowers, is it?' Clicking his tongue he bent to rummage in a cupboard. 'Women! As if I hadn't got enough to do.' He dragged out a battered metal pot with no handle and a dented, ill-fitting lid. 'Here, you can 'ave this. Try a soak in seawater first.' He threw the advice over his shoulder as he busied himself at the stove. 'The salt will take the stain out. Then use your soap and hot water.'

'Th-thank you.' Was it possible to die of embarrassment?

But the advice proved invaluable and she managed to get the cloths washed and dried without their purpose being obvious to every passing crewman.

13 February. No wind for two days. The heat is intense. Mr Arthur's ulcerated leg is healing well since I applied stimulant lotion. The crew's demeanour toward us seems much improved.

The sea was a sheet of glass beneath a dazzling merciless sun. The huge booms had been pushed wide, but the canvas hung limp and useless.

'You never heard of an "angel's whisper"?' The seaman's voice carried clearly. 'Mind, 'tis only called that if you set'n above a skysail.

269

Set'n above a moonsail and he's called a "trust to God".'

Sitting on the hatch cover beneath an awning rigged from an old strip of sail slung between the main and mizzen masts Susanna had her journal open on her lap. Her simple dress of apple-green cotton clung damply to her back.

She wasn't writing, but with her head bent over the book she was able to listen unobtrusively, fascinated by the men's talk of ships and the masters who commanded them. If she appeared occupied they yarned and bantered as though she wasn't there. But if she showed the slightest interest they became either truculent or tongue-tied.

The sultry heat had even brought Meredith on deck. Shaded by the awning she reclined alongside the water tank on a day-bed fashioned from pillows wrapped in blankets. Lucy sat close by, reading quietly to her.

A shadow fell across her lap and she looked up. 'Good afternoon, Mr Lockhead.' The tow-headed second mate's easy blushes made him the butt of endless leg-pulling by the crew.

'The captain would like a word, miss. He says now, if you aren't too busy.'

Hearing the irony and underlying anger in those last five words Susanna felt her stomach dive. She stood up closing her journal. 'Of course. It's too hot to write anyway.' Trying to hide her apprehension and ignore the rigging gang's sidelong glances she turned towards the companionway. 'How is the burn?'

He lifted his bandaged arm. 'Coming on

270

fine, thank you, miss. I can hardly feel it now.' Beetroot-red, he mumbled, 'You can do magic.'

He did so remind her of William. She smiled. 'No, Mr Lockhead, no magic. Just linseed oil and lime water.'

He left her at the hatch and, as she descended the stairs, she heard the crew baiting him with cat-calls and whistles.

'What's going on up there?' Lowell growled as she entered the day cabin.

She hesitated. Though she was prepared for censure there was a tension in the air she didn't understand. 'I have no idea.'

It was obvious he didn't believe her. 'These treatments, they've got to stop.'

She clasped her hands, every muscle tense. 'Why?'

'The whole thing has got out of hand. I should never have allowed it in the first place.'

'How can you say that?' It had taken time and patience to win the men's trust. Even now their only acknowledgement was the briefest of nods. 'And what do you mean, out of hand? No one gets injured or falls ill on purpose.' One of his dark brows arched in silent irony and she knew he was thinking of Meredith. 'The point is that in treating one or two of the crew—'

'Four,' he interrupted. 'Let us not underestimate all the good you have been doing.' His sarcasm made her wince.

'All right, four. But all have returned to their duties far more quickly than they would have without treatment.'

271

'Miss Elliot,' he said with deceptive gentleness, 'I want to get this ship to Shanghai as quickly as possible. To do so I need a fit, disciplined crew.'

'But that is my point.'

'I haven't finished. I do *not* need men who are using your ministrations—no matter how well intended—either as a wager, or to boost their standing in the fo'c'sle.'

Susanna froze. Such a possibility had never crossed her mind. 'The injuries were real.'

'They are part and parcel of life at sea and something the men are well used to.' He leaned back stretching out his legs beneath the table. She shifted her gaze quickly. She had grown accustomed to the crew going without shoes, but seeing Lowell thus reminded her of his teasing concerning their intimacy. And that aroused feelings she didn't know how to deal with.

At Lansdowne Road, in stylish frockcoat, snowy linen, beautifully cut trousers, and boots polished to a mirror shine, he had been aloof, distant.

Now, barefoot and dishevelled, his shirt loose and unbuttoned to reveal a broad chest beaded with moisture beneath curling black hair, he looked untamed. Meeting his piercing gaze she caught her breath. Propriety was simply a garment he put on when occasion demanded and discarded with equal ease. Looking away she felt perspiration break out on her forehead and upper lip.

He tapped the table with a pencil. 'Perhaps you were unaware, Miss Elliot, that in the absence of a doctor on board it is customary for the ship's master to deal with injuries and medical problems.'

'Then why didn't you? If you had, the men would never have come to me. Especially as they believe that having women on the ship brings bad luck.' It was Oliver Lockhead who had confessed the reason for the men's hostility.

His fist tightened and the pencil snapped making her jump. 'Because until you came on board such incidents were simply shrugged off.'

'B-but that's inhuman.'

'What use is a sailor who can't walk or haul on a rope? Who will give him a berth? And without work how will he live? The sea is a demanding profession, Miss Elliot. Ships cannot be run on sentiment. In future *I* will decide if treatment is necessary, and if it is then *I* will administer it. I have managed perfectly well in the past.'

'And should you fail, who is to know?' she responded furiously. 'After all, you have an entire ocean in which to bury your mistakes.'

28 February. Mr Binney tells me we are in the South Atlantic. It is cooler and we are enjoying the fresh westerly breeze. Captain Hawke is a most contrary man.

'I was *not* flirting with him.' Her vehement denial made no impression.

'I am not passing moral judgement on your behaviour,' he drawled. 'However, discipline aboard this ship depends on—'

'Captain Hawke,' Susanna interrupted, 'I am

273

aware of Mr Lockhead's ... regard ... for me. The feeling is not mutual. I have never flirted. I do not know how. I smiled because he smiled. He—he reminds me of my brother.'

'I see.' Not for the first time she wished she could see behind the expressionless mask.

'I would remind you that I am *not* a member of your crew.'

'One must be thankful for small mercies.'

She refused to be distracted. She did not expect an apology. No matter how many times she proved his censure unfounded, he *never* apologized. But of all his criticisms this was the most unfair. 'It was never my intention to cause Mr Lockhead any difficulty.'

'*Mr Lockhead?*' Lowell exploded.

'So I will be more circumspect in future. Now if you'll excuse me, I—'

'*Damn* it, Susanna.' He raked a hand through his thick rumpled hair. 'I have *never* met a woman so—so—' He threw his hand up in sheer frustration. Footsteps clanged on the stairs.

'Ready for tea, are we?' John-Henry bustled in. Pushing the charts carefully aside he set the tray down on the widest part of the table. Then, looking from one to the other, he clicked his tongue and bustled out again.

'Join me.'

'I beg your pardon?'

'I'm sorry. That sounded more like an order than an invitation. And, as you say, you are not a member of my crew. Please?' He indicated the seat.

Not at all sure she was doing the right thing

she resumed her seat and watched him pour the tea, a picture so incongruous it was like a dream. He pushed a cup towards her.

'Tell me, why did your cousins choose China?'

She shrugged. 'All I know is that it has been Meredith's dream for a long time.'

'I can't see her coping with the demands of missionary work.'

'Some people are not good travellers,' she defended, setting down her tea cup. 'But once we reach Shanghai, I'm sure Meredith will soon be—'

'Her old self?'

To openly agree with him was treachery. Yet she could not deny her own doubts were growing.

'And why is Lucy so self-sacrificing?'

'You make it sound like a fault.'

'Isn't it, when taken to such lengths?'

She tried to ignore the disquiet he was stirring. 'The Quaker faith requires us to strive to improve the well-being of humanity. Lucy lives by that code. She's a truly good person.'

Lowell toyed with his broken pencil. 'The Quaker faith also appears to require its members to pour vast amounts of money into their favourite charities. Which might be seen as an attempt to buy their way into Heaven.'

These same thoughts had tormented Susanna for a long time. But loyalty to her family demanded she deny them. 'If God is all-wise and all-knowing, He won't be taken in by such people. Besides, Friends never give money.

Money is spent on drink, and drink provokes violence. Instead they give food, clothes and education.' She was startled by Lowell's cynical snort of laughter.

'Education is likely to provoke even more violence once the poor realize how badly society treats them.'

'Possibly. But people have a right to knowledge. Without education how can they fight injustice? How can they challenge old beliefs unless they know what alternatives exist? People have a right to try and change things for the better. And to determine their own destiny.'

The urge to reach out and touch her was almost irresistible. Her skin was downy, like a ripe peach. Sunshine angling down through the skylight lit the curling tendrils in front of her ear so they shone like filaments of gold. It fell across the bird's-wing curve of her brow and that stubbornly tilted little chin. Her eyes were the colour of new grass, their gaze intelligent and direct now self consciousness had been forgotten. His heart twisted. She was so young, so fresh. While he ...

Chapter Twenty-Four

12 March. Off the Cape of Good Hope. Huge seas make the ship seem very small. But with the wind in our favour we are covering great distances each day.

A knocking echoed through the bulkhead.

'Let me go this time.' Susanna started to rise. 'You get so little rest.'

'No, it's better if I do.' Lucy laid a hand on her arm. 'Do bear in mind the captain's many responsibilities.' Then, as the knocking started again, she hurried out.

'Your cousin has a delightful turn of phrase,' Lowell observed drily. 'What exactly did she mean about my responsibilities?'

'She's anxious that I don't impose too much on your time or good nature.' Susanna watched one corner of his mouth tilt upward, a reaction she was beginning to know well. 'She does not realize such advice is unnecessary as you would never permit either.' His glance and the slow smile that accompanied it made her heart skip a beat.

He rested his chin on his clasped hands. 'Why did you leave Falmouth?'

Resisting the flood of memories Susanna concentrated on folding her napkin. 'To assist my cousins in their mission.'

'You have already told me what you hope to do. I asked why you left the security of a comfortable home to join this hare-brained venture?'

When they were alone he often said things to deliberately provoke her. Richard had done the same. But Richard had been driven by spite. Lowell's motive she realized was a desire to hear, not what she believed she ought to say, but what she really felt. That he should even care what she thought was dangerously seductive.

Goaded into abandoning the restraints imposed by convention she was exploring and expressing her ideas, beliefs, and responses in ways she had never dreamed were possible.

He clearly enjoyed their debates. But would her nonconformity eventually alienate him as it had her family? What bitter-sweet irony that the only way to gain Lowell Hawke's esteem was to risk losing it.

'I left because I want something more from life: something to which I can dedicate myself.'

'Surely marriage—?'

She adjusted her cutlery. 'Marriage is not for me.'

'That is a statement usually made by those whom opportunity has passed by. You're far too young to give up hope yet.'

She shook her head impatiently. 'Perhaps I haven't made myself clear. It isn't a question of hope: I don't *want* to marry.'

'Why ever not? I understood that a suitable marriage was every woman's goal?'

'Not mine. The price is too high.' She sensed his gaze on her, and his sharpened curiosity.

'An unusual view indeed. May I ask your reasons?'

She thought of her sister, unable to speak of love but *relieved* to be married, even if it meant living with and looking after the whole Webber family. 'Marriage does indeed give a woman greater status in society, particularly among other women. But she surrenders her rights as an individual. From the moment the ring is placed on her finger her husband's needs and wishes take precedence over her own. In return for economic security, which if he is a drinker or gambler is by no means certain, she must do his bidding in all things.'

'You make it sound like slavery,' he mocked lightly.

'Isn't it? Men insist women are weak, foolish and helpless. No doubt some are. But certainly not *all*. Yet they must pretend to be in order that men may appear strong and capable. And what of the books outlining the duties of a wife? Written by clergymen and doctors.' Her mouth twisted. 'Men cannot possibly comprehend what it's like to be a woman but that doesn't stop them claiming to know what's best for us. Though I've noticed they operate a completely different set of rules for themselves.'

'And you consider such behaviour arrogant and unjust?'

'Yes, I do.'

'I see. So how would you describe the shy maiden who, once the ring is on her finger, becomes a domestic tyrant? What of the girl who tells her beau she loves him as he is then presses him to change his job, appearance and friends to conform to her ideas of suitability?' A new harshness entered his voice. 'And what of the sweetheart promising love and affection who, once a wife, discovers all manner of female ailments to keep her husband at arm's length?'

Contempt hardened his expression. 'The male arrogance you complain of is more than matched by women's duplicity and cunning.'

Having expected him to tease, this bitterness

and hostility shook her. Suddenly she felt very young and very gauche. It was difficult to shut out the images his scathing words conjured.

'So who is to blame?' She thought of her father, of his resistance to change and refusal to compromise. 'Women resort to guile because men won't *listen*. Why can't they respect women, not simply as wives and mothers, but as people? Given the same education and professional freedom as a man any reasonably intelligent woman could provide perfectly well for herself.'

'I think you might find Shanghai society less than receptive to such unconventional views.'

'I'm not likely to have much contact with Shanghai society.'

Lowell turned a brooding gaze on her. 'Perhaps that's just as well.'

21 March. Today is the vernal equinox. We are in the Indian Ocean. The glass has been dropping all day.

'It's not enough.' Meredith pushed away the glass. 'I want a double dose. If I'm asleep I won't be sick. Besides,' she said as she sank back on the pillow, 'if the storm overwhelms us and the ship sinks, I don't want to know about it.'

'We are *not* going to sink.' Touching Meredith's hand Susanna noticed how transparent the skin had become, revealing a tracery of blue veins. Her once-plump face was now thin and lined, her eyes sunk deep in their sockets as if to avoid seeing too much that was unfamiliar. 'Captain Hawke has crossed these oceans many

280

times. Storms are nothing new to him. He will bring us through safely.'

'And then what? There will be another test for me to fail.' Meredith closed her eyes. 'I'm too weak. I should not be here.' A tear slid down her temple.

Susanna stroked the frail hand. 'Don't, Meredith, please.' She was used to Meredith's detailed description of every discomfort. This was different, worrying. 'Seasickness is very tiring. You need time to recover.'

'It's all right, Susanna,' Lucy said quietly. 'You go along now.'

Ashamed of her relief, and of her inability to help, she returned to the day cabin. Too restless to go to bed she tried to ignore the worsening weather by reading her medical books.

Items on the shelf bumped against the guard as the increasing pitch and roll of the ship sent them slithering into an untidy heap. Concentration became impossible. Susanna glanced up at the swinging oil lamp wishing she had someone to talk to, anything to take her mind off the violence raging outside. She watched helplessly as one after another her books and the charts slid off the table.

The wind roared and howled. The coal bucket skidded sideways then tipped over, spilling its load on to the boards. A prolonged creaking was followed by a crash that made the cabin shake. Heart thumping, she looked up in fear at the deckhead and tried to wedge herself in the corner, aching all over from the ship's violent contortions. A falling spar crashing through the skylight would probably kill her. But she still preferred the padded seat to the suffocating darkness of the sleeping cabin.

The wind rose to a scream heralding yet another squall. Torrential rain hammered the deck and she cringed at the sound of another crash. *How much of this could the ship take?* She wiped her eyes with a shaking hand.

The schooner reared, climbing a wave. It reached the crest, hesitated, then plunged into the trough with a sickening corkscrew motion. She heard a high-pitched scream, shouts, and the sound of running feet above her head. *What was happening?*

The companionway doors slammed back. Thuds, scuffling, and voices raised in argument were barely audible above the shrieking wind. A series of thumps told her someone was coming down. Beating back churning fear, she hauled herself out of her corner, thrown to her knees as the ship canted again.

Gathering up the books she dropped them inside the padded seat on top of the spare blankets. She was trying to roll up the charts when the door burst open and John-Henry lurched in supporting a swaying semi-conscious figure.

Her throat tightened choking off a cry as she recognized Lowell. He was soaked, his shirt and trousers clinging to him like a second skin. Blood from a ragged wound high on one side of his forehead trickled in rivulets down his face. It dripped off his chin and ran down his throat, seeping into his wet shirt. The spreading scarlet patch already covered half his chest. He made a soft wordless sound then his eyes rolled up and his knees buckled. Staggering under the weight John-Henry lowered him to the floor.

Crawling across to the other seat locker Susanna pulled out several clean towels. Kneeling beside him she quickly folded one and pressed it against the gash. After a brief hesitation, shy of touching him, she began gently to wipe away the blood. He reminded her of a felled tree.

'Scally went overboard. Cap'n went in after him.' Still trying to catch his breath John-Henry pulled the grubby kerchief from his neck and mopped his own face. 'Got the little bugger too.'

Susanna was almost afraid to ask. 'How is he?'

John-Henry snorted. 'Not a mark on him. Once he's puked up all the seawater he swallowed he'll be right as a trivet. But the cap'n got smashed against the side.'

Susanna lifted the wadded towel to take another look at the cut. Immediately blood welled out of it again.

'That needs stitching,' John-Henry stated.

Susanna replaced the pad. 'You'd better fetch Mr Binney.'

'Can't do that. They need him top-side. He's in command til the captain's right again. You'll have to do it.'

'M-me?'

'Who else? You know about these things. You fixed Cecil's ulcer good and proper. And Joey's

283

bronchitis. And Mr Lockhead's arm.'

Susanna's thoughts spun as the ship lifted and plunged beneath her. *She had never stitched a wound.* Dry-mouthed she peered under the pad, *willing* the blood to have stopped flowing. It hadn't and the wound gaped, jagged and ugly. Without stitches healing would be slow, the scar prominent and disfiguring.

She wrapped a second towel around Lowell's head to hold the pad in place. How ironic that having derided her treatments and forbidden her to continue he should need her help now. She had no choice. 'Can you fetch me some fresh water? I don't suppose you've got any that's been boiled?'

John-Henry skittered crabwise towards the door. 'Sorry. I had to dowse the galley fire for safety.'

'And two clean bowls,' she called after him. From her bag of medical supplies she took out a bottle of carbolic acid. She dare not use chloroform or ether. If Lowell was sick he might choke. But if not those, then what? She picked up comfrey powder, lint and bandages, her hand trembling as she reached for the small flat packet of waxed paper containing silk-threaded needles. Why *him?*

Dropping the curtain behind her she saw John-Henry had returned and was rummaging in the cupboard below the guarded shelf.

'Here 'tis.' Grinning in triumph he held up a bottle of brandy. Below his soggy woollen hat his greasy hair hung in dripping rat's tails. 'Mr Binney said you might need this.'

Susanna knelt beside Lowell setting everything on the floor within easy reach. Crouching opposite her John-Henry pulled the cork from the bottle and thrust it at her. 'Here, have a swig.'

She shook her head automatically. 'I can't. I'm forbidden—'

'Go on,' he insisted. 'God helps them that help themselves. 'Sides, you'll do better with a steady hand.'

How could she argue? Tilting the bottle to her lips Susanna took a small mouthful, swallowed, and coughed. The aromatic spirit burned her throat and stomach, and her eyes streamed as she fought for breath. But within moments a warm glow radiated along her limbs infusing her with new strength.

'One more,' John-Henry urged.

Susanna obeyed, shuddered, and passed the bottle back. 'Will you hold his head?'

Taking a quick gulp himself John-Henry recorked the bottle and crawled forward. After preparing two bowls of antiseptic solution Susanna used one to wash her hands then, dipping a wad of lint in the other, she lifted the pad from Lowell's forehead and started bathing the wound. He stirred, winced, and tried to ward her off. Then he opened his eyes.

'Please lie still.' She did her best to sound confident. 'You have a deep cut on your forehead. I'm going to stitch it.'

He stiffened, his eyes widening. 'You?'

'I'll ask someone else if you prefer.'

His gaze flicked to John-Henry and back.

285

'No,' his voice was hoarse. 'No. You do it.' He reached for the bottle. 'Be quick.' He swallowed several times baring his teeth. 'I'd like it finished before this wears off.'

'So would I,' she muttered fervently and looked up at John-Henry. 'Will you hold the captain's head, please?'

'That won't be necessary,' Lowell mumbled.

'Oh for goodness sake!' Her nervousness spilled over. 'This'll be difficult enough as it is. If you move it will take twice as long. Neither of us wants that.'

A spasm crossed his face. *Laughter?* 'You're right.' He held his hand out for the bottle. John-Henry passed it over and after another deep swallow Lowell lay back and closed his eyes.

It probably took no more than fifteen minutes. But when she straightened up, rubbing her forehead with the back of her hand it came away wet with perspiration. Her chest hurt and it took a moment for her to realize why. She had been so intensely focused on *what* she was doing—the only way she could blank out who she was doing it to and the pain she was causing—she had hardly breathed at all.

She inhaled deeply, startled to realise that while stitching the wound she had been totally unaware of the lurching deck and the terrifying noise of the storm. Was it worse? Or had it started to ease? She sat back on her heels, one hand on the floor to steady herself.

'Bloody 'ell, that's a tidy little job, miss.' John-Henry was almost as pale as the man on the floor.

Lowell opened his eyes. 'Have you finished?'

'Almost. I just have to put a bandage—'

He started to sit up. 'No need for that.'

She caught his shoulder, felt warm skin and hard muscle beneath the wet cotton and snatched her hand away, trying to disguise the movement by tucking an untidy curl into the loosening knot at the back of her head. Embarrassment gave her voice an edge.

'Captain, the wound will heal more quickly and with less risk of infection if it is covered.'

'How long?'

'A few days only.'

'Oh, all right. Get on with it then.'

His sharpness rankled but she didn't respond. A few moments later the bandage was secured. His eyes were closed, his features tight.

'Captain?'

He looked up at her, his mouth twisting in wry self-mockery. 'What have you got for a headache?'

6 April. Through the Sunda Strait into the Java Sea, catching our first glimpse of land for many weeks. And such strange land it is. Steep mountains covered in forest that rise straight out of the sea.

Sitting on the hatch cover Lucy stared into the distance, fretting with her handkerchief. 'I shouldn't have brought her.'

'You couldn't have stopped her. She wanted it so much. Besides, it was her idea.'

'No.' Turning to Susanna, Lucy shook her head. 'No, it wasn't. Not in the beginning. It was mine. I prayed for guidance for a long time

287

before saying anything. When I did finally tell her God wanted me in China she was very quiet for a few days. Then she said it was what she had been waiting for. For so long her life had lacked direction. But now the light of God's purpose, shining through me, had illuminated the path she was to follow. We would go to China together.' She stared out to sea again. 'Meredith isn't strong and I'm not talking about her indispositions. She may appear confident and full of resolve but ...' Lucy pressed the handkerchief to her lips. 'Have I done a terrible thing?'

'No, of course not. Lucy, you didn't force her, Meredith wanted to come. Just as she wanted everyone to believe that the mission was her idea. You couldn't have known she would be such a poor traveller.' Susanna had tried hard to push her own apprehension out of her mind. Lucy's anguish stirred it up again like thick silt.

'Perhaps you're right,' Lucy murmured. 'Maybe once we reach Shanghai ...' But her eyes glistened with unshed tears.

Approaching the knot of men in the bow Susanna was horrified to see Tom Binney supervising the fitting of a machine gun with a cluster of barrels to a mounting on the deck. A few feet away Oliver Lockhead distributed small arms and rifles to the crew. Running back to the companionway she sped down the stairs into the day cabin.

'What are they doing?' she demanded breathlessly.

288

Leaning on his hands Lowell was studying a chart. 'What are *who* doing?' The wound on his forehead had healed cleanly leaving a thin scar that showed livid against his tanned skin.

'Mr Binney.' She tried to catch her breath. 'And Mr Lockhead is giving the crew guns.'

'That's right.'

'No. It's all wrong.' Her reaction was partly conditioning—Quakers were adamantly opposed to war—but it was partly fear. What she had learned about him for herself was so different from the rumours. But he was jeopardizing this new image. 'You can't. You have no right to take the life of another human being.'

Impatience flickered across his face. 'In these waters the choice is simple: to kill or be killed. English laws do not apply here. I'm not looking for a fight. But I have a moral duty to protect my ship and my crew, even'—one corner of his mouth rose,—'my passengers.'

'Yes, but—'

'No.' His smile vanished and his voice cracked like a whip. 'No *buts* Pirates don't capture. They kill. Do you understand? No prisoners. With one exception.' His tone sent a chill feathering down her spine. 'Pretty young women.' The bleakness of his features reminded her of Cornish granite. 'I've seen passenger ships after a pirate raid. I'd kill you myself sooner than let you fall into their hands.'

Susanna flinched back, hands flying to her mouth. His gaze held hers. His eyes, blue-grey and flinty, filled her vision, her mind, her world. She was drawn like a breath past the icy barrier

289

into black velvet depths that weren't cold at all. The heat bathed her. It permeated her body like a golden flame, filling her with sensations so exquisitely sweet, she shimmered and ached and burned.

'Susanna?' His voice, ragged and harsh, jerked her back to reality. Blinking as if she had woken suddenly from a deep sleep she clasped her arms around her body, trying to stop the trembling.

I'd kill you myself sooner than ... The moment the words were out, he was forced to recognize what had driven him to say them. He had never met anyone like her. He had known many women who lived independent lives, married women who did so on their husband's money. She was different. A little muddled perhaps, and naive, but clearly intelligent. She certainly had spirit. And courage. Not once had she complained. She made him laugh. It was a long time since he'd done that. *What was he doing? There was no place for her in his life.*

Looking into her eyes he recognized the hunger he knew she didn't yet understand, and felt the answering tug inside himself. She was his for the taking. Cursing the fates for bringing them together, and himself for a fool, he deliberately turned his back on her.

'If there's nothing else?' He bent over the charts again, his tone defying her to linger. Her soft gasp pierced him like a blade. He waited, leaning on stiffened arms, his nails digging into the underside of the wooden table. He heard the whisper of her dress as she left the cabin, heard her footsteps stumble on the brass stairs. Only then did he close his eyes and allow his head to drop.

Chapter Twenty-Five

10 April. To celebrate 'crossing the line' we were invited to the court of King Neptune—actually one of the older seamen dressed up. (Meredith remained in the cabin.) In strange ceremonies newer members of the crew were coated with flour and soap suds. I have seen little of the captain.

The air was stifling. A hot wind had driven the schooner past steep-sided islands where mist rose like steam from the lush vegetation; now it had dropped humidity enfolded the ship in a suffocating embrace. The crew were edgy and lookouts had been doubled.

Sitting in her favourite spot on the hatch cover Susanna looked up. A black velvet sky sprinkled with diamond stars looked close enough to touch. The night was heavy with the scent of exotic flowers and the sweet stench of decaying vegetation. Howls and roars from the dense tropical forest carried clearly across the water. An unearthly scream made her start and gooseflesh erupted on her clammy skin.

Lowell emerged from the companionway. She watched in silent yearning as he stretched, flexing his shoulders. Now they were in the

South China Sea he remained on deck from dawn to dusk, and during the hours of darkness never slept longer than one watch.

Night after night, though he took care to move quietly, the soft noises he made leaving or entering the cabin woke her. Lying in the hot darkness she would listen to the creaking deck and the slap of waves against the hull then drift back into shallow restless sleep.

Each morning as soon as the anchor was raised soundings were called every few minutes. Tom Binney and Oliver Lockhead took turns marking the chart while Lowell gave course corrections to the helmsman and kept one eye on wind and sails as the schooner crept forward through the narrow channel between sand bars that would hold her fast and rocks that would rip out her keel.

'Why so often?' she had whispered to John-Henry, indicating the sailor swinging the lead weight out over the bow. 'Is the chart not reliable?'

'Shouldn't think so.' Juggling pans on the stove he hadn't even looked up. 'I daresay this passage isn't marked at all. Cap'n likes to find shorter routes. Cuts down the time, see? And time is money.'

But while she recognized the demands, understood the responsibility he carried, and saw how hard he was driving himself, none of it explained why for days he had scarcely spoken to her. Though she filled the long hours studying, writing her journal, and doing the necessary personal chores for herself and her cousins, she missed their talks. She even missed his teasing.

Was it something she'd said, or done? Or was it simply her? As far back as she could remember she had been wrong; in the way she looked, her behaviour, her ideas, and her ambitions. Only William had accepted her just as she was. And William was dead. Even Edward, despite admiring her intelligence, had rejected her.

She had never minded solitude, but this past forty-eight hours she had felt so *lonely*. Though rarely more than thirty feet away, Lowell Hawke was as remote from her as Cornwall.

She watched him glance upwards even though all the canvas on the towering masts was furled for the night. He seemed to possess a sixth sense, knowing instantly when something wasn't right. He had told her the schooner sang to him and a fraying rope or a sail on the verge of splitting sounded a false note. She still wasn't sure if he'd been teasing.

She had learned from her visits to the infirmary how physically hard and emotionally demanding a life the men led, parted from their families for months at a time. But this voyage had shown her another side to life at sea—the close comradeship of men working together in extremes of climate, horrendous weather and almost constant danger. Their singing and banter made her own sense of isolation even more painful.

She hoped desperately that Lowell might pause for a few moments and talk. But she didn't approach him. The tattered remnants of her self-esteem forbade it. He turned towards her and she held her breath.

'When you retire tonight'—his voice held no emotion of any kind—'I suggest you leave the curtain fastened back. Foul air combined with this humidity is certain to give you a headache. However, the decision is yours.'

'Th-thank you,' she stammered. After a brief hesitation he started to walk on. 'Captain?' She hadn't meant to say anything at all. She certainly couldn't ask why he'd changed for that would show him how much it mattered. She gestured helplessly. 'Forgive me. I—I'm sure you're busy. Please don't let me detain you.'

He turned, a dark silhouette against the faint glow from the day cabin skylight. 'What is it?'

'It's just—I wondered ...' *Why won't you talk to me?* 'if you are from a seafaring family.' It seemed an age before he spoke.

'No. My father runs a large merchant house in Shanghai. We even have a branch in London. He considers himself a very astute businessman.' Sarcasm glinted like a splinter of broken glass beneath the weariness that thickened his voice.

'My father claims,' Susanna ventured, 'that the secret of success in business is to create a demand, then fill it. Does your father deal in tea or silk? Or jade perhaps?' This tiny clue to his background, of which she knew so little, brought home to her how keenly she missed his company and the cut and thrust of their conversations. He was the first man she had ever talked to in any depth—her conversations with Edward had been confined to infirmary matters—and he was certainly the first to rate

294

her opinions worthy of serious consideration.

'He's dealt in all of them,' came the laconic reply. 'And porcelain. But the company started life trading something far more lucrative—opium.'

A quick intake of breath betrayed her initial shock. It was followed by horror, and terrible disappointment

'Oh no,' her voice quavered. 'How could you be involved in something so evil?'

'I'm n—' he clamped his mouth shut. After a moment he enquired coolly, 'Considering your own family's connections with opium smuggling aren't you being rather hypocritical?'

'*What?* Don't be ridiculous. What are you talking about?'

'Have you heard of the Opium Wars in China?'

'Of course I have.'

'Do you know who was British Superintendent of Trade in Canton when the Chinese first declared war on Britain over the import of opium in 1839? Captain Charles Elliot. A kinsman of yours.' The words fell like hammer blows. 'He used his position to protect British ships bringing opium from India into Chinese waters, even though he knew trading in the drug was illegal.'

Stunned, speechless, Susanna stared at him. Yet it never occurred to her to accuse him of lying. He wouldn't. But a member of her family? Her father had spoken out many times and with great eloquence against what he called 'the filthy traffic in degradation and human misery'. Her kinsman? With an inarticulate cry she brushed past him and flung herself through the hatch.

As she clattered down the companionway he glared in anguish at the coldly mocking stars. It was the only way. He must drive her away, turn her against him.

That his marriage was a sham was something only he and Marjorie knew. Both were aware of his reputation among the ladies of Shanghai's international settlement: not only was he an accomplished lover he was also—so important to those with difficult husbands—exceptionally discreet. But they both ignored it; she because as long as she was his wife her position in society was unassailable, he because he simply didn't care what people thought of him.

Until now. His jaw was clenched so tight his teeth ached. Susanna Elliot was only nineteen and under the guardianship of her cousins. He was not free to court her. And no matter how much he might desire it—and her—an affair was out of the question. A bitter smile twisted his mouth. Of all the times to discover a conscience.

But he had no choice. Any hint of scandal would finish the Braithwaites' mission before it had even started. Regardless of his own opinion of their venture, they didn't deserve that.

Nor did she.

'Lucy,' Susanna blurted in a frantic whisper, as the door opened to her urgent tapping. 'Did you know about Lowell's father? Is Lowell involved in it too? He says one of *our* relatives—'

'Ssh.' Stepping into the cramped stairwell,

Lucy pulled the door closed behind her. 'Now, what is all this about? *Slowly.*'

Susanna repeated what he'd told her. 'Was Captain Elliot really on the side of the opium traders?'

'No, of course not.' Susanna knew a moment's unutterable relief before questions crowded in. She pushed them aside to concentrate on what Lucy was saying. 'His job was to protect British shipping from harassment by the Chinese. But the mandarins employed by the emperor to stop the opium smuggling were making even more money by turning a blind eye and allowing it to continue. This forced Captain Elliot into the unenviable position of having to support and protect his own countrymen while they acted illegally.'

'So what did he do?'

'It all came to a head when the emperor appointed a special commissioner and gave him a free hand to stop the trade in opium once and for all. Commissioner Lin imprisoned all the British in their factories. He blockaded the street, surrounded the buildings with soldiers, and forbade any Chinese on pain of death to give them food or fuel. You see, the British were only allowed to do business in Canton on condition that Chinese merchants stood security for them. When two of the wealthiest and most important of these merchants were paraded in full view of the factories with chains around their necks, implying their lives would be forfeit if the British didn't surrender, Captain Elliot gave the order for all the opium in the factories to be handed over to the Chinese authorities.'

'And the prisoners were released?'

Lucy nodded. 'But the emperor banished all the British, including Captain Elliot, from Canton.'

'What happened to the opium?'

'It was shovelled into water-filled trenches then spread with salt and lime to make it rot.'

Susanna rubbed her throbbing forehead. 'But Lowell implied Captain Elliot was on the side of the opium smugglers. Why would he do that?'

'Perhaps,' Lucy suggested quietly, 'because you jumped to conclusions about him? Lowell chose a life at sea rather than join his father's company. He has always refused to carry opium on his ships. I believe these decisions cost him dearly.'

'In what way?'

'I can't tell you any more than that.'

'Lucy, *please*. Surely you must have heard something?'

'Only gossip at family gatherings. If Lowell wants you to know he'll tell you himself.'

'He won't,' Susanna murmured in despair. 'He doesn't talk to me any more.' She turned blindly away before Lucy could ask questions for which she had no answers.

15 April. Lowell accepted my apology. But nothing has changed. I don't know what to do.

Staring at the words she had just written, blurred now by tears, Susanna closed her journal.

'Ah, there you are.' Meredith emerged from

the companionway. Her eyes had a fevered brilliance. 'I wondered where you'd got to. I don't seem to have seen you for such a long time.'

The reminder that they had spoken less than an hour ago dried on Susanna's tongue as she watched her cousin make her way to the shade of the awning. The ship was stable on an almost calm sea, yet Meredith clung and stumbled and lurched as if ... *as if she couldn't feel her feet on the deck.*

An image of the almost empty chloral hydrate bottle flashed across Susanna's mind. Fear for her cousin cramped her stomach.

'This heat is terribly draining,' Meredith's normally crisp diction was slurred. 'It makes me quite dizzy. I've had a headache for three days now. Lucy insisted I come up for a breath of fresh air. I think I'd have been better lying down. I love my sister dearly, but she does fuss. And always about the wrong things. Still, it's not long now. Only another two weeks till we reach Shanghai. I must admit I'll be glad to be back on dry land. This has not been a pleasant experience. In fact, if I'd realized—' She cut herself off with a glassy smile. 'But I mustn't complain. God wouldn't give us burdens heavier than we can bear. *Would He?*'

'No, of course not,' Susanna lied.

'One must be worthy, you see, to undertake ... only I've felt so inadequate.' Taking a deep breath she squared her shoulders, widening the grotesque smile. 'But I'm much better now.' She looked around vaguely. 'And what have you been doing with yourself all these weeks? I hope you've kept busy. The Devil makes work for idle hands.'

29 April. Only a few hours now and we will be at our destination. The blue waters of the Pacific have turned thick and cloudy.

'It's mud,' Tom Binney explained, 'washed off the plains bordering the Yangtze. That's why they call this the Yellow Sea.' As officer of the watch he was standing near the compass. Behind him two able seamen clung to the wheel, holding the schooner on course as she raced forward on the heavy swell.

There were other vessels in sight; steamships puffing black smoke from their funnels, square-riggers twice and three times the size of the schooner, and odd-looking craft with high square sterns and two masts, each supporting a huge slatted sail.

Susanna clutched her journal. Though Lowell's coolness and distance were torture she dreaded reaching Shanghai.

Chapter Twenty-Six

As the schooner sailed up Woosung River towards Shanghai, Susanna felt chilled to her soul in spite of her thick cloak of heavy brown wool.

She gazed listlessly at the stilt-legged birds

stalking about on the mud banks thrusting long curved bills into the soft yellow-grey ooze. Above a line of debris marking the high tide, houses of mud brick roofed with straw clustered close together.

As the schooner rounded a bend the clouds parted to reveal a sky the colour of cornflowers. Sunshine streamed down on a scene of such vitality that her misery was momentarily eclipsed by awe.

'Some sight, isn't it?' Tom Binney grinned. The river ahead was crowded. Huge five-masted barques rode at anchor in mid-stream. Smart steamers with tall funnels chugged towards landing stages. Schooners, mat-sailed lorchas, sampans, water-taxis and junks with large eyes painted on the bow for good luck all wove complex patterns across the teeming water.

Susanna's nose wrinkled at the pervasive smell of sewage, fish, rotting vegetables, incense, smoke, and hot cooking oil.

Shallow barges containing bulging sacks of grain were poled along by lean men with leathery skin and eyes slitted against the sun's glare. Above gnarled bare feet, they wore knee-length ragged trousers, baggy wrap-over jackets held in place by a knotted sash, and shallow conical hats.

A narrow houseboat, propelled by a single long oar, crossed almost under the schooner's bows. Small round faces thatched with straight black hair peeped out from the crude cabin made of woven mats fastened over a half-hoop bamboo frame. The instant they saw Susanna the children hid behind their mother who squatted by a wooden tub, washing clothes.

Lucy emerged from the companionway her drawn face brightening. 'Goodness me, what a view.' Meredith followed with obvious reluctance.

Before them lay the panoramic sweep of the British Settlement, breathtaking in its grandeur.

'Falmouth has nothing like this,' Susanna murmured, gazing in awe at majestic stone buildings several storeys high and topped by clock towers and cupolas. 'Oh Lucy, I wish Will was here.' She spoke without thinking, the words born of loneliness and immediately regretted. Pressing her arm Lucy said nothing.

'What's that dreadful smell?' Meredith grimaced.

'Er—fertilizer,' Susanna replied. 'Apparently the Chinese spread all animal and human waste on the fields to enrich the soil and produce better crops.'

Meredith groaned. 'Did you have to tell me?'

As well as banks, hotels, and offices belonging to important trading companies they could see private houses surrounded by gardens full of spring flowers and blossoming trees. Behind these loomed the larger shapes of two churches.

'What's that?' Lucy pointed to a building with a long elegant façade and wide lawns.

'The British Consulate,' Tom Binney answered from the compass. 'They hold all the mail there. Coming by steamer it arrives before we do.'

Lucy sighed. 'We're here at last.' Meredith's face betrayed momentary terror. Lucy patted her hand. 'It'll be all right.'

Would it? Susanna wondered, and was immediately swamped by guilt. There would be difficulties enough without her anticipating more. She scanned the deck, her heart lurching as she saw Lowell's broad back.

Talking to the mate he glanced at his watch then indicated the holds. Fighting an anguish that was almost unbearable she gripped the jade medallion and turned away to stare at a waterfront humming with activity.

All along the granite-faced embankment, jetties and wharfs jutted out into the river. At some the boats were moored three or four abreast. Labourers scurried to and fro like columns of ants loading and unloading.

The noise was incredible. Everyone shouted and she heard several different languages. Steamer sirens wailed and hooted. Adding to the din were the squeals of winches, shrieking gulls, and the rumble of wheelbarrows along the wooden landing stages.

'I think we should go below and make sure all our baggage is ready to be put ashore,' Lucy said. 'Lowell will have a great deal to do. We mustn't delay him from his own business.' Unable to speak, Susanna gave a brief nod and led the way down.

Half an hour later, the schooner made fast, she stood to one side as her cousins said goodbye to Lowell Hawke. Her mind felt like a creature trapped, hurling itself against the bars of a cage, desperately seeking a way out. There had to be a key, something that would make it all right. But she didn't know what it was. So she bit the inside of her lip, tasting blood, as she waited to utter the one word she would have given anything not to say.

'Goodbye, Susanna.'

She couldn't meet his eye. Couldn't allow him to see. With lowered lashes she took his hand for the second and last time, felt briefly its warm strength and the loss as he released it. Swallowing the painful stiffness in her throat she forced the word out. 'Goodbye.' A pathetic sound, little more than a croak. But it didn't matter because he was already turning towards the companionway.

After three months on board ship it took a while to adjust to solid ground under her feet. Before she reached the end of the jetty her head was pounding. There were so many people. Well-dressed men strode to and fro along the wide jetties, busy and purposeful as they issued orders to staff trotting alongside. She heard American and German accents as well as clipped British tones.

Two white-turbanned Indians took leave of each other. One wore a tunic-style coat of emerald green and baggy white trousers. The other was resplendent in crimson. Bowing over hands pressed palm-together the one in red said a few words. Susanna had heard them before from a Friend who had travelled with the first official delegation to India. It was a proverb which roughly translated meant *providence will provide.* The other raised his eyes heavenward and sighed.

'*Lucy,*' Meredith hissed behind her. 'Why are there so many Chinese? I thought this was a British settlement.'

Looking around Susanna realized she was right. The labourers unloading the ships were Chinese, so were the Aladdin-hatted coolies pulling rickshaws and strange-looking wheel-barrows which had a single large wheel, two long handles, and a flat platform. Some were laden with goods, others carried Chinese women and children who sat on the platform with their legs dangling over the edge. She glimpsed one piled high with lantern-shaped cages, each containing a small bird.

Clerks wearing high-necked, knee-length tunics over wide trousers continually kow-towed as if hinged at the waist. Sleek *compradors*—identified by Tom Binney as the treasurers, accountants and secretaries to western businessmen—glided by with half-shaved heads and long pigtails, dressed in rich silks embroidered with Chinese characters.

At the end of the jetty they stepped on to a wide, flagged pavement edging a broad road thronged with rickshaws, hansoms, and gleaming two-horse carriages attended by coachmen and grooms in colourful livery.

The crewmen piled their luggage into the nearest cab on the rank, sketched quick salutes accompanied by cheery grins, and turned back to the ship rubbing their hands at the prospect of a run ashore.

'Mr Hudson Taylor's residence, please,' Meredith directed the cab driver. When he shrugged, his expression uncomprehending, she flung up her hands. 'This is ridiculous. The man doesn't even understand English.'

Lucy leaned forward. 'The China Inland Mission?' she enunciated carefully.

With no discernible change of expression the driver clicked his tongue urging the horse into a trot and turned left into a wide road with shops and offices on either side. Some proclaimed their ownership and business with elegantly lettered signs in English. Others had flags and banners painted with Chinese characters fluttering from long poles. Beneath these, hanging in the open doorways, hung beautifully crafted bamboo cages.

Though the birds inside trilled and sang Susanna found the sight heartrending and looked quickly away, only to be awed by the brocaded satins and silk taffetas of European ladies promenading in the afternoon sunshine.

She had never seen such rich fabrics, or such glorious shades of mauve, buttercup yellow, pearl grey, rose, turquoise and periwinkle blue. There wasn't a crinoline to be seen. Every woman was wearing the new fashionable bustle, the overskirt caught up at the sides to reveal toning or contrasting flounces and frills.

Amid the feminine finery naval uniforms emblazoned with gold braid rubbed shoulders with superbly cut frock coats. Silk scarves, silver-topped canes, the flash of a diamond cravat-pin, and ruby cufflinks gleaming on snowy linen like drops of blood proclaimed their wearers men of substance.

As the cab drew up outside a gate Susanna looked out. 'I don't think he understood you, Lucy. According to the board this is the *Friends'* Mission.'

The cab driver looked over his shoulder pointing to the house. 'You go.'

'This isn't where we're supposed to be,' Meredith moaned. 'Why has he brought us here?'

'Excuse me,' Lucy called to a man crossing the courtyard. He hesitated then came towards them.

He made no move to open the gate but spoke through it. 'Can I help you?'

'We are missionaries,' Meredith announced. 'We've just arrived from England and we're looking for the China Inland Mission.'

'You've come to the wrong place.'

'We know that,' Meredith snapped, 'the driver doesn't unders—'

'Hush, dear,' Lucy cut in quietly. 'The driver must have brought us here for a reason.' She turned back to the man. 'Could you tell us where we might find Mr Hudson Taylor?'

'I'm afraid I have no idea.'

'You must have heard of him,' Meredith protested. 'Doctor James Hudson Taylor? The founder of the China Inland Mission.'

'I know *who* he is,' the man interrupted, 'but I can't tell you *where* he is. Since his sad loss—you are aware that his wife died?'

Lucy nodded. 'A tragedy indeed.'

He clicked his tongue. 'A miserable business. Anyway, he might well have gone upriver to Anqing. I believe that is his furthest outpost.'

'What about the CIM Mission here in Shanghai?' Lucy pressed.

'There isn't one. Not any more.'

As Meredith's clutching fingers tightened on her arm Lucy stroked the white knuckles. 'I don't understand. Why isn't there?'

'The main reason was the change of government in Britain last year. Hudson Taylor's part in the Yangchow riot gave Lord Clarendon the perfect excuse to try and disband the CIM.'

'It hasn't succeeded?' Lucy's face puckered in anxiety.

'No, they won't get rid of him that easily. I don't agree with his methods, but one can't help admiring his courage. He still has missions at Hangchow and Chinkiang as well as the one at Anqing. You'll have to try one of those.'

'Could you possibly allow us to stay here for a few days?' Lucy said. 'Just until we can arrange transport.'

'Do you have letters of accreditation?'

'Well, no. You see, we—'

'Oh dear, I should have guessed: more amateurs.' His manner hardened to barely-concealed annoyance. 'I can't help you. We only accept missionaries sponsored by an official body at home. This isn't an hotel, you know.'

Puce with indignation Meredith leaned forward. 'Now just a minute my good man—'

As Lucy grabbed one of her arms Susanna

caught the other and drew her back against the seat.

'Perhaps you'd be kind enough to tell me where I might find Mr Thomas Hanbury?' Lucy enquired politely.

'In Italy,' the man replied. 'He left Shanghai over a year ago.' With an abrupt nod he turned and walked swiftly away.

'What are we going to do?' Meredith wailed. 'Everything's going wrong. *Do* something, Lucy. This is all your fault. You would insist we came.'

Flinching as if from a slap Lucy swallowed audibly. 'I'm so sorry, Meredith. Please don't be upset.'

'Why shouldn't I be upset? We're in a strange country where we don't know anyone. Mr Hanbury might have helped us but he's gone. There's no China Inland Mission. Nothing is the way I expected—'

'Perhaps,' Susanna interrupted, realizing Meredith was on the brink of hysteria, 'the best thing we can do right now is find an hotel. At least we'd have a roof over our heads and a bed for the night while we work out our next move.'

'Oh what a good idea.' Lucy flashed Susanna a brief smile of gratitude.

'I don't know why you didn't think of it before,' Meredith complained.

Two hours later, having enjoyed her first hot bath in three months, Susanna sat at the dressing-table of her third-floor room overlooking the waterfront, the brush in her hand momentarily forgotten as she stared at her reflection. She still found it difficult to relate to the image she saw: wide, green eyes, skin unfashionably golden and glowing from exposure to sun and sea air, mahogany-dark hair tumbling over her shoulders springing into curls as it dried.

Over clean underwear she wore a plain white cotton wrapper fastened around her slim waist with a tie-belt. A few items from her now-empty trunk lay on the bed. The rest had been taken by the chambermaid to have the salt water and creases of the three-month voyage removed. Through the interconnecting door which stood ajar she heard Lucy helping Meredith into bed.

'I shan't sleep, Lucy. My nerves are in shreds. What are we going to do?'

'Put our faith in God,' Lucy answered simply. 'He brought us safely across thousands of miles of ocean. He won't desert us now. Try to sleep. When you wake we'll go downstairs and have a meal.'

'Sleep? How can I possibly sleep? I've got a terrible headache.'

'That will go. Just close your eyes. That's right. Remember all the plans we made back at Lansdowne Road? We didn't come all this way to be stopped by a little hiccup.' There was a mumble and the creaking of bedsprings.

Susanna turned on the padded stool to see Lucy back in, carefully pull the door almost shut, then lean against the wall and cover her face with her hands.

'Lucy?'

Forcing a smile Lucy crossed the room to sit

on the edge of Susanna's bed. 'I'm all right. A little tired that's all.'

'I don't know how you stand it.'

'She's my sister.' Lucy straightened. 'Now, what to do next? Whether we go south to Hangchow or up-river to Anqing it's going to deplete our financial reserves. We really can't afford to stay here in the hotel more than two nights, three at the most.'

'Lucy, stop fretting and get some rest while you can.' Snores issued from the adjacent room.

'What about you?'

Rising to her feet Susanna discarded her wrapper and took down the one dress the maid had left. 'I'm going to the British Consulate.' Raking the brush with swift determined strokes through her almost-dry hair she coiled the thick mass into a neat bun on the nape of her neck and secured it with pins.

'There's sure to be someone there who can advise us. Besides, we might have some mail.'

Lucy started to get up. 'Maybe I'd better come with you ...'

Susanna gently pressed her down again. 'What if Meredith should wake and find us both gone? I promise I'll take care.'

Sinking back, Lucy stretched out on the counterpane. 'If you're sure. I must admit this isn't quite what I envisaged.'

Turning away Susanna felt in her purse for the medallion. She looked at the gleaming pink jade, stroking its carved surface between her fingers. The Chinese believed it had magical

311

properties. Would they work for her? She slipped the cord over her head and tucked it down her bodice. Then, swinging her cloak over her shoulders, she took a last look at Lucy, whose eyes had already closed, and quietly let herself out.

There were few women on the busy approach to the consulate and all were accompanied by husbands or relatives. Some eyed her then looked away, others ignored her. Did the fact that she was alone make her somehow suspect? Surely it was obvious, if only from her drab, unfashionable clothes, that she was a newcomer in need of help?

Inside the elegant building with its ornate ceilings and tall windows she waited her turn among the people queuing for attention, aware of being studied and assessed. In response to glares of disapproval she simply lowered her eyes, smarting and bewildered.

When eventually she reached the polished wood counter, two men, one on either side of her, tried to claim the harassed clerk's attention.

'Excuse me.' Despite fiery cheeks her voice was firm. 'I was next.' She heard shocked murmurs, sensed curious critical eyes.

'Mail, is it?' The clerk was brisk, already half-turning to the wooden frame covering most of the wall behind him. 'Name?'

'Oh ... er ... Elliot and Braithwaite,' Susanna stammered.

Reaching up to two pigeon holes, the clerk took down several envelopes, thrust them at her, and turned away.

'Wait,' she called after him. 'Please, I need some advice.' But the clerk had already been cornered by one of the men who had tried to push in front of her. The other counter staff were equally busy. Susanna found herself edged out of the way. Overhearing snatches of conversation she realized many of those present were businessmen whose ventures were suffering through Chinese refusal to observe conditions set out in the treaties. The consular staff seemed able to do little.

'Diplomacy!' the irate man barked. 'While politicians talk, we're losing money and the Chinese are getting away with murder. They're laughing at us. Forget *talk*, what we need is a show of strength. Send the navy up-river with a few gunboats, that would soon teach them.' Murmurs of assent rippled through the crowded room.

To her left a door opened. The Indian in the emerald-green coat they had passed on the jetty was ushered out by an official obviously senior to those manning the counter.

'... no bail on such a serious charge,' the official warned.

'But what about my business? I am needing my secretary most badly. He is English. A gentlemanly person. I tell you he did not do this thing.'

'I'm sorry.' The official was firm. 'But I'm afraid your staff problem is something you will have to sort out for yourself.'

Susanna's mind raced. Just a short while ago she had wondered if the medallion's magic would work for her. Could this be the answer?

The official was already disappearing back through the door. Sighing and shaking his head the Indian turned towards the exit.

God helps them that help themselves. John-Henry's words echoed in her mind. But not believing in God any more she had only herself to rely on. Lucy was exhausted. And Meredith ... she didn't know what to think about Meredith.

She might never have an opportunity like this again. If she let it pass for lack of courage ...

'Excuse me.' She stepped in front of him, forcing him to stop. The rustle of disapproving whispers brought a painful flush to her cheeks. Accosting a strange man was brazen behaviour no matter how urgent the reason. She took a deep breath, her heart banging hard against her ribs. 'Do forgive me, but I couldn't help overhearing. My name is Susanna Elliot. I—' She flicked the tip of her tongue over bone-dry lips. 'I wonder if I might be of assistance? Just temporarily, until your difficulty is resolved?'

The Indian gazed at her in astonishment. 'You? But—'

'I am experienced in accounting and book-keeping. For a short period I ran my father's cargo-broking office. He is Samuel Elliot of Falmouth. I've also spent some time in the office of my uncle's ship-yard.' As his expression changed from astonishment to uncertainty desperation drove her on. 'Do you know Captain Lowell Hawke?'

The Indian nodded. 'Yes, of course, but—'

'We, my cousins and I, have recently come from England on Captain Hawke's ship. I am sure'—she crossed her fingers, her hand hidden by her cloak—'he will vouch for me. And no doubt you have heard of my kinsman, Captain Charles Elliot, who was British Superintendent of Trade in Canton?' She ran out of breath.

'Indeed you are having most impressive connections, Miss Elliot, but—'

'More important than my connections is my ability. Believe me, sir,' her chin rose. 'I can run your office. And it appears you need someone immediately which would suit me very well.'

After a long hesitation he beamed, his teeth very white in his brown face. 'I think, Miss Elliot, that the gods of good fortune have smiled on me today. I am Soman Prakash from Trivandrum.' He placed his palms together and bowed over them in the traditional Hindu greeting.

She offered him her hand shutting her ears to the shocked buzz behind her. Indicating the door he gestured politely for her to precede him. 'I am exporting jade and silk, and importing spices, ivory and cotton. Please come and meet my wife. She is waiting at my office. It is a short walk only.'

She had a job. Her heart was beating so fast she felt dizzy.

'What is the matter, Miss Elliot? You are looking most astonished, isn't it?'

'Forgive me, Mr Prakash. I *am* surprised, and very grateful. Where I come from a woman wanting to do this type of work faces

315

considerable difficulties.'

'Ah. But we are from Kerala State. My wife is belonging to Nair caste. She is very strong and independent. When she is not giving birth to our children my wife is greatly helpful to me in the business. She is wanting English secretary, not Chinese. She thinks is better for our business when lady customers are talking with English secretary.' He beamed. 'She is very clever woman.' He stopped, indicating a stone-faced building. 'This is godown.' Seeing her bewilderment he explained, 'Godown is what you are calling warehouse. The office is here at the front.'

Karnala Prakash was small and plump, her pregnancy barely visible beneath a fuchsia-pink sari edged with gold. Her lustrous black hair was braided into a thick plait which hung almost to her waist. She wore gold in her ears and nose, and the caste mark on her forehead was the same colour as her sari.

As she listened to her husband her brown eyes flickered swiftly over Susanna, then she smiled.

Releasing the breath she had been holding, Susanna smiled back. 'When would you like me to start?'

'Can you be coming tomorrow morning?' When she nodded he waved his hands. 'That is most excellent.' His wife touched his sleeve and murmured something. He looked momentarily sheepish. 'My apologies, Miss Elliot. You accept Mexican dollars? Most Europeans prefer. Shanghai currency very confusing.'

316

Gulping, Susanna nodded. 'Mexican dollars will be fine.'

Soman and Kamala Prakash both put their palms together and bowed. On impulse Susanna did the same, and repeated the proverb. The couple exchanged a look of surprise and delight.

'Indeed so, Miss Elliot,' Soman Prakash beamed. 'Providence has provided most generously.'

Clutching the mail and Soman Prakash's card Susanna hurried back to the hotel.

Chapter Twenty-Seven

Lowell found it hard to conceal his shock; his father had aged twenty years in the last eight months.

Once well built and handsome he had shrivelled to a husk of his former self. He made no attempt to get up, remaining hunched in the high-backed armchair at one side of the fireplace. He picked with claw-like hands at the rug covering his knees. His face was greyish yellow, the bones prominent beneath stretched skin. The once-luxuriant mane of golden hair had grown sparse and straggled over a collar at least two sizes too big. But illness had not mellowed him; despite the web of lines about his eyes and deep grooves on either side of his mouth, his cold gaze was as ruthless and determined as ever.

317

'Of course I know what's wrong: I'm not a fool.' He shifted slightly and this involuntary betrayal of weakness made him even more testy. 'I've seen doctors. There's nothing they can do.'

'Not here, maybe.' For the first time Lowell saw past the tyrant of his youth to the damaged, sick and lonely man his father had become. 'But back in England—'

'Don't be ridiculous.' Joseph Hawke's interruption held more weariness than irritability.

'A steamer could get you there in six weeks.'

'I wouldn't last the journey,' was the flat reply. One thin hand crawled across the gross swelling around his middle. 'It feels like wolves are gnawing at my vitals.'

'Has the doctor given you something for the pain?'

Joseph Hawke raised his head, his pale watery eyes glittering. 'Doctors,' he spat in contempt. 'What do they know?' With a jerk of his head he indicated the small table beside his chair on which several articles were covered by a fine linen cloth. 'I have my own remedy.' He bared yellow teeth in a gloating smile that raised the hair on the back of Lowell's neck.

Lifting one corner of the cloth Lowell saw a smoker's lamp and a box of lucifer matches, a small block of black resin, and a porcelain dish half-full of ashes. Also, incongruously, there was a jar of honey and a spoon. Carefully expressionless, he gestured. 'Why the honey?'

Joseph Hawke frowned impatiently. 'Black smoke burns the mouth. I find honey soothing.

Never mind that now. I've got a job for you.'

Lowell replaced the cloth. His father's use of the Chinese term for opium, plus the bowl of ashes ready for mixing with the resin, confirmed he had already reached the stage of addiction where the pure drug alone was not powerful enough to satisfy his craving. Lowell recalled the old Chinese saying: If you want revenge on your enemy it is not necessary to strike him, or take him to law: simply introduce him to opium.

But if it dulled the pain.

'Are you listening to me?' Joseph demanded, as Lowell stared sightlessly out of the window. 'I want you to find your brother and bring him home.'

Lowell didn't move. 'Do you have any idea where he is?'

'He said he was going prospecting for gold at Anqing,' Joseph sneered. 'Bloody fool. Anyway, I want you to find him.'

'Why?' Lowell didn't love his father. That had died long ago. But seeing him now—a shell of the man he had once been, destroyed by ambition, grief, and an unappeasable lust for vengeance—Lowell was surprised by the depth of his pity.

'I'm dying. You owe it to me.'

'I didn't mean why do you want me to find him, I meant why do you want him back?'

'To run the business of course,' Joseph snapped. 'Damn fool question.'

Lowell turned to face his father. 'Even if I do find him, which is by no means certain, what makes you think he'll even listen? He left because you destroyed his confidence. Why would he want to come back?'

'For the money.' Joseph's eyes gleamed with malicious pleasure. 'If he comes back to Shanghai the business is his. Tell him that.'

'He may not come,' Lowell warned.

'Yes he will,' Joseph said with absolute certainty. 'He'll come because he likes the easy life. It's what he's used to. Going off prospecting for gold was just a pathetic stab at proving his independence. But his place is here. He knows it, and he knows I do too. I'll lay odds he's already bored and looking for an excuse to return to civilization. Oh yes,' he nodded, 'he'll come.'

Lowell was curious. 'What makes you think I'll give him the message?'

His eyes bright with mockery, Joseph gave a cackling laugh. 'You'll do it because it's my dying wish. And because if you don't I'll leave it to you. With all you've got on your conscience you'd hate that.'

Lowell fought his anger. 'I have a cargo for Kewkiang. I'll stop at Anqing, but I can't stay longer than a day.'

'How long before you leave?'

'A week, possibly longer. It depends.'

'All right.' Joseph's face suddenly contorted, his eyes losing focus as his body tensed. Sweat formed on his pale forehead, standing out in great drops. With a shaking hand he pushed the cloth aside and reached for the pipe. 'Now get out.'

Entering the company office provoked a flood of memories. Lowell brushed them aside like so many flies. They no longer hurt. And with that realization came another: he could not go on as he was. He owned a house but had no home; he was married but had no wife. His voyages had gained him a reputation for bravery and daring but he knew it to be hollow, for without fear to overcome, courage couldn't exist. Life, death, he hadn't much cared which side up the coin landed. He still didn't. But things had to change.

He'd known a lot of women; many more beautiful, all more sophisticated, but none had affected him like Susanna Elliot. Sending her away had been the hardest thing he'd ever done. She would haunt him for ever. But though she deserved better than him he deserved better than this.

'So, honoured sir, it is important these matters are addressed.' Where the *compradore's* calm tones had failed to penetrate Lowell's introspection, his choice of words succeeded.

Focusing on the suave, cultured man who provided the link between the suppliers from whom the company bought and the merchants and wholesalers to whom Hawke & Son sold, Lowell pressed his fingertips briefly to his forehead. 'Forgive me, Tau. My thoughts were ... elsewhere. Outstanding accounts, you said?'

The *compradore* bowed. Beneath the pigtail that fell halfway down his back, he wore a gown of burgundy silk with a round upstanding collar and full sleeves over wide-bottomed trousers and black cloth shoes with thick white-edged soles. Now almost fifty years old he had been with Hawke & Son for as long as Lowell could remember. Without Tau holding everything together over the past year Hawke & Son would have collapsed.

'Polite letters of reminder have been sent, but from one there has been no response.'

'Which merchant is it?' Lowell held out his hand for a copy of the account.

'Soman Prakash, honoured sir.'

Lowell nodded. 'I'll call on him myself.'

'Goodness me, Susanna!' Lucy's astonishment gave way to uncertain laughter. 'You have quite taken my breath away.'

'I surprised myself,' Susanna admitted frankly. 'But Mr Prakash was most courteous and his wife was charming. He said our meeting could not have been more timely.'

'I'm not at all sure this is wise,' Meredith fretted, from the bed where she was propped up on pillows. Her thin hair fell in a narrow braid over one shoulder of her voluminous white nightgown. She fiddled with a button, her face anxious.

Susanna tried not to let her disappointment show. A few words of approval would have meant so much.

'What you did must have taken great courage.' Lucy touched Susanna's shoulder, adding quietly, 'I can only assume there wasn't time to come back and discuss your idea with us first.'

Susanna shook her head. 'It all happened so quickly. No one at the consulate would listen. They were all too busy. So when I overheard Mr Prakash it was too good an opportunity to miss. Perhaps I shouldn't have ... I certainly shocked everyone. But they aren't going to help us, are they? And we do need the money.'

'We do indeed,' Lucy sighed. 'It's just that—and please don't take this amiss, Susanna —but as new recruits to a mission we are particularly vulnerable to criticism. And that could all too easily undermine the work we have come to do.'

Susanna's hand flew to her mouth. 'Oh, I never thought—'

'Well, what's done is done, so let's not waste time worrying about it. Look, you read your letters while I help Meredith dress. Then we'll all go down and have some tea.'

'Can't I stay here, Lucy?' Meredith whimpered. 'I'm still awfully tired. You could have mine sent up. I really don't think I'm ready—'

Fighting the surge of impatience by reminding herself how much more difficult it must be for Lucy, Susanna returned to her own room.

She opened her father's letter first. It wasn't very long. After thanking God for her mother's improving health, he had written a few sentences deploring the Thurstan family. Apparently Mrs Thurstan and her daughters had been seen without bonnets. As she read Susanna's hand rose automatically to her own bare head. Perhaps if men had been forced to endure the restricting discomfort they would be less quick to condemn.

323

He ended with the hope that they were all well then added a reminder that it was her duty to repay her cousins' generosity by working hard in whatever capacity they might require.

Folding the letter Susanna speculated about his reaction when he learned that, to give her cousins precisely the support he advocated, she had found work with an Indian merchant doing the very same job he had refused her back in Falmouth. Might it be wiser not to tell him? But that was cowardice. She had done nothing to be ashamed of. All she wanted was to show that women were capable of living independently of men's well-intentioned but smothering paternalism.

Seating herself in the cushioned cane chair by the window she opened the second letter. It was from her sister and ran to several pages.

'*Mr Webber's business has failed,*' Frances wrote in her neat script. '*He was taken ill with what appeared at first to be just a bilious attack. But when his condition worsened, the doctor diagnosed degeneration of the liver. He was confined to bed for several weeks and during that time the bank foreclosed. We do not yet know whether his bankruptcy means he will be disowned by the Friends.*'

Susanna pictured Mr Webber as she had seen him at family gatherings, in a world of his own, neither overtly drunk nor entirely sober. He had always seemed to her a *sad* man. She read on.

'*Mrs Webber has taken the shame of financial ruin very hard and is staying with relatives in Devon. Mr Webber is recovering but remains frail.*'

He no longer drinks and is a most appreciative patient, always grateful for any little kindness. We have begun to know one another quite well. And though I never sought or expected it he has taken me into his confidence. He believes he has always been a disappointment to Richard's mother. Apparently she had certain expectations which were not fulfilled. And while he is pleased to see Richard doing well, they have never been close. What I am about to write now is most painful and embarrassing.'

Picturing Frances on the sofa by the fire, her face tear-stained as she unknowingly tore holes in her handkerchief, Susanna guessed what was to come.

'Richard was seen in Quay Hill with a woman of low morals. The person who saw him—I don't know who it was—reported the matter to Father. As an Elder his duty in such circumstances is to appoint Visitors to call upon the transgressor and warn him about his future conduct. But it put us all in a terrible dilemma. Can you imagine the shame? How could I attend Meeting, knowing everyone would be talking about my husband? I begged Father to show compassion, for me if not for Richard. And with Mother's help I prevailed upon him to respond, not as an Elder of the Society, but as Richard's father-in-law. This he did and reprimanded Richard most severely. So the matter remained within the family. As Mrs Webber was away we did not tell her. I would not be writing of it now except I wanted you to know that the difficulty we spoke of before you left has been overcome.

When I learned what Richard had done I am

ashamed to say that serenity deserted me. I was so angry and upset, for Mother and Father as well as for myself, that when he begged me for punishment I needed no great urging to oblige. As a result he was at last able to do his duty as a husband. I confess I find the business wearisome and cannot understand men's fondness for it. But it appears this is the price women must pay in order to have a husband. So, with the problem now resolved, we need never speak of it again.'

Holding the letter in her lap Susanna gazed down on to the waterfront. *Poor poor Frances.*

Entering his house Lowell surprised Marjorie crossing the cool spacious hall. As he dropped his bag she came towards him, her face alight with pleasure.

'Welcome home, my dear. I'm so pleased to see you.' Taking his hands she kissed him lightly on the cheek then linked her arm through his. 'Come and sit down. I'll order tea.' She led him towards the drawing-room. 'Have you visited your father yet?'

'I went straight from the ship,' Lowell said. 'Tau sent one of the clerks to the jetty so I was forewarned. But it was still a shock. I'd come to think of him as indestructible.'

Marjorie nodded sympathetically. 'I call on him every day or so. But you know your father. Illness may bring out the best in some people, unfortunately it has had the opposite effect on him.'

Summoned by the bell, a Chinese servant appeared. While Marjorie ordered tea Lowell

326

sank wearily on to the sofa. Resting his head against the crocheted antimacassar he watched Marjorie seat herself with studied grace in a chair opposite and carefully arrange her dress.

'You look well.' She had put on weight. Tight lacing beneath her cornflower-blue gown maintained the requisite hourglass shape, but her chiffon-swathed bosom was plumper and curve of her hip fuller and more rounded than he remembered. Spun-gold hair was drawn back from her rounded face with jewelled combs and piled high in a cascade of curls and ringlets. Her blue eyes, small pink mouth, and milk-and-roses complexion were not unattractive. But she looked more like a porcelain doll than a real woman.

Suddenly a different image filled his mind; wild, dark hair caught up in a rough knot, tendrils teased loose by the wind framing sun-gilded cheekbones, a nose dusted with freckles, soft lips untouched by salves and rouges, and emerald eyes a man might drown in.

An image so vivid, so *real*, that for an instant he couldn't breathe. Passing a hand across his eyes he focused on his wife. 'So.' He forced a smile. 'Apart from visiting my father what have you been doing to amuse yourself?' He needed a few moments to put such memories where they belonged—firmly in the past.

'There has been some excellent shooting this winter.' Hands neatly folded, Marjorie's head was angled in a manner that convinced whoever she was talking or listening to they were the sole focus of her interest. This little trick ensured her

327

welcome as a guest and enhanced her reputation as a hostess.

But he wasn't a guest, damn it. This was his house and he was her husband. He battled to remain calm. 'And the amateur dramatic society put on a most entertaining play a few weeks ago. Of course, the main topic of conversation at the moment is the Shanghai Cup. Franklin Beresford is favourite to win the breeder's trophy. His ponies have run very well this season.'

She glanced round as the tea arrived. 'Thank you, Chang.' Setting the tray down the servant left, bowing as he closed the door. 'Franklin's giving a party at the Steeplechase Club and we're invited.' She set out the cups and saucers. 'I'm so glad you're back in time. You'll be able to catch up on all the news.'

Leaning forward he rested his elbows on his parted knees and raked both hands through his rumpled hair. Feeling it stiff with salt reminded him of—'When is the party?'

'This evening. That's why I'm so glad you—'

'No. Not tonight.'

'But you enjoy Franklin's parties.' Her surprise was genuine. She passed the cup and saucer to him, a faint frown crumpling her alabaster forehead. 'You've always said you glean more information in two hours with Franklin than—'

'Marjorie, I've been at sea for three months.'

'Exactly.' She gazed at him in bewilderment. 'I'd have thought you'd welcome the chance to enjoy some intelligent and interesting conversation after being cooped up on the ship

328

for weeks on end with only the crew for company.'

'It wasn't like that. Not this time.' He couldn't stop the images tumbling through his mind: Susanna at the table engrossed in her medical books, her head propped on a slim workworn hand; Susanna bent over a bucket, the sleeves of her drab wool dress rolled up, using her willowy body to shield whatever she was washing from the crew's gaze; sitting on the hatch cover writing her journal or watching the sea, her gaze faraway, her lovely face inexpressibly sad. 'I had three passengers.'

Marjorie's eyes widened. 'Really? You don't normally.'

'No,' he rubbed the back of his neck feeling the tension like an iron band across the base of his skull. 'These were unusual circumstances.' *He had to expunge every memory, every emotion, every response. There was no place for Susanna Elliot in his life. He had duties, commitments. And she—she had her whole life ahead of her.* He looked up at his wife. 'Marjorie?' His voice was hoarse with desperation. 'Come to bed with me.'

Her recoil slopped tea over the rim of her cup into the saucer. In any other circumstances he might have laughed. Her face suffused with colour. But it wasn't the rosy flush of shyness that so often warmed Susanna's golden skin. This was a surge of shock and fear. It drained away leaving her ashen. With visibly trembling hands she set the fine porcelain carefully down on the tray.

'I th-thought we had an understanding.'

329

Uncoiling like a spring he leapt to his feet and paced the room, unnerved by the eruption of savage fury inside him. 'Did you? *I've* certainly been understanding.' He bent down his face only inches from hers. *'For five years.* Isn't it your turn now? Aren't I entitled to a little understanding from you?' He straightened up, pushing one hand through his hair in a gesture that betrayed helplessness and frustration. 'Damn it, woman, I've been away two thirds of a year. I've been at sea over three months. Is it so remarkable to want to sleep with my wife?'

'P-please, L-Lowell, c-calm yourself' Her tone mingled chiding and entreaty. Tremors shook her as she wiped her palms over her corseted stomach. 'You have been in the house less than an hour. I am well aware you have been away for eight months. You must allow me time to adjust. I—I believed we had reached an accommodation over this matter. Now s-suddenly you wish to change everything.'

'Marjorie,' Lowell forced himself to speak quietly. 'This can't go on. You must see a doctor.'

'I did,' she whispered.

His gaze sharpened. 'What? When?'

She looked away. 'A-about a year ago. It—it was an extremely difficult interview. I told him I loved you and wanted to be a proper wife. But when I tried to explain my ... difficulty he grew impatient. He said I wasn't expected to *enjoy* ...' She broke off, the motion of her hands betraying fear and distaste. Lowell felt despair envelop him like a shroud. 'But as your wife I had a duty to you. He said I should concentrate on the thought that my acquiescence would, in the fullness of time, be rewarded by motherhood.'

'Grit your teeth and think of babies?' Lowell exploded. 'God almighty! The man's a complete fool.'

Marjorie raised her head, her features slack with relief. 'Oh Lowell.' Against her pallor the rouge on her cheeks stood out in bright mocking patches. 'I hoped you'd understand. I did try, but—'

'He's not the only doctor in the settlement. You could see someone else.'

Her mouth trembled. Tears spilled over and ran down her face leaving silvery tracks through the powder. 'I can't go through that again.' She swallowed. 'I know—we both know'—she was hesitant, voicing their unspoken agreement for the first time—'that over the years you have formed certain brief relationships. And I have always appreciated your discretion. Please, can't we simply go on as we are?'

He looked at her for a long moment. 'No, Marjorie, we can't.'

Chapter Twenty-Eight

Picking up the sheaf of invoices Susanna gazed at the rolls of freshly dyed silk piled on the wooden counter and reverently touched the nearest one. So fine it was almost transparent,

331

the dove-grey silk had a pearly luminescence and trickled through her fingers like water. She looked slowly around, enraptured.

Stretching from floor to ceiling the deep shelves were crammed. And so that customers could see the range of shades available the first few feet of each bolt had been pulled loose to waft and stir on the faintest draught in a shimmering rainbow-hued waterfall of silk.

At the sound of light footsteps and female voices on the walkway outside, she glanced towards the door leading through to the rest of the warehouse. Mr Prakash had told her to check the silk that had come from the dye company against his order and their invoice, then separate the rolls for export from those required by shops and private customers here in Shanghai. The remainder was to be placed on the shelf for ladies who came directly to the warehouse, anxious to have first choice of any new shades.

As the two women entered Susanna slipped behind the high-piled counter and peered through the door into the warehouse. The coolies were all busy, Mr Prakash nowhere in sight. He hadn't mentioned waiting on customers. But in his absence she had little alternative. Unaware of her presence the women were talking.

'... wonderful evening. I was surprised not to see them there. I know they were invited.'

'Things aren't all they might be in that marriage.'

'In what way? She's always seemed quite content.'

'She puts on a good show but that's all it is.'

'What makes you think so?'

'Because, my dear, I know for a fact he had an affair with Martha Kennington last year.'

'No!'

'It's the truth. Martha was dreadfully cut up when he ended it. Alfred took her down to Hong Kong to help her recover.'

'I thought they went because of the cholera outbreak.'

'That's what they told everyone. But I know differently. I'd tried to warn her. But she wouldn't listen.' The laugh was brief and bitter. 'Martha's a fool. We all know Lowell Hawke has a heart of solid ice.'

'You mean—you too? Oh Geraldine.'

Lowell? His name had the impact of a slap. Then shock forced all the breath from her lungs. *Lowell* married? She gripped the counter for support. Why hadn't he said? *Why should he? It was none of her business.* Even so— There was a pounding in her temples and her heart hammered against her ribs. Married. Of course. It explained so much.

'All water under the bridge, my dear. But you can't tell me Marjorie doesn't know. So why does she put up with it?' Her tone grew impatient. 'Where is the man? Ring the bell, Sarah.'

Straightening up Susanna lifted her chin and swallowed hard. The woman was wrong. Lowell Hawke was not a cold man. She had glimpsed in his eyes a warmth that reminded her of toast in front of a winter fire, summer sunshine—*stop*. Catching her lower lip between her teeth Susanna opened the door behind her and, to pretend she had just entered, closed it with audible firmness. Carefully expressionless she walked out behind the counter.

'Good morning.' She watched the women's eyes widen and their mouths drop as she anchored the sheaf of invoices under a roll of scarlet silk. 'How may I help you?'

'Where is Mr Prakash?' This was the one who had done most of the talking, the one whose caustic tone betrayed pique and relish at a rival's misery. The one called Geraldine. Her striking looks made it obvious why Lowell had found her attractive. Susanna cleared her throat as jealousy knifed deep.

'He's had to step out for a moment. Perhaps I might be able to help you?'

'That remains to be seen.' Geraldine looked down her straight nose. 'Who are you?' Her chic lemon jacket was adorned with dark-green braid in a mock-military style. The matching overskirt, gathered into a full bustle, was looped up with rosettes of green braid to reveal fluted frills of pale cream silk. Black hair, dressed in an intricate arrangement of curls, was crowned with a narrow lemon hat decorated with dark-green egret feathers.

Glancing down at her plain brown dress with its simple white collar and cuffs Susanna felt like a sparrow alongside a bird of paradise.

'What are you doing here?' the other woman enquired. Though less striking than Geraldine

334

she was prettier, softer-looking. She too was stylishly dressed in shades of bronze, gold, and cream. Though her tone was one of intrigued amusement her eyes reflected the same wariness and disapproval apparent at the consulate.

Susanna smiled politely. 'My name is Elliot. I am Mr Prakash's assistant.'

'His wife usually helps him in the shop,' Sarah observed.

'My dear, she's expecting again,' Geraldine turned to Susanna. 'So where is James?'

'I beg your pardon?'

'James Napley. Mr Prakash's secretary.' Geraldine tapped one elegantly-shod toe impatiently. 'He usually assists us when Mr Prakash is not available.'

It seemed James Napley's detention in custody was not yet public knowledge. 'As you see,' Susanna gestured, 'Mr Napley is not here this morning.' Impulsively she indicated the rolls of silk. 'These only arrived yesterday. You are the first to see them.'

Both women immediately switched their attention to the silk, fingering it, comparing colours, discussing possible outfits. Susanna assumed the self-effacing pose perfected during her youth and was quickly forgotten.

As she listened to the gossip she realized that despite their sighs about never having a moment to catch their breath, their lives were essentially frivolous, selfish, and without purpose.

For the first time she understood that though her father had carried his principles to suffocating extremes, without that discipline she might have been one of these women.

'I'll have fifteen yards of the crimson and another fifteen of the ivory.' Geraldine's imperious voice sliced through Susanna's thoughts, and she stepped forward to set the silk aside for cutting. 'Have you been in Shanghai long, Miss Elliot? I don't recall seeing you at church.'

'My cousins and I arrived only a few days ago.'

'Have you come to stay with relatives then?' Sarah enquired, determined not to be overlooked.

'No. My cousins are missionaries.'

Geraldine eyed Susanna shrewdly. 'You're not though. So why are you here?'

Suppressing anger at the women's impertinence Susanna gave a bland smile. 'As I said, I am assisting Mr Prakash.'

'Quite so,' Geraldine interrupted, tight-lipped. 'Perhaps I should point out that while we may be a long way from England we do pride ourselves on maintaining certain standards.'

Susanna's bemusement was genuine. 'I don't understand.'

'My dear, it just won't do.' Sarah leaned forward. 'One cannot blame Mr Prakash. Being of a different culture he cannot be expected to understand, but your cousins should have realized. A young unmarried Englishwoman working? And in a godown?' She shuddered. 'It's totally unacceptable.'

'I see.' Tempted to ask if having an affair with a married man constituted *acceptable* behaviour in Shanghai, Susanna resisted. The answer was

336

self-evident. 'Then perhaps you could advise me. What are we to live on if I stop working?'

Above her sympathetic smile Geraldine's dark eyes were as hard as pebbles. 'My advice? I think you should go back to wherever you came from.' She started towards the door. 'Have the silk delivered to my house. Come, Sarah.'

'Your name, madam?' Susanna's polite enquiry was met with a faint sigh of exasperation.

'Wilbury. Lady Wilbury. Mr Prakash has the address.'

'Honestly, Lucy, she was horrible. But apart from that I really enjoyed my day. It's all so interesting. Did you know—?' Susanna stopped, realizing Lucy's thoughts were elsewhere. It was just after nine o'clock. Meredith, who had somehow managed to procure a fresh bottle of chloral hydrate, was already sound asleep.

'What about you?' Susanna asked. 'How did you get on?'

'We visited several of the missions.' Lucy shook her head. 'I'm reluctant to condemn. After all we are newcomers and know nothing of the difficulties. But I have to say the missionaries here seem far more concerned with their own petty squabbles and rivalries than with saving souls. I gather they rarely leave the settlement. Certainly none want to be away overnight. Very few speak any of the Chinese dialects and even fewer know anything about Chinese culture and beliefs.'

Susanna pulled a wry face. 'It sounds as though they are in need of missionaries themselves to remind them why they came to China in the first place.'

Lucy shook her head. 'There is nothing for us here. We must go up-river to Anqing.'

Susanna stiffened. 'Why Anqing? And what if Mr Hudson Taylor is not there?'

'Anqing is Mr Hudson Taylor's furthest outpost. If he is there it will be a privilege to meet him and receive his blessing and guidance. If he is not, at least we can establish contact with his people and offer them our assistance.'

Susanna didn't want to go. She was enjoying her work at the godown. It was her first true taste of independence. As well as being a challenge—which was how she had chosen to view her encounter with Lady Wilbury—the job had many aspects, all of them interesting. 'How does Meredith feel?'

'She would prefer to remain in Shanghai,' Lucy admitted. 'I think she's worried about the prospect of more travelling. And about being unable to obtain her medicines.' Lucy gestured helplessly. 'I didn't know ... she said we needed soap. When I saw the bottle ... she's taking too much. But she says she can't sleep without it.'

Lucy's drooping bony shoulders filled Susanna with compassion. Every decision was fraught with complications because of Meredith's increasingly fragile state of health.

'I've an idea. Why don't Meredith and I stay here and you go up to Anqing by yourself?'

Lucy straightened. 'What?'

'I don't mean remain in the hotel. We'll rent a small house. I'm earning quite enough to keep

338

us both. And it would give you the—'

'No,' Lucy shook her head firmly. 'It is a kind offer, Susanna, but no. What would Meredith do while you were at work? You couldn't take her with you and she couldn't possibly be left alone all day. She has to come with me. And it's out of the question that you should remain in Shanghai by yourself.'

Though bitterly disappointed Susanna had to concede Lucy was right. Lady Geraldine Wilbury had made it abundantly clear that arriving in Shanghai unsponsored and unspoken-for was definitely not the done thing. A young Englishwoman on her own, especially one refusing to conform to expectations would swiftly find herself a total outcast. Quite apart from the difficulties that would cause her, Mr Prakash's business might suffer which was no way to repay his kindness. She tried to put on a brave face.

'So how are we to get to Anqing?'

Lucy pushed herself to her feet. 'I'm not sure yet. I'll make some enquiries tomorrow. Goodnight, dear.'

'Lucy?' Susanna blurted the question that had haunted her all day. 'Did you know Lowell was married?'

'Is he?' Lucy's eyes rounded in surprise. 'I don't think he's ever mentioned—at least, not that I can remember. Are you sure?'

Susanna nodded, oddly comforted. If Lucy hadn't known then she needn't feel quite so stupid. 'Quite sure. Lady Wilbury was talking to her friend about Lowell's wife. Apparently her name is Marjorie.' She turned away so Lucy would not see how much it hurt. That he was married had been shock enough, to learn he had mistresses as well. Lowell Hawke's lifestyle was none of her business. But knowing that didn't stop the sword-thrust of grief and jealousy when she imagined him with Lady Wilbury.

Clad only in a crimson silk dressing-gown, his wet hair combed back from his forehead and curling thickly on his neck, Lowell returned to his bedroom. Apart from the large bed with its deep feather mattress and crisp, clean sheets the furnishings were spartan: a wardrobe, a tall-boy, a chair, and a lacquered table, its glossy surface almost hidden beneath letters and papers. It was, he realized, as impersonal, as anonymous, as a hotel room.

Scooping up a fistful of correspondence he pulled the pillows from beneath the counterpane and bunched them against the polished brass bedhead. Leaning back he opened the first envelope. He tried to read but the words wouldn't register. *Susanna.* Where was she? What was she doing? *Stop.* He tried to focus on the schooner's turnaround time. How long to unload, fumigate, deal with repairs, then reload with a fresh cargo to cover the costs of carrying the guns up-river to Ellis? But silent as a shadow she kept returning. Her image was crystal clear. Willow-slender, graceful, and always so serious that he counted each smile a treasure to be horded. *No!* Swinging his legs over the edge of the bed he buried his face in his hands. Sweat

340

trickled down his chest.

Roused by a knocking on the door he glanced up. 'Yes?'

The door opened and Marjorie came in. But this was a Marjorie he had never seen before, giggling, breathless, her face flushed and dewy. As he slowly straightened up she closed the door and leaned against it. She had brushed her hair out. Fluffed about her head it made her neck seem shorter, her face more rounded. She was wearing a filmy froth of pale-blue silk and white lace.

'Lowell, d-darling,' she stammered over the endearment and it sounded strange on her tongue. 'I'm sorry about ... earlier.' She waved one hand airily. 'Tha's all in the past now. Nothing to be afraid of. Not with you. You're my husband.' Her bosom heaved as she sucked in deep breaths and she seemed unable to look at him. 'This time's going to be all right. I promise.' She rushed forward, arms outstretched. He rose to his feet. It was the first time in the whole of their marriage that she had approached him.

Taken aback, trying to summon delight, telling himself it was what he wanted, he held her. As he felt the soft fullness of her breasts and her body's heat through the fine fabric he was unable to control his physical response. Battling feelings of treachery he drew her gently down on to the bed. Stretching out beside her he pressed his lips to her neck, feeling the rapid beat of her pulse against his mouth. She smelled strongly of lavender water. He would have preferred to discover the natural scent of her skin but now was not the time to mention it.

Fighting his own need for release from the tension that had plagued him for weeks he prepared himself to take as long as she needed. If this was to work she must be led slowly, with subtlety and kindness.

At least she was not trembling with fright as on previous occasions. Nor, as he caressed her lightly, tactfully, did she shrink away. But after a few moments he realized that despite her breathless sighs and the heat radiating from her body there was no real response. Something wasn't right. He struggled with his doubts, telling himself to be patient, that the rewards would be worth the effort. As he shifted to a more comfortable position his fingers brushed her lower belly. She gasped, her doll-like face contorting in a spasm of fear and pain. 'Please don' hurt me, Papa.'

Lowell froze. *Papa?* He reared up on one elbow.

She blinked slowly and smiled at him, *unaware she had spoken.* Lowell's breath stopped. Her pupils had shrunk to tiny black pinpoints. ''S all right now.' Her voice was soft and breathy, the words slurred. 'Not afraid. Not like before.'

In that instant he understood. It was all suddenly horrifyingly clear: her mother's cowed behaviour, his own father's warnings, Marjorie's terror of physical intimacy. Hurling himself away from her he sat hunched on the far side of the bed shaking with rage as he contemplated the wasteland that was his marriage, the trick she and her family had played on him. But gradually his fury lost its edge, tempered by overwhelming sadness. If she needed to be drugged before she could bring herself to approach him Marjorie was as much a cripple as the malformed beggars by the old city walls.

Fastening his dressing-gown he grasped her shoulders and shook her. 'Marjorie?'

Her lids fluttered and she forced her eyes open. 'Mmm?'

'The drug, what was it?'

'Jus' li'l something the chemist gave me. Don' worry.'

Lowell shook her again harder, then hauled her up. Her head lolled sideways. 'What did you take?'

She frowned and her chin began to quiver. 'Don't be cross. I did it for you. It's what you wanted—'

'No, I didn't. Not like *this*. What sort of a man do you think I am?'

'But you said—'

'Marjorie, I wanted a wife who loved me, wanted me.'

'But I do, Lowell,' she cried piteously. 'I do love you. Why else would I—haven't I just proved it?' She clung to him. 'Why are you so angry? I'm trying to give you what you want.'

Tearing himself free he jack-knifed off the bed and stood in the centre of the room every muscle knotted with tension. 'If you have to try so hard I don't want it.' He swung round. 'In God's name, Marjorie, why didn't you tell me?'

Huddled against the pillows she drew her legs

up, hiding them beneath the filmy négligée. 'Tell you what?'

Tired to his soul, he sat on the edge of the bed, careful to leave an expanse of white cotton bedspread between them. 'About your father. About what he did to you.'

She huddled lower. The drug-induced euphoria was evaporating leaving her pale and drained. 'Would you have believed me? And if you did, would you have married me?'

Unable to answer he looked away. What had happened wasn't her fault. But if he had known then the effect it would have on her ... She started to cry. Part of him was touched by her misery but searing rage forbade him offering comfort. Rage at the way she had used him, hiding behind the status of being his wife while giving him nothing in return. Not even honesty. Yet he *had* been warned. Only he'd chosen not to listen.

'Wh-what are you g-going to d-do?' she sobbed.

'I don't know.' He cradled his head in his hands. 'I need time to think.'

'I'm so sorry, Mr Prakash. I had hoped to be with you until—' Susanna broke off, realizing that the merchant might prefer his secretary's impending court case to remain unmentioned. 'But as my cousins' arrangements have now changed I thought you should know at once.'

Soman Prakash's limpid brown eyes made Susanna think of a spaniel that had just been kicked.

'I really am terribly sorry.' She wanted to tell him how much she would rather stay here and continue working for him. But to do so would imply criticism of her cousins. Her debt to Lucy was too great to permit that.

'This is very great shame as I am being most impressed by your work.' He sighed. 'So when do you leave?'

'I'm not sure. Perhaps within a week. But if you wish I could continue working until the day before we sail?'

He nodded, beaming. 'I am agreeing most heartily, Miss Elliot. Now I must go. My wife is needing me. Last night I am describing to her your great efficiency and she is most relieved and happy.' His smile faded and the corners of his mouth turned down. 'It is not good that she will start to worry again—'

'Don't tell her yet,' Susanna suggested. 'Wait until you've found someone to replace me.'

'You are most sensible young lady.' With a flash of white teeth he disappeared through the office door on to the Bund.

As she sat down behind the big desk, Susanna couldn't help contrasting the Indian merchant's trust and gratitude with the lack of either from her father and uncle. Pulling the tray of invoices forward she opened the big ledger and picked up her pen.

She heard the door open but took an extra few seconds to finish entering the figures she had just totalled before raising her head. 'Good mo—' She started violently, her intake of breath clearly audible. As she looked into Lowell's eyes

345

all the barriers she had so painstakingly erected were swept away by a tidal wave of joy.

'We've been here before,' he murmured, his voice unsteady. 'Five months ago I walked into the office at Braithwaite's Yard in Falmouth and saw you just as you are now.'

Five months and a lifetime of changes. 'No,' she murmured, 'I'm not the same person.' She hadn't expected to see him again, and now he was in front of her, almost within touching distance. It was torture, a bitter-sweet agony of longing and—*why was he looking at her like that? He had no right. He was married.* She began to tremble. 'I'm afraid Mr Prakash isn't here right now.' She avoided his gaze, terrified he would see things she had neither the strength nor the sophistication to hide. 'Can I help you?'

Gathering himself he laid a statement of account on the ledger in front of her. 'My father's *compradore* has sent several reminders—'

'Yes, I found—' Susanna opened the right-hand drawer, took out a cheque and a receipt and pushed them across the desk. She had to clear her throat before she could speak. 'Mr Prakash asked me to offer his most sincere apologies. His wife's illness, and ... other matters ... caused this to be overlooked.'

'May I?' Lowell indicated the pen. Scrawling his signature on the receipt he put the cheque in his pocket while Susanna returned the signed chit to the drawer. With business concluded the tension increased. The air was so charged it seemed to vibrate. *What was he waiting for? Why didn't he go?*

346

'You must excuse me, Captain Hawke.' The words stuck in her dry throat. 'I do have rather a lot ...' She indicated the ledger and the tray of invoices.

'Susanna, please.'

The chair flew backwards as she shot to her feet. 'How is your wife? She must be so pleased to have you home. Lady Wilbury was quite upset that you missed the party.' She broke off, bowing her head, pressing her knuckles on to the desk.

'You don't understand.'

Her head jerked up. Tears welled and his face splintered into glittering fragments. 'No I don't. But it's none of my business, is it?' Her brittle laugh was choked off by a sob. She blinked furiously, wiping her wet cheeks with her palm.

'Please listen to me,' he pleaded softly, urgently. 'There are certain things ... it's very difficult—'

Susanna knew she had no right to feel such heartache. But that didn't stop it hurting. 'It would be, with you away so much.'

'My wife prefers it so.'

Studying his face she saw lines of strain around his eyes and mouth. He looked more exhausted now than he had during the worst moments of the voyage.

'I don't underst—' The words dried as he nodded.

'Exactly. We have to talk. But not here, not now.' His mouth twisted in a weary smile and some of the tension seemed to leave him. 'How

347

are your cousins? Are they settling in?'

'No. There isn't a CIM mission in Shanghai any longer. That's why I'm working here. We've been staying in an hotel but our money's running out. We have to go to Anqing. Lucy is making enquiries about steamers.'

'I'll take you. I'm going up-river in three days' time.' His gaze held hers.

She looked away in despair. 'You're married, Lowell.'

He gestured impatiently. 'There's so much you don't know. Tell Lucy to forget the steamer. I'll take you to Anqing.' Reaching across the desk he caressed her cheek with his fingertips. The fleeting touch made her blood leap.

'Just one thing: the freight I'm taking up-river to Kewkiang.'

'Yes?'

'It's guns. Guns and ammunition.'

She froze. 'You're a gun-runner?'

A wry smile twisted his mouth. 'Not on a regular basis. This particular cargo was ordered by the British Consul in Kewkiang. The weapons are to protect British lives in danger because the treaties are being ignored.'

Listening to the complaints in the consulate she had felt anger and sympathy for the victims of Chinese refusal to obey the law. But her Quaker upbringing demanded she condemn violence. Torn, she looked up at him uncertainly. 'Why?'

'Why tell you? Because—do you remember saying how your whole life has been spent trying to be what other people wanted? And how you longed to be accepted for the person that you are?'

'Oh yes.'

He shrugged. 'You must see me as I am, Susanna, not as you might wish me to be. Do you understand?'

She blushed furiously.

'And will you trust me?' His expression was hard, almost arrogant. But the harshness in his voice told her how much her answer mattered.

Helpless, she nodded.

Chapter Twenty-Nine

Lowell watched as Susanna helped Meredith. Her shy uncertain smile wrenched his heart. What right had he even to hope? Yet when she looked at him ...

Tearing his gaze away he drew Lucy aside. 'Are you sure this is wise?' They both glanced at Meredith leaning heavily on Susanna's arm, a perceptible tremor shaking her head as she stared vacantly into space. 'Wouldn't she be better off staying here to be cared for by the nuns? I've heard they have a particular understanding for this—'

'I can't,' Lucy said simply. 'I'm sure the nuns are kind. But she's my sister. How can I ask someone else to take care of her? She is not always like this. There are times when she's perfectly lucid. How do you think she would feel to realize I had abandoned her? And what would the Chinese think? They have a great reverence for family. How could I ask them to listen to me talk about God's love for all mankind if I find caring for my own sister too great a burden? Please don't worry, we'll be fine.'

Reluctantly Lowell turned away and gave the order to cast off, watching Susanna until she disappeared from sight down the companionway. Patrolling the deck, ostensibly checking the condition of the ship, he thought about his wife.

Despite the disaster she had maintained their customary routine, particularly when the servants were about. It was a brave effort, for her entire future—her reputation, friends, position in society, social life—hung on his decision. *But he was no nearer making it now than he had been five days ago.* He could have killed her father with his bare hands. But the man was already dead, drowned with his mouse-like wife in a typhoon two years ago. Which meant Marjorie had no one. Yet, God knew, he owed her nothing.

When he told her he was leaving earlier than planned to go upriver she had made a valiant effort to hide her dread and behave as though nothing unusual was happening.

'Do you think John will come back?'

He shrugged. 'If I can find him I'll give him father's message. But it's his decision.'

'And the missionaries? Will they be safe there?' Seeing his eyes narrow she added

350

quickly, 'Geraldine Wilbury called yesterday afternoon while you were out. She mentioned them.'

Lowell felt a quick flare of anger. Geraldine had initiated their liaison, contriving meetings with a flair that demonstrated considerable practice. But at a party one evening at the height of their affair, overestimating her power she snubbed Marjorie. He had ended it there and then. She had never forgiven him. Yet driven by motives he did not pretend to understand she still called regularly on Marjorie. 'Did Lady Wilbury also mention how she knew they were going to Anqing?'

'Apparently she overheard one of them in the chemist's shop in Nanking Street, a rather excitable woman with a carrying voice. Geraldine was surprised to hear that you were carrying passengers. I told her these were unusual circumstances.'

'They are.' Lowell looked directly at her. 'Quite exceptional.' She nodded slowly her bruised eyes fixed on his face. He saw her throat work. 'I suppose I've always known that one day ... Lowell, if this is—'

He raised one hand, cutting her off. But his voice was gentle. 'When *I* know, I'll tell you.'

'Thank you.' She attempted a smile. 'It's just, well, I'd hate to hear it from anyone else.'

'Gossip never bothered you in the past.'

'No, but that was ...' She bent her head for a moment, then looked up at him. 'It's different this time, isn't it?'

'Yes. It's different this time.'

'I can't.' Susanna raised her horrified gaze from the derringer lying on the hatch cover between them, and shook her head. 'Please don't ask me to.'

'So someone else must carry the burden of your safety?' Lowell arched one dark brow. 'What sort of independence is that?'

'You're not being—'

'Fair? Do you think the river pirates or the renegade soldiers will be fair? Do you imagine that once they realize there are women on board they'll bow politely and attack some other vessel instead?'

She winced at his sharpness. 'This is a fast ship. Can't you simply avoid trouble?'

His laugh was brief and humourless. 'I wish it were that easy. I'd back my crew against any on the Yangtze. But in these waters skill with firearms is as important as seamanship. I can't spare men for guard duties, Susanna. You must share responsibility for your cousins' safety, and your own.'

She gave a shaky nod. 'Yes. I do see.' The dull metal gleamed like polished pewter. It looked like a toy. Yet those tiny twin barrels spat death.

'Pick it up.' When she hesitated his voice grew harder. 'Go on. It won't bite you.'

Stung, she reached for the gun then glared up at him only to meet a look of such tenderness and understanding that her heart turned over. How well he knew her. *And how many others?* Her answering smile faltered and she looked away, biting the inside of her lip.

'I never expected this ... you.' She had to strain to hear his whisper. 'I'd accepted ... thought I could cope. But everything's changed. Not just meeting you. There are things I didn't know about. Marjorie and ... it is not a proper marriage. It never has been. My bride wa ... is ... unable to be a wife. Do you understand what I'm saying?'

Blushing crimson Susanna nodded. 'I think so. But why? I know some women find the early days of marriage difficult—'

His brows climbed. 'How?'

'My sister. Her husband behaved in a most peculiar ...' She shook her head. 'But you wouldn't. I can't imagine you doing anything—' She stopped in confusion. She was betraying thoughts and feelings about him to which she had no right. He reached out to take her hand just as an able seaman trotted past, and brushed imaginary dust off his trouser knee instead. 'Surely this isn't the right place to be talking of such matters,' she whispered.

'It's the safest place.' He was grim. 'God knows I'd rather be alone with you, but you're sharing my quarters because your cousins trust me not to take advantage of the situation. It's a trust I'm finding very hard to honour.'

His burning gaze sent shivers of strange and exquisite sensation through her. The ship's bell clanged, making her jump and breaking the tension. Lowell explained how to load the tiny gun. 'Now come over to the rail.'

As the schooner rose and plunged on the

lumpy water she staggered. He caught her instantly, his hand warm, steadying. She glanced up in gratitude. And looked quickly at the murky water. 'Why is it so rough?'

'The melting snow draining down from the mountains causes the river to rise more than forty feet at this time of year. But even this volume of water can't hold back a rising tide. It's a battle between two powerful opposing forces.' His tone was dry and self-mocking. 'It creates enormous turbulence.' After a brief silence he pointed to a rock-fringed, wooded island. 'See the temple near the summit? Aim at that and pull the trigger.' As she swung round, eyes wide, he gently deflected the gun from his stomach.

'*Oh!* I'm s-sorry.'

'It's all right. No damage done ... this time,' he added darkly. 'You won't hit the temple. A gun this size has a very short range. Go on, fire. And don't close your eyes.'

He made her reload and fire until she no longer flinched at the report. 'Well done.' Sagging with relief she offered him the gun back. He shook his head. 'I want you to keep it on you at all times. Somewhere out of sight but easily reached. Wait here, I'll be back in a minute.'

She tried the gun in the pocket of her dress, but it thumped uncomfortably against her thigh when she moved. After a moment, shielded by her cloak, she felt for the garter just above her knee and tucked the little gun into her the top of stocking. Leaning her folded arms on the gunwale she stiffened as she caught sight of a large steamer lying on its side half-submerged in the yellow-brown torrent.

'He probably ran on to a mudbank,' Lowell said from behind her. 'The force of the stream is enough to capsize ships twice as big. But that won't happen to us. The schooner has a much shallower draft which allows for more leeway outside the channel.'

'Oh, good,' she croaked. Then saw he was holding a rifle.

Lying on her back, the curtain open just enough to admit a narrow band of comforting light from the oil lamp, she listened to footsteps on the deck above her head and the calls of the crew standing a double watch. Lowell was still on deck.

Though she was physically tired her thoughts wouldn't let her rest. Handling firearms out of necessity was one thing; discovering she had a natural aptitude with them was quite another.

Lowell hadn't been able to hide his amusement. She couldn't altogether blame him. Her own feelings were decidedly ambivalent. Ministers thundered 'thou shalt not kill' at every opportunity. Which was fine provided *everyone* obeyed the rules. But as she had seen for herself too many didn't. On reflection she was reassured rather than shamed by her competence.

She pictured Lowell's hands, strong and weatherbeaten, his fingers swift and efficient on the rifle. Those fingers had caressed her cheek. She had believed him gone from her life

355

for ever, now they were together once more. But for how long?

Trust me. His voice echoed in her head. And where for so long there had been only dark desolation hope glimmered like a newly-lit candle. She slept.

Men shouting. Feet pounding along the deck. The boom of cannon and scream of grape-shot. Susanna shot upright, eyes wide, heart racing. Was it a nightmare? Then more shouts from above and the piercing sound of Meredith screaming told her whatever was happening was all too real.

Leaping from the bunk she flung her cloak round her shoulders, pushed bare feet into her shoes, and seizing the tiny gun ran out through the day cabin. Her cousins' door was open revealing Meredith slumped on the floor hammering the deck with her fists, her mouth wide open in a non-stop scream. Crouched alongside Lucy had hold of her sister's shoulders.

'Meredith, please—' The clatter of a machine gun, loud and very close, made all three start. As Meredith whimpered and cringed Lucy's shocked gaze met Susanna's. 'Wait, Susanna, don't—' But as Meredith's moan rose swiftly to a shriek, she was already halfway up the brass stairs.

Bursting through the companionway hatch she stopped abruptly. Dense fog shrouded the schooner, made worse by thick, evil-smelling smoke. Screams and splashing came from somewhere near the bow.

'You got the bastards, Cap'n! Jesus, that Gatling's some gun.'

Coughing and gasping, holding the tiny pistol tightly in a shaking hand, Susanna covered her nose and mouth with her cloak and felt her way forward, clinging to the gunwale. The smoke stung her eyes and tears streamed down her cheeks. She tripped, crying out as she sprawled over a body. Coughing and gasping for breath she scrambled backwards pointing the little gun at the crumpled figure, terrified in case it moved.

'He's going to hit us!'

There was a crash and the schooner shuddered. Feet pounded down the deck towards her.

'He's capsized!'

'Bloody thing's sinking!' A ragged cheer went up.

''Ow many d'you reckon?'

'Eight, at least.'

'That'll teach the buggers!'

A crewman emerged from the murk. Seeing her and the body he skidded to a halt. *Jesus!* Don't shoot, miss. It's Cecil.' Crouching, he turned the body over and recoiled in disgust. 'He got hit by a stinkpot.' He yelled over his shoulder, 'Somebody bring water!'

Susanna stumbled to her feet. Her legs felt like jelly. It was easier to breathe now but the fog still drifted and swirled like veils. Lowell appeared with a bucket and threw water over the seaman who grunted then sat up, shaking his head.

'All right, someone give him a hand then get back to your duties. And keep a sharp lookout. There'll be others.' Gripping Susanna's upper arm he hustled her back along the deck towards the companionway. 'You shouldn't be up here.'

'I heard gunfire and—'

'You were supposed to remain below. You could have been hurt.' Beneath the dark stubble a nerve jumped in his jaw.

'So could you,' she retorted.

He hauled her round to face him. 'I gave you the gun to protect yourself, not me, or the ship.' He looked towards the companionway. 'What in the name of God is all that screaming?'

Susanna gulped. 'Meredith. She was frightened by the gunfire.'

'In future you stay below unless I tell you otherwise.' He shook her. 'Do you understand?'

She nodded, her hair blowing wildly in the wind. He caught a handful and gave it a warning tug. 'I can't be dealing with pirates *and* worrying about you.' His scowl softened. 'Scally'll bring your water in a minute. In the meantime for all our sakes try and shut Meredith up.'

Susanna swallowed the last mouthful of her tea. She was very tired. During her brief visits topside she had seen two other ships attacked. But Lowell's consummate seamanship had kept the schooner free of further trouble.

Beside her Lucy ate slowly, dark circles of fatigue beneath her eyes. Even her resilience

358

had eventually crumbled under the strain of watching Meredith reject every remedy Susanna prepared, and she had fetched the chloral hydrate. Meredith's transformation had been instant and miraculous.

'Thank you. Thank you both so much,' she had whispered as Lucy settled her down between fresh sheets and Susanna collected up the soiled towels and linen. The smile lighting her blotched haggard face had been as sweet and trusting as a child's as her swollen eyelids closed. Within seconds she had been deeply asleep.

'I'm so sorry.' Lucy pushed her plate away. 'I'm afraid I'll have to ask you to excuse me.' She made a brave attempt to smile. 'What with one thing and another ... Goodnight.'

Susanna watched as Lowell half-rose then resumed his seat.

He had shaved and made an effort to tidy his thick unkempt hair with water and a comb, but there was still an untamed air about him. With so many questions still unanswered and every hour bringing them closer to Anqing her nerves were as taut as the mast stays.

'I did love Marjorie,' he said quietly, 'once, a long time ago. Those other women ...' He sighed in despair. 'How can I expect you to understand? You're too young.'

'I know how it feels to be lonely.'

He stared at her, his black brows drawn down, conflict visible on his harsh features. 'I don't want to lose you.'

She caught her breath. 'Lowell, you shouldn't—'

'I know.' He raked a hand through his hair. 'But I can't—I *won't*—go on like this. An annulment will bring the whole wretched charade to an end.'

'And your wife? What will happen to her?'

'Why should I care?' He prowled the cabin like a caged tiger. 'When did she give a thought to what all this was doing to me?'

'You never told me why she ... what happened to make her the way she is?'

His back to her he drew a deep shuddering breath. 'She was brutalized by her father.'

'He beat her? Oh, the poor—'

'No, Susanna.' Lowell swung round, weariness and torment stark on his face. 'He used her as if she were his wife.'

Susanna's hands flew to her mouth.

Lowell rubbed the back of his neck. 'I didn't know. She never told me. I only found out last week.'

Susanna clasped her hands together on the table. 'I am very new to Shanghai but I've already seen and heard enough to know that great weight is attached to the way things look. Reality and truth are far less important than appearances. Your wife Marjorie enjoys a certain status, not only would she lose that, an annulment would make her failure a matter of public record.'

'What makes you so sure people would think *she*—'

'Oh come, Lowell. Who is going to believe, even for a moment, that the fault might lie with you?' She flushed. 'Too many ladies in

360

Shanghai know differently. Can you imagine what Lady Wilbury and her friends would make of it? They'd destroy her.' Digging her nails into her palms Susanna forced the words out. 'You can't do it.'

'I see.' The look on his face was devastating.

'No, Lowell, wait ...' But he had gone, his boots clanging on the brass stairs.

Leaving the women aboard the anchored schooner and arming the crew on watch, Lowell was rowed ashore in the jolly-boat. Below the slum shacks crowded together a short distance above the water, pigs snuffled and rooted feeding on whatever was thrown from the mean dwellings.

'Come back in two hours,' he instructed the seaman. As the row-boat returned to the ship he threaded his way between fishing boats pulled up on the steep shingle beach. Paved with stone slabs the main street was barely eight feet wide and restricted even further by stalls set up in front of shops. The houses were built of soft-looking grey brick. Roofed with bamboo and rice straw they had very wide eaves which offered protection from both monsoon rain and searing sun.

The street was busy but, as usual, he saw very few women. Even the poorest families tried to improve the marriage prospects of their daughters by binding their feet, but this deformity, so highly prized among men, made walking almost impossible.

In shirt sleeves, a Colt revolver at his waist,

Lowell made his way past men pulling heavily laden wheelbarrows, and others with huge loads on their bent backs.

Labourers crowded around a food stand shovelling strips of frizzled pork and stir-fried cabbage into already bulging cheeks. The odour of garlic and hot oil was heavy on the humid air.

Calling to one of the vendors in his own dialect Lowell asked where he would find the CIM mission. The man shook his head. Some of the men at the stall looked over their shoulders, exchanged brief glances, then returned to their eating. Accustomed to Chinese inscrutability Lowell detected wariness and felt new tension in his gut.

Mopping the sweat from his forehead and neck he walked on up the street, passing stalls piled with cabbages, purple aubergines, carrots, soy beans and onions. There were shops selling paper lanterns and incense sticks, cotton cloth dyed indigo, parcels of tea in oiled paper, sacks of salt, rice, earthenware pots, and thick felt. Shoemakers and tailors worked in open doorways or on the street. Everything bought or sold was haggled over. The noise was deafening.

Many of the shops had wicker or bamboo cages hanging outside their doors. As he drew level with one the bird inside began to sing. The linnet was small and brown, its plumage dowdy. But the notes pouring from its tiny throat were pure and clear and melodious. Gazing at the little bird he forgot the noise and smells and

362

hustle, and thought of Susanna.

Forcing aside the tempting torturing image he strode on; past a man skinning eels, his arms and legs splattered with blood; past the barber who carried his stool, towel and razor with him and shaved his customers wherever there was space to stop.

Turning up an alley he emerged on to a street of better quality houses owned by merchants dealing in tobacco, silk, tea and opium. Beyond them was the Catholic mission. And a pile of blackened ruins.

'You know what these mobs are like.' The elderly priest shook his head sadly. Beneath a black cassock that flapped in the breeze his lanky frame was stooped with age and disillusion. The fine red veins mottling his aquiline nose and thin cheeks revealed comfort sought from a bottle rather than prayer. 'Who knows what caused it this time? It takes so little.' He spread tremulous hands. 'A rumour, the weather. They took everything they could carry, and destroyed the rest. But at least they left the building intact.' Sighing, he indicated the burned rubble. 'As you see, the CIM was not so fortunate. No one was hurt, thank God. Hudson Taylor left some weeks ago for Hangchow.'

'Thank you.' Lowell turned to leave, then stopped. 'How far is it to the gold diggings?'

'Not far, perhaps a couple of miles down the coast.' With his pale crêpy neck, bald head and faded black cassock the priest resembled an elderly vulture. He peered at Lowell through

363

watery eyes. 'You don't have the look of a prospector.'

'I'm not. I'm delivering a message.'

The priest nodded. 'Before you go all the way out to the claims, try Murphy's bar.' As Lowell's brows rose the priest explained. 'Jack Murphy is an ex-navy gunner who managed to get left behind after the Taiping Rebellion. He was one of the first prospectors up here. But when he realized there are few places up-river a man can get a decent drink he hired someone else to work his claim and took a house down on the waterfront.'

'Whereabouts?'

'Lower side, the far end. He had a delivery a few days ago. Word will have reached the diggings by now. Chances are you'll find your man there.'

Taking a couple of Mexican dollars from his pocket Lowell pressed them into the priest's bony hand as he shook it.

'Bless you, my son.'

Lowell didn't recognize his brother. The golden hair, bleached almost white by fierce sun, was tied back with a ragged strip of blue cotton cloth. Physical labour had transformed pale flabby flesh into lean brown muscle. Dressed in a fraying shirt and worn trousers he sat astride a narrow bench rolling dice on the wooden table. Two more Europeans watched, slapping the table and arguing. A big burly man with tangled black curls wearing a faded red shirt stood behind a counter.

As Lowell approached he lowered the glass he was polishing. A puckered scar ran from beneath his left eye across his broken nose to his right ear.

'Look your fill, mister.' Jack Murphy's gaze was level and fearless. 'See what a chain will do.'

'And the man holding it?' Lowell enquired drily.

'Ah, well, now,' Murphy grinned, exposing blackened teeth. 'I've a suspicion I tore his arm off.'

While they were talking the man on the bench had turned. Now he stood up. 'Why are you here?'

It wasn't until he met the brilliant-blue eyes that Lowell knew. 'John?'

'Have I changed so much?'

Lowell threw several silver coins on the wooden counter. 'A drink for everyone, Mr Murphy.' Seating himself on to the narrow bench he waited. After a moment John joined him. The other two men moved tactfully away and leaned on the counter, talking.

Lowell glanced up, nodding at Murphy as he set two glasses of whisky in front of them. 'I didn't expect to find you so easily.'

'Why have you come?'

'Father asked me to. I have other business up-river so it wasn't out of my way.'

Cradling the glass between his hands, John stared at it. 'What does he want?'

'He's dying. If you go back the company's yours.'

Tossing the liquor to the back of his throat John swallowed. 'What about you?'

Lowell shrugged. He sipped his whisky, surprised to find it was of good quality. He raised the glass in brief salute to Murphy who winked. 'I promised I'd give you the message.'

'That's all? You get nothing?' As Lowell shook his head he sensed the tension leave his brother. 'The old bastard.' After gazing into the glass John pushed it away. 'I've found gold you know. Mostly dust, but a few nuggets. Enough to make it worth while. And I've got a woman.' He glanced up, unable to contain his curiosity. 'What happens to the company if I don't go back?'

Lowell took another sip. 'He's threatened to leave it all to me.' They looked at one another for a long moment.

'And you came anyway? The *bastard*,' John whispered. 'Take it with my blessing, Brother. And tell him ... tell him he chose his life, now I've chosen mine.' He stood up. Lowell followed.

'You're sure about this?'

John nodded. 'I'm sure.' He held out a scarred and calloused hand. 'Have a good life. And if you're up this way again ...' He shrugged. 'Maybe I'll be here, maybe not.'

Lowell gripped his brother's hand. 'I'm glad for you, John. Good luck.'

As he crossed the shingle to where the rowboat waited, he could still hear his brother's farewell. 'Go back to that rat's nest, Lowell, and it's you who'll need luck.'

366

Chapter Thirty

As Lucy wrung her hands, Susanna put a comforting arm around her shoulders.

'I'm sorry. But you cannot stay here.' Lowell turned to Tom Binney. 'Raise the hook and get under way as soon as possible.'

Tom blinked. 'The ladies aren't leaving then?'

'There's nowhere for them to go.' Lowell's gaze met Susanna's. 'The mission has been burned down.'

With a brief grimace Tom hurried forward, his shouts galvanizing the crew into action.

Lowell turned to Lucy. 'My next stop is Kewkiang. I'm carrying freight for Christopher Ellis, the British Consul. You can rest there for a few days while I go on up-river to collect a cargo of silk. Then I'll take you back to Chinkiang and arrange a passage down the Grand Canal to the CIM mission at Hangchow.'

'You dear man.' Lucy grasped his arm, pink with gratitude. 'Your kindness is more than we deserve. I fear we have put you to enormous trouble.'

'Not at all.' As his eyes flicked to hers Susanna felt tingling warmth spread from her toes to the top of her head.

Lucy braced herself. 'I'd better go and break the news to my sister.'

'I'll come with you,' Susanna volunteered,

guiltily relieved that her parting from Lowell had been postponed. So much still needed to be explained and discussed.

'No,' Lucy patted her hand. 'It'll be better if she and I are alone when I tell her.'

Watching her start down the companionway, Susanna turned to Lowell. 'I—'

'Later,' he murmured. 'Right now I must—'

'You may be too busy later,' she whispered urgently. 'I only wanted to say ...' She screwed up her courage. 'My sympathy for your wife's position is quite separate from ... my ... my great regard for you.' She pressed one palm to a crimson cheek. 'I just wanted you to know. You appeared to believe ... I couldn't let you think ... You can go now.' With a shy sideways glance she saw the bleakness fade from his grey eyes.

'Damn it, girl,' he grated, 'you certainly choose your moments.' Glowering with frustration, he strode away.

Leaning on the gunwale Susanna gazed at the water as the crew hauled rhythmically on the halyards. Despite the heat and humidity of the afternoon Meredith's cry of despair made her shiver.

Closing her journal Susanna slid along the padded seat to make room at the table. 'How is she?'

'Resting quietly.'

'Have you given her—?'

'It seemed the kindest thing to do. She's suffering so.' Sitting down, Lucy rested her elbows on the table and covered her face with both hands. 'She talked about our childhood, about Mother and Father, and all the plans we had for our lives. She believes her whole life has been a failure.' Lucy raised beseeching eyes. 'How can I make her see that's not true?'

The door opened and John-Henry backed in with a loaded tray. 'I want all this eaten,' he warned, unloading plates and dishes on to the table. 'These last few days 'aven't been the best of times for you ladies. You got to keep your strength up. All right?'

Despite being perilously close to tears, the contrast between his unsavoury appearance and mother-hen manner made Susanna giggle. Lucy, who had had little to do with him, simply gaped.

'Get on with it then,' he chivvied.

'Stop your bullying,' Lowell growled as he entered the cabin.

Tucking the tray under his arm John-Henry tutted as he stumped out.

During the night a squall lashed the muddy torrent to a fury and Meredith was sick again. Straightening up from the tin bath, a pile of clean washing on the hatch beside her, Susanna wiped her sweating forehead with the back of her hand. She glanced at the crewmen raising the topsails and marvelled at their stamina.

Rags of dark cloud with luminous edges moved with slow menace across a brassy sky. The sweltering heat and muggy air threatened another storm. After hanging the linen over a line one of the men had rigged for her, she stopped for a moment to look at the magnificent scenery.

Yesterday there had been low hills. Today there were mountains topped by stunted pines and firs. On the lower slopes she could see chestnut trees and oaks, tall stands of bamboo and giant ferns. Exotic blooms made splashes of red, orange and white amid the vivid green.

To her left, the river suddenly opened into a wide canyon of towering cliffs topped by giant trees. It must be the entrance to Poyang Lake. Lowell had showed her on the chart but she could remember little of what he'd said, aware only of him next to her, so close, so careful not to touch.

Approaching Kewkiang the helmsman steered carefully between countless junks, cargo boats, lorchas and bamboo rafts. On either side of the town and the hills behind, every bit of land capable of cultivation bore a crop of some sort. At one end close to an inlet a small fleet of narrow, shallow craft drifted. Each contained one man and several large black birds. More birds bobbed on the water. Every few moments one would dive, popping up again seconds later with a large fish in its long bill which the man would lean over and take.

'They're cormorants.' Lowell came to stand behind her. 'Each fisherman has a dozen or so. A ring around the bird's throat stops it swallowing the fish. But when the morning's work is finished, the rings are removed and they eat their fill.'

Acutely conscious of his nearness she tried

desperately to concentrate, pointing at great swathes of broken masonry. 'What happened?'

'The Taiping Rebellion. The town was totally destroyed.'

Above the shacks crowded together on the rubble between the river and the terraced fields, stood several new houses. Enclosed within high walls they had curved roofs of red tiles and were surrounded by tree-shaded gardens. Paved paths meandered between carefully tended flowerbeds ablaze with colour. These oases of opulence looked out of place amid so much abject poverty.

'The prefect has ordered a six-mile-long wall erected around the town to prevent such an invasion being repeated.'

A nuance in his tone made Susanna glance round. 'You don't think it will be effective?'

'It will certainly deter attacks from *outside.*' He motioned her forward. 'Come, Tom has found transport for you.'

'Look at the cherry blossom,' Lucy marvelled. 'Isn't it beautiful?'

'It's too hot,' Meredith whined. 'I don't feel well.'

'Try to be brave, dear. We're nearly there. Once we reach the consulate—'

'I need my medicine, Lucy.'

'I know, but it affects your balance then you find it difficult to walk. You shall have it as soon as we reach the consulate, I promise.'

Startled to see Oliver Lockhead, the bosun, and two ABs all armed with rifles waiting at the end of the gangplank, Susanna moved quickly to help her cousins. The transport turned out to be a kind of sedan chair slung between two poles and carried on the shoulders of two Chinese. Once inside with the door closed the passenger could not be seen but was able to look out through a slit at eye level roughly a foot wide and six inches deep.

As Lowell assisted Meredith and Lucy into their chairs Susanna heard shouting. She looked round. But before she could see what the trouble was Lowell grasped her arm and hustled her to her own chair.

'Sit well back,' he warned. 'A European woman is a rare sight this far up-river.' His voice softened. 'Especially one as lovely as you.'

'I doubt the Chinese think me lovely,' Susanna remarked drily, making a brave attempt to hide her growing disquiet. Though Lowell was pretending all was well she sensed it wasn't. 'My uncle used to tell me stories about China. He said they would find my colouring ugly and offensive.'

Ensuring her skirts were tucked in he smiled. 'What might be ugly to their eyes is enchanting to mine.' He fastened the door shut. 'Don't worry. We'll be right alongside.' Standing back he shouted an order to the bearers and Susanna felt the chair lurch as it was picked up.

The heat, stench and noise from the crowded street were indescribable. Some men glared in sullen silence as the chairs passed but others screamed and waved their arms, their faces contorted with hate. Jolted and sweating in her airless prison she was frightened, despite

Lowell's reassurance.

The sound of a rising shriek stopped her breath. The bearers ahead of her dropped the chair and backed away, jabbering and gesticulating. Knowing she must not show herself Susanna fought panic. Though sweat trickled down her temples her mouth and throat were dust-dry. She closed her fingers over the small gun tucked into her garter, hoping desperately she would not have to use it.

As Meredith continued to scream, Lowell bellowed an order. The two sturdy able seamen passed their rifles to Oliver Lockhead, picked up the poles, and the procession moved off again, faster this time amid the howling and yelling.

It seemed an eternity before they passed through a gate in the outer wall surrounding one of the new houses. The chairs were set down at once. As Chinese servants came forward with much kowtowing to meet them, the remaining bearers loudly demanded payment so they could leave at once.

Climbing shakily from her own chair Susanna met Lucy coming in the opposite direction.

'Have you got—?' She broke off as Lucy raised her hand, revealing the bottle.

Straining backwards, her body rigid, eyes tightly shut, Meredith's purple face was shiny with sweat and streaked with tears. Saliva drooled from one side of her mouth as she panted and whimpered.

As Susanna grasped her hand Meredith let

out a shriek 'It's all right,' Susanna shook her. 'You're safe now.'

Pale with shock Lucy leaned in and held the bottle to her sister's lips. 'No, not too much,' she cried anxiously, as Meredith seized the bottle in both hands and gulped the liquid down. Wrenching it away Susanna handed the bottle to Lucy and leaned in to help a shaking but quieter Meredith to her feet.

Lowell strode across. 'Is everyone all right?'

Susanna nodded, not trusting herself to speak. It was over. They were safe. What on earth was there to cry about? Meredith clung to Lucy's arm, her gaze unfocused, her head wobbling like a marionette.

With the servants carrying their luggage and Meredith supported between them, Susanna and Lucy followed Lowell towards the house. Inside the spacious hall, Lowell indicated lacquered chairs grouped at one side of a wide fireplace, protected from drafts by a woven bamboo screen.

'Why don't you sit down? Ellis might be—'

Alerted by the sound of briskly approaching footsteps he went forward.

'My God, but you're a welcome sight, Hawke.' Short and paunchy, Ellis carried himself ramrod straight. His hair had receded to a thick fringe at the back of his skull for which he compensated with a luxuriant black moustache. Seizing Lowell's hand he pumped it up and down. 'The guns?'

'My men are unloading now.'

'Thank God. We've got trouble, Hawke.

374

There's been—' Alerted by Lowell's signal Ellis glanced round, visibly shocked to see the three women. After inclining his head in a stiff bow he turned away. 'Who are they? What are they doing here? Surely *you* didn't ...?'

Lowell led him over to one of the windows too far away for her to hear what was said. But there was no mistaking Ellis's agitation. A quiet but intense argument followed with Ellis gesturing and Lowell shaking his head. Susanna heard the words 'Kwang Tsai.'

'Lucy, when can we go to our rooms? I need to lie down,' Meredith pleaded plaintively.

'Soon, dear,' Lucy soothed, stroking her sister's fretful hands. 'Lowell is making the arrangements now.'

'Everything is settled.' Lowell came towards them. 'Ladies, allow me to introduce your host, Mr Christopher Ellis. Ellis, may I present Miss Lucy Braithwaite, Miss Meredith Braithwaite, and their cousin Miss Susanna Elliot.'

Murmuring, 'How do you do?' Ellis shook hands with each of them. But his smile had no warmth and a frown scored two deep grooves between his brows. 'I think I should warn you that—'

'Come now, Ellis.' Behind Lowell's smile his tone and gaze were steely. 'Allow the ladies to settle in and freshen up first.'

'Yes, of course. Forgive me.' Ellis snapped his fingers, summoning servants to carry the luggage upstairs. 'Lunch will be served at one. The dining-room is through there. You'll meet my other guest, Mr Edgar Hutchins. As he too is a missionary no doubt you'll discover much in common.' He turned to Lowell. 'A word before you go?'

As Lucy helped Meredith towards the wooden staircase Susanna hung back.

'What's wrong?' she whispered to Lowell. 'And don't tell me *nothing*. It's quite obvious Mr Ellis is unhappy about us being here.'

'Ellis is under a lot of pressure. He's having difficulties with the local mandarin. Tempers are frayed and this hot weather is making matters worse. There's been an outbreak of disease in the poorest part of the town. Several children and old people have died.'

'Is there any way I could help?'

'No. You must not leave the compound.' She was startled by his vehemence. 'I know you probably *could* help, but the Chinese are very suspicious of all foreigners. Imagine what might happen if Meredith insisted on going with you, especially in her current state of mind.'

'I take your point.' They walked slowly up the stairs. She had so many questions and too little time. 'How long will you be away?'

'It depends on the weather. I'm hoping no more than four days.'

'When do you plan to leave?'

'In a few minutes.'

She stopped, facing him. 'So soon? But—'

He placed his forefinger gently on her lips. 'The sooner I go the sooner I'll be back.'

She wanted to ask why he couldn't wait a

day or two, just until the trouble died down. But she kept silent. He wouldn't go unless he had to. Nor surely would he leave them unless it was safe. Reluctantly she nodded and turned to continue up the stairs.

'I won't come any further.'

Bitterly resenting his will-power she flung a dark, angry look over her shoulder. The strain on his face filled her with shame. It was no easier for him. 'I know you're right.' Her shoulders drooped. 'It's just—please, *please* take care.'

Catching her hand he raised it to his mouth. But instead of kissing her knuckles he turned it over and, looking into her eyes, pressed his lips to her palm. She swayed towards him, her free hand rising to touch his face. His skin was warm, the dark stubble rough against her fingertips.

'Susanna, I—' Shaking his head he pulled free and ran swiftly down the stairs.

Leaving Meredith resting in bed Susanna followed Lucy down to the dining-room. Ellis and another man were already at the table. Both immediately rose.

'Do forgive us, Mr Ellis,' Lucy hurried forward. 'My sister will not be taking lunch. The heat and the effects of the journey ... I'm sure you understand.'

'Indeed. Miss Braithwaite, Miss Elliot, may I present—'

'Edgar Hutchins from St Louis, Missouri. Your servant, ladies.' Clutching his napkin

377

the American bowed to each of them. He was lanky and raw-boned with a wide jaw, a nose like a beak, and brown eyes full of kindness and shadows. His trousers and jacket of fawn-coloured linen were baggy and creased. But his shirt was clean and his brown wavy hair neatly brushed from a side parting.

As Lucy and Susanna took their seats servants glided in with bowls and dishes.

'Have you been in China long, Mr Hutchins?' Lucy enquired.

'Five years, ma'am. And I have to say there are times when it seems twice that. There's so much anger and resistance. I guess it's understandable when you hear the wild stories about those of our calling.'

'What stories?' Lucy enquired.

'I really don't think—' Ellis began.

'Come now, Mr Ellis,' Lucy chided briskly. 'If this tittle-tattle is likely to affect our work we have to know what it is.'

'That's the spirit, ma'am,' Edgar Hutchins' quiet drawl brought a faint blush to Lucy's sallow cheeks.

'As you were out there this morning, Hutchins,' Ellis huffed, 'perhaps you should tell the ladies the latest rumour.'

Hutchins' lopsided smile held a hint of apology. 'It concerns a wild woman with staring eyes. They say she's come here to steal children so she can make medicine from their hearts and eyes.'

Meredith. Glancing at Lucy, Susanna saw her throat work as she gulped. 'I see. Thank you for your candour, Mr Hutchins. It's clear we have quite a task ahead of us.'

When they had finished eating, Ellis excused himself and hurried back to his office.

Edgar Hutchins unfolded his length from the chair and stood up. 'Would you ladies care to join me for a stroll in the garden? It's a long time since I had such charming company. Maybe you'd like to hear about the work we've been doing at Chinkiang.'

'Thank you, Mr Hutchins,' Lucy smiled. 'That would be most agreeable.'

The paved paths were only wide enough for two so Susanna dropped behind, glad to be alone with her thoughts as she walked between banks of white, pink and yellow azaleas whose fragrance scented the hot still air. Bees hummed among the white blossoms of a Japanese cherry. Pausing by a magnolia Susanna inhaled the heady perfume. A large stone landed with a thud a few feet away. She looked round quickly. But other than Lucy, the American and herself the garden was empty.

The air stirred hot and moist against her face accompanied by the low rumble of distant thunder.

'Time to go in I think,' Lucy called.

As Susanna started towards them she saw their eyes widen. Both opened their mouths but before they could shout another stone crashed on to the path barely inches in front of her.

Startled, Susanna glanced over her shoulder and saw a chunk of rock come flying over the wall. She began running towards the house. Edgar hustled Lucy in the same direction. Thunder rumbled again, closer this time, and a large drop of rain splashed against Susanna's cheek. She arrived in the porch out of breath, more bewildered than frightened.

'What—?'

Edgar interrupted, 'Let's go inside before you ladies get wet.' He followed them in closing the door. 'There won't be any more trouble. The Chinese don't like the rain. Whoever was out there will be on his way home now.'

Glancing at Lucy who appeared equally bemused, Susanna recalled what had been said at lunch. 'It's because of the rumours, isn't it? Can't we explain to them that Meredith isn't well? That she was frightened?'

'I regret, Miss Elliot, they would not be inclined to listen,' Edgar said gently. 'Now don't you worry none. We're perfectly safe in here. Tell you what, why don't I order us some tea and you can tell me all about life in Cornwall.' He opened a door. 'This room has a lovely view over the garden.'

'I wonder if you'd both excuse me?' Susanna said quickly. 'Do stay,' she whispered to Lucy. 'Mr Hutchins will be able to give you all kinds of useful information.'

Lucy hesitated, her expression wistful. 'He has lived a most interesting life, but maybe I ought—'

'I'll look in on Meredith. She won't be stirring yet awhile.'

'You will come and fetch me if—'

'I promise.'

Meredith was still snoring heavily. Closing the door Susanna entered her own room. Seating herself at the small table she reached for a sheet of paper but made no move to pick up the pen. She really should write to her parents. Abruptly she stood up. Hugging herself she crossed to the window and looked through the streaked glass. Beyond the wall and the terraced roofs the great river roared in an ever-swelling torrent towards the sea. She couldn't see the mountains. They were veiled by rain that billowed like curtains of silk in the gusting wind.

She pictured the schooner battling up-river and felt a physical ache in her chest. The longer she spent with Lowell, the more they learned about one another, the stronger the bond between them became. It was nearly six months since she had left Falmouth and she was still travelling, still not sure of her ultimate destination. But he had said he did not want to lose her. Somehow, somewhere, he intended them to be together. But what about Marjorie? What about her cousins? Not to mention Shanghai society with which he was all-too-intimately acquainted.

As lightning flashed and growling thunder made the house vibrate Susanna tightened her arms, holding herself together as she struggled with fear and despair. 'Please come back safe,' she whispered. A plaintive cry reached her from the next room. The storm had woken Meredith.

Chapter Thirty-One

Standing in the porch Susanna looked up at a sky the colour of curdled milk. It was hotter than ever. But though the air was thick and heavy there was still no sign of rain.

With all domestic chores expertly taken care of by servants there was nothing for her to do. Yet she could not settle. She had washed Meredith's hair, tried to read, and failed in another attempt to write to her family. At lunch she had listened to Lucy discussing missionary work with Edgar Hutchins. Retreating to her room she had opened her journal. But that had immediately set her thinking of Lowell.

Missing him so much it hurt she had closed the book. Unable to sit still, feeling stifled inside the house, she had come out to the garden.

Every now and again a stone was hurled over the wall into the compound accompanied by curses and shrieks of *'Yang-kwei-tze'*, which Edgar had reluctantly translated as 'foreign devil'.

Throughout the day men in European clothes had arrived at the back gate of the consulate on horseback or by sedan chair. None stayed long. At first she had assumed them to be merchants coming to Ellis about problems with the Chinese, using the rear entrance to avoid the angry people at the front. Then, noticing that each left carrying a long rectangular box and several small square boxes, she realized: They were coming for the guns.

'I shall have to go and see the mandarin myself,' Ellis announced at dinner that evening.

'Is that wise?' Edgar was doubtful.

'Probably not. But it is necessary. The letter of protest I sent this morning was returned unopened. This intimidation cannot be allowed to continue. The people outside the main gate should have been dispersed by the militia.'

'You're not going tonight?' Lucy's frown reflected concern.

'No, I would lose face. I shall go tomorrow.'

Edgar tried to set their minds at ease. 'Those people out there are just plain scared. People always fear what they don't understand. If we could talk to them individually and explain that we mean them no harm, I reckon—'

'Out of the question,' Ellis cut in brusquely. 'For a start you aren't dealing with individuals. And an angry crowd is like a powder barrel. One spark—' He left the rest to their imaginations. 'We must on no account provoke them further.'

'But we haven't done anything.'

'With respect, Miss Braithwaite,' Ellis snapped, 'it's not what you have or haven't *done*, it's what you are. Missionaries are not welcome in China. The ruling classes view your activities as an attempt to destabilize the country for political gain. The peasants believe you kill and eat children. A belief possibly started, and certainly encouraged, by the mandarins.'

Lucy paled in horror and incredulity. 'Why would they do such a dreadful thing?'

'You threaten their power,' Ellis replied. 'They cannot accept that, any more than I can permit them to flout the treaty regulations.'

'Don't take on now,' Edgar leaned towards Lucy, his sad gentle eyes crinkling as he grinned. 'Mr Ellis does not hold us personally responsible, but I guess his position makes it hard for him to accept our point of view.' He turned to Ellis. 'No one in our line of work expects an easy time. I don't mind telling you there've been times when my faith was severely tested. But with God's grace I survived. And there is nothing more worthwhile than bringing a lost soul to the Lord.'

'Oh, bravo, Mr Hutchins.' Eyes shining with admiration Lucy clapped her hands. 'Bravo, indeed.'

'I do not doubt your courage, Hutchins.' Ellis wiped his moustache with his napkin. 'But I have to question the wisdom, even the morality, of deliberately exposing yourselves to danger.'

'How else are we to reach those who need us most?'

The logic was unassailable but Susanna felt increasingly uneasy.

It was late afternoon when she saw the consul coming in through the back gate, his face scarlet with barely suppressed rage.

'Mr Ellis is back,' she murmured to Lucy, setting down a jug of diluted lime cordial. 'I don't think he's had much success.'

'What are you whispering about?' Meredith croaked. Lying in bed, racked by spasms of shuddering and twitching, her shrunken features glistened with perspiration. 'It's about me isn't it? You're angry with me.'

'No, of course no one is angry with you.' Lucy wrung a cloth in the bowl of cold water on the bedside cabinet and gently wiped her sister's face. 'But we are concerned. We don't like seeing you so unhappy.'

'I'm ill, Lucy,' Meredith rasped. 'I need my medicine.' Suddenly Meredith's eyes narrowed and her lips retracted in a venomous snarl. She pointed a trembling finger at Susanna.

'She's trying to poison me.'

Startled, Lucy shot Susanna a look of apology.

'No, dear. Susanna would never harm you.'

'You don't understand,' Meredith clutched at Lucy's sleeve. 'I *know*. I can hear things.' She shrank into the pillows. 'I want to go home,' she whimpered. 'I don't like it here.'

'Lucy?' Susanna said softly. 'Do you think—'

'Keep her away!' Meredith shrieked, her eyes bulging with terror. 'Don't let her come near me! She'll bring snakes. Look, *Look!* They're everywhere!' Feverishly she slapped and brushed Lucy's skirt.

'It's all right, it's all right.' Lucy tried to catch her sister's flailing hands.

'Lucy, get them off!' Meredith sobbed, her face contorted. 'Get away from me!' Her voice rose to a shriek.

Appalled at the speed with which Meredith's condition was worsening Susanna wrenched

385

open the door and ran to her own room, grabbed her medical bag and raced back along the passage. Taking out the bottle Lucy had asked her to hide, she poured what she prayed would be the correct dose.

She knew from her books that Meredith had reached a state where even a few drops too many could prove fatal. But withholding it caused her cousin mental and physical agony. Watching such distress was harrowing enough; for Meredith, trapped inside the nightmare, it must be petrifying.

Catching sight of the glass Lucy shook her head. 'No,' she pleaded. 'It's killing her. Surely there's some other—'

'I haven't anything strong enough,' Susanna said helplessly. 'She should be in hospital. We must do *something*. The strain on her heart.'

'All right.' Lucy's voice was thin with anguish. 'If there's no alternative.' She knelt beside the bed, her head bowed. Ten minutes later, her frenzied terror soothed, Meredith drifted into unconsciousness.

Susanna gripped the jade disc, unable to remember a single formal prayer. All her chaotic mind could manage was *please:* for Meredith, for Lucy, for herself. And for Lowell. How she missed his strength, his sureness.

Lucy rose to her feet pale but calm. Through the window hate-filled howls and shouts were clearly audible above the low growl of thunder. 'We'd better go down and find out what's happening.'

'I waited for hours but he refused to see

me.' Furious at the snub Ellis was also clearly worried.

'Did you find out why?' Edgar asked.

'His reason, if you can call it that, "is that I am harbouring enemies of the people".'

'It is not we who are their enemies,' Lucy cried.

'I slipped out the back way this morning and talked to a couple of the local landlords,' Edgar said. 'We've got along OK in the past but today they were very cagey. It looks like there could be trouble.'

'Then we must prepare ourselves.' Ellis looked at his pocket watch and with a grunt of irritation glanced over his shoulder to the door. 'I particularly asked for dinner to be served early; I don't know what can be—' He stood up quickly. 'Will you excuse me?' He hurried out.

Susanna and Lucy exchanged bewildered glances. Edgar watched the door. Returning a few moments later Ellis looked shaken.

'They've gone. Every last one of them. This really is too much.'

'The windows,' Edgar muttered and hurried out. A few minutes later they heard him slamming the shutters across all the downstairs windows.

'You don't think they'll attack the house?' Lucy's voice was slightly higher than usual.

Ellis shook his head vigorously. 'Certainly not. The consulate is sovereign territory. Even the mandarin would not ... the repercussions.'

Edgar lurched into the hall, chest heaving,

sweat streaming down his face. 'They're trying to smash down the gate.'

Ellis stared at him. 'I cannot believe the mandarin would allow—'

'I reckon it's out of his hands,' Edgar panted. 'I've bolted the front door. I'd better check the back.'

Drawing himself up Ellis took command. 'While you're there, fill every container you can find with fresh water.'

'Sure thing. What about lamps?'

'And food,' Lucy added. Then her hand flew to her mouth. *'Meredith.'*

'Let her sleep as long as possible,' Susanna said quickly. She turned to the consul. 'Mr Ellis, I believe Captain Hawke brought you guns?'

'Guns?' Lucy gasped.

He looked sharply at Susanna. 'You're acquainted with firearms, Miss Elliot?'

She nodded. 'Captain Hawke insisted I learn.'

'He *what?*' Lucy was horrified.

Susanna spun round. 'I don't *want* to kill anyone, Lucy. But surely we have a right to defend ourselves?'

'I cannot condone—'

'Lucy, *think!*' Susanna shouted above the howls of the mob pouring into the compound. 'Who will care for Meredith if anything happens to us? And what about those people outside? How can you save their souls if you are dead?' A chunk of masonry thudded against the shutters.

A little while later, leaving Lucy beside a stirring Meredith, Susanna felt her way over to

388

the window and peeped out. Waving flaming torches the rioters surged all over the garden, their faces contorted with loathing as they screeched and hurled stones at the shutters.

Lowell, where are you? She could hear her heart pounding and clutched the medallion so tightly the edges cut into her palm. Fear was a sour metallic taste in her mouth. And it hurt to swallow.

Footsteps in the passage made her look round as Edgar's lanky figure appeared in the doorway. In one hand he had a pitcher of water in the other a rifle and a box of shells.

She had to clear her throat before her voice would work normally. 'What's happening?'

He set the pitcher down alongside the brimming bowl he'd carried up a few minutes earlier. 'Ellis has been shouting through the door trying to reason with them. But they're way beyond that.' He paused and Susanna heard loud, regular thuds. The screams outside reached a new level of ferocity that made her skin crawl and the hair on the back of her neck stand up. Handing her the rifle and shells Edgar sketched a brief salute.

'Wh-where are you going?' Lucy asked. In the lamplight Susanna saw Meredith's eyes open.

'Downstairs. They're trying to break through the front door.'

'Are they going to kill us?' Lucy asked, keeping her voice low.

'I don't want to hear that kind of talk, ma'am,' he chided gently. 'If they do manage to get in you keep real quiet, y'hear? Ellis 'n' me'll try and draw them to the other end of the house. I reckon we should be able to hold them off until help arrives.'

'What help?' Susanna demanded. 'Mr Ellis said the mandarin had refused.'

'Lucy?' Meredith quavered. 'What's happening? Who's that man?' There was a loud crash and the sound of splintering wood. She screamed and sat bolt upright. 'Lucy, I can't see. Why is it so dark?'

As Lucy tried to reassure her Edgar dashed downstairs leaving the question of help unanswered. Susanna quickly closed the door. The torches outside cast flickering shadows on the walls. Meredith was becoming increasingly nervous, her queries louder and more shrill.

Crossing to her medical bag, Susanna measured out another small dose of chloral hydrate. 'How much?'

She heard Lucy's fear. 'Just enough to calm her. She mustn't go back to sleep but we have to make sure she stays quiet.'

Seizing the glass Meredith gulped down the contents. Within a few moments she sank back on the pillows.

Replacing bottle and measure in her bag Susanna opened the door a fraction. Heavy thuds and a crash were followed by the crack of a rifle. The mob roared angrily. Then came the sound of breaking glass and more yells, this time of triumph.

'Get Meredith out of bed, Lucy,' she whispered urgently. 'There's no time for her to dress. Just put a cloak round her. Be sure you keep away from the window.' Crouching, she opened the box of cartridges then picked up the rifle. It felt heavy, the metal cold. The bed creaked. She heard shuffling and Lucy's reassuring murmurs. The tremor in her hands made her clumsy and she dropped a cartridge. Furious with herself she scrabbled desperately to retrieve it, biting hard on her lower lip to stop it quivering.

Shrieks and squeals were punctuated by rifle shots. The smell of smoke was growing stronger and her heart gave a sickening lurch as she heard the crackle of burning wood.

Leaning the rifle against the wall she peeped through the door again, and stopped breathing. A man was coming along the passage. Clad only in filthy baggy trousers, his naked, dirt-streaked torso glistening with sweat, he pushed each door open with a bare foot then peered inside. In one hand he carried a flaming torch, in the other a knife.

Frantically waving Lucy and Meredith down behind the bed Susanna felt beneath her skirt for the derringer then pressed herself back against the wall as the door flew open.

As the man stepped in holding the torch high, Meredith let out a piercing scream. Startled, he gave a blood-curdling yell, raised the knife and lunged forward.

Pointing the tiny gun as Lowell had taught her, Susanna squeezed the trigger. The report was deafening. The man jerked. His arms flew up and the torch rolled beneath the bed as he crashed to the floor. Fire raced along the loosened bottom sheet and licked the edge of the cotton-stuffed mattress. Dropping the little gun Susanna seized the bowl of water and flung it on to the flames, extinguishing them in a hissing cloud of steam. Another yell echoed along the passage then the sound of running feet. Susanna scrambled for the derringer as a second half-naked savage charged in followed by a third.

She fired wildly catching one in the upper arm. Throwing the little gun aside she reached for the rifle. But as the wounded man swung round on her the other raised his knife and lunged at Lucy.

'No!' With another piercing shriek—this time of rage—Meredith threw herself forward, fists flailing at the man's face. Aiming the rifle Susanna fired once, twice, and both men went down. One screamed, the other gave a choking gurgle. Smoke burned the back of her throat and made her eyes water. Glimpsing flames in the passage she kicked the door shut.

Outside the noise had grown louder. Amid the howls and shouting she heard ... *a whinnying horse?* Gunfire? There was no time to wonder. Had they survived a murderous attack only to be trapped by fire? Dropping the rifle Susanna ripped the rumpled counterpane and upper sheet from the foot of the bed where they were heaped, and poured the pitcher of water over them.

'Quick, Lucy.' She scooped up the sodden bedding. 'This will protect you' She froze. Lucy knelt on the floor cradling her sister.

The front of Meredith's white nightgown was dark with blood, the stain growing larger with every wheezing agonised breath.

'Oh no,' Susanna whispered crouching beside them.

'It should have been me.' Lucy was distraught. 'He was attacking me. Meredith tried to stop him, and the knife—' She flinched as a stone crashed against the window.

'*Miss Braithwaite, Miss Elliot!*'

'Mr Hutchins?' Lucy whispered, bewildered.

'*Outside?*' Susanna's eyes widened. Crawling forward she peered over the sill. 'They're running away,' she breathed incredulously. 'Men with guns are driving them out of the compound. There's a man on a horse.'

'What men?' Lucy didn't seem able to take it in. 'Soldiers?'

'They don't look like soldiers.' Ragged tunics were belted over baggy trousers tucked into knee-high leggings, their heads covered by roughly-bound turbans. 'More like brigands.' *With rifles?*

'Quickly, Miss Elliot! Open the window!'

'It *is* Mr Hutchins,' Susanna gasped and after a brief struggle with the catch heaved up the lower sash.

'Hurry,' he shouted. 'You must get out of there. We can't reach you by the stairs. Use the sheets to make a rope.'

Waving acknowledgement Susanna ducked back inside.

'Meredith won't be able to,' Lucy began anxiously.

393

'We'll make a sling.' Susanna spread the thin counterpane over the soaked mattress.

Trying to ignore Meredith's groans of agony they lifted her on to the bed. As Lucy gathered up the corners of the counterpane Susanna began knotting the sheets together. Smoke seeped, thick and choking, under the door. The crackling roar of the flames was horribly loud.

Fighting for breath Susanna tied one corner of the twisted sheet to the leg of the heavy wood-framed bed and motioned Lucy to help her drag the bed nearer the window. Leaning out she sucked in great draughts of air. Thunder rolled across the dark sky.

'Meredith's coming first!' she shouted and glimpsed men passing huge jars and pitchers of water from hand to hand as they fought the blaze. There was no time to wonder who they were.

Meredith's pain-filled moans shredded their nerves as they manoeuvred her over the sill. 'She's too heavy,' Lucy wept. 'We'll never hold her.'

'Yes we will.' Susanna gritted her teeth. 'We have to.' Every muscle in her back and arms quivered under the strain as they released the sheet inch by inch. She breathed in short gasps. It was too much. She couldn't ... . Her muscles were tearing.

'OK, we've got her!'

'Oh, thank God,' Lucy gulped.

Susanna pushed her cousin roughly towards the sill. 'You next.' She thrust the sheet into

394

Lucy's hands. 'I'—she started to cough—
'medical bag.'

'Leave it, Susanna,' Lucy cried.

Coughing too hard to reply, Susanna simply
shook her head and gestured urgently for Lucy
to go. Dropping to her hands and knees she felt
her way to the chest, fear screaming inside her.
Touching the leather she grabbed the handle,
stumbled to her feet, and lurched towards the
window.

She had almost reached it when the door burst
open and a fireball roared across the room. She
heard Lucy scream, felt searing heat across her
back, and smelled her hair singeing. Hurling her
bag through the window she scrambled over the
sill and grabbed the sheet. She tried to go down
hand over hand but the bunched cotton slithered
through her palms. With no strength left to hold
on she fell the last few feet, landing with a thud
that jarred every bone. Ellis ran forward to help
her up. Dizzy and sick she staggered towards
her cousins as another peal of thunder cracked
and rumbled.

Sitting on the ground, her sister's head on her
lap, Lucy smoothed damp strands of hair off
Meredith's glistening pain-racked face. 'That was
so brave. You've always been brave, Meredith.
No one knows that better than I.'

Susanna crept up alongside Lucy, about to
suggest they move Meredith under cover. Then
she saw the blood-soaked counterpane.

Meredith grimaced as she fought for air then
smiled wearily at her sister, her eyelids heavy.
'Not ... afraid ... any ... more.' Her breath

bubbled wetly in her throat. She tensed as a spasm of pain gripped her. Then, slowly, her features relaxed into the sweet smile Susanna had not seen since they left Falmouth. 'Light,' she whispered in wonder. 'Lucy, it's beautiful ... so bright ...'

Eyes tightly shut, lips compressed, Lucy raised her face to the sky for a moment, visibly fighting for control. Edgar Hutchins gripped her shoulder. She looked down at her sister.

'Go on, dear,' she urged softly, her voice warm and steady. 'Go towards the light. He's waiting for you.'

A heavy raindrop struck Susanna's cheek. Another hit her back and she flinched. Over by the house the bellows of urgency changed to shouts of laughter and relief as the soft pattering grew louder, harder. She was vaguely aware of someone trying to help her to her feet. The sound of the rain grew louder and all she could see was Meredith's face, only it wasn't because Meredith wasn't inside it any more, then darkness swallowed her and she was falling.

Loosely wrapped in a sheet Susanna picked up the scissors and held them over her shoulder, wincing as her strained muscles objected. Her burned back was so sensitive even the tiniest movement hurt. How would she bear to put clothes on? 'You'll have to cut it.'

'Oh, my dear, I wish ...' Lucy shook her head as she surveyed the scorched and shaggy remnants of Susanna's hair. Already bathed she was wearing one of two long, wide-sleeved gowns of indigo blue cotton Ellis had procured from the servants.

'My father would consider it a fitting punishment for my vanity.' It really didn't matter. Nothing mattered.

Though the fire had destroyed the guest wing the remainder of the consulate had suffered little damage. Daybreak had seen the servants silently back at their duties and the mandarin's soldiers strutting back and forth past the smashed gate in their flashy uniforms. It was an empty gesture for the road outside was deserted, the trampled garden and scattered debris the only signs that a riot had occurred. From this angle it wasn't possible to see the blackened ruins. Even the smell of wet charred wood had to compete with the fragrance of incense and the mouthwatering aromas of cooking.

They had lost everything but Susanna's medical bag and the clothes they'd been wearing, presently being washed and pressed. Susanna's dress was so badly scorched she wasn't sure it would survive laundering.

Ellis had gallantly insisted on giving them his room. In the adjoining bathroom the servants were refilling the hip bath for Susanna.

'You really should have woken me.' Susanna closed her eyes as Lucy snipped. Her back throbbed and she was so stiff and sore she could barely move.

'You needed rest.'

'But you shouldn't have been alone, not—'

'I wasn't. Mr Hutchins sat with me. He

understands you see, about Meredith. His wife was a missionary too. They came out to China six years ago. She had read about conditions here and thought she knew what to expect. But the reality ... she blamed herself, believed she was unworthy. After three years of struggle against the demons of fear and self-doubt, she took her own life.'

'Poor woman,' Susanna whispered. 'How could he face staying on?'

'How could he leave?' Lucy enquired gently. 'The person who was most precious to him is buried in Chinese earth.' She stood back. 'There. At least all the burned bits have gone.'

Susanna opened her eyes. *She looked like a street urchin.* Raising one hand stiffly to the spiky crop she forced a smile. 'It will certainly be cooler.' Struggling awkwardly to her feet she started towards the bathroom, careful not to look at the hair scattered around the stool.

As she clambered stiffly out of the water Susanna asked, 'Last night, who was the man on the horse?'

'A local warlord. Apparently Lowell was worried in case our arrival sparked off more trouble and when he left to go up-river this man's camp was his first call.'

Pouring a lotion of linseed oil and lime water on to a wad of soft lint Susanna handed it to Lucy, trying not to flinch as the soaked pad was gently dabbed against her burned back. It all made sense now. 'No wonder the soldiers arrived so promptly this morning. I can't imagine the mandarin's superiors being very happy about foreigners seeking the protection of a warlord.'

Lucy slipped the simple cotton gown over Susanna's newly washed head then carefully drew a tortoiseshell comb through the cropped curls. 'Do you feel a little better now?'

Susanna turned to face her cousin. 'How can you be so ... you and Meredith were so close.'

'And now she's dead why am I not grieving?' Still holding the comb Lucy crossed to the window. 'Life had become unbearable for her. Such terrible fear.' She gazed up at the brilliant-blue sky. 'She's at peace now and her body will be laid to rest this afternoon. Mr Ellis has kindly consented to her being buried in a corner of the garden where there is no danger of her grave being—' Susanna saw her swallow as she composed herself. 'I miss her dreadfully, I always will. But loving her as I did how could I wish her back? I shall continue with the work we planned. I'll do it for both of us.'

At five, Edgar and Lucy led the way out into the garden. Thick dark clouds had bubbled up to hide the sun and the air was heavy and humid.

Taking Ellis's arm for support Susanna forced her aching limbs forward. As they crossed the ravaged earth she saw the servants gathered at a respectful distance. One held burning incense sticks, another some white cash notes. Several more were carrying bamboo cages. Suddenly all the cages were opened and with a great fluttering of wings the captive birds soared skyward.

'Well, who'd have thought ...' Edgar Hutchins shook his head.

'What does it mean?' Lucy asked.

'The Chinese put great store by *virtue*. Buying caged birds then setting them free is one method of gaining a spiritual merit mark. I guess they're ashamed of what happened yesterday.'

'Really?' A tremulous smile lit Lucy's pale face. 'Then perhaps all ... this ... was for a purpose.'

'Ha!' Ellis muttered under his breath. 'I'd as soon trust a snake as a Chinaman.'

Edgar Hutchins led the short service. His words were simple and moving. But Susanna stopped listening. Suddenly she was beside a different grave in the chill of a raw-edged November wind. Something tore inside her and through the jagged rent poured months of pent-up grief, loneliness and strain. Covering her face with her hands she sank to the warm moist Chinese earth, sobbing as if her heart would break.

Chapter Thirty-Two

'Come on, come on! Don't take all day about it!' Lowell roared at the men lowering the mainsail.

'They're doing their best, *Captain*.'

Lowell spun round. 'When I want your opinion, Mister Binney, I'll ask for it.'

'We'll be alongside in a few minutes. Bellowing at them won't get us there any quicker.'

Furious, Lowell opened his mouth to give the mate a tongue-lashing and abruptly shut it again, raking both hands through his salt-stiffened hair. 'You're right. I'm sorry.'

For the past four days he had driven the ship and everyone on board mercilessly. He had eaten without tasting what he swallowed and hardly slept at all. Delivering the guns to Kwang-Tsai had been his first priority.

They had just set sail again when a squall had blown out two of the topsails and damaged some spars. He had insisted they keep going despite the horrendous conditions. After loading the silk he'd begun the return journey immediately, deaf to the grumbles of his weary storm-battered crew.

'Don't tell me you're sorry, tell them.' Tom jerked his head towards the panting, sweating men.

Lowell started towards the companionway. 'I'll stand the drinks for those who go ashore. The watch remaining aboard can have their pay made up by the same amount.'

A grin split Tom's seamed and weatherbeaten face. 'I daresay that'll help.'

As he stepped off the gangplank Lowell sensed his worst fears confirmed. Something had happened. His requests for information were either ignored or waved away with angry jabbering. Then a toothless old man cackled that one of the female foreign devils had been killed.

Dread paralysed him for an instant. Then he was running, pushing his way through the narrow crowded street, leaving Oliver Lockhead and the able-seaman to follow as best they could. His lungs burned as he gulped in humid air as thick as treacle. Sweat poured down his face stinging his eyes. It slid down his chest and sides and soaked the back of his shirt, the waistband of his trousers. Licking his lips he could taste the salt.

As he reached the consulate he saw carpenters working by the outer wall rebuilding the smashed gate. Glimpsing the blackened brick and timbers beyond he slowed, terrified of what he might find. *If anything had happened to Susanna.* He plunged forward.

'Ellis?' He stepped through the blackened doorway into the damaged hall. Glancing up at the charred staircase he felt a sick churning in his stomach. *'Ellis!'* he bellowed then hearing footsteps swung round.

'Thank goodness you're back. You really must get them out of here. I cannot take further responsibility.'

'Who was killed?' Lowell's voice cracked.

'You heard?' Ellis was sombre. 'There was nothing anyone could have done. She'd lost too much blood. A remarkably brave woman. A few of the mob managed to get upstairs. Apparently one went for her sister with a knife.'

Lowell released the breath he'd been holding and passed a shaking hand over his face.

'Are you all right?' Ellis peered at him.

'Not used to running. Which Miss Braithwaite?'

'Miss Meredith. We buried her yesterday.' He indicated the garden then grimaced, leaning forward. 'We couldn't wait. The heat ... I'm sure you understand.'

'Lowell!'

He swung round as Lucy came towards him from Ellis's private quarters followed by a thin lanky man who appeared vaguely familiar. Though pale she was calm and composed.

After a swift glance past both of them he clasped her outstretched hand in both his. 'I'm so sorry.'

'Thank you.' She indicated her companion. 'May I introduce Edgar Hutchins? He's—'

'Captain Hawke and I have already met.' Edgar extended his hand toward Lowell. 'At Chinkiang, about eighteen months ago?'

'I remember.' Lowell shook hands briefly. 'Good to see you again. Where's Susanna? Is she all right?'

'She's resting.' Folding her hands Lucy moved slightly to block his path. 'She'll join us later.'

'I have to see her.'

'I don't think that's wise.'

'Why? What's wrong? Is she hurt?'

Lucy laid a hand on his arm. 'Nothing serious. But the strain—she's very tired.'

'I won't disturb her. I just want to see—'

'Please,' Lucy tightened her grip. 'Your ... interest ... will only do more harm.'

He gazed down at the slight figure determinedly barring his way. *Harm?* A wild laugh

403

tore itself from his throat. 'What are you talking about? I could never harm her. She's everything to me.'

Startled, Lucy removed her hand. 'As a married man you have no right to say that.'

'You don't understand. There is much more to the situation than—'

'Please believe me, Lowell, I have nothing against you personally. And if you are experiencing domestic difficulties you have my deepest sympathy. But I cannot permit my cousin to form a relationship with a man who, in the eyes of God and society, already has a wife.'

'*Lowell?*'

His head snapped up. Holding the wall for support Susanna moved slowly and stiffly towards him, her wan face alight with joy. 'I was asleep. And then I heard ... was afraid it was a dream.'

He felt a great wrench in his chest and started forward. Lucy put out a hand to stop him but Edgar Hutchins drew her gently back.

'Let them be.'

'But ...'

'Look at their faces.'

'*Oh.* Even so.'

'Come away, ma'am. Let's you and I take a turn in the garden. I've an idea I'd like to discuss with you.'

Lowell didn't hear them leave. 'Why can't you walk properly? Why are you wearing a servant's tunic?' He caught his breath, his eyes narrowing. 'And what in the name of God happened to your—' He bit the words off as she hesitated under his scrutiny, sliding one hand self-consciously to the back of her neck. He saw the violet circles beneath her eyes, the pallor of her sun-kissed skin. He saw the flicker of anguished uncertainty as she bent her head and looked away. His eyes pricked. Reaching out he tenderly fingered the spiky uneven curls and swallowed the thickness in his throat.

'I see you've changed your hair.'

She glanced up, eyes overbright, a wry smile lifting the corners of her trembling mouth. She tried to shrug and winced instead. 'It got too hot.'

With a muffled wordless sound he pulled her close, releasing her instantly as she gasped.

'What?' he demanded urgently. 'What is it? What's wrong?'

She shook her head. But even that small movement made her face crumple and she caught her bottom lip between her teeth. 'My back ... the fire.' His indrawn breath hissed sharply. 'Nothing serious,' she said quickly. 'It's a bit tender, that's all. I'm fine, really. A few aches. Nothing to worry about.'

He cupped her face in his hands, studying every curve and hollow, seeing the delicate bones too close to the surface, the smudges of exhaustion.

'I'm all right.' She smiled to reassure him.

'No, you're not,' he growled softly and rested his forehead against hers. 'I might have lost you. I don't know how I'd have ... .' He closed his eyes briefly, a future without her impossible to contemplate. Drawing his head back he looked down into her eyes, frowning. 'I've never ...' He heard his own bewilderment. 'I didn't know it was possible to feel ...' He paused. 'I love you so much.' The words, spoken once many years ago, sounded strange. He had never imagined saying them again. He watched her eyes open wide, saw the shadows dissolve.

'Oh, Lowell.' Her smile was radiant. 'I *am* glad.' The gong sounded, announcing lunch.

Immediately they had finished eating Ellis excused himself and returned to his office. Susanna kept her gaze lowered. She was finding it difficult to contain her happiness. It threatened to spill over in smiles and sighs and tiny giggles of delight. But mindful of Lucy's bereavement she held it tightly in check. An added restraint was the uncertainty surrounding her future.

'I suggest we leave as soon as possible,' Lowell said. 'The journey down-river shouldn't take more than a couple of days.' Susanna watched his strong fingers turn an unused spoon over and over and felt a delicious stirring deep inside her.

Lucy cleared her throat delicately. 'It is most generous of you, Lowell.'

He waved her thanks aside. 'I simply want to get you and Susanna to a place of safety as quickly as possible.'

'I understand. And I'm most grateful for your concern. But we will not be going down-river after all.'

Susanna's head flew up. The sudden movement sent needles of pain through her tender skin and aching muscles. Her eyes sought

Lowell's, the news as startling to her as it was to him.

Lucy explained. 'When that arrangement was made my sister's welfare was our main concern. But circumstances have changed.' Shaded with sadness her voice contained new resolution. 'Mr Hutchins believes I could be of help at the mission station in Hangkow. Susanna and I will accompany him.'

'No,' Susanna blurted. 'Forgive me, Lucy. It isn't that I'm not grateful, I am, truly. But I'm not suited to missionary work.'

Lucy smiled. 'I know that, dear. No one expects it of you. You will be useful in other ways. Your medical knowledge, perhaps even teaching.'

'Susanna is coming with me,' Lowell said quietly.

Susanna's softly caught breath was quite audible in the sudden silence.

Lucy blinked. 'I'm afraid that's out of the question. Susanna is my responsibility.'

'Please, I'm not a child,' Susanna blurted. 'I don't want to be anyone's *responsibility*. I'm perfectly capable of supporting myself. Lucy, I'll always be grateful to you. If it hadn't been for you and Meredith ... But as you said, everything's changed now. At last you have the opportunity to do what you've always wanted. I beg you, don't deny me the same chance. I want to go back to Shanghai.'

With a brief glance at Lowell, Lucy spread her hands, her face taut with concern. 'My dear, you must know it isn't that simple.'

'You have a calling to serve God,' Susanna rushed on. 'That's why you came to China. I'm good at something too. My talent is for business. I wasn't permitted to develop my gifts at home, except when Father and Uncle Joshua found themselves with no one else to turn to, it's different here. Mr Prakash was delighted to employ me.'

'That's not the point,' Lucy began.

'It's *exactly* the point! This is what *I* want, Lucy,' Susanna pleaded. 'I want to run a business.'

'And so you shall,' Lowell cut in. 'But not for Soman Prakash.' She looked at him quickly. 'My father is mortally ill.' His voice was flat, emotionless. 'On his death I will inherit the company. At the moment it is being run with commendable efficiency by my father's *compradore*. But Tau cannot carry that responsibility indefinitely. Nor do I wish him to.'

As he looked directly into her eyes, everything —Lucy, Edgar Hutchins, the dining-room— faded from her consciousness. Only Lowell existed. His warm gaze reached deep into her soul. 'Though I intend making fewer long-distance voyages,' he continued quietly, 'I have no wish to give up the sea entirely. So, during my absences I shall need to leave the company in the hands of someone I can rely on, someone in whom I have absolute trust.' As Susanna listened she felt an unfurling inside her.

'Will your *compradore* have time to teach me

the local dialect? I have an ear for languages and—'

'Stop!' Lucy cried. 'Both of you stop this at once. Lowell, Susanna cannot possibly return to Shanghai without a chaperone. How can you even suggest such a thing? If you have no regard for your wife's position at least consider Susanna's. She will be the target of all kinds of gossip and speculation.'

Lowell's mouth was set in an implacable line. 'She will not be alone. I meant what I said, Lucy: Susanna comes with me.'

'She *can't.*' Lucy wrung her hands. 'You're a married man.'

'A farce,' Lowell muttered, his face darkening. 'I intend to petition for—'

'No, Lowell.' Reaching across the table, Susanna rested her fingers briefly on his provoking another anguished gasp from Lucy. 'I will not be responsible for destroying Marjorie's position in society.'

Lucy's face was a study of worry and confusion as she looked from one to the other. 'And what of *your* position?' she cried. She turned to Lowell once more. 'You profess to love her but your selfishness will make her an outcast.' She was visibly startled by Susanna's peal of laughter.

'Lucy, you surely can't have forgotten so soon? I have *always* been an outcast.'

'But you will never be accepted in society.'

Susanna gave a wry shrug. 'Having met two examples of Shanghai society I don't consider that a great loss.' Catching Lowell's eye she blushed.

He leaned forward. 'Susanna will be under my protection, Lucy. I will ensure no—'

'Protection?' Lucy's voice rose. Susanna had never seen her so agitated. Bright colour blotched her sallow cheeks. 'Your protection will bring her dishonour, sir.'

'*No!*' Susanna and Lowell spoke in unison, both emphatic in their denial.

'The circumstances are not as I would wish,' Lowell said grimly. 'And it would be naive to imagine that our relationship will go unnoticed. But most will, I fancy, keep their opinions to themselves. I am not a man to cross.'

'Lucy, if you must blame, then blame me.' Susanna took a breath knowing what she was about to say would be difficult for her cousin to comprehend. 'Yes, Lowell has a wife. However, circumstances exist which could resolve that. It is *my* choice that he leaves matters as they are. I love him with all my heart. Nothing, not marriage, or lack of it, will change that.'

Lucy made a despairing gesture. 'What will your parents think?'

Moving to Lucy's side Susanna bent to put an arm around her shoulders. 'I shall tell them you tried your utmost to dissuade me,' she said gently. 'Was I not always difficult and contrary?' She crouched in front of her cousin ignoring the protest from her strained muscles. 'Go with Mr Hutchins to Hangkow.'

'How can I?' Lucy demanded in distress. 'I would be failing in my duty.'

'What about your duty to yourself?' Susanna broke in. 'You have spent your life caring for

410

others, first your parents, then Meredith. I don't want to be your excuse for not doing what you want to do.'

Lucy stiffened. 'You surely can't think—'

'I am going with him, Lucy. I'd like to go with your good wishes. Do you recall what my life was like back in Falmouth?' After a moment Lucy nodded. 'And do you remember the birds we saw in Shanghai? We've lived like that, you and I. Trapped in cages of expectation, of duty, and convention. But the doors have been opened, for both of us. *Please*, Lucy. I want to fly.' She rested her head on the bony knee utterly drained. There was nothing more she could do or say.

After several long moments she felt her cousin's fingers stroke her shorn hair and heard her whisper, 'God bless and keep you safe, child.' Raising her head she saw Lucy trying to smile as tears rolled down her cheeks. 'Promise you'll write to me?'

As the schooner eased out into the river Susanna looked up from the pink jade lying on her palm. How much had happened since the Portuguese pressed it into her hand. She had suffered but she had survived. Magic? A stubborn refusal to give in? Or something else. Loving and loved, she had discovered within herself reserves of strength, compassion and understanding as powerful as they were unexpected.

Filled with gratitude for all that was good in her life, she closed her fingers over the medallion. She thought of Meredith but saw

411

instead the mound of fresh earth in a corner of the garden. Her mind shied away. Some memories were still too painful.

The crew's shock at her appearance had been quickly replaced by a clumsy inarticulate solicitude she found deeply touching.

Hearing Lowell hand over command to Tom Binney she felt her heart quicken as he crossed the deck behind her. His large hand covered hers on the wooden rail. She leaned against him. Her dress had survived its washing. Before she put it on Lucy had applied more linseed oil and lime water to her back. Already it was much less sore. She watched with Lowell as Kewkiang receded into the distance.

'Tom and Oliver were quite prepared to let you have their cabin,' he said drily as he led her below.

'That was kind.'

'But unnecessary. You will remain here,' he indicated his bunk. 'And I,' he added as she glanced up quickly, 'will use the seaberth.' He caressed her flushing cheek with his fingertips. 'You need rest and time to heal.' She looked down knowing he was right yet obscurely disappointed. He cupped her chin and gently raised her head. 'Susanna.'

Glimpsing the hunger in his eyes she felt a leaping response. His lips brushed hers. Her eyes closed and she held her breath, entranced by the sensation of his mouth against her own. Her head swam and her pulse raced. He drew away. Bereft she forced her eyes open. His jaw was knotted with tension and she saw his throat

412

work as he swallowed.

Anxiety fluttered like a swarm of butterflies. 'Wasn't it ...? Didn't I ...? Don't you ...?'

He lay his index finger on her lips. 'Hush. It was perfect. Now try to rest.'

'What will you be doing?' If he couldn't be with her she wanted to picture him in her mind.

His mouth twisted. 'Keeping extremely busy.'

Stepping on to the jetty Lowell took Susanna's hand, feeling her grip tighten as she surveyed the bustling waterfront and broad avenue beyond. Aware of the curious glances her cropped hair and scorched dress were attracting he drew her arm protectively through his.

'I'll take you to the hotel. After you've bathed and rested you can choose colours and materials for your new wardrobe. I'll ask Soman Prakash to send—'

'Where are you going?'

'To see my father.'

'I'd rather come with you,' she said quickly. 'If it's not inconvenient?'

He squeezed her hand. 'Of course it isn't. I want him to meet you. I thought you might prefer to wait until ...' He indicated her dress. 'I understand women attach great importance to such matters.'

'That is something else of which I have limited experience.' She made a wry face. 'I love colour but my father required us to dress as plainly as possible. It's funny. I've spent my life trying not to be noticed, but with my hair

413

like this I shall be stared at regardless of what I wear. Anyway,' she sobered, 'if your father is so very ill you really should see him as soon as possible.'

'I love you,' he whispered.

Her smile was radiant. 'And I you. With all my heart.'

Entering the elegant high-ceilinged room Susanna was at once aware of a strange smell. She had prepared herself for the particular odour of incurable illness. But this was different. The air in the room was hot, close, and hazed with smoke. She glanced quickly at Lowell. His face was totally devoid of expression, the mask with which he concealed deep and powerful feelings. She loved him so much.

'Father, I want you to meet Susanna Elliot.'

Susanna walked towards the skeletal figure hunched under a rug in the high-backed armchair and held out her hand. 'Good morning, Mr Hawke.' Fever-bright eyes flickered over her. The gaunt face was greyish-yellow but for twin blotches of hectic colour on the prominent cheekbones. A spasm which might have been amusement or pain briefly tightened the thin mouth. Then he looked straight past her to glare at his younger son.

'Where's John?'

Susanna folded her hands, glad Lowell had warned her, and thankful for the training that enabled her to appear undaunted by his father's rudeness.

'I gave him your message.'

'And?'

'He's not coming back.'

Though Joseph Hawke remained totally still Susanna sensed something crumble inside him.

'You told him I'd leave it all to you?'

Lowell nodded.

'I don't believe you. You can't have.'

Lowell shrugged. 'I told him. He said he'd chosen a different life. He looks well. And he's happy.'

'Happy?' Joseph spat venomously, but his thin mouth trembled. His head jerked up. 'Why is she here?'

'Because if you leave the business to me Susanna will be running it.'

Deep grooves furrowed the thin skin stretched across Joseph's forehead. He glowered at Susanna, his gaze brutal and intimidating. 'A *woman?*' he sneered, deliberately offensive. 'What's wrong with your hair? Some ridiculous new fashion?'

'That's enough.' Lowell took Susanna's arm. 'Come along, I'll—'

'It's all right,' she reassured him. Turning back to Joseph she forced a smile and found it less difficult than she expected. 'I wish it were a new fashion. I wouldn't feel quite so conspicuous.' Suddenly she recognized in Lowell's father the same fear, the same awful sense of isolation, that had destroyed Meredith. Filled with compassion she calmly folded her hands. 'I was in a fire, Mr Hawke. Believe me, it looked far worse before it was cut than it does now.'

He fixed her with a narrow glittering stare. 'Sit down,' he snapped, waving a bony claw at her. 'You're making my neck ache.'

'Father,' Lowell warned as Susanna sank gratefully into a chair on the opposite side of the fireplace.

'Are you another of his fancy women?' Joseph demanded.

'*Father!*' Lowell's roar made them both jump.

Susanna raised a hand to forestall him. 'It is a fair question.' A scalding blush flooded her face. 'Not polite perhaps, but understandable.' Though Lowell would do his utmost to protect her she had to share the responsibility. 'Not yet, Mr Hawke, but I hope to be soon. And I shall be the last.'

Joseph Hawke began to shake and his gaunt face creased into a strange grimace. Then she realized he was laughing. 'Damn me, girl, I like your spirit.'

'Come along, Susanna.' She felt Lowell's hand on her shoulder. 'You've put up with quite enough for one day.'

'Where are you going?' Joseph demanded, his gaze darting between them.

Lowell answered. 'I have some other business.'

'Go on then,' Joseph waved Lowell away. 'But leave her here. I want to know what makes her think she can run my company.'

Chapter Thirty-Three

Hearing the front door close and the sound of voices in the hall Susanna lifted the black crêpe over the brim of her hat.

Joseph Hawke had died two days ago. It was four weeks since her return to Shanghai. She had been reading to him. A sudden stiffening, a caught breath, a long slow exhalation: all over before she could move.

'An easier death than he deserved,' Lowell had muttered looking down at the shrivelled figure, but Susanna had seen tears in his eyes.

For years the house had known only anger and grief. But Joseph's departing spirit had taken with it the rage and pain that had encased him like a shell and tainted the atmosphere. Now tranquillity permeated the house. *Her house.*

She still found it hard to believe. Joseph hadn't said a word to her about his intentions. He had told Lowell, but sworn him to secrecy. She hoped that Joseph had at last found peace and that he knew how grateful she was.

Footsteps crossed the landing and Lowell appeared in the doorway. Her heart quickened as it always did each time she saw him. His black coat and trousers gave him a slightly saturnine air. His thick hair was neat for once, the scar on his forehead now a thin white line against his tanned skin. Less than three hours ago the big double bed with its neat coverlet had been a tangle of damp sheets and pillows as they clung together, hot, breathless, melting into the subtle rhythm that deepened, gathered power, rose like a curling wave and swept them both to gasping shuddering fulfilment. Then holding her with infinite tenderness he had rained kisses on her face and whispered his adoration.

Their eyes met and he smiled; knowing, calming, encouraging. 'Ready?'

Nodding, she followed him down. But at the door to the drawing room she caught his sleeve. 'Will you give us a moment alone?' He hesitated then stood back and Susanna entered by herself.

Marjorie was standing by the window. Her dress of black silk and taffeta was styled in the very latest fashion, and decorated with rosettes, bows and inserts of lace. A froth of fine black veiling crowned the small hat perched on top of her elaborately coiffed blonde hair. At first glance she epitomized sophisticated elegance. Then Susanna noticed the pallor cosmetics could not hide and the constant smoothing of the black silk gloves over taut knuckles.

Closing the door, Susanna was face to face with Lowell's wife for the first time. 'Thank you so much for coming.'

'I'm not at all sure why I did.' Lines of strain surrounded Marjorie's blue eyes. 'Except ...'

'You're curious?' Susanna smiled. 'Do sit down. Would you care for some tea?'

'No, thank you.' Marjorie perched on a rosewood and green velvet sofa. 'I should have replied to your letter.'

'It's of no consequence.' Susanna seated herself opposite. 'We both had much to consider.'

Marjorie's alabaster forehead furrowed. 'You are not at all what I expected. I confess I am astonished at your decision. I know Lowell would have preferred—' She looked away, her composure on the verge of cracking.

'Lowell loves me,' Susanna said quietly. 'And I love him. I hope you will forgive my candour but I see no other way of making my point.'

Marjorie stiffened. 'Which is?'

'That as you have no desire for the intimate privileges of married life it cannot be said I am depriving you of them. Nor do I wish to usurp your position and status in society as Lowell's wife and Joseph Hawke's daughter-in-law. So with those facts in mind it seems only proper that you and Lowell should receive the funeral guests together, and in *your* home.'

Marjorie's gaze widened in comprehension. 'I wondered ... thought he might want ...'

Susanna clasped her hands in her lap, happiness shimmering through her like liquid sunshine. 'I already have more than I ever dreamed of.'

Marjorie stared at her. 'You are content to remain his mistress?'

Susanna nodded. 'In fact, strange as it may seem, my position gives me certain advantages. Particularly in relation to the business. As *Miss Elliot* I am an unknown quantity. Naturally, I am still required to prove my ability, but I don't

419

have to worry about my decisions reflecting badly on a husband. Nor do I have to put up with patronizing condescension from men with loud voices and empty heads who consider the only place for a married woman is at home.'

Marjorie's burst of laughter took them both by surprise. 'Forgive me, Miss Elliot.'

'Please call me Susanna. I hope you see now that there is no reason for us to be enemies.'

Marjorie rose gracefully to her feet and smoothed her glove again. 'I believe you're acquainted with Geraldine Wilbury?'

'We have never been formally introduced, but I met her, and a friend of hers, while I was working for Mr Prakash.'

Marjorie nodded. 'Not a kind woman.' She held Susanna's gaze. 'The gossips have had sport with me long enough; if you and I were to present a united front ...' Her brows rose.

Relief spread a slow smile across Susanna's face. 'My thoughts exactly.'

Marjorie's lips twitched. 'My dear, I can hear teeth grinding already.'

The door opened to admit Lowell whose first glance was for Susanna. 'Tau is waiting for you in the carriage. You're sure you want to go?'

'Quite sure.' A frisson of nervousness tingled down her spine. 'As Mr Hawke was so well known in Shanghai I imagine there will be a lot of people paying their last respects.'

'Oh yes,' Lowell smiled grimly.

Marjorie's sigh held regret. 'I did not find him an easy man.'

'Few did,' Lowell mumured, then smiled at

420

Susanna. 'Except you. I don't know how you put up with his ranting.'

She gave a small shrug. 'He reminded me of Meredith. And it wasn't for very long.'

Marjorie addressed her husband. 'Susanna and I have reached a most amicable understanding. I would like her to join us at the house after the service.' She turned to Susanna. 'Will you come? We might as well start as we mean to go on.'

Seeing the light of battle in Marjorie's eyes Susanna gave an impish grin. 'I should be delighted. Thank you.'

Bowing briefly to his wife Lowell caught Susanna's hand. 'You are amazing,' he murmured, raising it to his lips. 'And I adore you.' Then the corners of his mouth tilted in an ironic smile. 'I can see this being a most interesting afternoon.'

A bitter December wind howled outside the bedroom window but the icy blast was mild compared to Lowell's eyes. Despite the glowing fire Susanna shivered and drew her quilted silk robe more closely around her.

'How long would you have tried to hide it from me?' he demanded.

'I wasn't—' Susanna began, but his anger and hurt were such that he didn't even hear.

'Do you think I did not see the difference? Feel the changes? I know your body as well as I know my own.'

'Lowell, please—'

'I will not have my child born a bastard, Susanna.'

421

'That's why I didn't tell you immediately.'

'What do you mean?' He glared at her, black brows drawn down.

'As soon as I suspected, I guessed you would want ...' She gestured helplessly. 'Surely you understand I needed to be sure?'

'But not to tell me.' He shook his head, turning away.

Scrambling on to her knees Susanna threw her arms around him and pressed his shaggy head to her swelling breasts, ignoring their tenderness as she sought to comfort him. 'You knew,' She kissed his thick rumpled hair.

'Of course I knew.' He held her close. 'That's not the point: I wanted you to tell me.'

She kissed him again, then sighed. 'Are you really determined?'

He reared back, features hardening. 'You are carrying my child. That changes everything. But you are not to worry. *I* will tell Marjorie.'

'No, Lowell. It was my promise. It's my responsibility. I'll call on her this afternoon.'

Though there was much about Marjorie she would never understand, Susanna had found her a staunch ally. Together they had calmly ignored the flurry of rumour and gossip. And her dignity in the face of what must surely be every married woman's nightmare won Susanna's boundless admiration.

'A baby?' Marjorie's expression betrayed a tangle of conflicting emotions. Beneath her primrose tea gown her posture was stiff and defensive. 'How nice.'

'I haven't come to gloat,' Susanna reproved gently. 'You should know me better than that.'

The fragile porcelain cup and saucer rattled as Marjorie passed it across and her mouth trembled as she tried to smile. 'I'm sorry. When is it due?'

'Mid-June I think.'

'And how are you feeling?'

'Wonderful. Perhaps a little more tired than usual. But apart from that I feel marvellous.'

'And Lowell?'

A bubble of happiness burst softly in Susanna's chest flooding her with radiant warmth. 'He's thrilled.' But the mention of Lowell's name reminded her of why she had come. 'Marjorie—'

Gazing at her delicately patterned teacup Lowell's wife set it down very carefully. 'You want the annulment.'

'Not me. But Lowell does. For the sake of our child.'

Marjorie glanced up. 'So why did he not come himself?'

'He wanted to. But I persuaded him it was my responsibility. I was the one who promised you nothing would change. And now I'm going back on my word. I'm so sorry.'

Marjorie looked at her hands. 'I'll have to leave Shanghai.'

'I don't see why. It won't be any worse than the last six months, and we survived that. In fact I'd say we've come through it remarkably well.'

'Yes we have, haven't we? Do you really

423

think—? You see I don't know anyone ... I have no relations anywhere else ...'

'Stay here then.'

'How odd that I should think of you as a friend.' Abruptly Marjorie's face closed into the social mask she rarely permitted to slip. 'Of course I know why.'

'We enjoy one another's company,' Susanna said simply.

'No. Well, thank you. But that's not the only reason. You know the truth about me and yet you aren't ... it doesn't disgust ...'

Compassion welled. Susanna said softly but vehemently. 'What happened was not your fault. You were shamefully abused by someone you should have been able to trust. All the guilt is his. Given those circumstances marriage must have been a terrible strain for you. That at least has been resolved. As far as you and I are concerned I never wanted to add to your pain. I still don't. Perhaps I am asking too much but I wondered, do you think, would you be willing to continue our relationship?'

'Do you mean that?'

'Why not? We are still the same people. All that will change are a few legal details. Over the past six months I have gained many acquaintances but few real friends. To a certain extent that is *my* choice. I am considered either an object of curiosity or a means of reaching Lowell. I have no family here either.' She laid one hand protectively over the barely noticeable curve of her stomach. 'Your friendship means a lot to me. Marjorie, I—would you consider being godmother to this baby? It might be unconventional but,' she shrugged, 'our relationship is unconventional.' She smothered a sudden giggle with her fingertips. 'Books on etiquette don't cover situations like ours.' She leaned forward, suddenly anxious. 'You're not offended are you?'

Marjorie looked up. Though her cornflower-blue eyes brimmed with tears, her smile was radiant. 'No, I'm not offended. I'm ... overwhelmed. *Thank you.* I cannot tell you how much—For all your unorthodox behaviour you have a truly Christian soul. What is it? What did I say?' she asked in bewilderment as Susanna began to laugh.

This Large Print Book for the Partially sighted, who cannot read normal print, is published under the auspices of

THE ULVERSCROFT FOUNDATION

THE ULVERSCROFT FOUNDATION

. . . we hope that you have enjoyed this Large Print Book. Please think for a moment about those people who have worse eyesight problems than you . . . and are unable to even read or enjoy Large Print, without great difficulty.

You can help them by sending a donation, large or small to:

**The Ulverscroft Foundation,
1, The Green, Bradgate Road,
Anstey, Leicestershire, LE7 7FU,
England.**
or request a copy of our brochure for more details.

The Foundation will use all your help to assist those people who are handicapped by various sight problems and need special attention.

Thank you very much for your help.

Other MAGNA General Fiction Titles In Large Print